DISCARD

OCT 3 2017

D1297422

At Drake's Command

The adventures of
Peregrine James during the
second circumnavigation
of the world

By David Wesley Hill

Temurlone Press • New York

Published by
Temurlone Press
www.temurlonepress.com

This is a work of fiction. Names, characters, incidents, and places are products of the author's imagination and are used fictitiously. Any resemblance to actual persons, living or dead, events, or locales is entirely coincidental.

Copyright © 2012 by David Wesley Hill
All rights reserved. No part of this book may be reproduced or transmitted in any form or by any means, electronic or mechanical, including photocopying, recording, or by any information storage-and-retrieval system, without the written permission of the Publisher, except where permitted by law.

Cover design by Christine Van Bree
Cover art: "The Golden Hinde off New Albion" by Simon Kozhin, oil on canvas, 2007. For information: http://www.kozhin-art.com. Used with the permission of the artist.

ISBN-10: 0983611726
ISBN-13: 978-0-9836117-2-1

To Gail Pamela Dubov
For a love encompassing the world

Contents

Acknowledgements

No man is an island entire of itself. Writing a novel is both an intensely personal and an intensely public endeavor. I could not have written this one without the friendship, advice, and support of many people. Thank you all for believing in Peregrine James:

Mike and Carol Bisker, William DeSeta, Barbara Earley, Ray Edelstein, Jim Farrell and Jamie Stiller, Geoffrey Felder, Susan Fishgold and Jay Molishever, Josh Frank, Rachel Galan, JoAnn Hill, Sara Hill and Michael Winkler, Judy Klein, my agents Howard Morhaim and Caspian Dennis, Annalee Pappas, Forrest Todd Parkinson, Bernie Passeltiner, Pat Roberts and Harry Breger, Lorraine Shemesh, Carol Soskil, Martha Stelly, and Hugh Van Dusen.

Chapters Eight and Nine were written during a residency at the Blue Mountain Center in the Adirondacks—for this period of peace, comfort, and creativity, thank you, BMC! For the loan of her log cabin in which to finish the final chapter—thanks, Karen Kennedy!

Most of all I must thank Gail Dubov. The book would never have been written without her love and encouragement.

Historical Preface

The Drake circumnavigation was one of the best documented Elizabethan voyages of exploration. Francis Fletcher, parson and preacher to the adventure, kept a meticulous diary. Testifying before the lordships of the Admiralty, John Winter, captain of the *Elizabeth*, provided a concise account of the expedition up until the point when he abandoned the *Golden Hind* and returned to England. Another sailor, Edward Cliff, also wrote at some length about the journey, as did Francis Pretty, "one of Drake's gentlemen at arms."

Nuño da Silva, the Portuguese pilot kidnapped by Drake in the Cape Verde Islands, maintained a daily logbook, which still exists. We also have the record of his interrogation by the Inquisition after he was released at the Mexican village of Guatulco. Dozens of eyewitness accounts from Drake's victims are scattered throughout archives in Spain and Mexico, as well as correspondence by the Spanish imperial bureaucracy about how to deal with the English pirate's incursion into the Pacific.

The gentleman investor John Cooke, who sailed on the *Elizabeth*, left behind an unflattering appraisal of Drake, which was suppressed until 1854, when it was finally published by the Hakluyt Society.

In the early twentieth century a draft plan of the expedition was discovered in the archives of the British Library but the manuscript had been damaged by fire and much of the text burned away. The words that remain tease the reader by almost, but not quite, making sense.

Unfortunately, Drake's own rutter, which he worked on with his cousin John, was confiscated by Queen Elizabeth and never seen again.

The wealth of information about the voyage has allowed me to follow the adventure almost on a daily basis as the fragile wood ships proceeded across the brine. Google Earth has allowed me to look down upon the places where they anchored and to see the large black rock where the crew caught fish five hundred years ago. Although this is a novel, I have attempted to present an accurate portrayal of the voyage, embellishing history rather than manufacturing it. Wherever possible, I have used the actual words of my characters, allowing them to speak for themselves across the divide of time.

Of the 164 men, gentlemen, and sailors who set forth from Plymouth, the names of one hundred have come down to us.

Peregrine James is not among them.

A Fine Morning to Be Whipped

November 15, 1577
Plymouth, England

It was as fine a morning to be whipped as any I had ever seen. The November sky was cloudless except for a puff or two of pure white fleece above the Hoe, the high greensward beyond Plymouth, which was just visible past the rooftops of the city. A stiff sea breeze was pushing back the usual stink and the air tasted as sharp and pure as dry sack. I took in a deep breath, trying not to think of what lay ahead.

Chained by the wrists to the tail of the parish beadle's cart, I was being led toward Sutton Pool, the city harbor, where the civic ducking stool, stocks, and whipping post were located.

I had been stripped of my doublet and boots and now wore only breeches and a thin shirt. The cobbles were icy against the soles of my naked feet and I began to make a point of stepping in the piles of slop littering the street. This helped warm my toes but did little for the rest of me. I was shivering by the time the cart turned onto the quay side.

"Say, Hal," I called to the beadle. "Could you hurry a trifle? It is uncommonly cold and I am not attired properly."

Hal Audley had been clanking a bell to draw the attention of passers-by. He spared a glance over his shoulder, only his melancholy blue eyes and huge beak of a nose showing between the brim of his hat and the woolen scarf swaddling his neck and the bottom of his face.

"Now, Perry," he answered, "how long would you say we have been acquainted, you and I?"

"All my life, at least. You were a friend to my parents well before I came onto the scene."

"In that time have you ever known me to neglect my duty? To shirk from the task when a jack needed emptying or a woman required sympathy? No, not Hal Audley! If a thing needs doing, it needs doing well, that is my philosophy. Constable Felix has ordained a solemn march to the post, and a solemn march I will provide. You could do worse, Perry, than to heed my example. Chin up, lad, eyes forward, and let us continue our pavane at its proper tempo."

Hal resumed his dismal clanking and to my discomfort we proceeded along the waterfront at the same slow cold pace as before.

Sutton Pool was a basin of deep water two hundred yards wide. Most of its circumference was hemmed in by buildings occupied by establishments catering to the maritime fleet—taverns and lodging houses, chandlers, coopers, sail makers, and victuallers. At the far end of the pool was a narrow channel allowing passage out into Plymouth Sound. This was guarded on the west by a blockhouse and on the east by a square stone fort with round towers at each corner. In times of war a great chain could be strung between the castle and the blockhouse, denying enemy ships access to the harbor.

In the center of the pool a dozen vessels lay at anchor, rocking on the choppy water, their cables and rigging creaking, timbers groaning, the pennants at their mastheads snapping in the wind. Small boats went between them and the quay, taking off cargo and ferrying out casks of wine and barrels of salted pork and beef, sacks of oats and barley and dried peas, marine hardware of diverse sort, and huge bales of combed gray wool. Closer at hand weather-beaten fishing smacks were lodged right against the dock, bumpers scraping with unnerving screeches against the pilings while their crews unloaded the morning catch, sole and plaice and halibut as wide as both arms outstretched, buckets full of wriggling brill, angry tunny, and sluggish codfish with bloated orange innards popping from their mouths and vents.

The dock was crowded with the typical bustle—longshoremen and sailors, wives in search of bargains, servants in blue livery, merchants, whores, idlers, and onlookers. All this commotion slowed our passage and allowed everyone to take note of me. Those with nothing better to do, and this was a fair number, fell in behind the cart and accompanied us to the stocks, so that we formed a straggling parade. Many of these people knew me, and so I was not abused as much as I might have been if I were a stranger or disliked, which is to say, only an urchin or two pelted me with clods and fish heads during the journey.

Sam Goodman, a cordwainer who spent more time in his cups than at his trade, clapped my back with a leathery hand and said:

"Perry, bring forth a tankard of your best ale since I have a burning thirst. What? What stops you? Have you no ears with which to hear? I have made an honest request and yet see no action. Your master must have report of this!

Tardiness is not a virtue."

"I fear you must be blind as well as thirsty, Sam," I replied. "If you had eyes, you would see I am chained to the cart and thus prevented from doing you service."

"Indeed, indeed," Goodman answered with heavy humor. "I had not noticed. Tell me, Perry, what circumstance has reduced you so low? Was the roast underdone? The capon poorly seasoned? Or have you—and this is an offense sublimely criminal—singed the porridge? *Awk!*"

This exclamation was caused by the impact of Beth Winston's palm against his cheek. She was a tiny woman but by no means frail and the slap left behind a blushing imprint. "Have you no shame, Sam Goodman?" she asked, stretching on tip toes to meet his eyes. "To taunt the boy is poor sport. Leave off, else your wife will hear what occurred between us on your last visit."

"Please, Beth," Sam gulped, "I meant no harm. I merely wanted to take Perry's mind off his troubles."

"Tell that to someone who will believe it. Now away with you before I surrender to a Papist urge and confess *your* sins."

Her glare followed him until Sam had retreated among the crowd. Then she turned me a softer glance.

"How do you fare, Peregrine James?" Beth asked.

"Well enough, I suppose, all things considered."

"Brave child. To suffer cruelty without complaint, when innocent of wrong, is the heart of martyrdom. There is little justice in this world, where those with wealth may purchase judgment against those without."

"It could have been worse, Beth. I would be facing the

gallows had the jury valued the brooch more."

"They would not have dared! It was sufficient travesty you were convicted when every man present understood the truth." She walked beside me a few paces, a pensive expression on her face, which was naturally pale and needed only the slightest dusting of alabaster to achieve beauty. Over her bodice Beth wore a tippit, a short cape of scarlet cloth, and the brisk wind was spreading it behind her. Perhaps the wind had reddened her eyes, too. She rested her fingertips on my wrist just above the clasp of the manacles.

"I bear a token from Annie," she said.

"What is it?"

"She sends you five shillings, her entire savings, enough to carry you to London with some remainder so that you may establish yourself."

"I do not want the money."

"Listen to what I say. There is nothing for you in Plymouth. Who will employ you with the stripes of a thief on your back? Especially with Annie's father spreading lies like manure on a field. By springtime even those who know what really happened will believe his falsehoods since it is the character of men to enjoy slander above fact and to forget what they know to be true in favor of evil gossip."

"I will not go to London, Beth. Nor will I accept Annie's money. Return it to her. Or keep it yourself."

I shrugged away as she sought to tuck the small cloth sack of coin in my breeches. Then the bells of St. Andrew's began ringing—Yogge's Bells, as they were known, after the merchant who had financed their construction. Once, twice, eleven times in succession sounded the knell and then all eight bells in the tower clapped together.

On the brink of the quay side was the civic ducking stool, an ungainly contraption of wrought iron, which was generally used for the chastening of women although on occasion quarrelsome married couples were ducked together, strapped back-to-back, as well as slanderers and brewers of sour beer and bakers of adulterated bread. Beside it was the pillory, this wooden, in which was jailed a man I did not know, his ears nailed to the board restraining his neck and hands, a dull grimace on his face, his beard dirty with egg and bits of fish gut.

The whipping post was planted in front of the stocks and stool. It was a stout chunk of ship's mast as thick around as my thigh and half again as tall as I was. An iron ring was sunk into the wood at shoulder height and I could not help but notice the cobbles beside the post were discolored with dried blood.

Hal swung his legs to the ground and stood upright with an audible clacking of the knees for he was forty years of age and not a young man. He paused to brush dust from his jerkin and then walked around to the tail of the cart. Upon noticing Beth, he tipped his hat, a copotain of blue felt in the shape of a loaf of sugar, and gave her a quick bow.

"Mistress Beth."

"Beadle Audley."

"If you have come for the entertainment, I fear that you are early. It still lacks an hour of noon."

"I have not come for the entertainment. Such spectacle is not to my taste, particularly when an innocent boy is to be misused. No, Master Audley, on the contrary, I have come to ask for your leniency. Spare the rod and do not insist Perry suffer for a felony he did not commit."

Hal pulled at the tip of his immense nose, a nervous gesture. "Mistress, I cannot."

This did not deter Beth. Placing her hands on either side of her waist, which thrust her bosom tight against her bodice and made it plain she was generously proportioned although of slight build, she tilted her head and stared aslant at the beadle with a coquettish look.

"I do enjoy performing favors for good friends," she remarked slyly. "With equal fervor do I shun the company of boors and ingrates."

The bobbing of Hal's Adam's apple as he swallowed caused the scarf around his throat to bulge and shrink and bulge again.

"Pray, do not take offense," he said at last, "but you are not the only whore in Plymouth, Mistress Beth. Still, let us not argue," he went on hurriedly, observing the twin spots of color catching fire in her cheeks. "I love Peregrine James as if he were mine own son and would not do this thing save that it is my obligation. What is more, Constable Felix himself has promised to attend. He is a stern master who will judge my efforts with an expert eye. No, Beth, you ask me for what I cannot give."

Their argument went back and forth while Hal unclipped my manacles from the cart and attached them to the whipping post.

I was not listening. All the week I was in jail awaiting trial, and during the half hour the procedure actually required, and during the days since my conviction, and even through the long cold walk to the quay side, I had managed not to think about the situation I was in. Now, however, the iron encompassing my wrists and the hard trunk of fir to which I was joined made forgetfulness impossible.

One Sunday had already passed. In another two, Annie would be standing at the door of St. Andrew's with her flaxen hair loose to the waist while another man placed his ring upon her finger.

London? A bitter laugh escaped my lips and was swept away by the wind. London was too near—a thousand miles too near. No, I told myself, I could travel half the world around and still not be far enough from Plymouth.

Beth had drawn Hal Audley aside and they were continuing their conversation while the crowd formed an irregular semi-circle around me and waited for the show to begin. Hucksters went among them selling trinkets, oranges from Seville, mugs of hot cider, roast beef ribs heavy with fat, and crisp fried smelts doused with vinegar. After a week of little but oat gruel and stale beer and bad cheese, the sight and smell of this good fare wet my mouth and caused my belly to churn. So I turned away from land and looked instead upon Sutton Pool.

Although I had been conceived in Plymouth and had spent my life in one of the busiest of English ports, I had never considered going to sea myself. In all my twenty years, in fact, I had never been aboard a vessel grander than a wherry, when my father would take me fishing for salmon and pike on the Plym and Tamar rivers, which framed the city and drained into the sound. Now, though, the ships straining at their cables upon the choppy water held new interest for me—not the smacks and trawlers, nor the swag-bellied coastal traders that never sailed farther than the

Low Countries or Calais, but the larger ships bound for distant shores. One such lay directly in my view, the flagship of a fleet of five, which was about to embark, or so rumor had it, on a voyage to Alexandria in the land of Egypt, where the Nile flowed into the Mediterranean. She was the *Pelican*.

Even as I gazed upon her, out of the corner of my eye I observed her captain striding along the quay side with the swaggering bow-legged step of a man more accustomed to having a heaving deck under the soles of his boots than the solid stone upon which he was walking. He had a slight limp in one leg, where a piece of lead shot still lodged, a souvenir of battle. I recognized him by the gold of his hair and by his fiery beard and by the boom of his laughter as he bantered with a companion. This was no great achievement, however, since everyone in Plymouth, from the lowest scullion to the highest aristocrat, knew him or knew of him. His name was Drake, Francis Drake.

The man at his side was a different sort. A full head taller than the robust mariner, he was slender instead of stocky, dark-complexioned where Drake was fair, and he moved with the languid motion of a gentleman rather than with the jaunty energy of a seafarer. His doublet was of burgundy silk, the codpiece of rich plum velvet embroidered with gold, and his boots of supple leather reached above the knee. I recognized him, too. He was Thomas Doughty, the second of the three captains in command of the expedition to Africa.

The pair halted twenty paces from the whipping post and each turned me an incurious glance before resuming their discussion. A watch had evidently been set for them aboard the *Pelican* because a ship's boat soon put forth toward the dock, propelled across the white caps by the oars of the sailors crewing her, spray jetting from her bow. I realized that if I was to speak, it must be soon or never.

"Captain Drake, sir," I asked. "Have you a moment?"

I had to call three times to gain his attention. At first I feared Drake would ignore me in spite of his reputation for being approachable by even the meanest citizen but after a word to Doughty he strode to the post and looked me up and down with a calculating eye, turning upon me the scrutiny of a man accustomed to evaluating other men.

"What is it, boy?" he asked. "Quickly."

Despite the chill Drake was not wearing a scarf. His clothes were plain, practical rather than showy, tailored of hardy wool rather than velvet, satin, or silk. His boots, although well-made, were well-used, the leather bearing the whitish stains of brine and weather. Not that Drake disdained fashion—I would later see him dressed as gaudily as any courtier, trussed in finery and as brilliant as a peacock. But Drake was a sailor first and he possessed the practical temperament that was essential for survival upon the ocean.

"They say you sail for Alexandria, Captain Drake."

"God's blood, is my business known to every vagabond and ragamuffin littering the streets of Plymouth?"

"I cannot speak to that, captain, since I am not one nor the other. My name is Peregrine—Perry—James."

"Well, then, Mr. James, who is neither vagabond nor ragamuffin, what would you have with me?"

"I would have a position among your crew, sir, if there is need for another man."

A Fine Morning to Be Whipped

Drake's complexion, as I have mentioned, was fair despite the years he had endured on deck beneath the sun and despite exposure to the fury of gales and tempests beyond counting. This allowed the blood now suffusing his cheeks to be easily noticed and I feared my request had angered him. But he threw back his head and laughed with such enjoyment that people across the quay turned to discover the cause.

When he had collected himself, he asked, "Damn me, lad, what need have I for a thief?"

His tone was not unkind but the words stung even so. "I am no thief, captain," I protested. "I am innocent and unfairly convicted."

"That I have heard before and from men eminently guilty of crime."

"In my case it is fact, Captain Drake," I exclaimed with as much sincerity as I could muster. "My only wrong was to love my master's daughter. But her father had a more favorable marriage in mind. I was an unwanted suitor and for that offense he resolved to see me hang."

Drake approached nearer, until mere inches separated us, and stared into my eyes without blinking. His own were bright blue framed by the brightest white, the eyes of a raptor, cold and pitiless and without sentiment. It required all my strength to meet his gaze without flinching.

Finally he said: "Do you vow by Jesus and by our holy Lord that what you say is nothing but the truth."

"By Jesus, Captain Drake. My oath as a Christian."

"Yes, I do believe you, lad, for it is well known I am an admirable judge of character."

"Then you would have me, sir?"

"I did not say that. While 'tis true I could always find employment for a sailor, it is clear you are not one. Have you some other skill?"

"I speak Spanish, Captain Drake. And some Portuguese, which is not so different a tongue. My mother, God rest her, was from Cordoba."

Drake was not impressed. "What else?" he asked.

"I am a cook, sir."

"Hardly a remarkable distinction, Perry James. To boil salt pork is no great accomplishment—"

"A word, Francis, if you please."

This was the moment Thomas Doughty entered my life. At the time I did not care for him. The difference in our stations was too great for there to be easy sympathy between us. Nor did he possess the common touch that came so naturally to Drake, who had risen from humble origins. Doughty was a gentleman and moved among the highest circles in the land, hobnobbing with Walshingham, Hatton, Burghley, and other familiars of the queen, while I was a convicted felon awaiting the lash. I doubted he meant me well when he pulled Drake out of earshot and engaged the sea captain in conversation. No, I was certain Doughty was convincing Drake to have nothing to do with me and I was surprised when they both returned to my side. It was Doughty who spoke first:

"Are you not the cook at the Jack and Rasher?" he asked.

"I was, sir. Although I distrust the owner will have me back since he charged me with theft and bore witness against me in the assizes."

"And you are familiar with cooking as it is done on the continent, which is to say, in the manner of the Italians and French?"

"Aye, sir. God bless my mother, she taught me the secrets of gravies and sauces, the use of spices, how to braise and roast, and the trick of decorating food so that the dishes are well presented upon the table."

"Indeed. I have had an excellent meal at the Jack and Rasher, better than I had hoped to discover in Plymouth. Francis—" this while bowing politely to Drake—"may I suggest we find a place for Mr. James among our company. He could be useful. In particular when we are obliged to entertain certain foreign *dignitaries*."

I did not understand the emphasis Doughty placed upon this last word but what he meant was no mystery to Drake. He slapped Doughty on the back, a gesture that the gentleman, by his studied expression, endured rather than enjoyed.

"God's blood," Drake exclaimed. "You have the right of it, Tom. Let no one say Englishmen lack proper culture! Damn my eyes, we will instruct the dons in the meaning of refinement, will we not?"

"Then you will have me, sir?" I repeated.

"Perhaps, lad. It is a brave expedition we are embarking upon and I have no sympathy for cravens. Tom, I must return to the *Pelican*—" the ship's boat had come up against the quay side and was being fended off the pilings by the oars and brawny arms of its crew—"and I cannot linger. Stay awhile, and observe how Perry accepts the lash. If he whimpers, well, leave him to his life and we will be quits. But should he meet the sting with a roar and bear his anguish with indignation, then include him in our roster."

"As you wish, Francis," replied Doughty just as Yogge's bells tolled, signaling the noon hour and the execution of my sentence.

The crowd had quieted in anticipation of the entertainment. It had grown in number, too, certain parents having summoned their children so that they might be instructed in the peril of wrongdoing and profit by my example. Beth was in the first row, clasping a pomander to her face. Not far from her side was Constable Felix, Hal Audley's master, a portly man dressed in robes trimmed with beaver and wearing a tasseled hat garnished with ostrich feathers. He was drinking tobacco from a pipe and spitting the smoke into the air with a bored look, his attendance evidently a matter of responsibility rather than of pleasure.

"On with it, man," he called to Hal. "We do not have all afternoon."

The beadle unfolded a broadside and recited the charges against me and the punishment to be inflicted upon my person, "two dozen strokes, stout and true and delivered without stinting." Then he hefted the handle of the lash in one hand and ran its tails through the fingers of the other while approaching the whipping post with a solemn tread.

"How goes it, Perry?" he inquired. "Are you prepared?"

"As prepared as any man," I answered with such bravado as I could summon.

"Remember what I instructed," Hal went on. He spoke with unusual urgency, as if his words carried deeper import than their surface meaning, although I lacked the sense to decipher the riddle. "Heed my example, Perry, and give your all to the role fate has prescribed for you. As I have said occasionally, a thing worth doing is a thing worth doing well. This is my firm belief."

"Aye, Hal, I hear you," I replied and braced myself against the post, unable to prevent my shoulders from tightening, or to stop my heart from racing, or to keep my mouth from going dry. I pressed my cheek against the wood and stared out on Sutton Pool—there swam the *Pelican*, a bustle of activity about her as the final stores for the journey to Egypt were hoisted aboard—and attempted to ignore the noise Hal Audley made while stepping away to gain room for a round-up, the rustle of cloth as he raised his arm, the grunt he uttered while swinging the lash.

"One!"

The cry wrenched from my throat came not from pain but from surprise.

I hardly felt the lick of the cattails. To all appearances the beadle was delivering the sentence with authority, lifting the whip above his head and sending the thongs toward me with such velocity that they whistled and hissed as they cut the air. Yet I did not notice the caress.

"Two!"

This time, my wits dulled by amazement, I failed to make any response. Not until the third stroke did I finally catch on. Through flattery or bribery or by using a feminine inducement whose nature I did not care to know better, Beth had convinced the beadle to hold back. Belatedly I understood the message Hal had sought to convey in the guise of philosophical advice. Craning my neck around, I saw him once more drawing the thongs of the lash through the fingers of his free hand, and I realized he was secretly coating the leather with red ochre or a similar dye so the cattails would leave evidence of their cruelty even though my skin remained unbroken.

"Four!"

Entering into the spirit of the sham, I pretended to be wounded. "God damn you, Hal Audley," I cried.

"Five!"

Again I cursed the beadle and wrenched at the manacles, attempting to persuade the crowd of my anguish while impressing Thomas Doughty with my rage. Unfortunately, I was unskillful at deception.

Lounging against the ironwork frame of the ducking stool, Doughty had been taking exact note of the proceedings. Soon he was tugging at the point of his beard and peering my way with a puzzled expression. Constable Felix, too, by the nature of his profession a connoisseur of such sights, proved unconvinced of my sincerity.

"Put more vigor in it, Audley," he called. "Need I provide instruction in every detail?"

"As you wish, sir—eight!"

I redoubled my efforts, tearing at my restraints like a madman and cleaving the air with all the oaths known to me, to no avail. Muttering peevishly, the constable came forward until he was standing beside the beadle. As Hal raised the whip for a tenth stroke, Felix lifted his cane, a strong piece of oak with a knob carved to resemble a snarling wolf, and applied the stick with a thump to Hal's back just as the whip touched my own shoulders with a far kinder stroke.

"'Tis how the job is done, Audley," the constable informed his subordinate. "Do you require further illustration?"

"I am striving my best, sir," Hal protested.

"Your best is not adequate. Harder now."

Perhaps because of friendship, perhaps because of prior arrangement with Beth, or perhaps because of simple kindness, Hal failed to increase the power of his strokes enough to please Constable Felix. He matched Hal blow for blow, falling on the beadle with unkind energy when Hal refused to do me any harm. This strange show caused the crowd to quiet. It enraged Beth, however, and she strode into the melee. Grabbing the love-lock curling beneath the constable's hat, she pulled down his head and slapped his face.

"Leave off," she said. "Leave off, you ugly toad."

Her assault took Constable Felix so aback that he could not find his voice nor come up with a coherent plan how to deal with the angry woman. Instead he sought refuge in habitual activity, which is to say, he continued striking poor Hal each time the beadle pretended to strike me. Beth, in turn, applied the flat of her hand to the constable's cheek whenever he hit Hal.

"Fourteen," grunted Hal, going on with the count in a stolid voice while Constable Felix protested:

"Get away from me, harlot, or I will clap you in the stool myself and quench your temper in Plymouth harbor."

"I dare you!" Beth replied. "What amusing tales I could tell of certain unnatural notions you hold regarding intimate congress with the female sex, had I the necessary inspiration."

Beth, it would appear, possessed intriguing knowledge about more than a few of the men of Plymouth. Constable Felix did not cease beating Hal but he said nothing further to Beth about bathing and endured her attentions with a stoic grimace on his plump face. It seemed curious to me that I, who was supposed to receive the reprimand, was receiving the least injury although I could not decide whether Hal was worse off than the constable or vice versa. At last the beadle allowed his arm to rest and the lash to relax upon the cobblestones.

"Why have you stopped, man?" Constable Felix asked, giving Hal another knock in emphasis. "Continue."

"The job is done, sir," Hal replied.

"You are mistaken! 'Tis not half done. Go on, else you will take the boy's station at the post."

"Hold, hold."

Thomas Doughty was sauntering toward us. A twitch at the corner of his mouth betrayed that he was having difficulty maintaining a solemn demeanor. This did not endear him to Constable Felix, who freed his love-lock from Beth's hold and settled his hat upon his head.

"Who are you, sir, to interfere with the execution of justice?" he replied, passion getting the better of sense for it was plain Doughty was a gentleman even if Constable Felix was ignorant of his exact identity.

"Why, I am little when compared to a dignitary such as yourself, sir," Doughty answered in so smooth a tone that the sarcasm was lost upon the constable. "Most recently I had the privilege of serving his lordship Christopher Hatton in the capacity of private secretary. At present I am engaged on an insignificant venture on behalf of her grace Elizabeth to negotiate a trade agreement with the sultan of Alexandria. My name, sir, is Thomas Doughty."

This revelation had a sobering effect on Constable Felix and for a moment I hoped he would swallow his tongue in a fit of apoplexy but he recovered his poise and regained enough temerity to argue.

"Your permission, sir," said the constable, "my charge was to ensure the delivery of two dozen strokes of the lash upon the back of this young felon, Peregrine James."

"Which you have done, sir. I myself noted each one as it was dealt and your man provided an exact measure."

"If your worship says so," said Felix, plainly unconvinced. But another thwack of the stick upon Hal's back put the constable in better spirits. "Audley, you laggard," he exclaimed, "what are you waiting for? Undo the boy and get on with business."

The audience began to disperse, some returning to their shops, others to their homes, most to idleness along the waterfront. Soon Hal, Beth, and Doughty were my sole companions.

While the beadle freed my wrists, I said, "You have my thanks, Hal. I only wish I were not so dull and a better player besides. I fear the constable will not be kind to you."

"Do not worry on my behalf," he answered. "I can handle Felix. A shilling or two, or even better a kidney pie baked by a widow I know, will do wonders toward easing his temper."

As I rubbed my wrists where the manacles had chafed them, Thomas Doughty came over and regarded me with amusement. Hooking his thumbs in the belt supporting his blade, a slim rapier of the kind used on the continent, he said, "You intrigue me, Mr. James. I did not expect cunning from such an earnest fellow. I supposed you to be a simple lad."

I did not think it right to reveal Beth's leadership of the affair. "Sir," I said hotly, "even a simple lad or earnest fellow will go to extraordinary lengths when wrongly convicted of crime by the slander of evil men."

"Hold, Mr. James. I speak in admiration, not in censure."

"Then you will have me on the adventure, sir?"

"As the matter stands, no. Captain Drake charged me with bearing report of your fortitude under the lash. In conscience, this I cannot do since I have not seen it. Would you have my recommendation, there is just one thing to be done and one thing only."

"Tell me what that is, Captain Doughty."

"Why, Mr. James, 'tis child's play. You must endure another stint at the whipping post. What is more," Doughty went on, "so that I may have confidence the strokes fall true, this time I must wield the rod myself."

Bathing in Plymouth Sound

November 15, 1577, later
Sutton Pool, the Barbican

Once again I approached the whipping post, on this occasion of my own accord and not because I was being dragged to it in chains, which made some difference in my attitude but not much. I took hold of the ring and readied myself, allowing my gaze to return to the *Pelican* and the hubbub around her, trying to think of the future and not of the present. Behind me I heard Doughty take the cat from Hal and come within striking distance. I understood the reason behind his insistence that I accept the beating at his hands and I did not disagree with it. Captain Drake, after brief acquaintance, had impressed me as having little tolerance for less than precise obedience to his commands. Yet it required all my will to submit to the lash.

As he had promised, Doughty did not hold back.

The first time the cattails stroked me I thought I was burned by fire. The second time by acid. The third time by the claws of a demon.

"Sweet Jesus, give me courage," I muttered between clenched teeth, clinging to the ring in the post as if to a mast in a storm. My throat was so raw, I did not recognize my own voice.

In a louder tone I called: "Could you hasten the procedure, Captain Doughty? I fear the ship will sail without us."

"Everything in its season, Mr. James," he replied, unleashing another stroke as stern as the ones previous. "Five!"

I no longer had the breath to speak. My greatest fear was that I would shame myself, as I had seen others do while undergoing similar treatment, and lose ownership of my body in public before everyone. This worry allowed me to forget for complete seconds the anguish I was enduring, but then there it was again, piercing like nails. My eyes clouded and I could not see. The knowledge that I was crying, albeit soundlessly, made me furious with myself. I could not afford the embarrassment of weakness and I filled my lungs with a shriek of rage, venting the noise in a wordless howl.

"Six!"

Anticipation was an evil thing, allowing my mind to summon a hundred dreadful phantoms and to live through a hundred dreadful fancies while I waited for the next stroke to fall. Yet I refused to shrink away, and I bit my bottom lip until it bled. Then Doughty said:

"That is all, Mr. James. You may stand down."

These words, coming when I expected another stroke, caused me such astonishment that I gave an inarticulate bellow before sagging to my knees. "How can it be done, sir?" I asked. "The sentence was two dozen blows and you have not delivered half that."

"It was not my concern to punish you, Mr. James, but to test your courage. Having done so, I may now carry a good report to Drake."

"Thank you, sir."

"Do not thank me. I am a practical man, not a kind one.

You would be of little worth to our venture if you were crippled. Now, harlot—" Doughty was addressing Beth, and I did not care for his manner—"see to the boy. Wash him and tend his scrapes. The expedition sails with the ebb, which comes just before nightfall."

We rode in Hal's cart to Beth's lodgings, which were in the neighborhood known as the Barbican and close by the Jack and Rasher, the inn that had once belonged to my parents, and where I had been employed by the new owner, Annie's father, until he learned of our courtship. Hal helped me negotiate the narrow staircase to the third story and laid me down on my stomach on the bed. My next clear memory was of pain as Beth applied a damp cloth to my back.

"Must you torture me?" I protested. "Have I not suffered enough."

"Lie still, Perry. Wounds must be cleansed, else they fester."

"I would prefer the festering."

"'Tis not an option." She went on swabbing my back, pausing only to dip the cloth into the earthenware crock of vinegar that rested on the table beside the bed. Then she said, "There is no need to journey to Alexandria, Perry. It is a distant place and the voyage is sure to be perilous. Take the money I have for you and go to London instead."

"I told you, Beth. I will not go to London. I cannot explain why, but I have an urge to travel, and the farther the better."

"I understand. You think you will escape your memories."

"Maybe. I do not know."

"Peregrine, memories cannot be left behind. You carry them with you wherever you go, even if it is ten thousand miles."

Beth helped me sit up and wrapped a length of clean linen around my torso as a bandage. Then she studied me, and apparently arrived at a decision. "I must tell you something I should have told you long ago," Beth said slowly. "You must forget Annie. She is not worthy of you."

"That is not so!"

"Perry, she is a pretty girl and has what all pretty girls have between their thighs. But Annie never returned your love. She was lying with Kit Gibbons, who is to be her husband, even as she lay at your side."

"A whore's lie."

"Who would know a whore better than another one? Have you ever wondered how her father learned of her gift? You never wore the brooch but concealed it beneath your pallet."

"He was always going through my things on one pretext or another, as all masters do," I answered weakly. "It was discovered by accident."

"By accident? She is a conniving wench who took her pleasure. When she feared your affection might interfere with her profitable marriage, she informed her father of the circumstances."

"Beth, you are breaking my heart."

"Better your heart than your neck. Oh, Perry, I have failed my duty. I pledged your mother on her death bed I would regard you as my brother and guide your progress to manhood. But look at you. Has there been another so innocent?"

I turned my face to the pillow and hid my eyes in order to hide my tears. But I could not hide from the truth in Beth's words, and a sob wracked me as I contemplated Annie's betrayal and my own stupidity. Then Beth was cradling my head against her bosom.

"Do you suppose Annie ever loved me?" I asked.

"Who can say? But love is fleeting and without endurance. The calculating person, whether man or woman, does not build a future upon such an infirm foundation."

"I hear you. On my oath, I swear I will never love again."

"I would not want that, Perry. Rather say you will bestow your affections more wisely and with discretion."

"It will be so."

There was the slam of a door and a heavy stumping tread as someone ascended the staircase. Wheezing from the exertion of the climb, Hal Audley entered the room. "Damn it, Beth," he said, massaging his knees, "why must you dwell at such an altitude?"

"'Tis to weed out those without the stamina to provide me proper service," she replied.

"Well, mistress, we shall soon put your philosophy to the test."

Hal had brought with him a canvas bag, from which he pulled an assortment of clothing and gear. "Put these on," he told me.

"They are not mine," I said.

"Certainly not. Your belongings were sold to defray trial expenses."

"I cannot pay for them."

"Do not forget the sum I have for you," Beth interrupted.

"I said I will never touch Annie's money."

Beth sighed. "You still believe it hers?" she asked.

Finally I understood—the money was Beth's. Only Hal's presence prevented me from breaking into fresh tears at this demonstration of tenderness. "I cannot accept your charity," I protested.

"It is not charity," she said, "just repayment for the many mercies Dolores"—my mother—"showed a silly girl newly come from the countryside to this hard city. Now, Hal, how much do I owe?"

"Nothing, mistress," he answered. "I, too, owe a debt, mine to Nicholas—"Audley was referring to my father "—who gave me license to run up a tab for victuals and drink without pressing for compensation. When Nick passed, knowledge of the debt died with him except in mine own brain, where it has been a guilty canker. In any case, I have spent your money outfitting the boy and some of my own besides."

The clothing Hal provided was worn but serviceable: sailor's breeches of thick blue wool, cut loosely to afford freedom of motion; shirts of gray canvas with matching sleeves; a leather doublet; several sets of knitted hose; and a pair of leather knee-high boots known as cockers. These things were wrapped within a woolen cloak along with some other small items and a sturdy belt, from which hung a knife. The hilt was plain wood wrapped in rawhide to prevent the grip from slipping, the iron was stained and discolored, and the edge was blunt, but I could tell by its full tang that the blade was good. I knew a little effort with a whetstone would restore its bite, if not its beauty.

The beadle helped me into shirt, doublet, sleeves, and jerkin, and secured the cloak across my shoulders with a brass clasp. I buckled the belt around my waist, slinging the knife from my hip. I placed my new hat, a jaunty thing of gray felt with a velvet band in which was stuck a dove's feather, upon my head at a slant.

"Marvelous, Perry," Beth exclaimed, clapping her hands together as if amazed. "If I did not know better, I would believe you a gentleman indeed although somewhat come down in the world."

Then Hal Audley gave me his arm and we descended the stairs to the ground floor, stepping outside as the bells of St. Andrew's struck four o'clock. Due to the lateness of the season, the sun was already well along toward the west, its orb hidden by the buildings of the neighborhood, and the narrow avenue was cloaked in shadow as we hastened to the waterfront. The ebb was approaching.

Here the angle of the setting sun permitted its light to spread upon the water like a skein of fire. The southern horizon was rich indigo streaked with violet, against which the masts and spars of the anchored merchant and fishing vessels were a darker tracery. I went to the lip of the wharf and peered into the twilight. For a moment I could not find her, and I feared we had arrived too late, but at last I made out the *Pelican* swimming in the gloaming like the bird that was her namesake. With each heave against her cables she seemed to strain to take flight and flee the land, and although I was no sailor, by the bustle of activity on her deck I knew she would soon cast off.

I began to doubt I would reach her in time.

Beth, however, had not paused to gawk. She had found a wherry further along the quay, hired it, and was spurring its oarsmen toward where Hal and I stood. "Put your backs into the work, you evil animals," she chastised the pair while keeping pace ashore as the boat sped along the pilings. "Sweet Jesus, a woman could pull with more vigor. Stroke, I say. The lad must board the *Pelican*."

"Unlikely, mistress," answered one wherry man.

"Most improbable," said the other, shaking his huge block of a head in the manner of a scholar rendering verdict on some question of logic.

"I will give you *unlikely* and *most improbable*," Beth replied, undaunted by the fact that each of these men possessed arms thicker than her thighs and thighs fatter around than her waist. "More to the point," she went on as they backed their oars and slowed the wherry from its headlong rush with such expertise that the prow nudged the pilings without a noise, "more to the point," Beth continued, "I will pay you not a groat should you fail but three pence a man should you succeed."

"And what of our gratuity?" asked the first with a broad grin, which split his face in half and revealed a mouthful of square teeth colored black and yellow.

"Aye, mistress," said the second. "A gratuity is customary in such circumstances."

Beth was already herding me to the ladder that led down to the water. "We will speak of gratuities if there is need," she replied. "Perhaps I could arrange you five minutes with an old sow of my acquaintance. That should be ample reward for such a sorry pair of louts."

"Ten minutes and no less will I accept," said the first man. "Is that not my firm rule, Harry?"

"You may keep the sow for all of me," replied his companion. "My preference is for tender piglets with soft ears and tails. I am partial to their squealing."

Beth ignored this repartee while the wherry men laughed at their own drollery, a deep booming rumble. I clasped the top rung of the ladder, searched with the toe of my boot for footing, and climbed down with care. The tide was high and I did not have far to go before a hand took my wrist in an unbreakable grip and assisted me over the gunwale and onto a plank seat in the stern of the boat.

"Keep your rump still and do not squirm, lad," instructed the man named Harry. "My mate and I must pull with all our might if we are to meet the *Pelican*. Can you not hear the capstan working?"

"Peregrine!"

I raised my eyes and saw Beth silhouetted against the sunset. Her hair was loose in the breeze and her short cloak was streaming behind her. The wind pressed her dress to her body, outlining her figure and demonstrating how diminutive a woman she actually was. I could never think of Beth as small since her character was so much larger than life.

"Take care, Perry," she called, waving slowly. "Please, take care."

Hal stood beside her, also silhouetted, but in his case the effect was more comical than touching since his nose gave him closer resemblance to some grotesque animal than to a human man. "Here, lad," he said, tossing down the canvas sack containing my belongings. "Remember my principle, Perry," he went on. "If you would do it, do it well!"

"Aye, Hal, you have my promise," I answered.

The wherry men, one sitting before the other, braced themselves for the task at hand, all humor set aside as they found their rhythm. The blades of their oars rose and fell in precise sequence, cutting the water in silence but leaving behind eddies of foam, bright whorls upon the dark surface. Both wore vests without sleeves, which allowed view of the slabs of muscle that were their chests, and the tree trunks that were their arms, and the action beneath the skin as their thews knotted and relaxed and knotted again. They understood their job so well, and were so familiar with the harbor and the position of the resting ships, that never once did either spare a glance over his shoulder, but held and restarted their strokes as if in obedience to commands I could not hear. Their breath issued in long plumes from their mouths as they breathed but neither was breathing hard. Nor were they sweating.

Recognizing good advice, I kept my seat still on the plank and tried not to squirm. As I took a final look at where Beth and Hal were outlined by the last light, I felt a strange ache of emotion. It was unlikely I would see either again for years, if at all, and I was already missing them both. I doubted I would ever find other friends as steadfast and true.

On either side of the rowboat were clutters of fishing smacks, river barges, and coastal traders, some tied to buoys, others with their anchors out on either side of their bows. Most were dark, their crews ashore except for skeleton watches, bow and stern lanterns lighting their decks and the lower shrouds, the only noise the creaking of rigging and the mutter of timbers. All the vessels were being pulled in the same direction by the ebb tide, toward the harbor mouth.

We were fifty yards from the *Pelican* when I had my first good look at her. She was lit brightly enough so I could see the color of her paint in the gloom—deep blue along her sides, with a bit of scarlet showing at the waterline, and ribbons of gold detailing her gun ports and upper decks. Her railings were trimmed with alternating bars of red and yellow, as were the windows of the captain's cabin at the stern of the ship.

She was a slim galleon, one hundred feet in length and just over twenty feet wide. Three towering masts rose skyward, the foremast and mainmast square-rigged but the mizzenmast lateen-rigged, its spar pointing backward instead of at right angles to the ship's hull. There was no figurehead beneath the bowsprit but she was an imposing vessel nonetheless, at least in my eyes. At the stern, a half deck and a poop deck were built above the main deck and on top of one another, so that the rear of the ship rose higher than the forepart, something like the posture of a cat crouching to strike. On the half deck I saw Drake, his fiery hair unmistakable, as was his pose of command.

The ship's capstan was located just below the half deck in the waist. It was a round device with stout spokes, known as handspikes, radiating from the central core. A capstan was essentially a rotating horizontal wheel allowing the cable and anchor to be lowered and raised despite their combined weight. There was room at each spoke for two men, but even so working the capstan was never easy. As the sailors heaved at the handspikes, everyone sang together to synchronize their efforts:

"In Amsterdam there lived a maid,
Mark well what I do say,

In Amsterdam there lived a maid
And she was mistress of her trade.

"I'll go no more a roving with you fair maid
A-roving, a-roving
Since roving's been my rue-I-ay
I'll go no more a-roving with you fair maid. "

With each repetition of *a-roving* the men put their shoulders to the handspikes and pushed. As they recited the final words of the chorus, and gathered breath to begin the next verse, the anchor suddenly came loose and sped to the surface.

Hearing this, the wherry men lengthened their stroke, levering their oars against the thole pins in the gunwale at such a steep angle, and with such force, that the blades dipped into the water parallel to the bow and did not return into the air until they were alongside the stern. I could only admire such a fine display of effort and think their talk of gratuities had not been so empty of credit as I had assumed.

The rattling ceased and after a silence there were a couple louder clunks, the sound of the anchor being fastened to the cathead beam that projected from the side of the bow.

The forward wherry man glanced around at the *Pelican*. "No tugs," he observed. "The cheeky devil will not be warping out."

"Aye, Wilbert," said Harry after a glance of his own. "Drake is a proud bastard. Ah, now I hear it. Listen, the fore course is being raised."

Even I, with my limited nautical experience, understood

Drake had chosen the more difficult method of departing the harbor. Instead of allowing the *Pelican* to be towed safely to open water by oared boats, he had decided to advertise his seamanship by steering with the ebb tide. Without a good wind behind her, however, the ship would be sluggish and respond badly to the rudder. Ahead was the mouth of Sutton Pool, which must be squeezed through, a channel thirty yards wide.

"So we are too late," I said as the *Pelican* began to slip away with the current, taking with her my dreams of good fortune. It was impossible to imagine that a day beginning with a whipping could become worse, yet such was the case.

"'Tis never too late for the stout of heart," replied Wilbert. "Is that not so, Harry?"

"Aye, mate. For the brave, all is possible."

The fact that this odd pair of philosophers continued to stroke without let-up allowed me to hope they knew some detail I did not. "Will you speak plainly," I asked. "I do not understand you."

"There is a boarding ladder not yet secured, hanging amidships. Did you observe it, Wilbert?" inquired Harry.

"I did. Someone will suffer when the sloppiness is discovered since Drake is unforgiving of slack. In any case, lad, some fool's fault provides your window of opportunity. Harry and I will draw nigh the ladder, whereupon you must leap up and grab hold and clamber aboard as easy as one, two, three."

I suspected the procedure was not as simple as Wilbert described but I knew I had no other option. "Let us be about it quickly," I said.

The *Pelican* was approaching the harbor mouth, her speed

increasing as the current funneled through the narrow gap. The fore course had caught a bit of wind, not much but enough to heel the ship a little, exposing her red belly. On her present heading the *Pelican* would enter the passage less than ten yards from the embankment upon which rose the squat blockhouse guarding the east side of the channel. This was a windowless square of stone three stories high. On the flat roof a signal fire burned, providing guidance for marine traffic and spilling a bloody glow on the jagged rocks that surrounded the point like teeth in a jaw. The full moon in the cloudless sky cast down a glowing silver radiance on the ship and the water.

From the city behind us came the somber peal of Yogge's bells noting the hour. "Prepare yourself, lad," muttered Harry. "At my word, seize the moment."

"I am ready."

I slung the canvas bag by its strap across my shoulders and crouched on the plank seat on all fours.

For the first time the wherry men began sweating, forcing each stroke to come faster than the last. The tiny boat shot into the narrow gap between the *Pelican* and the land, passing so close by the bank that I could have stepped ashore without getting wet. Then we were alongside her, coming up from the stern toward the ladder, which lay flush to the hull due to the angle at which the ship was leaning. With naked strength, Harry and Wilbert took us right to the ladder and held the wherry in position using only their port oars, bringing the starboard blades inboard so to get as close as possible to the target.

"Now, lad," Harry grunted. "Luck!"

At his command I sprang for the ladder and caught a

rung with both hands, flailing about with my boots until they, too, found support. The cord was thick but moved around alarmingly. The rungs, strands of thinner cord coated with black tar, sank in the center when I put weight on them and made each step an effort. When I had climbed a length above the water, Wilbert and Harry rested their oars and allowed the wherry to fall back. Then I looked up, and wished I had not. Although the actual distance could not have been much more than a dozen feet, the gunwale seemed a mile overhead.

Taking each rung only after careful preparation, I began the ascent.

That was the moment the *Pelican* heeled over in the other direction. Instead of being pressed against the hull, the ladder fell away from the planking, carrying me into the air. My pretty new hat flew off my head as I swayed back and forth and my boots skidded from the rung they were on, leaving me suspended by just my handholds.

The ladder bent away from me each time I tried to kick my feet back onto a rung. Then my grip slipped and I slid down for a terrible second, my palms burning from friction and because of contact with the brine soaking the cord.

The toes of my boots were a foot above the surface when I managed to catch the third from last rung with a desperate grab. But the next instant I was in saltwater up to my thighs, and then up to my waist, as the wind freshened and the *Pelican* heeled further on her side. The pressure of the water dragged me behind the ladder and threatened to break my hold. Spray was striking me like shot and choking my mouth and nostrils. I was sure I would lose my grip and sink into the cold depths of Plymouth Sound. Yet another lurch of the ship hoisted me back into the air. The respite let me regain my footing and clamber up a couple rungs before the *Pelican* dipped again and dunked me once more in the sea.

This time I kept hold and continued fighting upward until I was well above the water. The trick, I discovered, was to clasp the ladder between my knees and scale it sideways instead of from the front.

I was passing the gun ports—ominous square windows battened down with thick shutters, these colored the same blue as the hull except for an outline of gold paint—when there was a sharp report. The ship shuddered like a horse preparing to gallop and then surged forward as one sail after another was set.

I craned my neck and watched them swell with wind, a garden of strange and beautiful flowers blooming in the moonlight. The highest sails, the topsails, had square red crosses in their centers but the lower ones, the main courses, were plain white. Small dark blotches against the canvas were sailors balancing on lines far above the deck.

With a last desperate lunge, I caught hold of the gunwale and dragged myself upright. Soaked and bleeding, chilled to the marrow, bedraggled, and bare-headed, I hoisted one leg after the other over the railing, stepped on deck, and so came aboard the *Pelican*.

Bad Weather Aboard the *Pelican*

November 16, 1577
Off the Coast of England

"Welcome aboard, Mr. James," said Captain Drake, observing my arrival from the half deck, where he had a commanding view of the ship, the sails that rose above us, and the water on either side of the vessel. "I had begun to think you would not keep your appointment."

Behind him Thomas Doughty was leaning against the mizzenmast, a trunk as thick as my arm from elbow to fingertip yet girdled by iron bands for additional strength.

"I suspect Mr. James was delayed by the need to console his lady friend, who is a rare vixen," Doughty remarked. "Do you know, it seems our new cook is a whoremaster of enviable reputation."

"Is he, by God? I like that, Tom. It is a fine quality in a man. But what I do not care for—" now Drake was addressing me—"what I do not care for, lad, is allowing pleasure to interfere with business. You are aboard my ship and in my service. I demand obedience in all things, great and small. Do you understand, Mr. James?"

It was clearly the wiser course to agree with Drake and not to contradict his false impression of my qualities and of my relationship with Beth.

"Yes, sir."

"Blacollers!" Drake called.

"Aye, captain!" answered someone behind me.

"Have a firm conversation with the man who left the port ladder unsecured."

"I will, captain. It will not happen again."

"See that it does not." Now Drake returned his attention to me. "Are you ill, lad?" he asked. "You do not look well."

"To be honest, sir, I am not feeling my best."

Much had happened in the six hours since I began my walk to the whipping post and now all my hurts began clamoring with one voice.

What was worse was the swaying of the deck as the *Pelican* made way into Plymouth Sound. Turning to the railing, I heaved my guts into the ocean and then did it three times more.

"Do you suppose Mr. James is seasick?" Doughty asked.

"My God, I believe you have hit on it, Tom," Drake laughed. "'Tis hard to credit, considering the gentleness of the water. Lackland! Lackland, where are you? Move your tail when I call."

"Aye, sir, I hear you," replied a breathless voice.

With the sails set, men were descending from the rigging and beginning new tasks. Some came down by way of the shrouds, the lines connecting the masts to the sides of the ship. Others slid along the back-stays that stretched from the mastheads to the deck and braced the timbers against the pull of the sails. Most of the sailors went about their business with the surety that comes from knowing a profession well. Many, I would learn, had sailed with Drake before, during the famous raid on Nombre de Dios, which had made his reputation.

The boy who answered Drake's summons was two or three years my junior. "What would you have, captain?" he asked.

"Escort Mr. James below deck and find him a berth. In the morning introduce him to Mr. Stydye, who will be his master."

The look Lackland turned me expressed little enthusiasm for this duty but his reply was prompt enough.

"Aye, sir," he said and then opened a hatch and disappeared into it without waiting to see if I was following. A short ladder led into the dank gloom of the gun deck. Here there was not much more than five feet of overhead and taller men had to go about stooping, as I discovered after receiving a hard knock when I stood upright.

"God knows where to put you in this stinking rat's nest," Lackland said as I rubbed my new bruise.

What took up most of the room were the cannon—seven on each side of the ship, monstrous hulks barely visible in the shadows. They were demi-culverins, bronze guns that could shoot nine-pound balls fifteen hundred yards, or drive the rounds through two feet of oak at shorter distances. The tapered barrels were mounted on solid wood carriages with thick wheels and secured in place by turns of cord. Shorter lengths of cord clamped the carriages to the deck, and wedges at each wheel further restricted the motion of the weapons.

Brazil beds—hammocks—were strung from gun to gun, bags and bedrolls were stuffed wherever there was space, and every inch of bulkhead held cabinets or shelves crammed with supplies, enough to allow the *Pelican* to remain independent of the land for a year. Toward the bow were the carpenter's shop, the smithy, the armory, and a half dozen cabins and storerooms, mostly separated from one another by sheets of canvas instead of by true bulkheads. In the center of the deck—where the main hatch opened, allowing cargo to be lowered into the hold or hoisted from it—was a corral of wood slats, in which were five pigs, an equal number of sheep, and six calves. Smaller crates held flocks of ducks, chickens, and doves.

Neither the birds nor the livestock were happy and they were all loudly venting their displeasure.

They did not smell sweet, either.

"Spew into the bucket," Lackland instructed, shoving one into my hands. "No puking or pissing elsewhere, not even into the fire box, captain's orders." Then he buried his face into a pail of his own. "God rot all ships and the fools who sail them," he gasped from below the rim.

"My guess is you are no more a sailor than I am," I observed when I had breath.

"A sailor?" Lackland snorted contemptuously. "Never. I am a musician, a lutenist of destiny, although unappreciated by this sad world and forced to slave for my inferiors."

It was with a feeling of familiarity that I eventually found a place among the cooking supplies, surrounded by casks of carrots, peas, barley, apples, and walnuts. Undressing was a miserable affair and the effort of wrapping myself in a blanket and crawling onto the straw pallet left me weak. But as I lay swaddled in coarse wool, I began to feel warm, and the rocking of the *Pelican* became comforting, as if I were in my mother's arms. "*Mi hijo*," she had called me. "My son." I had missed her each day of the six years she had been gone.

When I awoke, the snoring and grumbling and more intimate noises of many men sleeping in close quarters reminded me I was aboard a ship at sea. The gun deck was covered by a latticework grate, which allowed some fresh air below, and I could see a patch of sky and a bit of topsail, above which flew a pennant bearing the design of a globe of the world with the North Star on it. I sat up and in one blinding instant recalled every place I hurt. Most of the stiffness had worked from my muscles, however, by the time I pulled on my boots. Then I did what I could with my appearance, which was not much, and made my way onto the main deck. The horizon was blue along its entire circumference.

A half mile astern were the sails of three other ships, their canvas bellied with the same wind that was moving the *Pelican*. Close to starboard was another galleon—the *Elizabeth*, whose captain was John Winter, the third of the expedition's leaders, a man I did not know nor knew much about. She was a smaller vessel, only eighty feet in length, her hull painted glossy black with a blood red trim.

"There you are, Mr. James," said Tobias Lackland in an aggrieved tone. "I feared the worst when I found you missing from your place."

"I could not sleep. Is it not a glorious morning?"

Lackland's morose temperament did not allow him to share my perspective. "If you broke your neck wandering about, whose fault would it be?" he asked rhetorically. "Mine, of course. Drake would be sure to hold me accountable for your demise. I swear, the fates conspire to make my life living misery. Why else would I be aboard this foul ship with a pirate for a captain and nursemaid to a cook?"

"Tell me, Tobias. Why are *you* aboard? Are you not a

lutenist of destiny, after all?"

"That I am," he replied seriously. "But I am also apprenticed to John Bruer, the master of our musical company and a dear friend of the captain's. Unforgivably, Bruer never thought to ask my opinion before accepting the engagement. Worse, he lends me out as a page whenever the consort is not rehearsing. I do not appreciate this."

"Why would Drake need musicians—" I began but then recalled Doughty's remark that it might be necessary to entertain certain foreign dignitaries aboard the *Pelican*. "I follow. It is to advertise that the captain is no penniless adventurer but a man of refinement who travels in style with money to waste on luxuries."

Lackland shrugged sourly. "You must visit the grand cabin, where the young lords bivouac. There is silver for the table and other extravagant appointments."

I nodded in admiration of Drake's cunning. "The sultan of Alexandria will have no choice but to recognize him as a gentleman and deal with him accordingly."

"The sultan of Alexandria?" Lackland asked, raising one brow in an arch of condescension. "Somehow I doubt we will be encountering that worthy any time soon."

"But in Plymouth everyone said Drake had license from the queen to negotiate with the Turks."

Lackland shook his head in wonder of my naïveté. "Do not believe all you hear," he said in a whisper although no one was close by. "We are no more going to Alexandria than to the moon."

"And our true destination?"

Lackland shrugged. "Who can say? Wherever there are Spanish or Portuguese ships to rob. But I will tell you what I think on your word not to reveal it to any soul."

"I will be quiet."

"All right. Now look here." Lackland climbed the ladder to the forecastle deck and led me to a stack of lumber tied to the deck behind the foremast and covered by a tarred canvas tarp. Each piece of wood was sawn into shape, planed smooth, and stenciled with a number. "It is a pinnace, do you see?" Lackland explained—a small boat that could be rowed like a galley or sailed before the wind. "The thing is in parts. But if you followed the ciphers and had a hammer and nails, you could assemble her in a day. There are three others besides this down in the hold, also in pieces," he went on. "Each can carry twenty men. All are reinforced to support artillery. And the *Pelican* has extra cannon stowed in the ballast."

"Your point?"

"What do you know of the captain's last expedition?"

"Just tavern rumors. It was five or six years ago, am I right?"

Lackland nodded. "Many of our crew of ruffians were on the voyage," he went on, "and I have had the truth from them. You know the Isthmus of Panama—'tis the Godforsaken land that divides the American continent. It is where the Spanish transport their wealth from the Pacific coast to the Atlantic—silver from the mines of Peru, mostly. They carry the stuff by mule across the isthmus and then ship it to Europe. Drake planned to ambush a caravan and take the treasure."

"Yes, that is what I heard."

"Less well known is that Drake scouted the terrain in the company of a man named John Oxenham. Panama, and we will learn this on our own, never fear, Panama is a stinking jungle, full of biting gnats called mosquitoes and venomous worms and other creatures I would rather not know better. Their guides were Cimarrons, a bastard race of escaped slaves and native Indians. They led Drake and Oxenham to an ancient tree with steps cut in its trunk, which brought them to a platform among the leaves. From this vantage point it was possible to see this very ocean and then, after turning your head, to see the Southern Ocean. 'Damn me, John,' Drake told Oxenham. 'Damn me as a liar if I do not sail that water on an English ship. You are witness I will, or die trying.'

"Well, Oxenham is dead," Lackland finished, "or as good as dead, seeing the Inquisition has him, and 'tis well known the fate of Christians in the hands of Papists. So the task of bearing witness has fallen to us. Drake is carrying onboard the disassembled parts of four small armed ships and I do not wonder why. Mark my words, we will have to lug the damn things on our backs eighty leagues across the isthmus and rebuild them when we reach the Pacific coast. This will allow Drake to fulfill his oath and have an English deck under him as he sails where he pleases on the Southern Ocean, and what pleases our captain will displease the dons, if you follow my logic."

"So the true agenda is a raid over Panama into the Pacific?"

"You did not hear it from me."

This was a lot to think about and I was not sure whether I accepted Lackland's conclusions or what I felt about being on a privateering voyage instead of on a peaceful merchant venture. But I had little time to consider the matter since Lackland had begun leading me about the ship in order to introduce me to the men I needed to meet.

The first was Thomas Blacollers, boatswain or chief mate of the *Pelican*, who had authority over the sailors and the routine of the vessel. He was a short burly man with a pockmarked face sanded into fissures by sun and brine and a tangle of yellow hair reddened by salt. His fist swallowed mine as we shook hands, calluses as hard as stone on his fingers and on the heel of his palm.

"Saw you come aboard," Blacollers said. "Bless me, I never laughed so hard in my life."

"In the future I will try not to be as entertaining," I replied stiffly.

"Never be ashamed of innocence, lad," he told me. "It is, God be praised, a condition for which there is a cure. Now climb the mast to the level of the fighting top."

"Pardon me, sir?"

Blacollers placed a hand on my arm and with the other pointed skyward. "See the mast, lad?" he asked patiently.

"I do."

"It is the foremast, coming as it does at the fore of the ship. Is that not simplicity itself?"

"It is, sir."

"At the juncture of the lower foremast and the upper foremast is the platform known as the fighting top, where archers perch during battle. Do you see the thing to which I refer, lad?"

"Aye, sir. It is a precarious roost perhaps forty feet above the deck."

"The precise place I mean. Now listen with both ears. The survival of a ship at sea depends on the effort of all her men without the exception of one. Since you are a member of our crew, lad, you must be a sailor in deed as well as name. The first step in this process of learning is to become acquainted with altitude. Soon you will enjoy the experience aloft as much as young Lackland does. It is difficult to believe that less than a week ago he was no more a mariner than yourself but only an effete instrumentalist. Tobias, boy, precede Mr. James up the mast, if you would, and provide demonstration of the correct procedure."

"Aye, sir," Lackland replied in a loud voice while turning me a reproachful glance and saying more softly:

"One day I will slip and break my neck and the world will have lost the flower of an age. God almighty in the heavens, I deplore heights."

"Is there some trick?" I asked.

"First, discard your boots. Second, do not look down."

Lackland jumped onto the ship's rail, caught hold of the shrouds, and began clambering up them while muttering under his breath.

The shrouds were rigging, six lines to a side, that provided the mast additional stability by pulling it between them. They attached to the mast just below the fighting top and fanned out downward to opposite gunwales, where they were connected to the hull by pulleys, which allowed them to be tightened or loosened. Each shroud was tied to its neighbor by shorter horizontal lengths of tarred line—*ratlines*—and I followed Lackland's example by using these like the rungs of a ladder to make my ascent.

At first I focused my eyes on where I was placing my hands and nowhere else but at the halfway point I looked around.

The deck was just twenty feet below but seemed many times more distant and the elevation made it feel like I was flying through the air whenever the *Pelican* surmounted a wave and descended into a trough. Only the sight of upturned faces watching my progress prevented me from publicly giving in to vertigo. Then the width between each shroud began shrinking, as did the vertical spacing of the ratlines. Soon the gaps were so tight I could no longer fit my feet between them.

"'Tis not much further," Lackland called. "Remember—do not look down."

The fighting top was built around the brace that held the upper part of the mast to the lower section. The main shrouds had become too narrow to climb but a second set, known as the futtocks, led up to the platform. These angled back away from the mast at such an incline that I went the last few rungs hanging fifteen degrees from vertical in the wrong direction. Nor was there an easy way to get from the futtocks onto the landing.

"Take my hand," Lackland said. "Everyone needs help the first time."

"No, I will do this on my own."

It was hard letting go of the line with one hand to wedge an elbow on the platform and even harder to swing my right leg away into space so I could wrestle a knee over the edge. For a moment I stuck in a position half above and half below the rim, unable to complete the motion that would carry me to safety.

A final lunge brought the rest of my weight onto the landing.

After this achievement all I wanted was to breathe

deeply while my heart slowed down. But I was determined to earn the respect of Thomas Blacollers and the rest of the audience on the deck below. Beside me another set of shrouds rose into the air, bracing the upper mast. I grabbed a line, hauled myself upright, and glanced around with what I hoped was a fair imitation of nonchalance.

"Well, we have done as the bastard instructed," Lackland said. "I cannot say I am enjoying the experience."

"The height does require getting used to," I agreed.

"Wait until you climb the topsails, Mr. James. Then we can talk of altitude."

Far below the *Pelican* was a toy boat at the mercy of the endless sea while far above the mast dwindled into the sky. Immediately in front of us the sails formed an immense vertical wall, the canvas quivering like a living thing as the wind filled it.

Nearly thirty feet more of the mast still rose above my head, the thin spire becoming a thinner splinter.

"Lackland," I began and had to clear my throat. "Lackland, not long ago I was advised to do a thing well if I were to do it at all. Let us continue to the next spar. What do you say?"

"I say we begin heading in the exact opposite direction."

"Then I suppose I will have to go it alone."

Without allowing Lackland time to argue, or giving myself chance to reconsider, I swung into the shrouds that led up the mast. The rigging narrowed quickly and I could barely get my toes in them. Each roll carried the mast overboard in a sweeping arc that made my stomach twist, and I knew I would miss the *Pelican* if I fell, never to be rescued.

The wind was making the rigging clatter and moan and

there was a sad whistling that did not stop. I felt the sheets vibrate in my grip and heard the mast complain in its socket, the doleful creaking of strong wood under pressure. Above me, seeming to float between the clouds and the ocean, was a narrow platform formed by a pair of crosstrees, known as the crow's nest. Shaking cold sweat from my forehead, I went up the last few yards and pulled myself onto the narrow ledge.

"Take heed where you put your clumsy feet," wheezed an old man with a mane of wild white hair and eyes so gray as to be almost white. "There is scarcely room for one here."

"Sorry," I said and squeezed around to the other side of the mast, which rose in the center of the framework and further reduced the available footage. "I did not know anyone else was up here."

The crow's nest swayed and creaked as I adjusted my position and the wind cried through the rigging, the sound of a child alone and abandoned. Beneath us, the *Pelican* was invisible, obscured by sails. The other ships of the expedition were smaller piles of billows upon the blue of the ocean, arrows of wake spreading behind them. Lifting my gaze to the horizon, I could see the curve of the world as it became a globe.

"Take care, *filos*," said the old sailor, clamping my shoulder with spidery fingers. "'Tis unwise to look at such a view for long."

The sound of his voice in my ear wrenched my attention back to earth. "Why not?"

"I am certain of nothing. But I have seen strong men come down from watch babbling like children, never afterward able to perform the most simple personal task. I have always supposed they stared too long into the distance, allowing their souls to wander from their eyes and become lost. Infinity is a dangerous condition. Mortal men must drink it in small doses, like *aqua vitae*."

It was clear from his accent that my companion was not English although I could not decide whether he was French or Italian, Spanish or Flemish, or from some other country entirely. I suspected, too, that he had been staring at the horizon despite his own warning. "Thank you for the advice," I said at last. "I will keep it in mind."

"Ah, you do not believe me. No, no, I take no offense. I have become accustomed to doubt. After so many decades it amuses me. Do you know why, lad?"

I shook my head. "No."

The old sailor cackled at a joke he had not yet told. "Because I have never mentioned to a living soul half the truth of what I witnessed. Is that not irony? For a man to hold his tongue and yet still be thought a liar?"

"I would have to say so, yes."

As if my pity had forged an intimate bond between us, the old sailor embraced me with a bony arm. The stink of wine on his breath provided an immediate explanation of both his fervor and his lunacy. He drew me close with surprising strength and pressed an unshaven cheek to mine. Mingled with the reek of liquor was a musty smell, like rotting onions.

"Now this is a pretty scene," Tobias Lackland observed, bringing his head over the rim of the crow's nest. He looked pointedly from me to my companion and then at the bottle poking from the old sailor's jacket.

"I climbed to this damnable aerie because I supposed

you needed help," Lackland went on. "Perhaps Mr. James has been overcome by altitude, I thought. Perhaps he requires aid. Instead I discover you carousing with Francisco Albo, as notorious a drunkard as any of our misbegotten crew despite his antiquity. Ah, why should I have expected different? 'Tis God's will no good deed of mine shall remain unpunished.

"And you, Albo," Lackland said to my companion, "it is a mystery beyond comprehension why the captain endures the company of such a decrepit wastrel."

This remark caused the old sailor to laugh so hard I thought he would strangle. "Truly you are a stupid boy," Albo wheezed, tears running from his eyes into the white stubble on his cheeks. "Nonetheless, your pretensions are endearing. In time I might become fond of you."

"Do not trouble yourself," Lackland replied. "I care nothing for your regard. Come, Mr. James, we must return below. I must introduce you to Master Stydye. Can you manage the descent?"

"I tell you, Lackland, we have not been carousing, nor am I drunk."

"As you like. Pray, do not embarrass me by plunging to your death. Drake will insist I clean up the mess."

Instead of descending by the shrouds, we took a faster route down by way of the stay, which was a cable stretching from the masthead to the deck at a steep angle. "Your feet control the descent," Lackland explained. "It is simple."

"In theory, yes."

"In practice, too."

Following his example, I grabbed on with both hands and swung my legs off the crosstree. Then I got the stay between my knees, clamped the line with my feet, and began letting myself downward hand over hand. Twilight engulfed me as I dropped among the sails and was surrounded by acres of canvas, then I was again in light. When I reached the deck, Lackland was already heading toward Thomas Blacollers, who was directing a gang of sailors at some task.

"God bless," the boatswain said when he noticed us, wiping grease from his hands with a rag and the last smudges from his fingers with his bristly beard. "There you are, lads. I had begun to wonder when you would be done skylarking."

"We were not skylarking, sir," I replied. "On your advice, I was deepening my acquaintance with altitude."

This answer amused Blacollers. "How did the friendship progress?"

"I cannot say we are bosom companions."

"Give it time. You will be surprised how even the plainest woman blooms after courtship."

"Sir—" put in Lackland. "The captain's instructions were that I am to introduce Perry to Master Stydye and get him started at his duties."

"I will handle that, lad. You may be about your business."

With a gesture that I should accompany him, Blacollers shambled to the main hatch, where the grating had been removed so that casks could be lifted to the deck by tackle attached to the spar of the mainmast. This operation was being supervised by a man with a pointed mustache and a vertical strip of beard between his bottom lip and chin, who was leaning forward and peering down into the hold. "No, no, you fool," he exclaimed to someone out of sight in the gloom. "The salted pork, not the beef. 'Tis marked clearly. Can you not read?"

"Certainly I can read," replied an affronted voice. "I know the alphabet as well as the next man."

"Then you can describe the symbol we require?"

"Easily. 'Tis a scrawny letter and has but a single tit instead of two. I believe it is known as a *P*."

"Truly your literacy comes as a pleasant surprise. Now get a barrel of pork on deck."

Blacollers chose this moment to interrupt. "Stydye, let me introduce Perry James. He is to be numbered among your staff as a cook."

"Is he, Blacollers? I have heard nothing of this."

"Drake signed Perry on just before we weighed anchor at the advice of Tom Doughty. The lad is well regarded in Plymouth."

"Then I suppose 'tis remotely possible he might be of use." Stydye looked me up and down and drew his mustache through his fingers with a dubious air. "Are you familiar with peeling carrots?" he asked.

"Aye, sir."

"And with cooking porridge so it does not burn?"

"The trick, sir, is to stir the pot over low heat."

"And do you know how many men are aboard this ship?"

"No, I do not."

"There are, including yourself, sixty-seven boys, sailors, men, and gentlemen. Each is entitled to a full pound of beef, pork, or mutton per day, with cod or ling served on Fridays, not to mention equal portions of vegetables and biscuit. Are you prepared to work hard and for however long necessary?"

"Without question."

"Excellent. Now let me see your knife."

"Sir?"

"Your knife, boy. Hand it over."

He was referring to the dagger Hal Audley had given me the day before. I had not thought of it since, nor had I repaired its bluntness. Stydye brushed a thumb across the edge and shook his head sadly. Returning the hilt to me, he observed, "An expert craftsman maintains his tools in ready condition. You would do well to follow this dictum in the future. Preparation is the key to all excellence."

"I will take every word to heart, sir," I answered, attempting to ignore my burning ears while replacing the dull blade in its sheath.

"I will say nothing more. Do you know what I mean by the *orlop*?"

"Aye, Mr. Stydye. It is the second deck below, just above the hold and beneath the gun deck."

"Exactly. There you will find Lancelot Garget, who is now your superior. Place yourself under Lancelot's command, heed what he says, and offer every assistance. Is any part of what I have said unclear?"

"No, sir."

"Then what are you lingering for, boy?"

Going below was a descent into hell from heaven. Above was clean air, open sky, limitless ocean. But as I went down the ladder to the lower deck, I reentered a dark narrow fetid world, dank and chill when it was not hot and stifling, and always unquiet with the noise of water against the hull and the creaking of the ship's timbers battling the pressure of the ocean. Some sailors were playing dice, rattling the bones excitedly before releasing the cubes, calling out bets in a babble of different languages since Drake's crew hailed from a dozen nations. Others, oblivious to the bedlam, snored in Brazil beds or on straw pallets.

Another ladder took me further down to a place where there was no light or air at all. The orlop, between the gun deck and the hold, was where the bulk supplies for the voyage were stored, as well as cable for the anchor and additional sails. Very large items, such as spare masts and spars, and heavy goods—including cannon, cannon shot, and anchors—were stowed in the bottommost deck, the hold, where they also served as ballast to keep the ship on an even keel.

Lancelot Garget was baiting a rat by the light of a lantern, dangling the animal by the tail while pricking its belly with the point of his knife as it writhed and squealed and tried to get away.

Then he slit its throat and tossed the corpse aside. "A waste of good meat," he observed. "But 'tis too early in the voyage for such cuisine to be appreciated."

"Forgive me if I doubt that time will ever come."

Garget regarded me with a knowing expression. "'Tis evidently your first occasion at sea, pretty boy," he said. "In a month or two you will be more than glad for a haunch of ocean fowl, or a rib of water coney, or perhaps a ragout of 'tweendeck venison."

His laughter was as thin as the rest of him, a nasal keening separated by quick hiccups, which expelled a warm mist into the air. Stepping back as far as permitted by the casks surrounding us, I said: "I hope you are incorrect, Mr. Garget. Still, it could be an interesting challenge to make such poor fare palatable. Perhaps enough rosemary or ginger would do the trick. There should also be a sufficiency of cracked black peppercorns and cloves, as well as gravy fortified with sherry wine."

Garget peered at me suspiciously. "Who are you, pretty boy?" he asked.

"I am your assistant, sir. My name is Peregrine James. Mr. Stydye instructed me to place myself at your service."

This revelation caused Garget to pinch his lips together in a displeased frown. He stepped forward until I had to endure his breath upon my face since there was no room to back away. "Let us get the situation straight between us from the start," Garget continued. "I am master, is that clear? I will hear no debate about the proper method of doing things. Nor do I wish advice, helpful suggestions, or polite recommendations. I am a simple Englishman and I cannot abide foreign flavors, particularly the stink of garlic. What I enjoy is food plainly cooked in the style my mother taught me, God rest the good woman."

"I, too, strive to follow my mother's example," I answered, meaning something entirely different since she had loved what Garget abhorred.

As I hoped, he did not understand me. "Then we are agreed. Now come, pretty boy. The beef requires boiling."

In order to prevent fire from escaping and running wild, all cooking aboard ship was done within an iron box a yard deep. We hoisted this on deck, packed it with tinder, and then filled the container with larger logs once the kindling was lit. Above the blaze went two heavy cauldrons, each supported on a tripod of metal legs. After I filled the pots with buckets of fresh water and rounds of meat, Garget had me peel and chop onions and carrots and add them to the stew. As the water came to a boil and began to throw off scum, I took a ladle and skimmed the broth, tossing the dirty foam over the side with a flick of my wrist. Garget appraised my efforts with a disbelieving air and said:

"Pray explain just what you are doing."

"Is it not evident, sir? I am removing the froth, which will impart a bitter or sour flavor to the dish if it is allowed to remain."

A long tired sigh issued through Garget's teeth as he shook his head in disapproval. "Do not bother," he said, "since no one will note the difference. Put your labor to better use by going below and fetching a round of cheese and a sack of biscuit. Is there a question, pretty boy?"

"I am thinking, sir, that now would be an opportune moment to add pepper and a handful of laurel leaves."

"Did you not listen? Did you not hear me? Did I not say I wanted no advice whatsoever, large or small?"

"Yes, sir, you did."

"Then heed my words, else I must complain to Mr. Stydye. Are we understood?"

"Aye, sir."

The crew of the *Pelican* ate their meals in separate groups, or messes—common sailors in one, craftsmen and petty officers in another, Drake and his staff in a third. Supper consisted of the boiled beef, wedges of hard cheese, apples, biscuit, and butter. Each mess sent representatives to carry their food back to them. As Garget had predicted, no one complained— except for Tobias Lackland. He arrived in the company of a boy his own age, a page named John, who was Drake's cousin.

As I speared chunks of beef with the point of my knife and dropped the meat into the pewter tureens they had brought to transport the stew, Lackland's countenance became melancholy.

"Learning of Mr. James's reputation, I had hoped for better," he said while regarding the grayish hunk of flesh steaming in its gray broth. "Alas, disappointment is my life's reward."

John Drake was as fair as the captain, his eyebrows and lashes so fine as to be almost invisible, the sparse fuzz of beard on his cheeks glinting gold in the sun. He also had the captain's square build, broad shoulders, and thick forearms and legs. To distinguish him from others with the same name, he was referred to as Little John. "I do not reckon," he replied in a broad Devonian accent. "It seems neither better nor worse than usual, and that is good enough."

"'Tis my point exactly. Well, I suppose mustard will render the stuff agreeable."

I did not argue the remark since I could not find fault with Lackland's evaluation. But I did not care to accept ownership of the meal, either. "Do not thank me. Offer your compliments to Mr. Garget," I said. "I have followed his instructions without interpretation."

Lackland glanced at Lancelot Garget, who was wolfing his portion of beef and biscuit with relish, washing the stuff down with great gulps of beer, which caused his Adam's apple to bob violently. "A fruitless exercise," Lackland said. "I have already informed the man of my opinion and was told to go straight to the devil."

Garget allowed me a little time to consume my own supper and then kept me busy shelling peas, chopping cabbage, and performing similar culinary duties. The weather began to worsen and the wind turned against the ship, coming hard against us from the southwest, and soon it became impossible to make headway. I watched with half an eye as Drake held a conference with Blacollers, Thomas Cuttill, and other important men on the half deck. Then there was a flurry of activity as the boatswain and mates ordered gangs to the braces, the lines attached to the ends of the yardarms, which were used to swivel the sails horizontally. Soon the *Pelican* was once again going with the wind—but toward land and not out to sea. We were heading for Falmouth Haven, said one sailor, to seek refuge from the storm in the harbor.

Still the weather failed. Garget and I doused the fire and brought the box below and prepared a cold dinner of sliced hard sausage, biscuit, and cheese. By early afternoon the clouds were so thick the sun could not be seen. The wind picked up and then grew stronger. We were riding what was called a following sea, where each wave approached the *Pelican* from behind, lifted her high, and sped off into the distance after dropping her into the hole before the next crest. This imparted a sickening, corkscrewing motion to the ship and my queasiness returned with redoubled vigor.

Garget observed my affliction with amusement, being himself untouched by seasickness, then or ever. "What seems to be the matter, pretty boy?" he asked. "Was the supper not to your liking?"

The mention of food caused me to grab the bucket again. Garget sighed, as if my illness was a hardship for him to bear personally. "Oh, go lie down," he said. "You are of no use in such sorry condition. Perhaps in the morning you will be fit to do a man's work."

"Thank you, sir," I replied weakly, too nauseated to take offense, and staggered to my straw pallet, where I curled up hugging my stomach. It was small consolation that I was not the only person affected by the weather. The deck was noisy with groans and the sound of vomiting since the rough water distressed even experienced seamen so soon after setting sail, before they had regained their sea legs. The motion of the ship sent loose things rolling and clattering and heaved me from side to side on the pallet. It felt like an eternity as I lay with my eyes closed, hoping to die, before I fell asleep.

The *Pelican* and the other four ships of our small fleet reached safe anchorage in Falmouth Haven while I tossed and groaned. But the weather worsened after we made harbor, and all through the following day, and by ten o'clock the next morning, which was November 18th, the water was so rough and the wind was so furious that you could not see the shore a hundred yards distant. Then there came the sharp rat-tat-tat of a drum and the shrill piping of a whistle. "All hands," boomed a voice over the roar of the storm. "All hands."

Somehow I managed to gain my feet and follow the others up the ladder leading above.

The sky was dark although it was not yet noon.

The *Pelican* was struggling wildly against her cable in what should have been protected water but which was as rough as the open sea, a nightmare world of wind and stinging spray At one moment, as a wave overtook the ship, the stern seemed a mountainside. Then, after an awkward adjustment, the deck tilted the other way, lifting the bow into the air. A hundred bolts of lightning slashed the sky, one striking so near that its thunder arrived the same instant as its explosion.

Blacollers was standing beside the hatch, grabbing the men emerging from below and directing them to their stations. The boatswain's hair and beard were matted. I saw his lips move but I could not hear what he said and I did not understand what he wanted until a shove made it clear I was to join the other men at the foremast.

Despite having all its sails furled tight to their yards, the pressure of the wind on the foremast was threatening to heel the *Pelican* on its side.

It had to be cut away before the ship capsized.

Two sailors were attacking it with axes while other men held fast to the clew lines—sheets attached to either end of the spars—so as to guide the mast when it fell. The trick would be to have most of it go overboard without damaging the ship or snarling another mast.

Cross waves slapped the *Pelican*'s gunwale, shooting sheets of foam skyward and sending a deluge of green froth across the planking.

The water knocked my feet out from under me and I rolled around for frantic seconds before I finally managed to claw myself to my knees. Suddenly the darkness was broken—not by a brief flare of lightning but by a cooler radiance that did not fade away. Lifting my eyes, I saw the tips of the masts and the ends of the yards surrounded by globes of yellow fire. The rigging, too, was outlined by light, the shrouds a spider's web of pale orange flame.

Gasping, and seeming to inhale as much water as air with each breath, I took my position with the sailors hauling on the clew line. The ends of torn rigging snapped in the gale like angry worms around the sailors hacking at the trunk.

"Bite!" directed Blacollers, his voice consumed by the scream of the tempest. "Bless your eyes—bite!"

Again the axes fell. Again we heaved on the clew line. Still the foremast resisted. The *Pelican* had reached the crest of a wave and it seemed that we were at the brink of a precipice, staring into an insane inferno where air and water joined in a comfortless unnatural embrace.

"Bless you all to hell," shouted Blacollers. "*Bite!*"

The axes rose. Again we strained at the clew line. Then there came an awful cracking sound and the mast tilted toward us. Splinters fired like shot from the point of fracture and the mast began falling, slowly at first and then faster as the weight of the upper rigging overbalanced the whole. To a man we scrambled backward as the mast fell, seemingly directly upon us but actually to one side. It hit the gunwale, tearing off a section as easily as you might pinch off a hunk of bread from a loaf, and then pitched into the sea. Someone caromed into me, propelling me against the edge of broken railing, so that I found myself balancing half within the ship and half overboard.

A surge of water swept across the bow. I began falling—

An Unsavory Stew

November 16, 1577 – December 7, 1577
Falmouth Haven, Plymouth

I never learned whose hand grabbed my collar and hauled me aboard the *Pelican* just as I was about to plummet into the roiling water of Falmouth Haven. That same hand pushed me toward the gang clearing the ship of the debris left behind by the falling mast. Then I was assigned to the pumps and for the next several hours I worked knee-deep in swirling foam while Thomas Blacollers blessed us to greater efforts. At each surge of wave the galleon came up short against her cable with a sickening lurch and every man tensed, fearing the line would part, separating the *Pelican* from her anchor and sending the ship to break her spine against the shore. Yet the cable held through the worst of the weather and while the rain slackened and the waves quieted.

When Blacollers finally permitted us to return below, I fell unconscious the instant I collapsed on my pallet.

"Shake your tail," commanded Lancelot Garget, prodding my ribs with his boot. "There is work to be done. Would you lie abed all day?"

It seemed that not a minute had passed since I had closed my eyes although an entire night had gone by. Garget allowed me to exchange my damp clothes for dry ones before sending me to fetch oats for gruel. I served a tureen to each mess, as well as slabs of butter and lumps of brown sugar and pots of weak beer. Then I thankfully gulped down my own cereal and almost felt ready to face the day.

Our fleet had taken shelter in Falmouth Haven, a bay opening from the Nyser River, thirty miles from Plymouth along the coast of Cornwall. The *Elizabeth*, the *Benedict*, and the *Swan* rode at anchor not far from the *Pelican*, their shredded rigging and broken spars testimony of the storm's anger. The *Marigold*, however, a small bark of only forty tons burden, had dragged her anchor even though her crew had cut down her mainmast. She had been driven ashore west of Pendennis Castle, the fort guarding the river mouth, where she listed at an angle on the sand, half in and half out of the surf like a stranded fish. It was obvious to everyone that the adventure could not go on.

Just before noon Drake dispatched boats to pull the *Marigold* off the beach. This was brutal work, as I learned after being assigned an oar, and I developed even greater respect for the skill and brawn of Wilbert and Henry, the wherry men who had delivered me aboard the *Pelican*. Despite the assistance of the tide, it required an hour of heaving and stroking before we finally floated the ship, by which time my palms were chafed and bleeding and I was sick of the entire business.

More than a week had to pass before the fleet was fit enough to limp back the way we came, back to Plymouth, where we would ultimately remain until the middle of December.

"Our voyage is postponed before it properly began," I complained to Lackland as we approached Fisher's Nose, the promontory of land jutting out before Sutton Pool, easily recognizable from seaward because of the tall stone chapel at its crest.

"Aye, Mr. James, is it not marvelous? Plymouth may be a wretched provincial village but I am very certain it is preferable to any other place on our itinerary."

"I do not share your enthusiasm, Tobias," I replied. "There are certain people I would dislike meeting again."

"Have no fear on that account," Lackland answered. "'Tis unlikely you will have opportunity to run into any of them. We are all to be confined aboard ship for the duration, that is my guess. Drake knows full well there will be no separating his ruffians from the whores and gamers should they be allowed loose in the Barbican."

Lackland's prediction proved on target. Although the captains of the fleet and their immediate circle of officers and gentlemen came and went as they pleased, common sailors were denied shore leave during the time we anchored in Sutton Pool. A two-man watch armed with staves was posted on deck day and night both to keep men from slipping over the side and to discourage enterprising vendors of both sexes from coming over the rail into the ship.

When I was not slaving for Lancelot Garget, I was put to work helping repair the vessel. Mostly this meant carrying tools and materials for the more proficient craftsmen but over time I became familiar with the basic skills necessary of a sailor, including stitching, tying knots, splicing cord, scraping paint, polishing brass and copper, and mopping and scrubbing—particularly mopping and scrubbing, with which I had had much previous experience and did not particularly care for. I also began to understand the language of the sea, which was a vernacular all to itself, almost indecipherable to landsmen, with a thousand unique words referring to the parts of a ship and to sailing her under any condition of wind and water. Although I would never be a sailor myself, and never desired to become one, I began to understand the experienced men when they talked of shipboard matters.

As the weeks passed, I also began to give Lackland's theory about the real aims of our adventure greater credit. There were the cannon, of course, and the disassembled flyboats. More convincing was the armory. Although I had never had martial training even I could recognize that no expense had been spared to provision the *Pelican* with the very latest in weaponry. The bulkheads were lined with row upon row of arquebuses and muskets, pistols, pikes and half-pikes and halberds, crossbows, daggers, hangers, bills and staves, and fire lances, which could be set ablaze and thrust into the faces of boarding enemies. Stacks of boxes contained incendiary grenades loaded with powder, pitch, sulfur, and camphor in varying combinations. These could be thrown by hand or fired from iron tubes with, as I would learn, great accuracy. Other cabinets held thousands of rounds of shot, a different caliber for each type of gun, as well as caltrops and mantraps. There was also armor for every man in the fleet, including helmets, morions, and padded jerkins known as brigandines, with protective metal plates sewn in the lining.

As I was soon to learn, however, the same care that had been taken outfitting the *Pelican* with armament had not been applied to the ship's provisioning.

The usual sustenance of a crew at sea was salt meat, either

pork or beef, and salt fish—stockfish, or cod. To render this stuff palatable was a time-consuming process known as *shifting*. The meat must be removed from its container, placed in a tank of fresh water, massaged vigorously to remove encrusted salt, and allowed to soak for three days, during which period the water must be refreshed daily.

Given the population aboard the *Pelican*, although it was diminished by the departure of the gentlemen adventurers for accommodations ashore in the Barbican for the duration of the refitting, the crew consumed several hundredweight of meat and fish each week.

Although the bulk was fresh, purchased by Stydye from the market, much came from shipboard stores. This meant that I had to descend to the orlop every day or two, hunt down the cask that Lancelot Garget had instructed me to obtain, and winch it on deck for shifting.

The orlop, where I had first been introduced to Garget, was a dark stinking maze. Hundreds of casks were lashed to each other and to the deck and to stanchions and bulkheads. Although some effort had been taken to keep similar material together, the stores had been organized with more concern for the ship's stability than to any consideration for easily locating a particular cask. One might contain meat, the one beside it nails or beads, and the next cask over might hold water or beer or linen. Worse, most were identified by only a scrawled character or two, almost impossible to read accurately in the shifting light of my lantern.

Working in a kitchen had taught me that only a poor cook, lacking both common sense and financial acumen, neglected to employ ingredients according to the order in which they were purchased and received into inventory. Simply put, the longer a perishable item sat on the shelf, the greater the likelihood that it would spoil and become valueless. Thus when Lancelot Garget dispatched me below for salt beef, instead of settling upon the first cask I found, I continued my search into the recesses of the orlop, assuming that supplies stored furthest from the center of the ship had been brought aboard earliest. Eventually I discovered a clutch of barrels, tierces, and hogsheads secured behind the stern bulkhead, covered by a tarpaulin. Turning up one corner of the canvas, I spied the Bs and Ps I sought. So I drew the tarp aside, released the knot binding the casks, and wrestled a barrel of salt beef to the deck.

Waiting beside the fire box were several wood troughs, which I had filled halfway with fresh water. These were to receive the beef after Garget popped off the barrel's upper hoop and levered open its head. But as the lid lifted, a foul stench assailed us and we both recoiled, unwilling to inhale another breath.

"God's mercy," I exclaimed. "Some animal has died in there."

For once Garget did not contradict me. "It is indeed an evil odor," he agreed, inching cautiously toward the barrel. "It might even be that the contents are somewhat disagreeable."

"Somewhat disagreeable, Mr. Garget? May I suggest that we condemn the entire lot?"

"Do not be so hasty, pretty boy," he replied, eyeing what could be seen of the contents with a certain hopeful speculation. "Possibly there are portions that are edible."

"Then you are welcome to grub through the slop to find

them, for I will not," I answered, more disposed to bear my supervisor's annoyance than to sort through the rank matter stinking in the cask. "Or let us bear the news to Master Stydye and allow him to decide what is to be done."

"No, no, 'tis unnecessary to disturb Stydye with every inconsequential detail," Garget snapped. He peered around quickly and arrived at a decision. "Come, let us replace the head boards and hoop and return the barrel below." So we sealed it again and winched it down to the orlop. Garget followed me as I rolled the barrel to its original resting place astern, clucking irritably all the while. "No wonder, no wonder," he hissed to himself as I tied the barrel into position beside its fellows.

"Yes, sir?" I asked.

"Never mind, pretty boy." Garget herded me forward. "In the future," he continued when we were beside the hatch, "you would be well advised not to exercise yourself unnecessarily."

"Aye, sir," I answered, perplexed by his kindness. "If you say so."

"Do you follow?" he repeated with a peculiar intensity that reminded me of Hal Audley's instructions prior to my pretended whipping. "Do not *exercise* yourself."

"Aye, I get you," I replied, although it was only after we returned above deck with a new cask of salted beef, this one found nearer the main hatch, that it dawned on me what Garget really meant.

I may never have been to sea before but my history in the kitchen had taught me that constant vigilance was the price of wholesome cuisine. From years of experience with farmers and purveyors I had learned that only the most scrupulous supplier hesitated to substitute inferior merchandise for good if given the slightest opportunity. Finding a putrid barrel before our fleet departed Plymouth did not promise comfortable tidings about the remainder of our provisions. How many more casks were rotten? How many had escaped Garget's scrutiny? How many had he been paid to overlook?

Either my superior was embarrassed by the airing of a professional lapse or else he was corrupt, but in either situation Stydye would never learn of the spoilage, not from Lancelot Garget.

I began to suspect that I would have to take action personally to bring the matter to light.

"Do not prove yourself more a fool than you are already," Lackland chastised me after I explained my reasoning. We had climbed to the fighting top and were sitting with our backs to the mast while staring idly toward the city—privacy was rare aboard the *Pelican* and generally could be only found aloft. Luckily, as the boatswain had predicted, our acquaintanceship with altitude had increased our tolerance of it, and we were now able to sit easily, if not happily, with our legs dangling over the edge of the narrow platform. At least while the vessel was in port and not heaving across open sea.

"Do you believe Garget has sufficient intelligence to plot such a scheme himself?" Lackland continued. "Or to dissemble before Stydye? I will not bet on it."

"True, Garget is not the wisest man in Christendom," I admitted. "But that would mean someone else is profiting."

"Ah, my child, now you begin to comprehend."

"And that person would be Stydye."

"You have hit the nail home, Mr. James," Lackland observed with languid cynicism. "'Tis the way with stewards and purchasing agents since antiquity, after all."

"And Garget?"

"Too dull and indolent to notice or paid to look elsewhere. He is Stydye's henchman, no more."

"Then I must talk to Blacollers. Perhaps to Drake himself."

My companion had to grab the shrouds quickly to prevent himself from rolling off the fighting top. "Do not bother," Lackland said when he could finally stop laughing. "No one will take your concerns seriously. At best they will be disregarded as the spite of an ambitious underling. More likely you will earn a stripe or two for your pains. Did you not know Stydye is a dear friend of Drake's? Of Thomas Doughty's, too. All three served under Essex in Ireland. They are as thick as thieves."

I recognized the wisdom of Lackland's advice but it still irked me to keep quiet. "I have proof," I argued.

"What is a single cask? Are you certain of others?"

"No."

"Well, there you have it. Not even Vicarye—" he meant Leonard Vicarye, one of the gentlemen traveling with the fleet, who was a lawyer "—not even Vicarye could prove the case on so little evidence."

Then Lackland regarded me with a frown. "Furthermore, and now I am sincere, you will receive no thanks if you discredit Stydye."

"Why?"

Lackland's theatrical sigh would not have harmed the reputation of a practiced player. "Do they breed nothing but idiots outside London?" he asked, once more aghast at my naiveté. "If Stydye is found guilty, it reflects poorly on those who appointed him. You would only be appreciated as the cause of their discomfiture. Do not become involved."

I could sympathize with Lackland's point of view but I could not let the matter rest. Perhaps he was right. Maybe I was simple. Or just stubborn, as my parents had insisted long ago. Or maybe I was taking Hal Audley's advice to heart, and doing a thing well. But that very evening after completing my duties, I returned below with a small drill and some other equipment that I had borrowed from one of the carpenters, Rich Joyner, without his knowledge. Since the orlop was so close and uncomfortable, there was little likelihood of encountering another person during my visit, but even so I took care to step quietly and to allow only a slim beam of light to slip from my lantern as I returned to the clusters of barrels and hogsheads lashed behind the stern bulkhead. If my suspicions were correct, most if not all would be rancid.

Stydye would have seen to it that inferior casks were positioned where they would not ordinarily be opened until far along in the voyage. By which point any rot would be easy to explain since even the best preserved meat went bad after too long a time.

Hanging the lantern from a nail at such an angle that its beam fell on the casks before me, I rolled aside the canvas tarp and began drilling into the barrel nearest the one Garget and I had broached earlier. The instant the bit penetrated the top and withdrew, curls of pine falling from the head, I again smelled the stink of decay. It was the same with a second barrel and with a third. I quit drilling after a fourth barrel proved foul, seeing no point in continuing.

Then I caulked the holes I had made, returned Joyner's tools, and settled onto my pallet on the gun deck among the carrots and peas.

Having my suspicions confirmed gave me no pleasure. Lackland's arguments were convincing. I was sure there was little chance any accusation against Stydye would be well received even if demonstrated to be true. If I spoke up, I would not be making friends.

Yet if I kept silent, I would be partner to Stydye's misdemeanor.

In the morning I awoke unsure which course to take and came no closer to making up my mind while serving breakfast and while cleaning up afterward. As I scrubbed out the cooking pot with sand brought along for that purpose, I noticed Francis Fletcher, the pastor of the fleet, going across the deck toward the stern. He was a tall man dressed all in black except for a white collar, a worn book in one gaunt hand and a sword belted across his long black canvas coat. Although we had not met, I had heard good reports of him, which encouraged me to introduce myself.

"Parson Fletcher, if you will, sir."

He stopped at my hail and regarded me with a stern expression. This did not concern me, however, for the man was not known to smile. "Yes, son. Peregrine, is it? Perry?"

"That is it," I answered, surprised he knew my name since Fletcher was among the elite of the expedition and slept in the main cabin with the gentlemen. Unlike the others, however, he had remained onboard during the *Pelican*'s refitting and had not moved into lodgings ashore. "I need advice," I continued, "and would appreciate your counsel."

"That you may have, freely. What is your question?"

"It concerns a friend," I answered and looked pointedly at the other men around us, most busy at their routine duties, some napping or idling where they would not be in the way. "Perhaps we could speak privately."

"Then we shall, my son," Fletcher replied. "Follow me."

A galleon such as the *Pelican* was divided into full and half-decks. From the bottom up, the full decks were the hold, the orlop, and then the gun deck. The half-deck at the bow was known as the forecastle and was originally used as a fortified battle station during ship-to-ship combat although in modern vessels it was typically employed as a storage area or barracks. The middle of the ship, the waist, was empty of construction, allowing access to the lower decks. Instead of solid planking, the decking of the waist was composed of hatches to allow light and air down below. At the stern rose the half deck, which served as the captain's command station as well as a recreation area for the officers and gentlemen. Behind it, at the very back edge of the *Pelican*, known as the poop, was a small cabin or round house, where Drake and his closest companions refreshed themselves during hot weather, particularly in the doldrums of our long sweltering passage to Brazil.

Two cabins were situated beneath the half deck. The first was the great cabin, with a table seating a dozen running its length and Turkish rugs covering the oak planking. Lattice-work windows along the port and starboard bulkheads allowed in dusky slats of yellow light. At the far end of the room was the door to Drake's personal chamber, which was forbidden to all but Drake and his manservant, Diego, the Cimarron.

The great cabin was empty when Fletcher led me inside although evidence of intense occupation was everywhere since a dozen men and their equipment shared the space. Indicating that I should take a seat at the near end of the table, the parson sat across from me and placed his book, a worn leather notebook or diary secured by a rawhide strap, before him.

"How may I help your friend?" he asked.

"Well, to be honest, Parson Fletcher, he is more of an acquaintance than a friend. But the point is, I know him for a cheat and I wish your opinion as to what I should do."

"How sure are you of your information?" Fletcher asked. "It is unwise to accuse a man of treachery on the basis of gossip or hearsay."

"I am absolutely certain," I answered.

"Then your duty, my son, is to let your voice be heard. Iniquity flourishes when God-fearing men fail to speak the truth. What if our lord Jesus had witnessed the world's sins and remained silent? History would have taken a very different course."

"But I am sure not to be thanked," I said, repeating Lackland's argument. "He is well liked by his friends, who are men of importance."

"Was being liked a concern of our savior? No, he spoke the word of God without doubt or fear. You could do worse than to emulate his example, Perry James."

As I would learn, since Parson Fletcher enjoyed talking about his own life to no lesser extent than most men, he was a seasoned traveler. He had wandered as far north as Russia and all through the countries and principalities of Europe and even across the Mediterranean Sea to the lands of the Moors. Years afoot and on horseback and aboard ships had left his hands rough and brown and his face as weathered as any sailor's. Traveling had also provided him with a severely practical temperament to augment his love of God.

"Specifically, my son," Francis Fletcher continued, "your challenge is to expose this scoundrel without incurring the retribution of his colleagues. First, ensure that you make your accusation loudly and before witnesses, so that it may not be ignored. His friends will attempt to dismiss the entire business, of course. Do not let them. Second, have any evidence immediately available or they will use its lack to their advantage. Third, do not frame your arguments with emotion or you will be accused of bias. Nor should you call upon God to bear witness since our Lord is unconcerned with petty affairs and his failure to appear will be employed against you. Last, be certain you do not stand to gain advantage in any regard or your every word will be undermined before it leaves your lips. Do you understand me, my son? Is there any part of what I said that you wish me to repeat?"

"No, no thank you," I said. "You have been quite particular."

"Then go with Jesus," Parson Fletcher replied, getting up from the table and leading me from the great cabin. "Listen to your heart and your direction will become clear."

That night I attempted to take his advice. As I lay on my pallet after my duties were over, I emptied my mind as best I could of its usual dialog. Trying not to think was an exasperating endeavor. Odd thoughts and fancies persisted like itches.

The harder I strove to clear my head, the more extraneous stuff filled it. And the moment I did manage to silence myself, fatigue rushed in to fill the void, yielding slumber rather than illumination. When I awoke, however, I knew what I must do and why I must do it. "The survival of a ship at sea depends on the efforts of all her men, without the exception of one"— Blacollers's words had come back to me and I could not ignore them. Although I was only the cook's assistant, the least boy on board, still I had to act as if the fate of our voyage rested upon my shoulders.

Parson Fletcher was right. I must speak up.

The more I mulled over the situation, the more I realized I needed an accomplice. Lackland, of course, objected strenuously.

"God forbid, Peregrine James, have you gone mad? Please, leave me out of your calculations. I have my destiny to fulfill."

We were at the bow of the ship, at the narrow point where the bowsprit, a mast about twenty feet in length, jutted forward from the prow of the vessel. Lackland had chosen this location in order to practice. He was sitting on an upended cask with his lute in his hands, idly picking out random chords.

"Your name will never be so much as whispered," I told him earnestly. "I will swear I acted alone."

"What of Garget? The oaf is sure to become suspicious."

"I have not yet thought so far," I admitted.

"Perhaps if he could be distracted ... by some physical ailment."

"Then you will help?"

"With recommendations only. What do you know of

Electuarium Indium?"

"Nothing. I am not even sure whether it is animal or vegetable."

"It is neither," Lackland informed me with a tired air. "*Electuarium Indium,* as I have come to learn through melancholy experience, is a purgative of remarkable power. On first entering this misbegotten scow, I was afflicted by an irregularity of the bowels, which necessitated a visit to Master Richard Winterhey, our surgeon. Unfortunately, Winterhey mistook me for a larger man and prescribed more of the stuff than appropriate. I was in the head an entire day clearing my guts. I have never been so empty."

"Garget taps a pint of beer before supper," I mused. "Perhaps we could put some of this, this—"

"*Electuarium Indium.*"

"—in his jack."

Lackland sighed, accompanying the sound with a brief riffle of music. "Dawn at last," he said.

"How much is needed?" I asked.

"A teaspoon or two. One was enough to do me in."

"Did you notice where it is kept?"

"In a chest by the door of the surgery."

"So tell me, Lackland, is this chest locked?"

"Of course. But the key is kept in the lock. What sane soul would want to steal the stuff? The *aqua vitae* is another matter entirely. That key is hung near to Winterhey's heart on a silver chain."

"Is not Winterhey ashore at this moment?" I asked.

"Such is indeed the case," Lackland nodded.

"Excellent. Two teaspoons, you said? Better make it three. Garget has the constitution of a horse."

"Just one minute," he protested. "I am participating in your scheme in an advisory capacity. I refuse any deeper involvement."

"Look here," I told him, "like it or not, lutenist of destiny or not, you are part of our adventure and share our common fate. What if there comes a time when our lives depend on what is in one of the foul casks? I know of five. There is no guessing how many others are bad. What will we say to our companions? Sorry, friends, we knew of the problem but chose to keep quiet. Now we will just have to live off our boots and 'tweendeck venison. I would not want to deliver that message."

"Nor would I." Lackland sighed again, this time with less drama. "What will you be doing, Mr. James, while I am pilfering from our surgeon at grave peril to my reputation should I be caught in the act?"

"I will be in the orlop preparing the other props."

"When will this mad performance take place?"

"Nothing is gained by delay. Tomorrow."

"May God have mercy on us both."

"Do not be so pessimistic. Is it not true God favors the right?"

"God favors those with the most position and wealth. This is what I have observed to be true."

Despite my brave argument to Lackland I was anything but confident. I almost scrapped the plan when he passed me a twist of paper containing several spoonfuls of white powder, the *Electuarium Indium*. But I thought of what Francis

79

Fletcher had said and of what Blacollers had told me and I dropped the purgative into Lancelot Garget's leather jack before filling it with his afternoon beer. This he drank while lounging to one side of the fire box and watching me prepare the evening meal. The jack was dry long before he finished criticizing my efforts but by the time the barley came to a boil, so had Garget's stomach. With a strained expression he ordered me to continue without him and made his way toward the bow with a peculiar stilt-legged gait.

I did not foresee his return any time soon.

The meal that evening consisted of ham and peas and the aforementioned barley, along with bread and butter, cheese, and cider. This was the menu I served the sailors and petty officers.

Lackland gave me a quick nod when he arrived to pick up the food for the gentlemen's table. The signal meant the plot could proceed. Drake was present. The play would have its intended audience.

The tureen I handed Lackland held different fare than before. Instead of wholesome meat, it was full of rotten stuff, which I had retrieved from one of the corrupt casks in the orlop.

"I do not like this," he whispered. "It is not too late to reconsider."

"I am not happy, either," I told him. "Still, I see no better course."

"On your head be it. Prepare for the consequences. And remember —I do not know you!"

With this final warning, Lackland sniffed dubiously at the covered dish and held it some distance from his body while carrying it through the door into the grand cabin. I could not decide how much time passed before he returned but the interval felt like hours. I had an eternity to rethink my decision and to tell myself I had made a mistake and to agonize over my foolishness. I was sure to be expelled from the expedition, probably with additional stripes on my back to complement those left by Thomas Doughty. There was also a good chance I would be returned to prison. Francis Drake was an important man in Plymouth.

"They are asking for Garget." Lackland was standing with his back to the door of the cabin. "Nor is their mood sweet."

"That is to be expected."

"Perry—" For the first time since we had met, Lackland let slip his sophistication. "Take care."

"I will, with thanks, Tobias."

Then he opened the door and I stepped into the grand cabin. Drake was seated in his usual position at the head of the long table. His manservant, Diego, the Cimarron, stood behind his chair and scrutinized all who entered, a pistol on either hip and the hilt of a sword visible above one shoulder. Thomas Doughty was to Drake's right. To his left was John Winter, captain of the *Elizabeth* and the third commander of our expedition, a man not quite thirty years old but with the grim expression of an experienced mariner. Many of the places at the table were vacant since most of the gentlemen who generally bivouacked in the main cabin were ashore. Francis Fletcher was present, as well as several others, including Will Markham, John Cooke, Emanuel Wattkyns, and James Stydye.

Stydye spoke first.

"Where is Garget?" he snapped as Lackland pulled the door shut and then slipped quietly away from me.

"Mr. Garget is indisposed," I answered.

"Get him."

In the center of the table was the tureen I had given Lackland to serve. The lid had been replaced to hide what lay within but even so a noxious stench lingered in the air.

"There is no need," I answered.

"Why not?"

As steward of the fleet, Stydye was ultimately accountable for the quality of our provisions. He could barely restrain his embarrassment and anger at the situation. My answers were only enraging him further.

"Mr. Garget has taken ill," I explained. "I alone prepared the meal just now served. Any questions regarding the menu should be directed to me and to none other. What is your concern?"

"My concern—you ask my concern?"

Before Stydye could gather his wits and form a coherent response, Drake took charge of the discussion by slamming his fist on the tabletop, causing the silver plate and cutlery to clatter against the wood. "Damn it, lad! Do you have a reason for serving this foul stew or is it your mistaken idea of a good supper?"

"Yes, captain. I have a reason."

"Out with it before I lose all patience."

For a second I dared take my eyes off Drake. Parson Fletcher was nodding as he appraised me, as if he had some sense of what I was about. Thomas Doughty had a more doubtful look. I suspected he was regretting his role in securing my employment aboard the *Pelican*.

Returning my gaze to Drake, I said: "My reason, captain, is it was the best available."

"How can that be?" he asked with an evenness I found particularly ominous. "We have not yet departed Plymouth and our provisions are already sour. I ask again, lad—how can that be?"

Somehow I found the nerve to shrug indifferently. "I cannot say, Captain Drake. However, I broached five separate casks, three of beef, two of pork. All were rotten. What is before you is the best of the lot."

"I see," Drake said quietly.

"The boy is lying!" Stydye burst out, rising from his seat and stabbing the air in my direction with the point of his dagger. "God's truth, I do not know why but we will find out when we hang him from a spar a time or two and watch him flop."

"Enough," Drake said. "This is not Rathlin, nor is it Bruce's castle."

I did not understand Drake's reference, and it was better so, for if I had known what had transpired on that bleak island off the Irish coast, my tongue would have frozen in my mouth. It was not until months later that I heard the story from Tom Moone, who had been there. But Stydye understood and fell silent. I took advantage of the pause to speak up:

"If I am lying, sir," I said, "it would be easy to test the lie."

"Aye," Drake said, "that it would be." With the decisiveness for which he was admired, he turned to Doughty. "Tom, escort the lad below and ascertain the truth. Report back with what you discover. Diego, accompany them and render assistance as needed."

"Yes, captain, *yo me voy*," answered the Cimarron. It was

the first I had heard him speak. His voice was a melodious baritone, accented with Spanish or Portuguese and with some other language I could not place.

John Winter, on Drake's right hand, gained his feet. He was taller than Drake but somewhat under Thomas Doughty's height, clean shaven except for a thick mustache that he waxed into points. "I am curious also," he said. "I will join the party, if you will, Francis."

"And I," Stydye said.

"No, James," Drake told him. "Remain awhile. We have other business to discuss together, you and I."

After a detour to borrow Rich Joyner's tools, this time publicly, I returned to the orlop in the company of Thomas Doughty, John Winter, and Drake's man, Diego. There was still nothing to be seen of Lancelot Garget although a peculiar grunting could be heard coming from the bow. As it always did in such a narrow wooden world, news of an unusual occurrence had spread through the ship like wildfire but no one was sure exactly what was happening. Every man on deck pretended to ignore us but every eye followed our passage to the main hatch. While our party began the descent below, Doughty murmured:

"It is a dangerous game you are playing, Mr. James."

"I do not understand what you mean, sir," I replied. "This is no game and I am no player."

"Save such disclaimers for those who will believe them. Still, I am willing to be entertained. For your sake, Peregrine James, I hope the remainder of this production is as amusing as the first act."

Lighting lanterns, we proceeded to the orlop and I led the way sternward to the casks I had opened earlier and tapped them again while the others watched. Even John Winter, normally imperturbable, wrinkled his nose in disgust before covering it and his extravagant moustache with a handkerchief as the aroma from the corrupt barrels made an already close atmosphere even more fetid. Diego, forced to hunch forward almost in half since he was well over six feet tall, cursed: "*Madre de Dios,* this is not pleasing."

"Are there others?" Doughty asked.

"I do not know," I answered.

"Then let us find out."

"Begin with this one," Winter instructed, indicating a cask somewhat separate from the rest I had opened. It, too, was bad, as were five of the next seven I broached. Finally Winter told me, "Enough, lad, that will do." And to Doughty: "We will have to perform a thorough inventory, of course. For the *Elizabeth*, as well, and the other ships. Damn it, Tom, I thought you knew Stydye. Did you not serve together?"

"Under Essex," Doughty admitted. "Stydye commanded the frigate *Reindeer* in concert with Drake, who had the *Falcon*. Francis and I were both impressed by his character."

"With my apologies, sir, you were both deceived. Stydye has feathered his nest at our expense."

"Perhaps. Or perhaps there is some other explanation." Despite the dimness of the orlop I noticed Doughty flash Winter a sharp look. "Let us discuss the matter further with Drake," he said. Then he turned to me.

"Who instructed you to open these particular casks?"

he asked.

"No one," I replied.

"But there are others located more conveniently."

"Aye, sir, but I thought these barrels should be used first," I said and explained the principles of proper inventory rotation. "Do you see?" I finished. "First in, first out, that is the way of it, particularly with fresh produce but also with dry and preserved goods. To follow any other practice is to invite spoilage and loss. I was performing my duty."

"Your duty!" Winter laughed and said to Doughty, "'Tis obvious to me the lad seeks a bounty or an increase in rank."

"Absolutely not!" I protested, remembering Parson Fletcher's admonition. "I will not touch a penny, sir. Nor do I seek Mr. Stydye's position or Garget's. No one would credit my character if I was rewarded over the bodies of my superiors and I would not be well liked."

Winter accepted this answer but Doughty was obviously less content with it although I had little idea what his suspicions were, knowing nothing about the political background of the expedition except for what bits of conjecture Lackland had shared with me. But he did not press the issue, and led our return above deck to the main cabin. No one looked directly at us but I could feel the eyes of every sailor follow our progress to the door. Little had changed within. The tureen of unsavory stew remained on the table where Lackland had put it. Drake was reclining in his chair, the armrests carved in the shape of lions, while James Stydye sat uncomfortably in his place, shaving a piece of hard cheese into ever thinner slices with his dagger.

"What is your report, Tom?" asked Drake.

"I do not bear good news," Doughty replied. "It is as Mr. James described. We opened five casks and they were all foul."

"Let God be my witness," exclaimed Stydye, rising to his feet and stabbing the tabletop with such force that the point of his knife sank an inch deep in the wood. "I know nothing of this matter, Francis." Stydye's gaze settled on me. "It is the boy," he said. "He must be responsible."

"I doubt it, sir," replied Doughty. That was when I noticed his hand had gone to the hilt of his sword and that Diego was now standing behind Stydye. "No," he continued, "we broached eight additional barrels, selected at random. Six were bad."

"Eleven altogether, you are saying," observed Drake.

"Eleven that we know of. We will have to do a complete inventory to discover the true number. There is no accounting the extent of Stydye's perfidy."

"Damn you, Doughty—"

"Shut it!" Drake had risen from his chair. His fair skin had become fiery red and even in the dim light admitted into the cabin through the port and starboard windows I could see that his brow was spotted with moisture. "Just shut your hole, James, before I shut it for you."

"Have care how you address me," Stydye warned, reaching for the grip of the hanger at his belt. But Diego grasped his wrist and the blade remained within its sheath.

"*Silencio, hijo*," said the Cimarron, displaying no sign of effort although it was apparent that Stydye was straining to draw the sword.

Thrusting his heavy chair away with such force that it flipped over backward, Drake came around the table to Stydye until they were face to face. "By the life of God," Drake roared, "who are you working for? Speak the truth or I will nail your ears to the pillory. Are you a Spanish dog? Or is Burghley paying your salary?"

With the immovable bulk of the Cimarron behind him, Stydye was unable to retreat. Still he had the courage to answer:

"I do not understand your question."

As I would learn during the years I lived aboard the *Pelican*, Drake was in absolute control of his emotions. For all his bluffness and rough humor, his every expression was calculated for best effect, and not a smile or a frown took form on his face without premeditation, either to elicit sympathy or to inspire awe and fear. But on this occasion I truly believed his anger was real. No doubt he had expected a certain amount of peculation from Stydye, but even if no further spoilage was found, the amount already discovered represented almost ten percent of our store of preserved victuals. If not for a fluke—if not for my accidental discovery—the fleet could have been lost before we ever set sail. The realization of how narrowly the expedition had escaped tragedy filled Drake with rage.

"Damn it, Stydye! You understand my question well enough," he went on. "Which is it? Are you taking money from Cecil? Or Philip?"

"Francis—" said Thomas Doughty, "would you not think this a conversation better held in private?" Turning to the other men, who had been witnessing the exchange with studied impassivity, he continued: "Gentlemen, we have certain particulars to discuss with Mr. Stydye. Would you allow us this courtesy?"

It was not a request and no one understood it as such. Parson Fletcher was the first to rise, followed by

Wattkyns, Markham, and Cooke. Lackland, too, took this opportunity to escape the scene. But as I began to follow him out the door, my name was called.

"Not so fast, Mr. James," said Thomas Doughty. "Tarry awhile."

Ill Met at Mortlake

December 7, 1577 – December 11, 1577
Plymouth, Mortlake

What Doughty meant was that I should remain outside the main cabin and wait to be summoned. This was not an easy period of time. Within minutes every man and boy aboard had heard some version of what was going on, however garbled. Most believed I was a condemned man awaiting sentencing and gave me a wide berth as they went about their affairs on deck.

Through the door at my back came the muffled noise of raised voices. Then Lancelot Garget returned from the head. He did not seem well. Nor was he in a kind mood.

"Damn it, pretty boy," he said. "Why are you not breaking down the equipment?"

"I am awaiting Captain Drake's pleasure," I answered. "My instructions are to stay here until I am called."

"What is going on?"

"There was a question about the meal I served. They are discussing the matter with Mr. Stydye even now, I believe."

"God in heaven!" Garget exclaimed, his complexion becoming even paler. "Can I not leave you alone for five minutes without disaster? Do not think I am unaware you have been awaiting your chance to shoot at my credit, pretty boy. Have no fear! I will disavow any knowledge of your culinary activities. You will have to answer Stydye alone."

"I suspect Mr. Stydye will not be asking the questions," I replied just as the door to the main cabin opened and Stydye himself stepped out, accompanied by Diego. *Herded* by Diego, I should say, since the Cimarron had a firm grip on Stydye's elbow and was deliberately propelling the other man forward. Thomas Doughty appeared in the entrance way behind them. "Blacollers!" he called.

The boatswain made an unconvincing show of being interrupted at an absorbing task. "Aye, Mr. Doughty?"

"Have a boat made ready to taxi Mr. Stydye ashore."

Stydye wrenched free of Diego and turned to Doughty. His pale complexion matched Lancelot Garget's although I could not decide whether his pallor was caused by fear or by rage. "My possessions," he said through thinned lips.

"They will be delivered to your lodgings."

"That is bold thievery! I will make a complaint."

"Complain as you will, James," said Doughty. "Or perhaps you would prefer to discuss the matter with Drake?"

"Damn Drake to hell," Stydye replied, but more to himself than aloud, and he made no further argument as Diego escorted him to the rail and assisted him into the waiting boat. Diego threw down the mooring line and rejoined Doughty, who said to us:

"You two. Inside."

"I will deny everything," Lancelot Garget hissed while touching his cap in acknowledgement, and once again I found myself standing before the great table, the oak set with silver platters and cutlery and with crystal goblets filled with dry sack. The chair that Drake had kicked over had been placed upright but Drake had not resumed his seat. Even in the dim light admitted through the thick glass, I could see that his fierce blue eyes were ringed with white.

"How much did Stydye pay you?" he asked Garget. "Do not lie."

Lancelot, of course, had little idea what Drake meant, having been isolated in the head with internal complaints. "Pay, captain? Mr. Stydye?" he asked.

"Are you a complete idiot, Garget? You cannot have me suppose Stydye acted alone. Out with it, man. What other mischief is planned?"

"Mischief, sir?" Somehow Garget managed to look guilty although he misunderstood what was going on. His eyes flickered sideways to me and then back to Drake. Wetting his lips, he said, "If there was any mischief, it was the boy's fault. I warned Stydye, sir, that Mr. James was not to be trusted but he disregarded my guidance. I fear the lad has been corrupted by alien habits of cookery beyond hope of rehabilitation. Still, captain, one can encourage him to see reason. How many stripes do you wish me to provide, sir? I recommend a round dozen but would favorably consider a sterner suggestion."

Once again Drake's voice was ominously evenhanded. "Are you telling me, Garget, that Mr. James is our man?"

"Could there be any other culprit? Normally, sir, I keep a strict eye on him to circumvent any attempt at mischief. But it appears Mr. James was only biding his time and took advantage of my indisposition. What has he done, captain?

Fouled the ham with foreign seasonings? Spiced the barley with cloves and herbs? Give the word and I will offer him instruction he will never forget."

"God's blood!" Drake roared—this was a favorite technique of his, as I would learn, to vacillate between extremes of temperament in order to disconcert the person he was interrogating. "We are discussing a far graver matter than mere cookery."

"Are we, sir?—that is, *absolutely*, sir."

"Yet you still maintain you know nothing?"

"Have faith, captain," Garget protested. "My ignorance is thorough and all-encompassing."

"That, by God, is the first true thing you have said. Garget, I begin to believe you are indeed the complete fool you appear to be."

"Thank you, captain. Thank you."

"Even so I suspect you know more than you let on. Once more I ask—" Drake's voice returned to its previous volume and he came around the grand table to within arm's length of Garget—"what was Stydye paying you, man?"

"Nothing! That is to say, captain, nothing besides a penny or two here and there for incidental expenses. Master Stydye is notorious for his parsimony. Ask anyone."

"So Stydye did not rely on you?"

Obviously remembering the barrel we had replaced together in the orlop, or some similar incident, Lancelot Garget began to understand the true subject of the conversation. "Rely on me?" Garget asked, putting his hands before him as if to ward off the thought. "Would you rely on me, sir? No, no, I followed Stydye's commands exactly to the letter, captain, as is only right and fitting, and he relied on me that far and no further."

Garget shot me another sharp glance, unsure of exactly what I had confided to Drake. "As God is my witness, I know of no irregularity apart from one cask of bad beef Mr. James and I opened together."

"You may take my word there are others, Mr. Garget. How many others is yet to be discovered. As is the extent of your involvement."

"I have none!"

"That, too, is to be determined," Drake warned, dismissing Garget with a gesture. "For your sake, I hope you are as witless as you seem."

"I am, sir! Let no one say otherwise."

Clearly relieved to be thought simple rather than devious, Lancelot Garget backed out of the cabin. Both Doughty and Winter resumed their seats but Diego remained at my elbow. Ready, I realized, to restrain me as he had James Stydye not much earlier although I did not carry a fancy hanger at my waist but only a kitchen knife. Drake leaned against the table and drew the point of his beard between the fingers of one hand while letting the other hand rest on the hilt of his sword, once more appraising me with the air of a man who has judged others and found them wanting. Preparing for the worst, I stood straight and returned his study with as much aplomb as I could gather.

"By God's left bollock, Peregrine James," Drake swore, "what is to be done with you?"

"Sir?"

"You have served me damned well, lad. But to reward

you would be to do you a disservice. Understand me?"

"Aye, captain, I think I do," I replied, reminded of my conversation with Parson Fletcher. "But as I told Mr. Doughty and Mr. Winter, I am not looking for reward. I was doing my duty, plain and simple."

Drake's grin proved he believed my protests no more than Thomas Doughty had believed them. Then he narrowed his eyes, fixing me with the look. "I am in your debt, Mr. James," Drake continued. "Do not think I will forget. I never forget the actions of a friend, nor those of an enemy. There will come a time when I will repay you, maybe that time will come sooner or maybe years will pass, but when the moment arrives, I will return your favor even though I cannot thank you now. Am I allowed this leeway, Peregrine James?"

His gaze held me as firmly as a hand upon my wrist. Many who have heard Drake speak have described his accent as rough and provincial, the broad voice of a Devonian countryman. As I would discover, Drake was well aware of his reputation and often emphasized the simplicity of his language in order to impress his audience with his rough manliness and honesty. The tactic was remarkably effective. Few proved immune to his charm, neither sailors nor courtiers.

I was not an exception to this rule.

"Aye, captain," I said, ready at that instant to grant him any request and to follow wherever he led. "Whatever you will, sir, it is fine by me."

"Thank you, Mr. James. I will not forget this conversation."

Believing myself dismissed, I made as if to leave only to be brought up short. "Not so fast, lad," Drake continued.

"There remains the small matter of your sentencing."

"My sentencing, Captain Drake?" Somehow I had known this was coming. Perhaps I was becoming as pessimistic as Lackland.

"Precisely, Mr. James. By now the least boy aboard has heard how poorly my table was served. It would be unnatural if you did not receive some reprimand, particularly in light of Stydye's departure."

"Then let us get on with it," I replied before I could regret speaking. "As you know, sir, I am no stranger to the post. In my estimation, a whipping is business better remembered than anticipated."

"Well said, lad. But I mentioned nothing of whipping. No, I have another honor entirely in mind for you."

Which is how I came to be chained to the deck with a posy—a sheet of paper detailing my misdemeanor—threaded around my neck on a loop of cord. Doughty, who had the penmanship of a professional secretary, wrote out the charge in letters large enough to be read at a distance. Then Diego led me from the grand cabin and shackled me to a bolt in the deck by a length of iron chain. The waist was deserted when he put the clamp around my ankle but by nightfall almost every sailor in the crew had found an opportunity to pass by. Most read the posy and returned to their duties, some with a snicker or chuckle, others with a nod of encouragement or sympathy or, as in Lackland's case, with a disparaging shake of the head. Lancelot Garget, however, loitered awhile. Pretending difficulty making out the words, he leaned close and squinted.

"What does it say here, pretty boy? Peregrine James,

the—damn me, I cannot figure the letters."

"Meanest."

"Aye, you are right! The meanest cook who ever lived. Is that not the sense of the message?"

"It is," I admitted.

"I thought so!" By his tone it was obvious that Garget was well satisfied with this estimation of my abilities. Crossing his gaunt arms across his stained leather vest, he regarded me sternly and pursed his lips as if at the sight of something distasteful. "Did I not tell you not to exercise yourself?" he asked rhetorically. "Out of the loving kindness of my heart, did I not instruct you to leave well enough alone? But would you heed this wise advice? No, not pretty boy, who knows best in all regards. Now look where you are. Sweet Jesus, is it not remarkable how divine justice is meted out!"

Although Drake had warned that wearing the posy would not be easy, in my innocence I had not understood how very hard it would be. As instructed, I attempted to put aside my pride and to bear my pretended shame stoically. But I did not enjoy being lectured to by Lancelot Garget, and only an intense effort of will allowed me to hold my tongue until he grew tired of goading me and went below to get out of the weather.

Snow had begun falling from a low ceiling of leaden cloud. Soon the harbor frontage was no more than an indistinct whitish blur beyond the dark water of Sutton Pool. Dragging my ankle chain behind me, I took shelter in the lee of the mainmast, which provided some relief from the wind and snow but not much. Drawing my legs up to my chest, I hugged my arms around my knees and tried to keep warm. By midnight I was shivering and miserable.

The chattering of my teeth obscured the sound of Thomas Doughty's approach and I was unaware of his presence until he spoke aloud. "Ah, Mr. James, you are a sorry sight."

"I have felt better, sir," I agreed.

"Wrap yourself in this," he instructed, handing me a wool blanket. "And lower your voice, lad! It would not do for the entire ship to overhear our conversation."

"Aye, sir," I said, dropping into a whisper although there was no one nearby. Even the night watchmen, usually visible at the bow and stern, were out of sight, most likely huddling someplace warm.

Looking around carefully, making doubly sure we were unobserved, Doughty drew closer. The shoulders of his leather coat were dusted with snow, as was the brim of his hat, and the cold stuff sifted down onto my face as he leaned forward. "Now listen carefully," he said, "and do not mention our conversation to anyone, particularly not to that little princess Lackland. Your performance today impressed Drake, Mr. James, so much so that he trusts you, which is a rare courtesy."

"I am honored, sir."

"Do not be. For Francis Drake, trust is a cloth measured in inches, not yards. But a matter has come up that must be instantly addressed and we have need of an honest courier. Can you ride, lad?"

"Absolutely, sir," I said immediately, stretching the truth more than a little in my eagerness to be of assistance. "Tell me what I must do."

Doughty paused, obviously deciding how much information to impart. At last he said, "Tomorrow Drake will announce that I am to assume Stydye's obligations in regard to victualling the ships. I will then go ashore to market. You will accompany me as my assistant. This will not be remarked upon because everyone will believe you are being punished with the burden of additional duty. Do you follow me so far?"

"Aye, sir. But I am confused as to why such pretense is necessary."

"Perhaps you do not realize, Mr. James, that even now unkind eyes study the *Pelican* from many directions. Our enemies are vigilant and relentless."

"Enemies, sir?"

"There are many who would know our business," Doughty replied. "The Spanish and their hired dogs, most surely. Certain members of the Privy Council, whose names I will not mention. I also suspect the Muscovy Company of having a keen interest in our affairs."

"What is so remarkable about a trading voyage to Alexandria?" I asked, believing it best not to voice Lackland's suspicions, nor my own, as to our true destination.

"Precisely, Mr. James! What is so remarkable about a trading voyage? Maintain this exact air of naiveté in the event you encounter any of the parties I have mentioned, although with God's grace no one will be noticing what becomes of you, lad."

"I understand, sir."

"Once we are ashore, I will provide you with a certain item and we will part ways."

"A certain item?"

Doughty studied me, again deciding how much information to divulge. "I suppose it will not hurt for you to know," he said reluctantly, "especially considering the role you have already played in the affair. When we examined Stydye's sea chest, we discovered a notebook concealed behind a false panel. The writing is in no language we can identify. No, it is in cipher, and only one man in England has the skill to break the code. You must bring the book to him and return with news."

"I will, Captain Doughty, sir. You have my word. What is this man's name and where is he to be found?"

"His name is Dee," said Thomas Doughty, answering my first question. "Dr. John Dee."

"Dee," I repeated. "Simple enough. He is a physician?" I asked, thinking his medical attire would make the man easy to recognize.

"No," Doughty replied. "Dee is a doctor of metaphysics." This, although I did not know it, while not an outright lie, was such a monumental understatement that it served the same purpose. "He is also the foremost English student of the arts of encryption, both in antiquity and as currently practiced on the continent. Should any person be able to break the code and discover what information it contains and to whom Stydye was reporting, it is John Dee. As to where he may be found—"

Doughty pressed several coins into my palm. "We will separate at market," he instructed. "If luck is with us, your departure will be unnoticed. Hire a brace of horse and take the post road toward London but proceed to the Thames crossing just past Bagshot. Turn off onto the towpath and continue another seven miles until you reach the town of Mortlake. There will be a church with a white steeple on one side of the road.

Across from the church is Dee's residence. To him alone give the notebook and my request. If you make haste, you will be able to complete the journey and return in a week."

Doughty left the blanket behind when he reentered the grand cabin and I was warm the remainder of the night. Not that I could sleep. My mind was racing with thoughts of the task before me. It is said that pride lies ahead of a fall. No one was more prideful than I was, enjoying the idea that Peregrine James, newest aboard and the least boy of the crew, had been selected for so important a mission. I felt myself to be a player in large events and promised myself solemnly to live up to the trust placed in me by my superiors. These foolish ramblings were, of course, only further proof of my inexperience, not to mention further confirmation of Lackland's low appraisal of my common sense. Despite Thomas Doughty's warning, and despite the murderous glare in Stydye's eyes as he was chivvied overboard, I felt no premonition of danger. I understood correctly that my insignificance was a virtue. What I did not realize was that my expendability was another.

Thus I greeted Lackland easily when he arrived at dawn to free me from the posy. "There you are, Tobias," I said briskly. "I had begun to fear Garget would have to prepare breakfast alone and without my aid."

Lackland shot me a curious look. "You are certainly in better spirits than those in which I expected to find you," he observed.

"Things are not so dark as you make out," I replied. "For example, I have been assigned additional duties. Not only am I Lancelot's henchman, I am also to serve as Thomas Doughty's factotum and assist with the provisioning. He has been given Stydye's responsibilities."

"And how is that a good thing?" Lackland exclaimed. "Was my prediction not correct, Mr. James? No kind deed goes unpunished."

"So should I grumble and complain? Tobias, occasionally you must look on the brighter side." I began to assemble the rigging with which to hoist the fire box on deck and begin the morning meal. "I, at least, will be going ashore to stretch my legs at market," I went on. "Others with whom I am acquainted are to remain confined aboard ship without hope of escape for the foreseeable future."

"You have a point," Lackland admitted. As usual, however, he was not content to leave the situation alone. "There is always the chance that I might be appointed to assist Garget during your absence, an assignment I would not enjoy. The man's ugly disposition is equaled only by the character of his menu."

However, to Lackland's satisfaction, another boy was given this duty. In the end Garget alone was displeased with the arrangement since he had become accustomed to my abilities. Horsewill, the lad replacing me, possessed neither skill nor interest in culinary matters. I could hear Garget complaining long after the taxi pushed off from the *Pelican*'s side and began making way across Sutton Pool but his voice was swallowed by city noise before we reached the wharf and disembarked.

This was the first time I had been on land since I had joined the *Pelican*. The absence of motion beneath my feet, the subtraction of the eternal rocking that all sailors experience even in the calmest harbor, caused me to stumble across the cobbles as I followed Thomas Doughty about his business.

Doughty took lodgings in a house not far from the waterfront that catered to the needs of gentlemen delayed in port. He gave the keeper enough rent for a week, ordered a supper of pigeons and sausage to be ready upon his return from shopping, and set off through the narrow streets of the Barbican toward the market held twice weekly in a field near St. Andrew's. I followed a couple paces to the rear, carrying a satchel that would be presumed to contain account books, inventory lists, and other items necessary to a purchasing agent. What it actually contained was Stydye's private notebook, which I was to convey to Dr. John Dee. Along the way Doughty paused to peer in shop windows, as if inspecting the merchandise but instead using the small oval panes of glass to view pedestrians behind us.

"Do not turn around, Mr. James," Doughty said quietly, indicating a reflection with an unobtrusive jab of his chin. "We are not alone. That fellow has been observing us."

"Yes, Fred Roach is a great gossip," I agreed. "A greater mystery is how he manages to escape arrest since he is also a great sharper."

"I see." Doughty was silent a moment. "And what of the dowdy rascal on our left with the surly expression? I am certain he has been at our heels since we departed our lodgings."

"Harry Wirthy, do you mean?" I asked. "The poor old drunk has been gathering courage to beg a coin off you, that is his problem."

Doughty was silent again. "Tell me, Mr. James," he said at last, "is there any person within view with whom you are not acquainted?"

I surveyed the street as best I could in the streaky reverse image of the shop window. "No, sir. Not at the instant."

"Inform me if and when that situation changes."

"Aye, sir."

I had not looked forward to returning to Plymouth and encountering those who knew my history, if not Annie herself or her new husband. This fear turned out to be unfounded. Not one person passing by knew me even though several of them had been acquaintances for years. Part of the reason for this lack of recognition, I suspected, was that I was dressed as a sailor from head to toe and not in the cook's apron that had been my usual attire in the Jack and Rasher. But as I regarded my reflection in the glass, I realized that more than my clothing had changed during my weeks aboard the *Pelican*. I had lost weight, which advertised the ridges of my cheekbones and made me seem less English and more my mother's son. And because I had not shaved, my upper lip and chin were hidden under a fuzz of dark hair. Even to myself I seemed only another common dock side vagabond, and one who was none too scrupulous with his appearance at that.

I supposed it was just as well. I had no true friends in Plymouth save for Beth Winston and Hal Audley, after all, and it would not do to meet either of them given the errand on which I was embarking.

The market began five blocks further on, a bewildering maze of stalls, farmers' wagons, and makeshift livestock pens, and soon we were elbowing along the crowded aisles threading the place. Remaining in character, Thomas Doughty stopped to inspect goods for sale and ordered several casks of apples and walnuts to be sent back to the *Pelican*, as well as the meat of a young bullock, a gross of hen's eggs, and a firkin of butter. Then he drew me into the shade of a cart piled high with fresh straw, where we could talk privately, our closest neighbor a farmer's wife sitting on the beaten earth several yards away with a pyramid of onions in her lap.

"Are you prepared, Peregrine James?" he asked.

"Aye, sir."

"And you know your route and destination?"

"In every particular, Mr. Doughty."

"The recipient of your parcel?"

"Dr. John Dee, who is to be identified by his remarkable beard."

"Exactly correct. We separate now. With God's grace, no one will remark upon your departure and you will have an uneventful journey."

"But if I do not?"

"What would be Drake's phrase? Keep a weather eye out, Mr. James. It is better to avoid trouble altogether than to be forced to overcome adversity."

"And if that proves impossible?"

"I cannot ask more of you than you can give. Hand over the parcel and flee. You have neither the training nor the experience to make an accounting of yourself. It is your obscurity on which I am depending, not your martial skill. Now go with God! Head directly to Mortlake without detour. I will expect your return in seven days with word from Dee."

Doughty remained behind as I entered the throng of housewives, servants, vendors, farmers, and buskers. His warning had put me on edge and I found myself studying passers-by suspiciously. Although I could not hope to recognize every person, particularly at market, those I encountered seemed no more than what they appeared. Nor, to my inexperienced eye, did anyone demonstrate more than casual interest in my passage to Peacock Lane, opposite St. Andrew's. Here was a row of stables with mounts for hire by the hour, day, or week. The proprietor was burly man with tufts of grass in his hair, the pockets of his leather apron bulging with carrots and apples and other stuff horses find agreeable. Once Doughty's silver was on his palm, he indicated two mares of remarkable girth and said:

"Why, Bess here, and old Netty, they are the perfect mounts for you. Slow and steady, that they are," he continued. "But they will get a sailor there and back no matter how much sack you have aboard."

I had told the liveryman I was headed for London to visit relatives but it was clear he believed my real destination to be a neighborhood on the Thames known to mariners for less than reputable reasons.

London was two hundred miles distant. Allowing time for Dr. Dee's analysis of Stydye's cipher, I would have to move quickly to reach Mortlake and return in a week. Although I was no expert of horseflesh, I doubted the plump nags before me could maintain the necessary pace.

"Would you have any others, sir?" I asked. "I have only seven days leave and my business is urgent."

"Aye, lad, it always is." The proprietor thought a moment and then gave me a dubious study, evidently appraising my horsemanship. "Could you handle a spirited mount?" he asked.

"Within reason," I answered carefully. While not totally

lacking experience on horseback, what little I had consisted of riding the tavern dray to and from market.

The proprietor led the way out of the stable to an open paddock behind the building. This contained two geldings, one dappled, one pure brown. "Barnabas and Chompers," said the liveryman. "Chomps is easy enough but Barnabas is a right jealous bastard, let no one tell you different. Still, if he takes a liking to you, he will give you a fair ride. Offer him a couple apples, lad. If he leaves your fingers alone, you will generally have no difficulty with the perverse creature."

Heartened by this encouraging advice, I gingerly approached the dappled horse. Barnabas skittered back a couple steps, snorted, and eyed me with his head cocked sideways. Even the sight of the apple I held out failed to calm him. It soon became clear the beast was in no mood to be friendly. I would have to find some other way to secure his cooperation.

Appealing to his better nature had failed. Perhaps, I mused, it might be more helpful to cater to his worst side.

The liveryman had called the horse a right jealous bastard. I suspected this was nothing less than literal truth.

"So be it," I remarked aloud, as if Barnabas were capable of human speech instead of being a dumb animal. "I will not impose where I am not welcome. I will find someone else with whom to share my apples."

I bit into one to illustrate my point, making a loud business of it and chewing with gusto.

Although Barnabas refused to look at me directly, his ears twitched whenever my teeth snapped through the skin of the fruit into the crisp flesh beneath. Pretending to notice

Chompers for the first time, I exclaimed: "Why, perhaps this handsome fellow would care to have an apple or two with me. Meals are lonely affairs without company to enliven the atmosphere. What do you say, Chomps."

The brown gelding took the apple from my palm without hesitation, and three more besides, guzzling the fruit with relish. This sight proved too much for Barnabas to bear. He came up behind Chompers and spurred the other horse out of the way with a nasty nip on the rump.

"What is this?" I asked. "Changed your mind, have you? You are a spiteful animal, Barnabas, are you not? Here is an apple."

Barnabas was in a complacent mood now that he had vented his spleen on poor Chompers. He allowed me to approach without backing away and ate out of my hand while leaving my fingers unscathed. Nor did he contest being saddled although he blew out his belly to prevent the strap being cinched tight, an old trick even I knew how to counter. Giving the evil beast a firm elbow to the gut, which caused him to properly exhale, I buckled the saddle strap securely. Despite the liveryman's assurances that Barnabas and I were henceforth to be bosom companions, I did not trust the horse and suspected he would try to throw me at the first opportunity. But I was still astride him an hour later, and already five miles along the post road past the outskirts of the city. Chompers, unsaddled so as to provide a fresh mount when necessary, followed at the end of a short tether.

We kept up a brisk pace the remainder of the afternoon and covered thirty miles by twilight. At first the road was crowded with pedestrians and wheeled vehicles but soon traffic thinned out and there were long stretches where I was the only traveler. To either side the fields had been readied for winter, the bare ground tilled in preparation for the spring planting, drifts of snow lying here and there on the brown soil. We passed Pomphlett and Elburton, both small villages, and then Combe, just three houses and a church. Yealmpton, the next town east from Brixton, marked the furthest point I had been from home, excepting the *Pelican*'s aborted voyage to Falmouth Haven. And by the time I was looking around for a suitable campsite, we were just south of Exeter.

In the morning I rode Chompers in order to allow Barnabas to regain his strength and switched horses again just past Crewkerne.

The weather remained fair but chill. By afternoon, however, the sun had warmed the air enough for me to unbutton my coat. Despite my misgivings, Barnabas proved an amenable mount, his docile behavior fooling me so completely that I suspected nothing of what he had in mind for later. The apprehensions I had entertained at the start of the journey had faded away, too. The only person to overtake us had been a postal rider garbed in black moving quickly on a fresh mount and I had long since given up any idea that I was being followed.

We covered another fifty miles by nightfall, for a total of ninety-five for the day, excellent time, which brought us to Tidworth, somewhat north of Salisbury. Again I bedded down at the side of the road and shared a breakfast of windfall apples with the horses. I washed mine down with flat beer while Barnabas and Chompers drank from a nearby stream and then we were off again along the post road. Late afternoon found us approaching the Thames. For a full mile, and then another, I was alone on the towpath. To my left was the muddy blue water of the river, here about fifty yards wide, the bank rimed with ice. To my right spread a field prickly with the stalks of harvested grain. Soon I overtook a farmer, a man of about sixty years, pushing a wheelbarrow of manure.

I reined in Barnabas until we matched the farmer's speed and touched my cap. "Would this be the direction to Mortlake?" I asked.

"It is, sir," he answered. "The place lies three miles further. Veer neither to the left nor to the right and you should reach it easily."

"That is good advice and I thank you for it."

"Take the vineyard path from the green," he went on. "You will find the doctor's house just past the church to the west. 'Tis not a stone's throw from the water. You cannot miss it."

It was disquieting to hear that my business was already known to a passing stranger. "What makes you believe I am looking for a doctor?"

"Come, lad, I was not born this morning! Mortlake receives few visitors except those entertained by Dr. John Dee. Why, just last month her grace Elizabeth herself conferred with him. It was no great application of logic to work out your destination. Tell me I am wrong."

"No," I admitted, "that I cannot do."

"I thought so!" said the farmer, although he did not seemed pleased by the accuracy of his prediction. "Well, lad," he continued, "I suppose you know your own affairs and the credit of your associates. Nor is it prudent to speak poorly of neighbors. If you hurry, and stray not from the path, you will reach Mortlake before dark. God's mercy on you."

In the twilight I could just make out the steeple of the village church rising above a distant screen of trees. Thanking the farmer, I urged Barnabas forward. If I had been more observant, I would have heard the caution in the man's voice. If I had been wiser, I would have asked for more information before continuing onward. But I was neither one nor the other and I pressed ahead without second thoughts. Soon we were cut off from the sun by the deeper gloom of a spur of forest, which pressed close against the track and obscured views of any distance.

Then I was forced to rein in Barnabas. Thirty yards ahead the way was blocked by a wagon with a broken wheel.

An empty halter signified that the three men by the wagon had been pulling it themselves rather than employing a horse or donkey.

The broken wheel had been removed from its axel and propped against the side of the wagon. The men were inspecting it and evidently conferring among themselves as to what to do about the matter. Hearing my approach, they ceased their deliberations and faced me.

I still did not suspect that these men might have any connection with me—I had come upon them, after all. However, it was not unheard of for knaves to disguise themselves as common people in order to betray travelers, and it was only sensible to be wary in any unusual situation on the road. So I let Barnabas go ahead slowly while I took a careful look at the scene I was approaching.

"A good evening to you, gentlemen," I said. "Although I

fear I find you in difficulty."

"The damned rim has sprung loose," said one, a very thin man with a fair complexion. Like the others, he wore a leather jacket over brown homespun. "It needs a wheelwright to be put in order."

"You have articulated our problem in every detail." agreed the second man. "How unfortunate the nearest resides in town. One of us has a long walk ahead of him to summon aid."

Then the third snapped his fingers, as if at the arrival of an idea. "Perhaps the young gentleman could be encouraged to bear the news for us. You are bound for Mortlake, are you not?"

Due to my previous encounter with the farmer trundling the wheelbarrow of manure, I was not surprised by this observation. There was something about the conversation, however, I did not like, although I could not identify exactly what was troublesome. Maybe it was the fact the three men had separated from each other, leaving one at either end of the stalled cart while the third came toward me.

"Aye," I admitted. "I am indeed headed for Mortlake."

"Excellent," exclaimed the pale man. "Is it not a miracle how God provides a solution for every problem?"

"Truly the lad is an angel in disguise," agreed another.

"Hold a minute," I protested. "I would like to help but I cannot spare time for a detour. My affairs are urgent."

"My oath, you will not be greatly delayed," said the man on my left.

"Better yet," said the one approaching me, "perhaps the young gentleman would allow us the service of his spare mount."

"No, no," I answered. "I will bear your message into town.

Tell me where the wheelwright is to be found."

If all had gone according to plan, this was the moment in which I would have been captured. The nearest man grabbed for Barnabas's reins while the others drew short swords from beneath their jackets.

I should have been trapped between them but Barnabas, demonstrating his usual ill humor, bit at the fingers reaching for his bridle, drawing blood, and danced back with a whinny. The pale man cursed and began fumbling for his own sword with his uninjured hand in order to join the attack.

It was not until his henchmen were almost upon me that I fully understood I was in danger.

"What is this!" I cried out, wrenching Barnabas's head around in order to steer him away. "I have nothing of value, I swear."

"What of the burden you carry?" asked the leader, coming forward in a crouch.

"It is just a book."

"Precisely, young sir. This book we require. Stand and deliver, and I will spare your person. You are only the messenger."

If I had paused to mull over this argument, events might have gone differently. I was, after all, the least boy aboard the *Pelican*. I knew nothing of combat and carried no weapon but my kitchen knife. I would not have been faulted for handing over Stydye's notebook and fleeing for my life. Had not Doughty specifically charged me to avoid difficulty rather than to seek to overcome it?

But I did not pause to think. Instead I kicked Barnabas cruelly in the belly with my boot heels. Already in a foul temper, the horse gave a scream of rage and began galloping back along the towpath in the direction from which we had come, clods of half frozen mud exploding from beneath his hooves, steam pumping from his nostrils in angry jets. I dropped Chompers's tether but the brown gelding was a creature of habit and kept to his usual place behind Barnabas as we fled the ambush. Then the hiss of a bolt whipping by my ear caused me to throw myself flat against the horse's back.

Glancing over my shoulder, I saw one man cocking a crossbow in preparation for another shot while his companions retrieved arms of their own from the wagon.

"Listen to me, young sir!" called the leader while bending to one knee in order to aim properly. "You do not need to die."

I could not have stopped had I wanted to. Barnabas was determined to go his own way and continued straight forward even when an obstacle appeared directly before us in the form of the farmer I had met earlier. Seeing the maddened horse bearing right toward him, the old fellow threw up his hands with a squawk of surprise and dove off the path into the river. He left behind in the center of the track his burden of manure. This presented Barnabas the opportunity for which the malicious creature had been waiting. Instead of avoiding the wheelbarrow, he rushed for it and came to a sudden halt while pitching up his hindquarters, breaking my desperate grip around his neck and tossing me from the saddle.

The depth of the stinking pile into which I was thrown cushioned my fall and saved me from serious harm. Barnabas paused briefly to survey his handiwork, snickered with delight, and then cantered off with Chompers trailing behind docilely.

My enemies surrounded me as I dragged myself from

the wheelbarrow. The pale man cuffed me across the face. "That is for causing mischief," he explained.

I began to wipe my mouth until I noticed the filth smearing the back of my wrist. I let my arm drop to my side.

"Now hand over the notebook," continued the villain.

It galled me to have to do as I was told but I could see no alternative, particularly with two crossbows aimed at my heart. Not daring to answer for fear that I would say something I would regret, I opened my satchel silently and took out the wrapped parcel that had been given into my care. Knowing that I had failed my mission and betrayed the confidence placed in me by Thomas Doughty and Francis Drake hurt far more than my physical injuries, and I turned my eyes aside as the pale man ripped away the paper from the notebook. It was not until I heard his oath of disgust that I learned we both had been deceived. There was no notebook inside the wrapping but only more paper bundled together. He stripped leaf from leaf with mounting exasperation, letting the wind take the discarded sheets and blow them onto the Thames.

"Where is it?" he growled, grabbing my shirt in his fist and pressing me against the wheelbarrow. "Speak with care, young sir. Much depends on your answer."

"I—I do not know," I stammered, as surprised as he was. "I thought I carried the book with me."

"That is not what I hoped to hear but I do believe you. You are naught but a decoy, lad, of no use to anyone."

The leader made a quick gesture to his men, ordering my execution.

Setting Sail

December 11, 1577 – December 13, 1577
Mortlake, Plymouth

I have faced death on more occasions than I care to remember since the incident on the road to Mortlake. But there on the towpath was the first time in my life I knew with absolute certainty I would die and when the moment of my death would be.

That moment had arrived.

The hiss of twin bolts cut the air at the same instant. I braced myself and hoped the archers had aimed well and that my agony would be brief.

I was determined to keep my eyes open and to not perish in darkness but even so I blinked involuntarily. To my surprise I was still among the living when I opened my eyes.

A third hiss indicated the strike of another bolt. It took the pale man in the chest and beat him to the ground to join his fellows. These men were not breathing. The leader, however, was alive. He began struggling to draw the barb from his flesh as Thomas Doughty approached, followed by Diego and Tom Moone, a hulking giant who had served as Drake's carpenter during the raid on Nombre de Dios and who was now master of the *Benedict*, the smallest ship of the fleet. Both men carried crossbows, already reloaded. Doughty kicked the injured man flat and ground his boot heel into the shaft protruding from the man's chest.

"Out with it," he said evenly. "Who hired you?"

"I cannot say!"

"Speak or die, it is that simple." Doughty placed the tip of his slim blade against the nape of the other's neck.

"I cannot say because I do not know!" The pale man squirmed beneath Doughty's boot but could not escape the pressure pinning him down. "I received a letter and instructions," he panted desperately. "How can I say from whom? No name was given and I did not ask for one. Why should I care? I was paid in gold."

"What were your orders?"

"To intercept the lad and retrieve the notebook on his person."

"And afterward?"

"I was to be contacted, that is all I know, I swear it."

Then he coughed. With a look of incredulity, the pale man opened his mouth, allowing a torrent of blood to rush out and stain his beard. Not much later he was as still as his subordinates. Tom Moone rifled the pockets of all three, discovering nothing except a couple worn shillings and a few oddments of little value. Diego went into the trees and retrieved the horses that the villains had concealed a bowshot from the towpath and then fetched back Barnabas and Chompers.

Thomas Doughty said, "The rogues were dogging your heels since Plymouth, Mr. James. Last night they went ahead in the dark to set their trap. We, in turn, set a trap for them."

"You knew all along I would be followed," I said, realizing that the pale man had been incorrect. I was not a decoy.

I was bait.

"Of course. It is as I have said before. Our enemies are vigilant."

"Nor did I ever have custody of Stydye's notebook."

"It is in my own possession. There was too much certainty that you would be waylaid. Now do what you can with your hygiene, Mr. James. On my honor, I have endured nicer aromas in a sty."

"And I in the bilge," agreed Tom Moone.

Doughty's observation reminded me of the condition I was in, which is to say, my clothing, skin, and hair were splotched with manure. Even Chompers, usually obedient, had to be urged to accept me as a rider. Diego replaced the wheel upon its axel and pushed the wagon to the side of the path. We left the three dead men by the river bank. There was no sign of the farmer who had jumped into the water.

I had never liked Thomas Doughty and now I liked him even less. While I understood that it was the nature of things for every man to oblige another, from the least boy in the kitchen to the highest in the land, I resented the fact that Doughty had kept me ignorant of my true role in the proceedings. Moreover, I was appalled at myself for not suspecting how I was being used.

Doughty pulled his horse in line with Chompers. "Did I not instruct you to hand over the notebook if you were intercepted, Mr. James?" he asked in too low a tone for his voice to reach the others but loud enough for me to hear his disapproval. "Do you think me prone to idle chatter?"

"No, captain. Never."

"Rest assured, I am not pleased. Those dogs were professionals with military training. Had you not irked them, we would have had the leisure to capture them alive for questioning or track them to their master. Your theatrics forced us to take killing shots in haste. I tell you in all honesty it was a near decision whether to let them do with you as they willed. Do you get my meaning, Mr. James?"

"Aye, Captain Doughty," I replied weakly, thanking God the darkness hid the color burning my cheeks. "You are particularly clear, sir. I will do better in the future, sir. You have my promise."

To my relief our arrival at Mortlake ended this uncomfortable conversation. Diego turned off the towpath onto a narrow lane leading through neat aisles of grape vines trained around upright stakes. Then he reined up before our destination, a stone building that at one time had been a simple farmhouse but had been added to until it was now far more imposing. One wing, I learned, was a library holding thousands of volumes on a hundred different subjects, the selection representative of the far-reaching intellect of their owner. Behind this was an even more private library housing books whose contents were too dangerous for public view. In the other wing was Dr. John Dee's personal study, an imposing room with many windows. Every horizontal surface was piled with objects that had excited his curiosity, the clutter so pervasive that it was hard to find space to sit. I have been told that the door behind Dee's writing table led to a laboratory in which he conducted philosophical experiments but I cannot vouch for this since I was never invited within.

A servant answered Diego's knock and summoned Dr.

Dee to the door while another man led our horses to a stable behind the building.

Dee was recognizable from Doughty's description, a man in his early fifties with the full gray beard of a scholar brushed into a blunt point several hand's breadths beneath his chin. He was wearing a velvet gown with loose hanging sleeves, which almost swallowed his hands. His head nodded slowly up and down while he listened to Doughty, the motion reminding me of the bobbing a pigeon's neck makes as the bird walks. But it was his eyes that held me. In the dusk they glowed with light, so wise and warm I never suspected they belonged to the most dangerous sorcerer in all England.

"Yes, certainly," Dee said, stroking his beard from end to end in a habitual mannerism. "I am glad to be of assistance to yourself and to Captain Drake. Come inside, you and your men—but stop! What, pray tell, is that infernal stench?"

"That is Peregrine James," Doughty replied. "Mr. James suffered an unfortunate accident on the road hither."

"Are you injured, son?" Dee asked, addressing me.

"No, sir," I answered. "But there is no question I would benefit by a wash and change of clothes."

"A wash? No, what you require is more stringent, son. Nothing less than a bath will do! Roger! Assist Peregrine with his ablutions and see that he has something to wear. Sally, where are you, girl? A pitcher of sack and a bite to eat, if you would. There are sausages remaining from supper, are there not? We will be in the study."

Roger led me around back to a wattle and daub laundry shed. This was situated beside a stream, allowing easy access to fresh water. There was a hearth for warmth and a barrel for bathing and a bucket for filling the barrel. An hour later I was scrubbed clean and dressed in a borrowed outfit while my own clothes, which I had soaped and rinsed in my used bath water, dried on a line. I followed Roger into the main building and found Thomas Doughty, Diego, and Tom Moone sprawled on comfortable chairs upholstered in green silk while Dee, seated at a cluttered table, examined Stydye's notebook. Our host muttered absently to himself as he turned the pages but I could not tell whether this was a sign of success or of failure. Little was left of the sausages he had mentioned but there was a slab of cheese, some apples, and half a loaf of bread. At Doughty's nod, I served myself and ate my meal quietly while Dr. Dee continued his deliberations and the other men drank wine.

I did not grow bored despite the length of the wait. Everywhere I looked, another marvel caught my interest. Beside the desk was a globe of the earth, its surface illustrated in blue, black, and red ink, the outlines of the known world fading into vast expanses of *terra incognita*, which, although I did not suspect it at the time, I would eventually know well. The bones of a man, held together by a framework of wire, stood in a lifelike pose in one corner of the room. Opposite the skeleton was the carcass of an owl perched on a branch with the stuffed body of a mouse in its beak. One entire wall held shelves on which intricate artifacts of unknown purpose fought for elbow room with stacks of charts and books, chunks of crystal and unusual rock, and curios of foreign origin.

At last Dr. Dee closed the notebook. "I fear that I have both good news and bad," he said. "The first is that I can indeed translate what is here. Unhappily, I cannot do so in the allotted span of time."

"I had anticipated a better answer, sir," Doughty replied, "The expedition sails in a matter of days. Repairs were almost complete when we left Plymouth."

"I, too, captain, wish I had a better answer. However, I would not want to provide you with false expectations. Let me explain."

Dee held the notebook open and tapped the page with a finger whose tip was stained black with ink almost to the knuckle. "What I had hoped to find was a simple code, what is called a Caesar cipher, after the Roman emperor of the same name, a scheme in which each letter of a message is replaced by another, an *h* for an *a*, for example, an *i* for a *b*. The method for breaking such a code is, of course, eloquently explained by Abu Yusuf Yaqub ibn Ishaq al-Sabbah Al-Kindi in his seminal *A Manuscript on Deciphering Cryptographic Messages*."

"This is a work with which I am unfamiliar," Doughty remarked.

"I believe you, captain, since it is available only in the author's native Arabic. Essentially, Al-Kindi notes that each language employs letters with predictable frequency. By counting the number of times a letter is repeated in a document, it is possible to make an educated guess as to its true reference. In English, *e* is most common, followed by *t* and *a*. Z and *q* are much rarer, and *q* never appears by itself but only as part of a letter pair. By deduction, the other half of the pair would be *u*. Do you follow my reasoning?"

"I do, by God!" Tom Moone exclaimed, slamming the flat

of one fist into the palm of his other hand. "'Tis damned clever, is it not? The Moors are cunning devils, that is plain truth!"

"Unfortunately," continued Dr. Dee, "here we are faced with a more complex code, what is known as a polyalphabetic cipher, as described by Johannes Trithemius in his posthumous work *Polygraphia*, published, if I remember correctly, in 1519. Polyalphabetic ciphers combine several Caesar ciphers with different shift values. Thus the letter *a* could be enciphered as any of several letters at different points in the message, first by an *b*, then by an *s*, then by an *n*, and so forth. This, of course, defeats any ordinary analysis of letter frequency."

"Fiendish!" observed Tom Moone.

"Theoretically," Dr. Dee went on, "the alphabet could be shifted with each letter in the message, which would render the code completely resistant to decryption. In practice, however, most polyalphabetic ciphers are limited to a small number of shifted alphabets, whose sequence is determined by a secret keyword. Discover the length of this keyword and the solution to the cipher is in your hand. The problem is that the undertaking could take months."

"By then we will be well away from Plymouth," Doughty replied, obviously disliking the answer. "But you are the expert, Dr. Dee. I have no choice but to accept that the situation is as you describe. In any event, sir, please be so good as to forward what you learn to those with the power to act on the information. You understand to whom I refer."

"Without doubt, captain! I will do as you ask, have no fear. Your enemies are the enemies of our blessed country and sovereign and mine to the marrow." Dee's brows furrowed.

"May there be an anathema upon them," he continued. "May pestilence descend upon their ilk and upon all foul traitors and henchmen of Spain wherever they hide and wherever they turn and may God look aside and send them to hell."

As before, Dee's eyes were lit from within but now the light was no longer kindly. His voice had lost its academic quality and he pronounced his words as if he were muttering them in some malevolent ritual. I felt a strange sensation along the back of my neck and sensed the fine hairs standing on end. Only then did I remember the attitude of the farmer into whose cargo of dung I had been tossed by Barnabas. Doughty had assured me that Dr. Dee was a professor of metaphysics but now I did not doubt that our host's studies ranged more widely.

Diego, steadfastly Catholic despite his hatred of priests and all things Spanish, was unconsciously tracing the sign of a cross in the air. Tom Moone's chair scraped against the floorboards as he edged back.

Then Dr. Dee's voice returned to normal. "You must forgive me, gentleman," he said, closing Stydye's notebook and laying it flat on the desk. "Occasionally I become excited with an excess of patriotism when reminded of those who stand against England and our good queen. For far too long our nation has been denied its rightful place in history, I tell you— but I am forgetting myself again. Sally! Where are you, lass? Our guests require beds! Why are they not ready?"

Diego and Tom Moone were out of the room almost before Dr. Dee finished speaking. Thomas Doughty bowed more deliberately and then followed them through the door. But as I prepared to go after him, my name was called, bringing me to a reluctant halt.

"Peregrine, a moment of your time."

I looked at Doughty for direction as to how I should respond to this request. He gave me a quick nod and a stern frown, which I took to mean that I had best do as I was asked but to mind what I said. Then Doughty continued on his way, leaving me alone with Dr. Dee, who indicated that I should take the seat closest to his desk.

"You interest me, son," he said as I sat down. "Tell me in your own words how you unearthed the perfidy of this man, Stydye."

Once again I described the principles of proper inventory rotation and explained the necessity of using those goods received first into stock before those received later. Dee remained silent after I finished, stroking his beard thoughtfully. At last he said, "Improbable. Inconceivable. But what else is the inconceivable but miracle in disguise? It is apparent, Peregrine, that you have joined this expedition for a purpose."

"Yes, sir," I agreed readily. "I wish to make my fortune at sea and to be of service to my masters. Additionally, sir, I am looking forward to leaving the city of Plymouth behind and to visiting foreign countries."

"That is not what I meant, son," Dr. Dee replied. He pushed aside some papers and books, freeing a space between us across the desk. Resting on his elbows, he stretched out his hands. "Give me yours, Peregrine," he told me, and although I did not want to, I placed mine on his. He examined them from several angles and then turned them palms up. With a fingertip he traced a crease in the skin that ran from the wrist of my right hand toward my index finger. "This line represents the journey you are to take," he explained. "Even more interesting are the crosshatchings, do you see them? They intersect the travel line."

"This is a fair omen, I hope."

"To the contrary. They indicate moments of acute peril. However, this other line is of even more concern." Dr. Dee tapped the fold that extended from my middle finger down to my wrist. "The line of fate."

"The line of fate?" I repeated, not caring for the ominous title. "Why should that be of concern, sir?"

"Because it intersects the travel line and because it, too, is scarred by crosshatchings. This can imply only one thing."

"What is that, Dr. Dee?" I asked.

"That your fate is tied to a greater enterprise, and that through symmetry the fate of the greater enterprise is tied to yours. In what fashion and by what device I cannot say."

"Is there nothing more you may tell me, sir?" I asked, disliking such an amorphous warning, which seemed to me worse than useless. What was the point in being alarmed by unnamed dangers without being able to prepare for them?

"Specifics, no. The future is not yet born and exists only as potential, much as a child growing within the womb of a woman is but a shadow of the man to come. I can merely sense its general shape." Dr. Dee studied my hand and began muttering to himself in a language I did not understand. Then he indicated a point midway between the base of my index finger and the center of my palm. "This is where the travel line ends. 'Tis known as the Mount of Lower Mars and represents courage and fortitude. In your case, son, Lower Mars is raised somewhat from the plane of your palm. The import is unmistakable."

"Go on, sir. Pray do not stop now."

"Much rests on your stoutness of heart, Peregrine. You will be tested three times—here, here, and here." Dr. Dee touched my hand with each repetition of the word. "In the first instance I sense terrible aridity, an ocean of sand. In the second there is a sea of silver without limit. Last, son, beware of the burning hills, for they harbor tragedy."

"The burning hills?" I said. "You have my word, Dr. Dee, I will take pains to avoid such an ill-named place."

"That will not be possible. However, what happens there is conditional and depends upon your actions. You must be bold and resourceful or all will be for nothing."

"I have had similar counsel before," I answered, thinking of Hal Audley and of the wherry men, Harry and Wilbert.

Dr. Dee let go of my hands and faced me silently for so long I felt the urge to fidget in my chair and to drop my eyes but I forced myself to continue looking straight at him without moving. At last he said, "I wish I had more to give you than vague advice. These are dangerous times for our country. The accursed Spanish and the Portuguese, who are naught but Spaniards by proxy, have had the pride to divide the world between them by fiat of their false Pope. There is no room for England in such a scheme. The wealth of the Americas and the Indies pours into Spanish coffers while our ships are denied permission to trade and English crews are imprisoned at the whim of the dons. It is vital that Drake succeed in his mission if her grace, Elizabeth, is not to become just another whore to Philip, as was her sister, the bloody bitch Mary."

I could not come up with an immediate response to this

lecture. At last I said, "I had not understood that a merchant voyage dealing in currants and raisins was of such importance."

"Come, come, Peregrine! You are an observant lad."

"You cannot help speculate," I admitted. "Everyone has a different idea. Some say we're bound for Panama, to repeat the captain's raid on Nombre de Dios or to continue overland to the Pacific. Others swear we are sailing for the Caribbean to harass Spanish shipping and make ourselves rich. I do not know what to believe, Dr. Dee, but I sincerely doubt the *Pelican* will return home with a burden of dried fruit."

"Do not be so sure, young man," Dr. Dee replied, wagging an ink-stained finger in contradiction. "Much depends on the fruit."

"What fruit could be so valuable?" I asked.

"I can name many. The fruit of the tree of life, for one. The fruit that provides knowledge of good and evil."

"Surely, sir, our destination is not paradise. Few among our crew would be admitted within the gates."

"Most likely you are correct, Peregrine," Dr. Dee replied with a chuckle. Then he stood from the table, signaling that the conversation was over. "Sally! Sally!" he called. "Why are you always getting lost, girl? Another bed is required. Make haste, since dawn approaches."

The other men were asleep when I entered the bedchamber. It seemed that I had just closed my eyes when I was awake again and seated upon Chompers, pounding along the towpath that followed the course of the Thames and then galloping along the post road.

Doughty was in the lead and set an even faster pace than

I had set myself during my ride to Mortlake. At times we averaged more than a dozen miles each hour, an exceptional as well as an illegal speed, and we did so for a dozen hours at a stretch. Only the fact that we had additional mounts, courtesy of the men who had ambushed me and who no longer needed them, permitted us to keep going so quickly without exhausting the horses. By the time we arrived at the outskirts of the city, the insides of my thighs and knees were cramped and burning from being in the saddle for so long. Our return had required less than two days—it was now the 13th of December. Doughty and the others made straight for the docks but I detoured at St. Andrew's to leave off Barnabas and Chompers at their stable.

The liveryman provided them treats from his apron pocket and gave back to me a portion of my deposit after examining the horses to ensure they were healthy.

"How went the journey, lad?" he asked.

"Well, mostly," I replied, bending slowly at the knees in order to work out the pain in my legs. "Chompers is an obliging animal but I cannot say the same of Barnabas. He is a sly and spiteful brute and tried his utmost to do me harm."

Barnabas whinnied disparagingly and presented his rump to me with unmistakable significance. We did not part friends.

I followed New Street downhill through the Barbican and arrived at Sutton Pool in time to hitch a ride to the *Pelican* aboard a taxi laden with barrels of wine and beer, some final provisions for the expedition. When I came over the gunwale, Drake was standing on the half deck along with his immediate advisors, appraising the crew's efforts while Blacollers directed operations from the waist. The ship was being readied for departure and it was apparent we would embark soon. Everyone was working with energy, thankful to be finally setting sail after a month in port without leave. I, too, felt my pulse quicken at the thought of putting Plymouth to my back once and for all, no matter what lay ahead.

"Bless you, Luke Adden," called Blacollers. "Trim that sheet, smartly now."

"Aye, sir!"

A dozen men climbed the ratlines of the masts into the sky and spread themselves out along the spars, loosening the short lengths of cord known as gaskets that secured the sails.

"Peregrine James!"

"Yes, sir!"

"Why are you larking about, lad? To the capstan."

"Aye, sir!"

There was a free space on the handspike beside Tobias Lackland. As I put my shoulder next to his against the shaft, he said, "Welcome back, Mr. James. I was beginning to fear we would leave without you."

"A distinct possibility," I admitted, "except for one fact."

"Which is?"

"I was in the company of Mr. Doughty, who is of more account than I am. He would be dearly missed even if I were not."

"You are finally acquiring a modicum of intelligence," Lackland admitted, pressing nearer so our conversation would not be easily overheard. "Now tell me all that occurred."

"I do not understand you, Tobias."

"Come clean. Neither you nor Doughty remained long

in Plymouth. The story is you were seeking cheaper goods at rural markets."

"If that is what you were told, how can I say otherwise."

"Ah, but I also was present two nights past when Drake and his cronies were in their cups. Bruer kept me busy running for beer and sack but I did hear a certain name mentioned. Dee."

"He is a pleasant gentleman and a kind host, I agree."

"Have you no inkling of his reputation?"

"I was given to understand Dr. Dee was a scholar of philosophy, although I suspected his true expertise lay in other directions."

"Other directions, indeed," Lackland sniffed. "If you were not a simple provincial, you would be aware Dr. John Dee is a practitioner of certain arts forbidden to good Christians. It is said his very look has dire consequences should the recipient be in his disfavor."

"Then I suppose it was just as well we did not argue."

"That is God's honest truth. What did you talk about?"

"I cannot say, Tobias. I have sworn an oath."

"And what, pray tell, has that to do with the cost of pepper—"

"Gentlemen, will you inform me, for I truly wish to know—what do you do with a drunken sailor?"

The question came from Blacollers, and was addressed not only to Lackland and me but to the entire gang around the capstan.

"What do you do with a drunken sailor?" repeated the boatswain, and then asked the question a third time. With each repetition Blacollers's voice took on melody, so that he was singing when he finished the verse with the traditional "early in the morning."

Now it was our turn. Although I was a novice at seafaring, I had heard the shanty a hundred times echoing across the harbor as ships prepared to leave Plymouth. This allowed me to join in confidently as we pressed our shoulders to the handspikes and sang the famous chorus:

"Hooray, way–hey,
Heave-ho and up she rises,
Heave-ho and up she rises,
Early in the morning!"

We heaved in rhythm with the cadence of the song, and with each exertion the capstan moved more readily, drawing the cable from the depths of Sutton Pool and onboard the *Pelican*, and depositing it through a chute in the deck down into the orlop, where a gang looped the incoming cable into tidy coils, a process known as *flemishing*.

Having asked the preliminary question, Blacollers now proceeded to provide a series of solutions to the problem of what exactly may be done with an inebriated mariner. These began reasonably with advice to "Take him and shake him and try and wake him" and "Put him in the longboat 'til he's sober." But soon the suggestions became progressively more severe. "Shave his belly with a rusty razor," was followed by, "Hang him from the yardarm 'til he dangles." We reached, "Throw him in the bilge and make him drink it," when the cable started to come aboard.

Then the capstan fought against us and refused to turn. The anchor must now be pried loose from the bottom.

"Bless you, ladies!" said Blacollers. "May I see at least a show of effort? What do you say?"

Grunt. "Heave-ho and up she rises."

"I cannot hear you! What do you say?"

"Heave-ho and up she rises!" Still the capstan did not turn.

"Louder now. I cannot hear you!"

"Heave-ho and up she rises!" Grunt. "Early in the morning!"

The anchor came free at the end of the chorus with a suddenness that took us by surprise and we all staggered forward.

"God pity all ships and the fools who sail them," Lackland muttered, much as he had done when we first met. "No good will come of this adventure, my word on it."

Rubbing the spot on my chin where the handspike had given me a nasty knock, I replied, "Try to be more cheerful, Tobias. I have it on excellent authority that what is to be in the future depends on what we do now. It may be equally likely that we all return home as rich men."

"I do not think so."

"At the least, we will have had a memorable voyage and seen many interesting sights."

"Yes, those of us who survive."

Blacollers dismissed the capstan gang once the anchor was secured to the cathead and I joined Lancelot Garget at the fire box.

Instead of hoisting sail and steering with the tide through the narrow strait into Plymouth Sound, this time

Setting Sail

Drake had chosen a less flamboyant method of departure than in November. Oared tugboats now led each vessel of our small expedition safely into open water, letting us loose in the lee of St Nicholas's Island, which lay just beyond the harbor mouth. Only when the galleys had cast off the towlines were the sails set, exploding against the darkening sky, taking us east around the island to avoid the rocky shoals on the western side. The *Pelican* was in the lead, followed by the *Elizabeth*, the *Marigold*, and the smaller vessels.

As we reached Penlee Point, or Fisherman's Nose, as it was more commonly known, the ancient chapel there invisible in the gloom, my thoughts turned again to Dr. Dee's warning. Despite my encouraging words to Lackland, I had difficulty feeling as optimistic as I had sounded. An ocean of sand. A sea of silver. Burning hills. I could not stop speculating about the dangers these places held and whether I would have the courage to do what I must when the moments of peril arrived that had been predicted. I knew I was no hero. It was equally unlikely I was any braver than the next man.

Then a strong wind bellied the canvas and sped the *Pelican* ever faster away from land, foam curling from our bow, and our wake glowing with mysterious illumination.

The Death of Tobias Lackland

December 14, 1577 – December 19, 1577
The Bay of Portugal

We had fair weather all the next day and for several days thereafter. According to the more experienced sailors, we rounded the Lizard, which was the southernmost projection of all England, just before nightfall, but we were too far from shore for land to be seen, not that I knew enough to distinguish one point from another. For hours at a time the *Pelican* rocked to a succession of swells that were sufficiently calm not to trouble even a stomach as unseaworthy as mine. Lancelot Garget, glad to command my services again, dismissed the boy who had been filling in and set me to my usual tasks. I went about them methodically, taking pains not to embellish the plain fare my superior demanded with seasoning since I did not want to endure his complaints.

On our fifth day at sea we cut across the Bay of Biscay, which was the body of water lying between France and Spain.

For this information I relied on what I was told by other sailors since I, of course, understood little of navigation, an obscure regimen few men ever mastered. In sight of the main, or so I came to learn, captains relied upon their personal experience with a coastline, on secret books known as rutters, and on the services of local pilots for finding their way. But on the ocean far from shore, location was determined by performing complex mathematical calculations on the stars in the night sky and on the elevation of the sun above the horizon while taking into account such vagaries as the speed and direction of the wind, the strength of currents, and the effects of fair and foul weather. This was a tedious and inexact process, more in the nature of an art than a philosophy. Even the best navigators, and Drake was counted among the best in England, could rarely pinpoint where they traveled with any degree of certainty and often ended up scores of miles from their intended destination.

Toward evening the fleet veered further westward into the Atlantic in order to avoid Spanish naval patrols. In fact we avoided the Spanish and Portuguese coasts altogether on the voyage and did not see land again until we were well past the Gulf of Cadiz, remaining a week in deep brine, dark blue water on all sides, the coast a dozen leagues distant.

From morning until night Blacollers drilled the crew relentlessly, insisting that each man become expert at several shipboard tasks, not just at his own job. The waist and foredeck were busy with sailors clambering up and down the shrouds, adjusting the sails, scrubbing the planking with stiff brushes, polishing brass wherever there was a speck of tarnish, or performing some other maritime duty, however unnecessary. The crew learned quickly to spend their free time below or in the rigging to escape being assigned extra work.

The half deck backward to the stern belonged to the officers and gentlemen, perhaps a dozen in all. Most either had a financial interest in the voyage or were related to an investor or person of influence. Their number included Drake's cousin, Little John, and one of Drake's younger brothers, Tom Drake, who was as fair complexioned as the other two and whose speech had the same Devonian burr. Doughty also had a brother on board, a man four or five years older than I, who resembled his elder closely except his beard had not grown in. John Doughty carried the same slim continental blade as his elder and each afternoon they engaged in an hour of rapier practice on the poop deck, stamping back and forth with their points before them, first one on the offensive and then the other.

Their rapiers caused some of the crew to laugh behind their hands. Most could not credit that such effete blades would be worth much in a fray, compared to a cutlass or hanger.

"Aye," said Gregory Raymente, an assistant blacksmith, a thin man with wrists and forearms disproportionate to the rest of his frame, "aye, 'tis the edge that counts at close range."

I was sitting in the gun deck with my back propped against a cannon, shelling peas for the evening meal, only half listening to the off-duty sailors lounging nearby. Besides Raymente, the group included John Cowrttes, Pascoe Goddy, and Great Nele, who was Danish.

"I t'ink you are right, *ja*," Nele agreed. "One, how you say it—one chop, the steel, it snap like log."

"Like a twig, damn your eyes!"

Goddy, however, had a different opinion. He was a grizzled man in his forties with long gray hair and eyes pinched together in a perpetual squint. He put down the knot he was weaving in the shape of a flower and thrust out his marlinspike in imitation of the Doughty brothers' swordplay. "Do not be so certain, Nele," he said. "Such blades in educated hands are impossible to catch. One was almost my death, have no question about it. 'Tis a miracle I am here with you to tell the story."

"A curse, more likely!"

"Kiss my tail, Gregory Raymente."

"Peace, gentlemen, peace," urged Cowrttes. "Go on, Pascoe. I for one would care to learn of this miracle."

"For the hundredth time," muttered Raymente before falling silent under the glares of the other men. Goddy stared pensively at his marlinspike before continuing. "Nine years have passed, but still the scene's before me, as near as yesterday, and I doubt I would forget it even if I were to live my life twice over. I was serving under Hawkins, God save the cocky bastard, aboard the *Minion*. Aye, you all know the situation. Our fleet was dogged by foul weather and we were short on meat and biscuit and drink. There was no safe haven within sailing distance on that dreary coast save for San Juan de Ulua, which is the port for the city of Vera Cruz. Mexico is a festering place, I tell you, and we all could smell the stink of fever in the air as we drew near the shore. San Juan made a poor harbor, too, being just a bit of protected water in the lee of fly bitten reef not a quarter mile long, on which the Spanish had placed a battery of canon. But seeing as we were out of beer and boiling rawhide, it was not as if we had any choice but to weigh anchor and brave the channel. You know how it is."

"God's truth," muttered Raymente, caught up in the narrative despite himself. The others echoed their agreement.

"As I were saying," Goddy went on, "there was a battery of cannon on the southeastern point of the island. We struck our flags and kept the top-gallants furled, so as not to show our true colors, hoping they would mistake us for their own fleet, which was expected momentarily. Damn me, gentlemen, if we did not cut so close that I saw the gunners in the fort touch match to tinder, and I was sure we were all dead men, each and every one of us—but the shot was only in courtesy, thank God, black powder and no iron. Hawkins returned the salute, waving from the half deck to the commander on shore as saucy as you please, and we were all dear friends, were we not, until our men landed and pulled out pistol and cutlass. The garrison were so surprised that most dropped their weapons and fled to the mainland in small boats without resisting. Some just threw off their boots and jumped into the water. It was damned entertaining, watching them founder like sick tadpoles in their haste to reach the shallows, and we all had a good laugh, but that was the last laugh we had on that godforsaken adventure. The very next day we counted a dozen sail on the horizon, both merchant vessels and men of war. It was the silver *flota* under the command of Don Martin Enriquez, Viceroy of New Spain."

Everyone had obviously heard Goddy's tale before, almost certainly several times, but even so they listened attentively. As I would discover during our endless Atlantic passage, sailors feared boredom even more than they feared thirst and hunger, and valued a good story as much as they prized strong drink, hot dice, and amiable women.

"Captain Drake has mentioned this man, I t'ink," said Great Nele, referring to Don Martin Enriquez. "There is no affection between them."

"I should say not," agreed Pascoe Goddy. "Nor will I

myself ever name the treacherous scum without a toast." He cleared his throat and spat upon the deck.

"Do you get the circumstances, gentlemen?" Goddy went on. "We controlled the harbor, true, but the Spanish ships had us penned in like pigs in a sty. They could not enter but we could not leave, which was a losing proposition for us since we were already stewing leather for victuals and drinking water, which is a rank beverage. Nor would the town supply us any commodity without authorization from Enriquez, fearing his displeasure. There was nothing to be done but treat with the bastard so Hawkins agreed to a truce and we exchanged hostages, supposedly gentlemen, but here the Spanish played us false, sending ordinary seamen instead of officers, believing us too dull to know the difference. Hawkins saw through the scheme, of course, but pretended otherwise in order to gain time while privately ordering all hands to be ready for action. You may be sure we had axes beside the head warps and handspikes in the stern capstans."

Pascoe Goddy drew a line in the air with the tip of his marlinspike. "Here lies the reef," he explained. "Our ships, the *Minion*, the *Jesus*, and the *Juliet*, which was under Drake's command, were lined along the southern edge, our bowsprits overhanging the shingle, head-ropes secured ashore and stern anchors out to keep us steady, so close together you could walk from one deck to the next. The dons moored their own grand vessels cheek to jowl along the other end of the reef but there was so little room that their smaller ships had to anchor in exposed water and take their chances in bad weather. Between us and the Spanish was an old hulk lacking both masts and rigging, which usually served as an auxiliary warehouse for the port. On the second night of the truce Enriquez smuggled two hundred men into the hold of the hulk. Come morning her crew singled up their head-ropes and began warping toward the *Minion*, hoping to take us unaware. But Hawkins caught on to the trick and fired the first shot, aiming at the Spanish vice admiral but instead blowing abroad the guts of man beside him."

Goddy shook his head soberly in recollection. "As soon as they knew the truth was out, the Spanish sounded a trumpet and attacked. My battle station was in the waist of the *Minion* and I reached my place just as the bow of the hulk touched ours. Jesus, I can still hear the fiends screaming 'Santiago' as they leapt across the gunwales onto the foredeck. I thought we were done for since there were so many of them. My own opponent was the Spanish lieutenant, I could tell his rank because of his fancy clothes and by the gold on his sword, and because his beard was shaved razor-sharp in the style the dons favor. Which is not to say the lieutenant was a girlish catamite—far from it, gentlemen, he pressed me hard. Which brings me to my point."

"At last," said Gregory Raymente. "I feared you had forgotten it."

"How could I?" asked Goddy. "Do I not carry a memento of the occasion with me to this day?" He shook back his long hair, revealing a circle of scar where his left ear had been. "I could not touch the cunning devil," Goddy admitted, letting the hair fall to again hide the deformity. "I hacked and I hewed but he always deflected the blow and danced away as lightly as those two gentlemen—" meaning the Doughty brothers, who were facing one another in profile, blades extended, left arms akimbo behind them. "The lieutenant slipped his sword past my guard, first pinking me in the shoulder and then taking off my ear, and I reckoned it would not be long before he grew tired of the game and skewered me for good. Not that I was any worse off than the rest of our crew. The Spanish had come aboard the *Minion* like ants and it was only a matter of time before we were all overrun. But Hawkins flourished his sword and jumped into the fray not ten paces from my side. 'God and Saint George,' he roared. 'Upon the traitorous villains and rescue the *Minion*. Trust in God and the day shall be ours.'"

"Aye, Hawkins was always an optimistic bastard," noted Cowrttes.

I had neglected the basket of peas while listening to Goddy. "What happened next?" I asked.

"There is not much left to tell, lad. Hawkins turned the tide, sure enough, for the crew of the *Jesus* rallied to his call. As they came across to the *Minion* to help us repel the Spanish, I could see in the lieutenant's eyes that he was considering how best to withdraw with his men without appearing to be retreating, and I knew the instant he decided to avoid any charge of cowardice by returning to his mates with the blood of an Englishman on his sword. That was when he beat my cutlass out of line and caught my hilt with his point and twisted the whole thing right out of my grasp. By God, I would have pissed myself except I did not have a moment to spare. I dove backward and came up hard against the mizzenmast and was pinned there by the lieutenant. He worked his blade bare inches from my eyes, toying with me as a cat plays with a mouse, while he decided whether I should accept his displeasure through the throat or through the heart. It was this arrogance that saved me. Thanks to Jesus, pride truly does go before a fall."

Goddy shook his head slowly, as if considering the melancholy state of the human condition. This pause went on so long that I began to fear he had lost the thread of the story.

"Did you regain your sword?" I prompted.

"No, Perry, it were far from my reach and useless, anyway, as had been justly demonstrated."

"What, then?"

Instead of answering with words, Pascoe Goddy reached behind himself. In the blink of an eye he held a cocked pistol pointed at me.

"Why, I shot the peacock dead and was done with him."

The other men found the conclusion to Goddy's account to be hilarious and their laughter drowned out the more usual noises of the gun deck, including the bleating of the livestock penned nearby. Great Nele pounded a fist the size of a ham against the planking. It was only with effort that Gregory Raymente managed to gasp:

"Aye, Pascoe, pride is indeed a deadly sin."

"Vanity, vanity, all is vanity," put in John Cowrttes, beside himself with mirth, although it was not until many months afterward, when I had lived in harm's way and seen many people die, that I came to understand my companions' brutal sense of humor. In the view of men hardened by experience, the Spanish lieutenant was a fool for failing to dispatch an enemy straight away when provided opportunity to do so, and richly deserved his end. It was proof of divine justice.

Just then Blacollers bent his head through the hatch and

called down: "Peregrine James, to the half deck with you. Our general requires your company."

By "our general" the boatswain meant Francis Drake. It was a term that would be used more frequently as the voyage went on, until the crew rarely referred to him in any other way. "Coming, sir," I replied, bidding Goddy and the rest farewell and scrambling up the ladder into the open air. The Doughty brothers had finished their practice and were drying themselves with monogrammed towels. Francis Fletcher, apparently deep in thought, strolled back and forth across the beam of the ship, his hands clasped behind his waist and his black coat flapping around his legs. Two other men, Nicholas Anthony and Gregory Cary, both junior representatives of a London merchant company, were lounging on chairs borrowed from the great cabin and talking together idly while drinking sack from pewter mugs. Diego stood behind Drake, who was speaking with a sailor I did not know.

"There you are, Mr. James!" Drake said. "I have a task for you."

"Tell me what it is, captain."

"You must go aboard the *Benedict* and take command of the galley for a while. The cook has fallen ill with the ague or some similar complaint—knowing Tom Hogges, I would guess the pox to be a better diagnosis. I am informed his assistant lacks appropriate skill, or so swears Bartelmyeus Gotsalk here."

"It is not just my opinion, general! Hogges's cuisine was poor but now that Artyur is tending the stewpot, we are all afraid for our lives."

"Well, we cannot have you living in fear, can we? Mr.

James will provide you proper service, is that not true, lad?

"I will do my best to make it so, sir."

"We had hoped you could loan us Lancelot Garget," said Bartelmyeus while eying me suspiciously. "Lancelot's table reminds me of my very own auntie's. I particularly relish his boiled beef and onions, which is precisely as the old woman prepared the dish."

"I hear you," agreed Drake, clapping the sailor on the shoulder, once more demonstrating the common touch for which he was famous, and which endeared him to the crew to such extent that most would—and did—follow him to the ends of the earth. "But the rub is," Drake continued, "Garget's the senior man and needed on the *Pelican*. Do you get my drift? I cannot spare him."

"Aye, captain, how could it be otherwise? Everyone knows the runt of the litter sucks hind tit."

Drake's laugh boomed across the deck. "On my oath, Bartelmyeus, Mr. James will not disappoint you. It is possible even your dear auntie might be favorably impressed."

"That is unlikely since she was a woman of high standards."

Another indication of Drake's common touch was that this grumbling amused rather than irritated him. He was still chuckling when he noticed Tobias Lackland arrive with a jug of wine to refill Nicholas Anthony's and Gregory Cary's tankards. This evidently inspired Drake.

"I have the perfect solution, my friend," he exclaimed. "Lackland, lad, put down that sack and take up your lute. Accompany Bartelmyeus and Perry James to the *Benedict*. Should the victuals not prove to the crew's taste, by God, soothe their hearts with melody so that they forget their disappointment."

Neither Bartelmyeus Gotsalk nor Tobias Lackland were pleased by this decision but they were sufficiently wise not to argue with Drake once he had settled on a course of action. For my part, I was content with the assignment since it gave me license to cook as I liked without interference from Lancelot Garget, although I knew I would have to take care not to offend the tastes of my new masters. It was also an opportunity to repair my reputation after my disastrous performance on the road to Mortlake, which had annoyed Thomas Doughty.

I made a brief visit below deck to retrieve my sea bag and then joined the others in the boat that was to ferry us to the *Benedict*.

Lackland was hunched over his lute, hugging the canvas-wrapped instrument close to his chest. "The *Pelican* may be a filthy scow," he complained as I settled onto the plank seat beside him, "but the *Benedict* is sure to be even more pestilential, see if I am mistaken. Thank you, thank you, Mr. James."

"How am I at fault? Drake volunteered you of his own accord. I had nothing to do with it."

"Yet had Bartelmyeus more trust in your abilities, my presence would not have been required."

This observation stung, particularly since I could not refute Lackland's logic, and we said nothing further to each other and sat together in silence during the passage to the *Benedict*. The trip took a full hour even though the distance was only five hundred yards since there was a strong chop and many white caps on the water. We were all tired of fighting our oars when we finally came up against the side of the smaller ship. The *Benedict* was the least of our expedition's five vessels, carrying only fifteen tons burden and a crew of twenty. Gun ports had been cut hastily in her hull and she had been outfitted with cannon but she was still little more than a fishing smack.

She stank like one, too. Lackland's nose wrinkled as he placed his lute carefully on the deck before following it over the railing.

"God save us," he muttered, "we are at the very spot where all maritime creatures come to die."

"And where all birds come to shit," I said, eying the layers of ancient droppings staining the rigging and woodwork.

The *Benedict* was commanded by Tom Moone, who had trailed me from Plymouth along with Thomas Doughty and Diego and participated in my rescue from the mercenaries hired to retrieve Stydye's notebook. According to what I had heard from other sailors, Moone had served under Drake on a half dozen voyages and was his trusted henchman. He was a hulking giant several inches past six feet in height, with placid brown eyes and a stillness of expression that encouraged you to believe him to be slow-witted. Having seen how fast he could cock a crossbow, however, and how quickly he had comprehended Dr. Dee's lecture on modern cryptography, much of which had been too complex for me to follow, I was not deceived by this outward show and knew Tom Moone to be a professional killer of high intelligence.

"Where is Garget?" he asked Bartelmyeus Gotsalk.

"Drake would not part with the man."

"No surprise there. Lancelot is too fine a cook to surrender."

"Drake swore the lad here would do as well. Let us take

heart, captain, at least he is not Artyur."

"Truer words were never spoken. I have been experiencing curious intestinal twinges since breakfast and I am not looking forward to supper. Artyur! Artyur! Where the devil are you?"

"Here, *meneer.*"

"This is Peregrine James, who is to be your superior until Hogges is back on his feet."

"Let him return to the *Pelican, kapitein.* I need no assistance."

"You have it wrong, Artyur—you are to assist Mr. James, do you understand me?"

Artyur was a Hollander of about my own age. His head was almost perfectly round and he cut his hair in a line above the ears and shaved his cheeks and neck clean, a style that emphasized the globular nature of his cranium. Artyur's features were in constant motion and he could not keep his hands still and he was always worrying the joints of his fingers.

"Aye, *kapitein,*" he muttered sadly, "I understand all too well, *ja.* You did not appreciate the morning porridge."

"Pepper does not marry easily with oatmeal."

"And what of the *taart?*"

"In the future remember that the flavor of sugar should overpower that of salt in sweet pastry. Now no more argument, Artyur. Provide Mr. James all courtesy."

My first challenge, I realized, would be to find Artyur harmless work since he was sure to do me injury through incompetence, if not through malice. It was plain that he resented my presence aboard the *Benedict* and coveted my station.

"Be so kind as to peel twenty onions," I told him, "followed by an equal number of carrots. Wash a couple bunches of celery. Cut each vegetable into pieces the size of your knuckle."

"*Ja ja.* Which knuckle? The first one or the second?"

"The knuckle does not matter. The point is for the pieces to be uniform, so that they cook evenly."

Going below, I found a haunch of beef that had been rinsed of salt and was ready for cooking. I butchered it into square chunks and began browning the meat in bacon grease as my mother had taught me, guiding my hand with her own as we turned the sizzling cubes with a wood spoon, murmuring, "*Mira, mi hijo.* Pay attention so that all sides receive equal color. *Es muy importante.*" Without Garget breathing over my shoulder, I was also able to skim off the impurities that would impart a bitter aftertaste if allowed to remain in the liquid. Frying together some butter and flour until golden, I employed this mixture to thicken the broth instead of using a paste of water and flour, which was quicker but brought nothing to a dish except a raw taste and a muddy color.

"I am done, *ja*," stated Artyur, giving the last carrot a couple chops before sweeping it from the cutting board into a bucket with the edge of his knife. "What now?"

"Fetch eggs, sugar, milk, raisins, and stale bread. A cup of sack, too. We will have pudding for dessert."

When Artyur left to get the required items, I carried the bucket of vegetables to the iron pot in which the stew was simmering. Some premonition, however, prevented me from tossing in the contents all at once and instead I added the ingredients handful by handful.

This allowed me to intercept the dead rat hidden among

the carrots, onions, and celery before it fell into the stew.

Artyur's strategy was obvious. He planned to publicly discredit me before Tom Moone and the rest of the men.

More saddened than dismayed by this evidence of perfidy, I tossed the rodent overboard without advertising that I had discovered it. I figured my silence would lead Artyur to suppose his intrigue remained undetected, and it did. He shot me a couple sideways glances and then began whistling happily while stirring the pot, no doubt anticipating my upcoming humiliation and his consequent elevation to my position once I was disgraced. I did not doubt he was composing a rousing speech to recite when the rat was sighted in the stew.

"How is the flavor?" I asked as I finished kneading the old bread with the sugar, eggs, and milk and began to press the dough into a greased tin. "Is more pepper necessary?"

"*Nee, nee,*" Artyur answered. "I believe there is ample."

"Taste it to be sure."

"I have done so, *ja.* All is good."

"Lift your spoon, Artyur."

"*Ja, meneer?*"

"Lift your spoon from the stew, place it to your lips, and tell me whether additional seasoning would be appropriate."

Artyur regarded the spoon as if he had never encountered such a utensil before and had no inkling why the thing was in his hand. Finally he brought it to his mouth, hesitated briefly, and flicked out the tip of his tongue. "Very good," he said, obviously relieved that his unwelcome addition to the recipe had not soured the dish.

"Excellent. Now, Artyur, please take a generous helping,

chew it thoroughly, and inform me if the meat is tender."

Unlike on the *Pelican*, where the men were separated into different messes, the sailors and officers of the *Benedict* all dined together. At the clang of the ship's bell, they lined up with their bowls before the fire box and Artyur began dispensing portions of stew while I handed out slabs of bread pudding. "Here you are, captain," I told Tom Moone. "Speak up if you wish more. There is a little extra."

"I will let you know when and if that is necessary."

Behind him Bartelmyeus was receiving his meal from Artyur. "Do you swear you had nothing to do with the preparation?" he asked.

Artyur, of course, was as anxious to disavow any connection to the stew as Bartelmyeus was to determine its origins. "*Nee, nee,*" he exclaimed, "except I did peel and chop certain vegetables that went into the pot, *ja*. That was my entire contribution."

Bartelmyeus sniffed the stew and then shrugged fatalistically. "If it is my time to join Jesus in heaven, so be it. Should I not recover, gentlemen, inform your wives I loved them all."

Next in line was Tobias Lackland. "Careful, careful," he instructed Artyur. "Do not slop the stuff everywhere."

"Speak to my arse, fancy boy."

"Why, do you possess ears there?"

Evidently still holding me responsible for his presence aboard the *Benedict*, Lackland went straight by without a word after accepting a slice of pudding. I did not know whether to be amused or offended by the slight but in any case other issues concerned me more. Artyur had begun looking puzzled as he continued to dole out the stew without discovering the dead rodent he thought to be hidden in it. His confusion gave way to anxiety when all the men had been served and only two portions remained in the pot, which he assumed to mean that one of us would be dining on rat that evening instead of on beef. I fell to eating without delay while he hesitated before touching his meal.

"Come on, Artyur," I encouraged him. "A hearty supper is God's reward for hard work and a clean conscience."

"*Nee, nee,* I not hungry," he replied, prodding the meat in his bowl in hope of identifying what lay beneath the gravy.

"I insist, Artyur. Or is there some fault with the stew?"

"*Nee!* How could there be—"

"Are you meaning to eat that?"

Bartelmyeus Gotsalk had rejoined us at the fire box and was referring to the full bowl in Artyur's hand.

"*Nee, meneer,* I—"

"Allow me to claim ownership." Bartelmyeus instantly appropriated Artyur's ration and began spooning the stew into his own mouth. "Forgive my doubts, Mr. James," he went on, "but this is damned agreeable. 'Tis almost on level with Lancelot's efforts, and he is a master with few equals."

"Mr. Garget has taught me much," I admitted.

"I am sure he is an excellent instructor. Is there pudding?"

"One piece is left and it is yours."

As Bartelmyeus returned to his seat against the starboard railing to finish his meal, I doused the fire and Artyur began scrubbing out the stewpot with sand. By the expressions that followed one another in rapid succession across his features while he worked—first a frown, then a grimace, next a perplexed scowl—it was easy to guess that Artyur was wondering furiously how his scheme had gone awry and where the rat had disappeared to. He was so deep in thought that he did not notice my approach, and he started in surprise when I spoke softly in his ear.

"Do not be alarmed, Artyur. I will say nothing this one time."

"I not know what you mean."

"Liar. I know what you planned. You took your best shot at my credit and you missed. I will not permit another shot, I tell you. Listen to me, Artyur, I would rather have you as a friend than as an enemy but I will accept you as either. Which is it to be?"

He would not look at me, nor answer my question directly. "It not fair," he muttered. "I should be in command of the station, not you. Was I not Hogges's man? Have I not slaved for him like a dog?"

"I will be blunt," I replied. "You are not qualified."

"*Nee?*"

"No. I have seen myself that your knife work is good. But you lack the basic education required for the job."

Artyur did not argue with my analysis. "Hogges always turns his back to me when adding ingredients," he explained. "He is fearful I aspire to his position and guards his secrets jealously."

"I have met people like that," I answered, remembering certain cooks hired by my father to help out at the Jack and Rasher during fairs and festivals and other occasions of heavy business. I was only a boy but even so these men would send me on errands at crucial moments in the cooking process in order to keep their recipes secret. I never cared for the practice and understood something of Artyur's resentment. "Look," I said, "I will make a deal with you. Promise to be my friend and to do as I say and I swear I will be your teacher and share with you what I know."

Again Artyur's features reflected a succession of thoughts. Then his round face settled into a doubtful expression. "What was the slurry you added to the stew?" he asked. "I have not seen it employed before."

"It is known as a *roux* and is composed of approximately equal proportions of flour and butter. *Rouxs* are used to thicken a variety of preparations, including soups, sauces, and gravies. Add hot *roux* to cold liquid, and cold *roux* to hot liquid, in order to avoid lumping. The darker the *roux*, the more flavorful it is, but it also loses strength and must be added in greater quantity. The rule of thumb, however, is that one part of *roux* can bind six times its weight in liquid. Do you follow me?"

"Six times its weight."

"Splendid. I can see you are a quick study."

"I have never been told that before," Artyur replied, mulling over the idea that he might possess hidden potential. "Who knows?" he said at last. "It could be true."

"Then we have an agreement?" I asked. "No further mischief?"

"*Ja*, Mr. James, you have my word I will be your friend."

"So the matter is settled. Now let us go and tap another barrel of beer, as this one is empty. In the kitchen many hands make light work."

"That I have heard before, *meneer*, chiefly from Tom Hogges. The thing is, he cannot calculate higher than two and ends the count before including his own hands in the total."

By this time we were traversing the Bay of Portugal, which was the span of water between the city of Oporto and a headland known as Cintra. The ocean here had never been plumbed, becoming fathomless within forty miles of shore, and I did not enjoy thinking of the bottomless abyss beneath the *Benedict*'s keel. Because we were now considerably south of England, the weather was warmer, and it was sufficiently comfortable for the crew to linger on deck, finishing their beer together as night fell, talking or listening to the wind tease the rigging and to the rhythmic flapping of the main course. Some drank smoke from pipes as Constable Felix had done, a habit whose appeal I did not understand, since the weed they burned had a foul smell. Bartelmyeus Gotsalk stretched out his legs full length and scratched his chest. Tom Moone, standing on the half deck, studied the horizon, where the topsails of the *Pelican* and the *Elizabeth* were outlined against the sunset. He spoke a few words to the helmsman and then joined the sailors in the waist. His gaze settled on Tobias Lackland.

"Drake said you are a musician." Moone said.

"I am, sir."

"That is glad news. I cannot think of a better end to a day than a good feed followed by comforting music. Does anyone disagree?"

"Not I, captain," called out one sailor, a sentiment that was echoed by the others, and soon they were all demanding Lackland get his lute and play a tune or two. I could tell this did not please him—most likely he thought it beneath the dignity of a lutenist of destiny to be commanded to perform before such an audience—but he stifled whatever he really wanted to say and went below to retrieve the instrument. After unwrapping its protective canvas swaddling, he spent the next ten minutes tuning the strings, a complex process since there were a dozen of them and each must be aligned melodically with its neighbors. The delay caused several sailors to urge him to greater speed but Lackland continued plucking notes at the same deliberate pace until he was satisfied all was as it should be. Then he spread his fingers across the frets and drew a chord from the instrument with a quill plectrum but something did not sound right to him and instead of proceeding with a melody, he went back to adjusting the pegs, twisting each by fractions of a rotation in his quest for the correct pitch.

"For the love of Jesus, lad," said one man, "will you get on with it?"

Although the words were spoken with good humor, Lackland took offense. "Patience," he replied stiffly. "The salt atmosphere adversely affects the gut of the strings, requiring meticulous correction."

He plucked a few more notes before conceding satisfaction with the tuning by settling the lute in his arms and looking up from the instrument. "I will play an air of my own creation," Lackland informed the group. "I call it *Seep My Misery*."

The performance did not go well.

Seep My Misery was a plaintive tune with melancholy lyrics, quite sad and beautiful in its way. The audience, however, was not interested in expressions of anguish, no matter how prettily sung. They had slight tolerance for such lamentations as, "No caverns are deep enough to hide those that in misery their lost treasures grieve," and by the time Lackland approached the final verse, and its observation that, "Gladsome, gladsome are they who in the abyss feel not the earth's cruel sting," the sailors were making their displeasure loudly known.

"God save us," groaned one man. "I do feel an inclination to end my life this very instant."

"Lend me your knife so I may slit my own wrists," said another.

"Stay your hand, Roger," urged his friend. "Suicide is a mortal sin. Although given the circumstances I suspect even Jesus himself would condone the practice."

"That is enough, Luke Adden," said Tom Moone, coming over to Tobias Lackland and pressing his shoulder sympathetically. "Speaking for myself, I enjoyed the tune, lad," the giant went on, "but it was uncommonly pessimistic, no argument there. Sing us another, only something easier in spirit."

"Aye, boy," said Roger. "How about *Sailor's Holiday*?"

"Or *Love's Fancy*," volunteered another man.

"I am sorry," said Lackland stiffly, "but I am unfamiliar with either of those—" he paused before completing the sentence— "compositions."

"Surely you know *The Maiden's Dream*? The one that begins: 'Slumbering she lay all night upon her bed, no creature with her but her maidenhead.' It is played in the manner of *I Often for my Jenny Strove* and is my particular favorite."

"No."

"Not *Woman Belly Full of Hair*?"

"Definitely not."

"Nor *Nine Times a Night*?"

"I do not know it."

"Why, you do not know much, do you, lad?"

Lackland was already seething from being, as he saw it, unfairly relegated from the flagship of the fleet to its smallest member. The poor reception received by *Seep My Misery* had rankled him further but it was this last comment that proved too much for his composure.

"Perhaps I do not know much compared with you, sir," Lackland replied. "Of course, it is also true I have not spent half as much time frequenting whore houses and taverns."

"When you grow fuzz, you will, lad," answered the sailor, which amused everyone except Lackland. Scowling, he turned his back on them and began binding his lute in its canvas wrap. Then he stalked off with the instrument, presumably to sulk alone, for he did not return the remainder of the evening.

Having finished cleaning the galley, Artyur and I sat with the other men and learned the words to many of the songs they had requested of Lackland. I was still humming the refrain to the last we sang—*The Unlaid Maid*—as I went below for the night to the space I had been assigned between the starboard cannon. Lackland's straw pallet was next to mine but although his bag was there, he was not. Nor had he come to bed when I woke with a natural urge just past midnight. I used the bucket and lay down again but now I could not sleep. With his haughty airs and high opinion of himself, Lackland was often annoying, yet he was my friend, and I began to be troubled by his absence. At last I put on my jacket and went on deck to look for him.

The wind had freshened and there was a gibbous moon, which shed sufficient light for the ocean to be distinguished from the sky and outlined a dark cloud bank approaching from the west.

Although the *Benedict* was less than fifty feet in length, I could not see from one end to the other since the deck was cluttered with stacks of supplies. Starting my search at the stern, I worked my way forward and finally found Lackland when I reached the stem of the ship.

He was sitting astride the bowsprit, the mast projecting out from the prow. Some vessels had netting strung beneath their bowsprits to protect against accidents. The *Benedict* did not.

There was nothing beneath the soles of his feet but dark water. Even so, instead of holding fast to the oak with both hands, he was holding his lute and picking out *Seep My Misery*.

Noticing me, he said sadly, "Do you know, Mr. James, I doubt I shall ever play it again."

"You may never play anything again unless you take care," I told him but he ignored my warning and continued in the same vein as before:

"I shall erase the lyrics and scourge the melody from my thoughts," he vowed. "The world is too cruel for such beauty."

"Let us discuss the matter on deck," I urged. "You have chosen a dangerous perch and I do not enjoy seeing you balancing so unsteadily."

"I do not mind."

"But I do, Tobias. Come, give me your hand."

"No."

"Would you deprive the world of a lutenist of destiny? The flower of an age?"

"It would be the world's loss."

"And mine. I would miss you."

"That I do not believe, Mr. James. We are not friends. Were you not laughing at my expense with the others?"

"It was the situation that was entertaining," I protested. "I do not understand what you were thinking, Tobias, but you did not match well your performance to the audience. It is as if I were to serve this crew refined cuisine when they are content with hash. Do you get my point?"

"I do not."

"I will explain once you join me. The water is becoming choppy and you are not safe where you are."

"True artists care little for personal safety."

"Pass me the lute and I will hold it for you and free your hands."

"No, I prefer to remain here."

"Then you may suffer misfortune."

"Misfortune is my fated lot in life—" Lackland agreed, shrugging eloquently. Sadly, circumstances confirmed his somber philosophy almost at once. A wave slapped against the *Benedict* with just enough strength to cause him to begin slipping from the bowsprit. He flailed with the lute in order to regain his balance but the effort only caused him to tilt further to the side. I lunged forward and stretched out my hand but I could not touch him. For a second we were on level and I saw the panic in his eyes but then Lackland was falling past me into the Bay of Portugal. Still holding the lute, he hit the water in a burst of foam and was battered aside by the hull of the ship.

His body was not recovered.

Kidnapped on Mogador

December 20, 1577 – December 28, 1577
The coast of Barbary

Tom Moone refused to bring the *Benedict* about or to dispatch longboats in search of Lackland. "The poor bugger is down below even as we speak," he observed, rubbing his eyes clear of sleep and peering out vaguely into the dark ocean beyond the taffrail, the railing at the stern of the ship, where I had ended up while trying to keep Lackland in sight as his limp body, still accompanied by the lute, disappeared in the murk. The moon had passed beneath the horizon and now it was hard to distinguish water from sky because both were spangled by stars. My calls for help had roused the ship and we were surrounded by the entire crew. Most agreed with the captain.

"Aye, sir," said Luke Adden. "How could it be otherwise?"

"Let me take out a boat if you will not," I insisted. "We must attempt to find Lackland."

"No, our duty lies elsewhere, lad," Moone said and clasped my shoulder, squeezing it with fingers as hard as iron pegs. "Even if he floats, he would be impossible to find. There is naught but countless miles of salt out there and no way to locate a speck in the midst of it."

The others nodded solemnly. "I only pray the boy cannot swim," said Bartelmyeus Gotsalk.

"Aye, Barty," said Adden. "What is the point in knowing how?—that has always been my question. To prolong your despair before you ultimately go under? I would not wish such torture upon an enemy, not even a Spaniard. No, mates, I have never studied the trick myself and, by God, I never will. I prefer to sink like a stone."

Several of the men shook their heads in confirmation of their personal commitment to avoid knowledge of the dread expertise.

"We must do something!" I protested. "We cannot go on our way."

Tom Moone again squeezed my shoulder. "Nothing could be done even if I myself were the one overboard. I cannot risk losing men in a vain and dangerous undertaking. Nor can I risk lagging behind and breaking contact with the other ships."

"It is a human life we are discussing," I argued.

"Yes, that is always the fix. However, it is the commander's lot to do what is best for the company. In this situation that means to continue onward without pause." Moone released me and raised his voice in order to be heard. "Gentlemen," he said, "let us come together and pray for the comrade who is now lost to us. May God have mercy on his soul."

"What was the boy's name?" asked the man beside me— Will Pitcher, a veteran sailor, who covered his right eye with a black patch since there was no orb in the socket.

"Lackland," I answered. "Tobias Lackland."

"Aye, that was it. He had a sweet voice, did he not? Alas, it was also abundantly plain the lad lacked compositional ability."

"Nor was his temperament endearing," contributed another sailor. "Even so, I now wish I had lied to him and said I enjoyed his song."

He pulled his cap from his head and crushed it between his hands as he dropped to his knees on the deck.

Soon we were all on the same level, our heads bowed together in memory. The guilt that wracked me was as painful as the heartbreak I felt. The way I saw it, if not for my failings, Lackland would never have come aboard the *Benedict* into harm's way. It was also my fault we had not parted as friends. He had sunk into the brine thinking I disliked him and now apology was impossible forever. Worse, although I had told the rest that Lackland had fallen by accident, I wondered if this was true or if he had deliberately committed the unpardonable sin of suicide. Given his dramatic character, it was easy to imagine Lackland releasing his grip in a fit of pique and wounded pride.

These questions and similar ones soured my disposition during my tenure aboard the *Benedict* and I went about my tasks without a spare word for anyone. Eventually, as is natural when time passes after a tragedy, my mood lightened and I thought of Tobias Lackland less often, but I never completely forgot him. Sometimes it seemed that I would only have to lift my eyes to find him sitting in the fighting top, the wind tousling his hair as he bent over his lute. When I looked, however, no one would be there and I had to resign myself to his loss.

My stay aboard the *Benedict* was cut short by Tom Hogges's recovery to health. I returned to the *Pelican* and resumed my duties under the eye of Lancelot Garget, who resented having been deprived of my assistance and soothed himself by finding fault with my work.

During my absence Thomas Doughty had instituted a

routine of military practice and was leading the crew in drills on a daily basis. The next morning after breakfast I was issued a cutlass by the master gunner and armorer, a man named Oliver, who directed me to join twenty other similarly armed sailors in the waist. My companions carried their weapons with an ease that came from long acquaintance but my own cutlass felt awkward in my grasp since I had never held one before.

The cutlass was a short sword, useful for close quarters fighting but heavy enough to let a man hack himself free if trapped in the debris of naval warfare, such as snarl of cable or a tangle of fallen rigging. The ones we were given all had the same type of handle, a functional steel basket protecting the offensive hand and wrist. Each basket was wrought in the shape of a globe and impressed with the mark of the North Star, identical to the design on the pennants flying above the *Pelican*.

Thomas Doughty instructed us to assemble into a single line and for the next hour we rehearsed procedures for repelling boarders, stamping our feet in unison as we charged the gunwale, yelling to intimidate and confuse our enemies as we pressed forward, and slashing the air with our cutlasses in order to create a wall of steel that would prove lethal to anyone attempting to come aboard.

"Slash—then cut down to the right," said Doughty as he strolled along the line of sailors and studied their efforts. "The first blow is for your enemy, the next is for the enemy of the man beside you. But you must act together for the trick to be effective."

He paused beside a seaman in the center of the line. "No, you have it wrong," Doughty said. "Surely you can distinguish left from right?"

"Aye, sir. Except sometimes I get the directions confused."

"In the future keep an eye on your friends and copy what they do."

Then Doughty addressed me. "Put your weight behind the blow," he said. "A cutlass is not a kitchen knife, Mr. James. You are not slicing a side of roast beef—strike harder."

On the following day, however, instead of sword drill we had artillery practice.

The cannon aboard the *Pelican* were bronze demi-culverins with eight-foot barrels and had a range of half a mile. Each was manned by a team of four sailors led by a petty officer, who was also responsible for aiming and firing the piece. It was only at this point that I came to realize a fact that would have been clear immediately to anyone with a modicum of maritime knowledge. Including officers and gentlemen, the *Pelican*'s crew numbered almost seventy men. This was four times the personnel necessary to manage a true merchant vessel of similar tonnage.

Warships and privateers, on the other hand, needed the extra men to operate their cannon, which each required a large gang of handlers.

I was assigned to a starboard gun and, as the newest member of the team, given the task no one else desired and sent down to the ballast to fetch the ammunition to be used in the exercise, a half dozen nine-pound iron balls. Another man visited the magazine and retrieved an equal number of linen bags containing charges of black powder, as well as smaller explosive cartridges that would be used to prime the cannon. These were placed temporarily in a wooden chest and taken out only when needed, to avert premature contact with fire.

"What should I do next?" I asked our chief, a sailor named Willan Smythe, after I regained my breath. It had required three trips to bring the heavy shot from the bottom of the ship up to the gun deck.

"Do you see the bucket, lad?" Smythe asked. "Your duty is to keep it filled, no more, no less. Can you handle that?"

"Yes, I believe so."

"Good. And, Perry, stay out of Fat Jane's way—" he meant the demi-culverin, which the crew had baptized with a feminine name—"she is a right mean bitch and has a nasty kick."

The other men were familiar with the routine. One flung open the gun port, allowing daylight to burst into the gloomy deck. A second sailor removed the *tompion*—a wooden cork or plug—from the muzzle while a third loosened the ropes securing the gun in place, taking care to arrange them so that they would not be snagged when the cannon recoiled. Through the port I could see a longboat towing a barrel painted with a white circle with a red bullet in the center. The target was set adrift a hundred yards away and was only visible when a swell lifted it into sight above the other waves.

"Arm your weapons, gentlemen," called Oliver, the master gunner, who was moving from cannon to cannon to ensure that the crews were prepared and that their efforts met his standards.

At each gun a man slid a bag of powder down its throat and then a wad of hay. Another took a ball and shoved it in and the whole was pushed home with a wood stick called a *rammer*.

At the other end of the cannon, the *breech*, Willan Smythe inserted a cartridge into the touch hole. When he was done, we pulled Fat Jane hard up against the side of the ship using the tackle attached to the carriage. "Point her down a hair," Smythe said, peering through the gun port at the distant target. Then he lit a slow match.

"Gunners, take your mark," Oliver instructed. "Starboard cannon, are you ready?"

"Aye, sir."

"Fire at will."

I had, of course, seen and heard artillery go off before, during celebrations and when important ships were welcomed into Plymouth harbor by the battery situated above the city on the Hoe. This did not, however, prepare me for the experience of being a yard away from a big gun when it was fired in an enclosed space.

The *Pelican* was hove to, her sails furled, and she was stationary in relationship to the barrel. Even so, determining the precise instant to fire was not a simple calculation since a gunner must take into account such variables as distance, the angle of the muzzle, the rocking of the vessel, the amount of powder in the charge, and the weight of the shot—even the speed and direction of the wind often played a part in his decision. Smythe frowned and muttered to himself before making up his mind and sticking the burning end of the slow match into the touch hole of the cannon. Then he immediately moved aside.

The match ignited the powder cartridge, which in turn set off the larger charge within the barrel.

There was a boom louder than thunder. The cannon exploded backward until it was caught by a rope run through bolts in the bulwark and wound around the knob at the breech end of the gun—the *cascabel*.

More detonations went off as cannon discharged on either side. A cloud of smoke poured in through the gun port but was blown away quickly enough for me to see our barrage strike, tearing the water into froth around the floating barrel but never hitting it.

Most shots did not come within a dozen yards of the target.

The sailor beside me dunked his sponge—a staff with fleece wound around one end—in the bucket that Smythe had indicated earlier. Then he rammed the dripping head down the smoking bore to extinguish any embers before a fresh charge was introduced into the gun. His mate scraped clean the touch hole of powder residue with a pointed iron rod.

Willan Smythe was talking to me but I could not hear what he was saying because the cannon blasts still echoed in my ears. To make his meaning clear, he shoved me toward the bucket, which was now empty.

I picked it up and sprinted to a nearby barrel filled with saltwater. The artillery crew had already prepared Fat Jane for another shot by the time I returned with the full bucket.

Again we ran out the gun and adjusted it according to Smythe's directions, which were communicated mostly through gesture since we were all deafened. Again he put the sputtering fuse to the touch hole. Again the cannon leapt back with a roar and a belch of black smoke. Now, however, I had regained my wits and did not need prodding to do what I must, I had the bucket in hand almost before the sailor with the sponge finished soaking the fleece. This procedure was repeated four times, until Fat Jane's barrel was hot enough to burn flesh and we had used up the ammunition and powder allotted for the exercise. The gun deck was filled with reeking smoke and cinders and our eyes were bloodshot and our cheeks stained with tears. When I cleared my throat, I brought up a wad of black stuff.

Perhaps a half hour had passed but it seemed that I had spent eternity in bedlam.

I stuck my head out the gun port to draw a breath of fresh air and saw the target floating unscathed. The concerted fire of the seven starboard demi-culverins had not harmed it. Nor did the port battery so much as nick the barrel when Drake brought the *Pelican* around and allowed them their chance to shoot.

These results seemed poor to me and I expected the master gunner to criticize us when he came by while we were mopping down Fat Jane. Oliver, however, was congratulatory. "Your crew does you credit, Mr. Smythe," he said. "Gentlemen, I have ordered a double serving of beer for everyone this evening. What do you say?"

"Why not a triple portion?" asked Corder. "This is thirsty work."

"Aye, Mr. Oliver," said another sailor. "Fat Jane drains you dry, she does. A gallon a man would not be unreasonable."

"Get on with all of you," Oliver laughed.

"Sir?" I said. "My thanks for your kindness, but was not the point of the exercise to strike the target?"

"Not entirely, lad. 'Tis true accuracy is important in certain situations, such as when shelling coastal fortifications or when engaging in a long-range duel, where neither vessel can close with the other. But in most cases you will discover yourself neck and neck with your adversary, and here your rate of fire is more critical than marksmanship."

"Why is that, sir?"

"If you load and discharge your cannon faster than your enemy, you do more damage. Eventually you win. It is simple."

Oliver went off to encourage other crews and I helped Peter Corder lug the powder box to the orlop for storage. Like many aboard, Corder was a veteran of the raid on Nombre De Dios six years previously. He was a wiry man with bow legs who refused to wear shoes even in the coldest weather. "Did you hear, Perry?" he asked as I passed the box down to him. "We are bypassing the Gulf of Cadiz."

"I cannot say I know the place."

"That is because you are damned ignorant of geography."

"I will not argue. Where is this gulf and why is it significant?"

"The Gulf of Cadiz is located between the arse end of Europe and the head of Africa. What is significant is that it is intersected by a passage of water known as the Strait of Gibraltar."

"Does this strait not lead into the Mediterranean Sea?"

"Correct. And what lies on the shores of the Mediterranean?"

"Here my knowledge ends."

"The city of Alexandria lies on the shores of the Mediterranean."

Finally I understood what Peter Corder was telling me. It was now impossible to pretend our destination and charter were as advertised on the Plymouth docks. Overshooting the Gulf of Cadiz proved Drake had no intention of sailing to

Egypt and dealing in raisins and currants.

"So where are we bound?" I asked Corder.

He shrugged. "We are maintaining a southeasterly course and that could lead anywhere. If we keep south, we reach Guinea, which lies beneath the land of Barbary and is home to men with black skin. Or we could veer west at Cape Verde, which is the westernmost extension of the African continent. That would take us to Brazil or to the West Indies, or to the Spanish Main, depending on whether we sail north or south when we make the coast."

As might be expected, the question of our real destination was the main topic of conversation among the men on the gun duck. One enterprising sailor established odds and took bets from the others. Even money on the Main, which was rich in towns to ransom and shipping to harass. Equal odds also on the islands of the Caribbean, where wealthy plantation owners could be intimidated. Tobias Lackland's suggestion, however, of an overland expedition across the Isthmus of Panama to the Pacific, received little credit and consequently paid better odds of three to one. To the amusement of the rest, Pascoe Goddy bet three pennies at five to two that we were bound around the cape of Africa on the Portuguese route to India. Not a single person laid a bet that we were heading for the Straits of Magellan, the deadly channel between the Atlantic and the Southern Ocean.

The next morning, December 22nd, was a Sunday. After breakfast a polished table was brought from the grand cabin and set upon the half deck. Behind this went an embroidered cushion and a small box, which were placed one upon the other to make a low dais for Francis Fletcher to kneel upon while he conducted Sabbath prayers. The parson struck the table twice with his palm and everyone removed their hats.

The officers and gentlemen sat around Fletcher on the half deck while ordinary sailors and petty officers sat below in the waist. Service consisted of prayers, hymns, meditation, and readings from the Bible and from Foxe's *Actes and Monuments*, also called the *Book of Martyrs*, a thick leather tome with many florid engravings of the Papist ritual known as the *auto de fé*, in which good Christians were forced to publicly repent their faith before being burned alive. The reading was usually followed by a homily from the parson but this morning Drake took Fletcher's place to deliver the sermon.

To respect the holy day our general wore a velvet vest embroidered with gold braid and a half cloak with purple lining, which streamed behind him as the wind teased it. "Gentlemen," he said, "it has come to my attention that many of you are confused. This does not surprise me, as sailors are confused whenever they are sober. Am I right or wrong?"

The laughter that greeted this statement demonstrated the crew's agreement. Drake studied the crowd until the amusement died away.

"I have also heard that some scurvy dogs among you are asking just where, by God, their captain is steering. Can this be true?"

Although the words were harsh, Drake's manner of delivery took the edge off them and encouraged the men to reply.

"Aye, general," answered several at once.

"No, general," answered others.

Drake chuckled. "Do not fear speaking honestly, gentlemen. How could I blame you? In your place, and everyone knows I have sailed a year or two before the mast—in your place, I would have questions of my own. I doubt there is a man aboard who does not understand by now that our course is different from what was given out publicly." Drake came around the table and walked to the edge of the half deck to better address the crew below. "Do you trust me, gentlemen, when I say you are all my friends and it is my privilege to be your master and general?"

"Aye, sir." The response rose unanimously from many throats.

"Then trust me when I tell you I cannot say anything further. I have given my word to her grace Elizabeth herself that our destination shall remain confidential, else our enemies discover our plans and plot against us. We all know how the dons question honest English sailors with pincers and hot iron. What if one of us should fall to the Spanish? Is not John Oxenham, who is a dear comrade to many here, is not Oxenham even now suffering torment at their hands?"

I remembered what Tobias Lackland had told me about Oxenham. He was Drake's companion in Panama and witnessed our general's vow to sail the Southern Ocean in an English vessel.

Oxenham was now a prisoner of the Inquisition.

Drake allowed us a moment to consider Oxenham's gloomy prospects and then set out to rally our spirits. "I may tell you one thing more, gentlemen," he continued, slamming a fist into the palm of the other hand. "I swear to you we will all return to Plymouth better off than we were before. The least boy among us will profit, and greatly, you have my oath.

Why, it is within the realm of possibility that even young Perry James, for one, could return home a rich man and open a cook shop of his own with his share of the proceeds."

This raised another round of laughter and I heard Lancelot Garget snort, "God forbid."

Although I did not enjoy being singled out as an example of the least boy aboard the *Pelican*, I kept my thoughts to myself. Drake, as always, knew precisely how to talk to his men and how to gain their loyalty, convincing them with a combination of threats, flattery, and humor, and with appeals to their naked self interest. By the time he finished speaking, although we were no wiser than before, we were all content to go ahead blindly and to follow his lead toward an unknown destination without asking our bearing.

Three days later, on Wednesday, which was Christmas day, the lookout sighted the coast of Barbary.

Since morning a sailor had been taking soundings from the bow in order to determine the depth of the ocean, which was a measurement used by navigators to help identify their location and to provide warning of shallow water, an unpredictable danger when approaching an unfamiliar shore. Every so often he threw overboard a line with a lead weight and allowed it to pay out. Marks on the line ticked off the length of a fathom, which is the distance between a man's hands when they are stretched to either side, about two yards. At first the line could not find the bottom but just before noon the sailor began calling, "Fifty fathoms. Fine sand and pebbles."

The lead plumb was coated with tar and brought back a bit of the ocean floor whenever the line was hauled to the surface. This was another item of information employed by navigators to fix their position.

"Forty fathoms. Coarse gravel. Shoaling."

In celebration of Christmas, Lancelot Garget and I had been ordered to serve the men fresh meat instead of salted. We slaughtered half our flock of chickens, which somewhat reduced the din below deck, and I was delegated the task of cleaning the birds. I was sitting by the port rail, plucking the carcasses and discarding the feathers over the gunwale, when a voice floated from the crow's nest at the peak of the foremast.

"Land, ho! Land ho!"

"Thirty fathoms. Coarse gravel and mud."

I put down the chicken and shaded my eyes with my hand but some time passed before we were close enough for me to make out the shore.

The sailor with the plumb line began casting it more frequently. "Fifteen fathoms. Mud bottom."

Drake was standing on the half deck, studying the horizon and occasionally giving an order to Blacollers, who echoed the command to the sailors in a booming voice. As the water continued to shoal, the top-sails were furled to reduce the *Pelican's* speed and we proceeded forward cautiously until we were a couple miles from the beach. Then Drake ordered gangs to the braces, the lines attached to the yardarms. Fighting the wind, the sailors swiveled the sails so that the canvas caught the breeze from a new angle, sending us southward parallel to land.

This was an expanse of sand rimmed by white cliffs two hundred feet high. The rocks shimmered with heat even though it was winter.

"Fifteen fathoms and holding. Gravel and mud."

Drake conferred with Thomas Cuttill, who was the sailing master, and with some other sailors, men with African experience, evidently attempting to pinpoint our position on the coast. Then he retrieved a book from his private cabin, his personal rutter, which was a sort of diary that all navigators maintained, where they wrote down the details of their voyages, including sailing directions, soundings, bottom composition, current speed, and other nautical particulars. A rutter was a pilot's most valuable possession and all guarded theirs vigilantly. The only person allowed to touch Drake's book was his cousin, Little John, who possessed remarkable artistic talent. As our journey progressed, he would become a regular sight on the poop deck, hunched over the rutter and drawing pictures of headlands and promontories as they appeared from sea with meticulous accuracy using both ink and color pigments.

Drake studied the rutter and then closed the book with an air of decision and said a few words to Cuttill. Soon everyone had the news:

"Cantin! We have reached Cape Cantin."

Apparently this was important. Sighting the landmark signified that we had indeed crossed to Africa and were sailing along known territory. As Lancelot Garget dropped the chickens I had cleaned into a kettle of boiling water, he gave the coast a long stare and muttered:

"This is a cursed shore, pretty boy."

Watching the searing cliffs pass by without sign of human presence, for once I agreed with my superior. "It does not seem hospitable."

"Hospitable? 'Tis a miserable waterless hell inhabited by filthy savages. Pity the poor mariner with the misfortune to be cast away in Barbary. He will not receive a kind welcome since it is common knowledge all Moors are buggerers and worship Satan."

"That is not entirely accurate, Lance," said a sailor named John Frye, who was working near the fire box. He could not have been a half dozen years my senior but looked older since his face and neck were as brown as rawhide and creased with weathering. "In actuality Moors pray to a god they call Allah and consider Jesus and Moses to be blessed saints, albeit of lower stature than their favorite prophet, Mohammed. Nor is it easy to believe Moors are buggerers, considering that each man is by law allowed four wives."

Garget disliked being contradicted. "How would you know, Frye?"

"Three years ago I sailed under a captain named Fenton for the city of Tunis, which is controlled by the Turks. We remained in port several months and I learned the local customs. A few words, too."

Frye cleared his throat and spoke in a language that bore little relationship to English or to any of the other tongues I had heard on the Plymouth docks or aboard the *Pelican*.

"That is how you say 'good day' or 'good bye,'" he explained. "The literal translation is 'peace be on you.'"

"Peace be on you," I said, liking the wording. "*Assalamu alaikum.*"

"Very close."

Despite its bleakness there was something beautiful

about the landscape and when I finished my duties, I brought my mug to the railing and watched the coastline pass by while I drank the sack we had been issued instead of beer in honor of Christmas. As the sun set, the last light of day colored the cliffs and the surf breaking at their base with bands of pink and orange and saffron. Gulls cried in the distance, a lonely noise. Then night fell suddenly, cloaking the land. At the moment of darkness a terrible roaring rose from the shore, not one voice but many. The sound caused the fine hairs on my neck to lift from my skin and I could not stop a shudder from running through me.

"What in God's name is that?" I asked out loud.

"Lions."

I had been joined by the parson, Francis Fletcher, although I had not noticed his arrival. Having spent years abroad on dangerous and uncivilized frontiers, Fletcher had learned how to move with the caution of a seasoned traveler. In his knee-length black canvas coat and broad rimmed black hat he was almost invisible in the shadows.

"Lions," he repeated and leaned on his elbows against the railing at my side, clasping his hands together while he gazed shoreward, where a rising quarter moon gave the land a ghostly presence. "There was once a city amid this desolation, Peregrine," he told me. "I do not know its name but I do know that it was famous in its time and frequented by merchants of many nations. But the inhabitants were proud and wicked, rivaling the people of Sodom and Gomorrah in their depravity."

"What were their sins, sir?"

"I am ignorant of specifics. It is enough that they displeased the Lord, who sent an army of lions against them, sparing neither man, woman, nor child and consuming all from the face of the earth. To this day the lions remain in possession of the ruins of the wicked city, which has been known as *Civitas Leonum* ever since. It is said the lions come forth at night with great fierceness to rage along the shore. Their roaring is what we hear. Thanks to God, the beasts cannot endure water else they would enter the sea and make prey of our boats."

The dimness was too intense for me to spy the lions prowling the beach no matter how I strained. Nor was there any sign of the animals in the morning, just more miles of sand and broken rock with little evidence of greenery except for a rare tuft of scrub. Before noon, however, the *Pelican* approached a wide bay, where the cliffs gave way to gentler land and a stream poured into the ocean from a ravine, giving life to a growth of strange trees, which had no branches and were topped by thick clusters of fronds. On the north slope of the bay there was a small town surrounded by a thirty-foot wall of gray rock or brick, before which was a dry moat. Because of the fortification I could see nothing of the place but the roofs of buildings and the square tower of a castle.

The *Pelican* was noticed the moment we entered the bay and a bell rang out to carry news of our presence. Other bells echoed the alarm and soon the air was filled with clanging.

A dozen boats were tied to piers extending into the water below the town. Most were single-masted fishing dinghies painted the blue of a robin's egg. Two were oared gunships, sleek galleys with ten men on a side and with brass guns pointing forward from their prows. Clearly these vessels were both fast and deadly.

Soon after our arrival, the galleys were manned and cutting through the bay toward us.

I was chopping the chicken remaining from Christmas into hash. These shreds were to be combined with suet and baked in a crust. This was a favorite dish of Garget's. I suspected he had learned the recipe from his mother since it was particularly unappetizing.

"The fat is where the flavor is, pretty boy," he said while watching me mix the flabby chunks into the pulled meat. "Aye, when I smell the pies baking, and hear the lard bubbling, I cannot help but dream of home. There is nothing like English cooking."

I chose not to differ with Garget although I could have offered a dozen ways to improve the greasy forcemeat. In any case I was more interested in studying the approaching galleys.

The men crewing them all had complexions as dark as Diego's and black beards and mustaches. Without exception each covered his head with a white or red skullcap or with what appeared to be a cotton scarf wound in a knot so that it would stay in place.

Perhaps Moors were as peaceful as John Frye claimed but at the moment I would not have cared to test their mercy since these men clearly comprised a hardened company of warriors. All were armed with swords and I saw a couple carrying arquebuses with flared muzzles.

The *Pelican*'s officers, however, spared the galleys only indifferent glances. Nor did anyone else seem more than casually curious.

"Why are we not being called to stations?" I asked Garget as the galleys slid toward us, their oars rising and dipping with a precision that the Plymouth wherry men, Harry and Wilbert, would have admired.

Garget whistled through his front teeth in disgust. "The galleys will soon turn aside, of course. Jesus save me, I did not knew it were possible to be so uninformed."

I did not care for his ridicule but told myself the cure for ignorance was curiosity and that in order to learn, I must bear his ill humor. "Why will they turn aside?" I asked in a tone as flat as I could muster. "Sir."

My humility inclined Garget to elaborate. He motioned to the sails rising overhead. "For one thing, pretty boy, given a fair wind a masted vessel will consistently outrun a galley, which depends on oarsmen who eventually tire. Second, 'tis obvious from our course that we are heading elsewhere and do not pose a threat to the town. Last but not least, our cannon could easily blow the dogs from the water, which they well know. Moors may be heathen savages but they are not stupid fellows."

As Garget predicted, the galleys kept their distance although they trailed the *Pelican* until we traversed the bay, when they fell back and returned to their berths. Someone claimed the town was called *Saphia*—another said, no, it was *Asafi*—but soon the place was behind us and forgotten. For the next several leagues the shoreline consisted of low sand hills that sometimes grew into cliffs and sometimes inclined to the beach. In the distance I could make out a range of crags known as the Atlas or Iron mountains, depending on whom you asked, although no one was really sure since few Europeans ever ventured inland. Then, looking south, I saw we were coming upon another town. This one was larger than the first, its wall enclosing dozens of buildings as well as two castles and a tall structure topped with a gold platform.

According to several sailors, the town—Mogador—was a famous haven for bandits, pirates, slavers, and smugglers.

The town itself was unapproachable from seaward since it was surrounded by a collection of detached rocks. The actual harbor lay a half mile further on, in the lee of a barren island of black stone.

We rode in place a mile off Mogador for the night since it would not have been safe to proceed without better knowledge of the water ahead. In the morning, which was December 27th, Drake dispatched a small boat to take soundings and then the *Pelican* led the rest of the fleet around the black island to its eastern side, where we anchored a cable's length away in five fathoms of depth.

Since there would not be another anchorage as good for hundreds of miles along the African coast, Drake ordered that the fleet would remain in the harbor several days, using the time to make repairs to the ships and to replenish our provisions, if the natives would trade with us. He also gave the crew leave to stretch their legs upon the island when they were not on duty. Blacollers noticed me lingering idly a moment too long at the gunwale and assigned me to the gang delegated a special task.

"Bless you, lad," said the boatswain, "do you see the tarp? Be so kind as to begin untying it."

He meant the canvas protecting the parts of the disassembled flyboat, or pinnace, that Tobias Lackland had pointed out to me when I first came aboard. This one, at least, would not be carried on our shoulders over the Isthmus of Panama, as we were instructed to ferry the pieces to the island and to begin putting the boat together under the direction of Rich Joyner, the carpenter, so that the pinnace could be employed as a scout or reconnaissance vessel for the fleet. Getting the components ashore was hard work and we were all soaked with sweat and saltwater when the last length of pre-cut timber had been hauled onto the narrow beach. Our presence disturbed the birds nesting in the scrub and a flock of doves with black faces and yellow bills flapped away cooing angrily as we dragged the lumber above the high tide mark. I had just put down my piece when Blacollers called my name.

"Perry James! Where have you taken yourself?"

"Here, sir."

"You are commanded back to the *Pelican*. Step smartly, lad. It is Drake himself who wants you."

When I returned to the ship and climbed the ladder from the waist to the half deck, I discovered our general surrounded by a group that included Parson Fletcher, both Doughty brothers, Lancelot Garget, the sailor John Frye, and John Winter, captain of the *Elizabeth*. They were discussing the party of men on the mainland opposite our ships, who were waving seaward to attract our attention, ankle length robes flapping in the breeze as they jumped and hopped on the sand. Despite the intervening distance I could hear them hailing us. The shrill yelping impressed upon me how far I had traveled from home. I had never heard anything like it before.

Drake made up his mind. "It is agreed. Permit two men aboard. Allow them daggers but no other weapons. In return

Mr. Frye will serve as hostage. You speak something of their tongue, do you not, man?"

"Aye, general. A few words."

"Keep your ears open and report back what you hear."

Then Drake regarded me. "What do you know of Moorish cookery, Mr. James?" he asked.

"Why, nothing," I answered honestly.

"Do you see, sir?" Lancelot Garget said. "The boy is ignorant and we do not need his opinion. Let me prepare the feast. There is a young sow ready for slaughter. I will bake a fine blood pudding according to a secret family recipe."

"That would not be appropriate," said Francis Fletcher. "Moors consider pig flesh to be unclean and abstain from eating pork in all forms. It would be a mortal affront to serve them such a repast."

"General Drake—" I had to raise my voice to get his attention since everyone had begun talking at once. "I may not know Moorish cookery, but I have learned something of Spanish food, since my mother was from Cordoba. It could be that the two cuisines are similar."

"Aye, possibly," Drake agreed. "John, your opinion?"

Winter turned me a grim stare while running the point of his exaggerated mustache through his fingers. "The last meal I recall being served by the lad was not of good quality," he replied.

To my surprise Thomas Doughty spoke in my defense. "I believe there were extenuating circumstances," he said. "Francis, let Mr. James demonstrate his skill. Was it not to prepare against this exact situation that we agreed to allow him on our adventure?"

"By God, I well remember the occasion. Mr. James, you

have two hours to have all in readiness for our visitors. Show us your best efforts."

Heartened by this display of trust, and determined to live up to my masters' confidence, I went below and searched among the supplies for what was needed by the menu I was putting together hurriedly in my mind. Our stores included a variety of spices and dried herbs although Lancelot Garget, shunning most flavorings save for salt and pepper, rarely used them. First I sweated several pinches of saffron in butter, added rice, peas, and water, covered the pot, and put it to one side of the fire to steam until ready. With little time available for preparation, I had decided to cook *pinchitos*, a favorite dish of my mother's from her girlhood, which was simple and quick and, I hoped, somewhat familiar to the Moorish palate. *Pinchitos* were made by marinating chunks of skinned and deboned chicken in lemon juice, chopped garlic, olive oil, salt, pepper, cumin, hyssop, and paprika, and by then threading the chunks on skewers with a sliver of onion between each piece.

Garget gave my work a baleful glare. "What is that stench?" he asked when the *pinchitos* began grilling. "Christ in heaven, pretty boy, 'tis enough to make a man puke. Must there be so much garlic?"

"It is a necessary ingredient, sir."

"Of course. What else would buggerers and idolaters enjoy?"

Knowing the question to be rhetorical, I did not answer and concentrated on having the meal finished when the longboat returned from the mainland with the Moor emissaries.

These men resembled the crews of the galleys we had encountered earlier and had dark faces covered by long black beards and mustaches. One wore a white robe while the other's garment was woven with brown vertical stripes. Both had heavy gold hoops dangling from their earlobes, gold bracelets around their wrists, and gold torcs studded with carnelian circling their necks. By their finery it was obvious our guests hoped to impress upon us that they were important persons.

Drake, however, was not to be outdone. He had changed from his typical sturdy outfit into clothes as fine as those Thomas Doughty wore—velvet breeches sewn with silver thread, a silk codpiece of enormous girth, and a cloak of plum welt embroidered with roses. Our general bowed floridly while doffing his scarlet hat, its feather scraping the ground due to the grandness of the gesture.

This was a cue to our musical consort, of which Tobias Lackland had served as the most junior member until his untimely demise. All six players wore blue satin uniforms and matching caps with tassels. Led by John Bruer, who was the master performer and the director, five of them lifted shiny trumpets to their lips and blew a clear peal while the last man struck a drum in counterpoint to the brass.

"By the grace of God, and by the benevolence of our blessed queen Elizabeth, whose servant I am, welcome to the *Pelican*."

The Moors returned Drake's salute, making complicated motions with their hands as they lowered their heads.

"*Assalamu alaikum*," they replied.

It soon became evident the Moors spoke no English although they did recognize a word or two of Portuguese. Francis Fletcher knew some phrases in their tongue but not

enough to hold a conversation. This proved only a slight barrier to communication, however, for the Moors were expert
at conducting business through a language of signs and gestures accompanied by a battery of sighs, disgusted looks, and
disdainful whistles. In short order they made us understand
that they would bring a caravan to the waterside the next day
and trade us provisions for either gold or manufactured products, specifically weapons and luxury items. As a token of good
faith, Drake presented our guests with a dozen yards of linen,
a pair of leather shoes, and a steel lance with a bone grip. The
gifts seemed to please them.

One Portuguese word, however, appeared as familiar to
the Moors as any in their own dialect. "*Vinho*," they said, mim-
ing a man holding a cup and pretending to drink. "*Vinho*."

I was standing beside Parson Fletcher since the meal was
ready and I was waiting to serve the first course. "I thought all
Moors abstained from wine and beer as well as from pork," I said.

"Indeed, my son," answered Fletcher, "they are in fact
forbidden all spirits by their blasphemous bible. But Moors
are like other men in that it pleases them well to do in stealth
what they deny publicly. They will have to be carried off the
ship. You will see."

The group retired to the grand cabin and were seated at
the massive table, which was set for the occasion with Drake's
own silver plate and cutlery embossed with his personal ensign,
the world with a star above it. The Moors, however, ignored
both knives and forks, preferring to eat with the fingers of
their right hands. Fletcher's prediction regarding their sobriety appeared to be on the mark since both men accepted glass

after glass of wine and sack and never once refused a toast. Perhaps this was the reason for their generous praise of the meal—both men kissed their fingertips after tasting the rice and wept with exaggerated pleasure while wolfing down the *pinchitos* despite the garlic suffusing the chicken. They were plainly drunk when the sweet was served, *buñelos de viento*, a basket of fried pastry rings dusted with sugar and cinnamon. The chief Moor took me in his arms and kissed my cheeks.

"Aye, what did I say? Buggerers, one and all," Lancelot Garget observed. Drake laughed and said:

"Why, I do believe you have made a friend, Mr. James."

"I hope that is a good thing, sir," I replied, attempting to avoid my admirer's thicket of beard without giving offense. But I could not avoid accepting the gift he pressed onto my palm, a leather pouch containing a silver pipe and a wedge of resin the size of my thumb. This bore little resemblance to the weed smoked aboard the *Pelican* and by Constable Felix in Plymouth. No one could identify the substance until John Frye returned from the mainland, having been released by the Moors after our visitors were rowed back to the beach, un-harmed but snoring.

Frye scraped a bit off with a nail and sniffed.

"It is a spice known as hashish," he said.

"I have heard of the stuff," said Pascoe Goddy. "Do Moors not eat it for pleasure?"

"Aye, they do. Its smoke is also drunk in place of hon-est beer or *aqua vitae*." Frye considered the quantity of spice I had been given. "This is of excellent quality," he went on. "Do you notice the black flecks? Those belong to another rare herb, which grows in the lands of China and India and is known as opium. Such a mixture is supposed to be especially potent. There should be sufficient here to make us all glad, and a score of men besides. What do you say, mate?"

"Be my guest, sir," I replied, not inclined to try the hashish myself as I did not care for its pungent odor. This, however, did not dissuade Francisco Albo from accepting my invitation.

Albo was the old sailor I had met in the crow's nest soon after I arrived on the *Pelican*. I had not seen much of him later since he kept to the high rigging in order, I supposed, to evade Blacollers's scrutiny and the consequent assignment of additional duty. With an expertise no doubt acquired through a lifetime of dissipation on the high seas, the ancient mariner crumbled a little hashish into the bowl of the silver pipe, lit it with a splint of tinder, and pulled the resulting fumes deep into his lungs.

"Aye, *filos*," he sighed after finally exhaling. "'Tis fine stuff, this is, as fine as any I have tasted."

The rest of us studied Albo as he put the flame to the bowl again. When he did not become ill or die, the others were encouraged to follow his lead and sample the hashish.

"Not bad," declared Pascoe Goddy. "Damn me if I do not feel a happy invigoration."

"Happy, yes," said Gregory Raymente after several pulls of his own. "Happy, happy, very happy."

Peter Corder accepted the bowl from Raymente, gripping the stem with his toes and bringing the pipe to his mouth with his foot in order to sip the smoke. Although the others had been entertained by Corder's dexterity often enough—so often, in fact, that the novelty had worn off—now everyone collapsed with laughter. This continued far longer than was warranted, until the sailors were gasping for breath and slapping the deck in an effort to calm down. Francisco Albo, however, was affected differently. Throwing a bony arm around my shoulders, he peered sadly at me from beneath his mane of tangled white hair. Once again I was impressed by how pale his eyes were and by the fetor of his breath.

"I heard of the loss of your friend," Albo said. "I wish you to know I share your grief."

"I am sure Lackland would have appreciated your sympathy."

"Ah, let us be honest, the prissy little catamite cared nothing for my regard. Did he not say so? Still, every man's death diminishes us all. To my sorrow, this is a lesson I have learned well. Did you know, *filos*, there were two hundred and sixty-eight of us? Two hundred and sixty-eight men and sailors and gentlemen. *Two hundred and sixty-eight!*"

"Aye, sir, I understand. Two hundred and sixty-eight," I agreed in an effort to soothe Albo, who was now clutching my shirt in his fist, as if he were afraid I would not listen.

"You understand nothing!" he exclaimed. "Eighteen returned. Eighteen out of two hundred and sixty-eighty!"

I did not know quite how to respond to this revelation. Pressing his grizzled cheek to mine, the old sailor held me close and began itemizing the tragedies his companions had suffered.

"Esteban Gomez died of starvation. So did Geronimo Guerro and fifty others aboard the *Victoria*. Diego de Mello drank his own piss and died of thirst. Hans the bombardier—he were a sweet boy—Hans took a spear in his lungs and expired with bloody froth on his lips. Louis Mendoça got his throat slit and was cut into quarters on orders of Captain Fernan, and the pieces were spitted on poles in the sand. Aye, it were a sorry sight, even though he was a mutinous dog who deserved nothing less. Cartagena, another traitor, met the same end and joined Mendoça in parts on the beach, God rest his soul."

There was no telling how long Francisco Albo could have continued reciting this grisly list but he fell asleep after naming only a dozen more men and their respective misfortunes. By this time everyone else had also lapsed into slumber, which appeared to be an effect of drinking the hashish and opium smoke, as their sleep seemed more profound than normal and most had pleasant smiles on their lips while they dreamed.

Just past daybreak, when light began spilling over the peaks of the distant mountains, a caravan of strange animals appeared on the beach.

I had risen before dawn to begin breakfast. Pushing the porridge to one side of the fire box so that it would not burn, I went to the gunwale and stared shoreward. The odd beasts somewhat resembled horses in that they possessed four legs but there the similarity ended. These animals had humps on their backs and long curved necks and they walked with a spraddle-legged gait that ate up distance despite its apparent awkwardness.

"Camels," explained John Frye. "Moors employ them instead of horses since they are better able to endure the desert and go without water. Some say they can withstand thirst for ten days at a stretch."

The camels carried cloth panniers or wicker trunks strapped

to their humps, evidently the victuals promised for trade by the men we had entertained. They knelt on the sand with a groaning that could be heard over the intervening water.

"These camels do not seem to be joyful creatures," I observed.

"Oh, they are generally well contented, albeit stubborn. But the beasts never forget ill treatment and can wait years to exact revenge."

"Then I must remember to be polite to any I meet."

I spoke these words lightly and without foreknowledge that soon I would have the opportunity to put my resolution into practice. Almost immediately Frye and I were summoned by Blacollers to the half deck and assigned to the longboat being dispatched to the beach under the command of Thomas Doughty.

"Frye, you know somewhat of the vernacular," said the boatswain.

"Less than I thought, sir. They speak a different dialect here than in Tunis. I can decipher only a few words."

"It will have to do! Your duty, sir, is to interpret for the landing party as best you may. And your duty, Mr. James, is to ensure the victuals are wholesome and provided in the correct quantity."

"I will be careful and exact, sir"

"Bless you, lad, that is the spirit!"

The dozen of us going ashore were issued cutlasses by Oliver, the master gunner. Thomas Doughty, in addition to his rapier, wore a brace of pistols strapped across his chest. "Gentlemen," he said, addressing us from beside the mizzenmast, "I urge you to be alert and vigilant! Moors are cunning rogues, as treacherous as the Irish. Do not so much as wander off to answer a call of nature else we may never enjoy your company again. Do you follow me?"

"Aye, sir!"

"God damn all Moors!" said another man.

"What, am I supposed to stifle the urge forever?" asked a third.

This question amused everyone but Doughty, who gave the speaker, Jhon Gribble, a stern look. "Only a fool would consider our security a humorous matter," he said.

"Sorry, sir," Gribble apologized, touching the brim of his hat while ducking his head in order to hide a grin. "I meant no disrespect."

Doughty scrutinized the sailor a moment further and then indicated with a curt nod that we should proceed to the longboat. John Frye and I took the forward seats, he the port oar and I the starboard.

As we approached the breakers, the sea turned brown with the muddy outflow of a small river.

The caravan had halted on its north bank and the camels had been turned loose to graze on scrub. Three men were waving to us and pointing toward the channel of slack water leading through the surf.

"Rest oars," ordered Thomas Doughty. He rose from his seat and balanced on bent knees while staring shoreward, obviously seeking evidence of betrayal. I gave the beach a hard look myself, not that I knew what I was looking for, since I lacked any military experience except for the drills aboard the *Pelican*.

"The coast seems clear," Doughty observed, which confirmed my own opinion, since I saw nothing out of the ordinary, either. "Mr. Smythe, what do you think?"

"I agree, captain."

"Mr. Wood?"

Symon Wood was less trusting. "A thousand villains could be lurking in the brush, captain, and we would be no wiser."

"The point is well taken, sir. Proceed with caution."

At Doughty's gesture we dipped our oars and propelled the longboat carefully through three lines of breakers, steering first to the left and then to the right and then right again until we came past the froth into calmer water fifty feet from shore.

Hundreds of black and white gulls dotted the sand, as motionless as statues. On the opposite side of the mud flats the ruins of an ancient fort baked in the sun, its tower collapsed and its crenellations tilted askew.

"Mr. Frye! Mr. James! Fend us off the beach."

The two of us shipped our oars and went overboard into the shallows. We each seized a gunwale and steadied the longboat while the Moors waved and made the curious yipping I had heard earlier, which seemed to be both an expression of excitement and a welcoming hail.

"Bring us in closer, gentlemen."

It required all our strength to wrestle the longboat to within a half dozen yards of the beach, and to hold her in position against the surge and ebb of the waves. The important thing was to keep her keel off the bottom, so that the boat could retreat in the event of treachery. Every time I braced myself, the sand underfoot was eroded away, forcing me to find new traction.

"Steady, steady," said Thomas Doughty.

"Aye, captain," I muttered, and promptly swallowed a mouthful of brine. The resulting fit of coughing caused me to miss Doughty's next command. It was not until I looked over my shoulder that I saw our peril.

As Symon Wood had cautioned, the vegetation growing along the riverbank concealed an ambush. Men were emerging from hiding and sprinting to the waterline, screaming and flourishing curved swords. The Moors who had pretended to be our friends were already splashing toward us, some holding daggers, others brandishing clubs.

"Back oars!" Doughty roared. "The dogs have shown their teeth!"

John Frye and I looked at each other. I am sure my own expression mirrored the alarm on his face, and we came to the same decision in the same instant, and tried to hoist ourselves on board the longboat. It was, unfortunately, already too late.

Frye failed to hold on and was left behind. I could not get over the side but did get a grip on the gunwale with one hand. As the longboat gained momentum, I was dragged off my feet and carried away.

"Let go or I will break your fingers," said the nearest sailor. I did not realize he was addressing me until his oar slammed onto the gunwale, just missing my wrist. He hoisted the shaft again and aimed it directly at my hand.

Thomas Doughty caught the oar before it touched down. "Use your strength to row," he said while shoving the sailor back onto his seat.

"God rot the boy. He will drag us all to hell, sir. Can you not see the devils are gaining?"

The rowers backed water even harder but still they could not get going fast enough. The weight of my body was acting as an anchor and slowing the vessel. I could hear the yelling growing louder. I tried to grasp the gunwale with my other hand but could not.

Thomas Doughty removed his pistols from their holsters, cocked the weapons, steadied himself, took aim, and fired. Neither shot struck a target. Nor did the reports discourage our pursuers.

Loud splashing and a string of furious English oaths indicated that John Frye was now being attacked.

"Mr. James!" said Thomas Doughty.

"Aye, sir," I coughed.

"We cannot come about to bring you aboard."

"No, sir."

"Do what is right for the good of the company."

He meant that I should release my grip and free the longboat to move without hindrance. That he asked this sacrifice of me came as no surprise—Thomas Doughty, by his own admission, was a practical man, not a kind one. Nor could I contradict his logic.

For the salvation of the rest, I must let go.

"Aye, sir, I understand," I said and drew in a breath to prepare myself for what I had to do.

Then a hand grabbed my ankle and broke my hold on the gunwale.

Other hands pushed my head under the surface and began drowning me in waist deep water. I struck out with my fists and kicked furiously at my opponents and managed to free myself and gulp down a lungful of air. Before I could take a second breath, however, four men bowled into me, two wrenching my arms behind my back while a third tore both my cutlass and my kitchen knife from my waist. The last Moor placed a dagger shaped like a scythe to my neck. "*Assalamu alaikum*," he said.

Peace be on you.

Marooned in Barbary

December 29, 1577 – January 2, 1578
Mogador, the desert

The dagger's edge bit into my neck. Only the slightest pressure would be needed to cut the artery beneath the skin. By the wild look in the eyes of the Moor facing me, I could tell he wanted to sever my throat. But he was restrained from murder by the captain of the ambush, no one else but the chief of the two scoundrels we had entertained aboard the *Pelican*. Wading into the shallows, he wagged his finger at the man with the dagger while barking a string of indecipherable orders.

These evidently constituted a pardon or a stay of execution. With a scowl my captor returned his knife to its sheath. Then he shoved me to the beach and made me sit beside John Frye on the sand.

"I thought they killed you, John," I said. "Thank God I was wrong."

"It seems we are more valuable to the bastards alive than dead. This may not be a good omen."

"Surely the Moors cannot hope for ransom. We are not gentlemen, that much should be obvious even to them."

"Aye, mate, but we are mariners, and seamen make fine galley slaves. Still, it is promising we have been neither robbed nor bound."

I had been relieved of my cutlass and cooking knife by my captor, who had appropriated them for his own use, but he had not stolen anything else, not even the valuable little silver pipe in its tooled leather pouch. Remembering Lancelot Garget's lurid ideas about buggery and Satanism, I asked nervously:

"Then what do you think they want from us?"

"I cannot begin to guess."

In the lee of the black island the longboat had reached the *Pelican* and men were clambering into the ship. By now Drake would know of the ambush and of our capture. But I was not foolish enough to believe he would send men after us and risk bloodshed for our sake. What was I but a cook's helper—the least boy of the crew? Frye, an ordinary sailor, was equally insignificant. As I had learned on the road to Mortlake, we were expendable. No one would come to our assistance.

In any case we were taken from the beach well before any rescue could have reached us. Within minutes the Moors rounded up the camels and herded them together. My guard pushed me toward the fourth in line, an animal with a particularly supercilious expression and white bursts of fur around its eyes.

Getting astride was simple—simpler, in fact, than getting on a horse since the camel was trained to go to its knees to make mounting easy for its rider. Before I finished settling myself, however, the camel suddenly pushed up its hind legs, flinging me into the front saddle horn. Then it jerked up its fore legs and sent me reeling backward.

Both impacts hurt. Shifting painfully on my bruises, I stifled the words that came naturally to mind, remembering how the animals were rumored to hold grudges, and instead patted the ugly brute in an effort to make friends. But it only looked disdainfully at me, puckered its lips in a sneer, and blew a wet belch. Then the camel lurched into motion, following the leader away from the coast, past the thicket of greenery growing along the stream, and into a barren wilderness.

For miles the landscape consisted of stony hills and dunes of sand, their surfaces rippled by the wind in parallel lines. The only signs of life were infrequent thorny shrubs and a few white flowers growing in crevices. Sometimes I heard whispering as the breeze shifted dust from a ridge but otherwise the wasteland was quiet. There was no cover except for occasional rock outcroppings and I envied my captors the scarves wrapped around their heads since my own was bare and the sun beat down without mercy.

Somewhat short of noon the camels halted in a ravine with walls sixty feet high. A slight overhang provided shade but there was no open water. Several men dismounted and put their shoulders to a round boulder and pushed together. Eventually it rolled aside, revealing the mouth of a well paved with irregular blocks of stone. A bucket splashed down into the hole and was hauled back overflowing with clear liquid.

My guard made sure I was last to drink. When he grudgingly passed the bucket, I only just stopped myself from thrusting my entire head inside to satisfy my thirst.

"Slow down, mate, else you will develop cramps or worse," warned John Frye. "I have heard stories of men saved from the desert. They drank so much that they drowned themselves and died."

"I do not believe you!" I sputtered but swallowed more

carefully after that and returned the bucket to the guard before my belly was full.

One man handed out loaves of flat bread and chunks of goat sausage, which were spiced with pepper and cumin and very tough to chew. When the meal was done, most of the company lay down and napped. Following their example, I stretched out on a clear patch of ground and soon joined the others in slumber.

When I awoke, I was unsure where I was.

I knew I could not be on my straw pallet at the Jack and Rasher because there was no window by the hearth where I slept and now I was looking up at a brilliant blue sky. Nor was I aboard the *Pelican* since around me was a desert of sand and not of brine. Then I remembered I was marooned in Barbary and I felt lost and far from home in an alien place among enemies.

"Do not move or you will die."

I could not see John Frye but I recognized his voice.

"What is the matter?" I asked, careful not to make any motion.

"There is a viper by your right shoulder. It must not be startled."

Now I could feel the thing slither upon me. I wanted to leap up and fling it away but knew that rash action would be fatal. Instead I made my breathing as shallow as possible and whispered my words through clenched teeth without moving my jaws or lips.

"Get it off, John."

"I will do what I can."

The snake continued exploring and came within range

of my sight. Its head was flat and broad and covered by bronze scales and its pupils were dark vertical slits. Above each eye rose a small spike. Instinctively I knew the worm was venomous. How could it not be?

Its tongue flicked out repeatedly, as if tasting the air.

By now I could not have moved if I tried since every muscle in my body was locked with tension.

Nonetheless the viper appeared to notice my presence. It curled in a circle and exposed its fangs while hissing angrily.

Then it struck.

The attack came so quickly that I was unable to react. The only reason I continued living was because the strike was not aimed at me. The worm had lunged at one of the men summoned by John Frye.

There was a flash of steel before it could retreat to its coils. The snake's head flew to the ground, where the mouth continued gnashing even though it was separated from its body.

I threw the remains away while scrambling to my feet. I could not stop myself from brushing at my clothes again and again, as if the snake had left behind a taint that must be removed. "Jesus, Jesus, Jesus," I repeated. It was some time before I could say anything else.

"Are you whole, mate?" asked Frye. "The serpent did not scratch you?"

"No, I am fine, thank God. And thank you, John."

"Thank the bastard over there. He decapitated the worm."

Frye meant my personal guard. Knowing the man would not understand my words, I bowed to express my gratitude. This gesture of respect, however, only increased his malice and he vented his annoyance by stabbing the dead viper until both the head and the body were tatters of meat. Nor did he ever stop glowering meaningfully in my direction while mutilating the snake.

"That man is not my friend," I observed to John Frye. "He has hated me since we first met. I cannot figure out why."

"Tell me, mate, did you by chance kick the villain while you were wrestling together in the shallows?"

"Aye, it could be so."

"Here is the explanation. For Moors 'tis a mortal insult to be shown the sole of a man's shoe. To be kicked is equally offensive."

"This is not good news. When I think about it, I believe I kicked the fellow more than once. Several times, in fact."

Despite the lateness of the hour the sky was a searing cauldron when the camels again set out into the desolation. Both John Frye and I had borrowed head scarves from our captors. Mine evidently had been employed as a wrapping for something unpleasant but I was glad to have it despite the smell. The scarf—the *cheche*—provided protection from the heat but not enough to suit me. Whatever moisture the sun did not bake away was sucked from my skin by the wind. It was not long before I believed I knew what damnation was like although I doubted hell was as hot and dry as the desert of Barbary, which was an ocean of sand.

An ocean of sand.

Suddenly I remembered Dr. Dee's warning in Mortlake when he had read my future and I realized that I was approaching the first of the three dooms that were my lot on the voyage.

An ocean of sand.

I knew I was now in deadly peril. Unfortunately, I was ignorant of both the nature of the danger facing me and the direction from which it would come. I glanced around carefully, scrutinizing my surroundings, determined not to be taken by surprise although I lacked any idea what to look for. By the time we reached our destination, a ravine similar to the first, my eyes were burning from squinting through the glare.

Here there was a shallow stream and living greenery. Beside the water was an encampment of black tents. The one to which we were led, evidently the captain's own pavilion, had scarlet pennants flying from its carved wood stakes and an interior lit by clay lamps and floored with thick carpets woven in intricate patterns. By gestures we were informed to remove our boots and to wait as a manservant attended the chief and his subordinates. Then we were made to stand before them while they reclined on embroidered pillows and conferred among themselves. Finally an old man hobbled forward.

Pinching my cheek between swollen knuckles, he moved my head from side to side while studying my features. Then he said:

"*Quando você vem?*"

"That is Portuguese," I said to John Frye.

"Aye, I recognize the language but know nothing of it. Do you?"

"A little. He is asking where we are from." Then, haltingly, I replied: "*Não, não somos Português. Estamos Inglês. Nós somos da Inglaterra.*"

"*Inglaterra?*"

"*Sim, Inglaterra.*"

My answer appeared to confound the old man and I

doubted he had any idea what I was talking about but I was proven wrong when his next words were delivered in clear, if accented, English.

"You no *Inglês*. *Inshallah*! *Inglês* pirates are as pale as snow. You are too dark. You *Português*."

"My mother was a Spanish lady," I protested, "but I was born in Plymouth, which is an English city."

"And I color easily, damn it," declared John Frye, who was even darker than the Moor himself due to his years on the sea.

The old man translated our replies for the chief—Sheikh Al-Rabí'a seemed to be the leader's name. He, too, doubted our honesty. For the better part of a hour the sheikh shot questions at us in an effort to catch us lying. Often we were asked the same question twice or several times in order to bring to light any inconsistencies in our answers. As might be expected, the sheikh was focused on our expedition and its purpose. We answered truthfully and told him what little we knew—there was, after all, nothing to be gained by evasion. Even so the Moor remained suspicious. "If you *Inglês*," he asked, "what is the name of your king?"

"We do not have one," answered John Frye. "Our ruler is a queen."

"*Bismillah*, I have heard rumor of this abomination!" Sheikh Al-Rabí'a's shudder of distaste at the idea of a female monarch was repeated by his subordinates. "I have also heard this woman—what is she called?"

"Elizabeth."

"*Sim*, I have heard this Elizabeth is a notorious—" the interpreter searched for the proper English word but had to settle for its Portuguese equivalent— "*prostituta*, yes?"

I was, of course, personally ignorant of the queen's private character but I could not remain silent while she was
slandered.

"No, sir, that is a lie," I answered.

"A damned lie, mate!" John Frye put in with equal heat.

It was not until later that I realized the sheikh was test-
ing us to determine whether we were really Englishmen and
not pretenders to the nationality. Fortunately our display of
patriotism proved sufficiently heartfelt that he was convinced
of our sincerity.

"Peace be on you, *Inglês*. I must beg your pardon since it
is impolite to defame any woman, whether scullion or sovereign. But now, thanks be to Allah, I am assured you are who
you say you are and not lackeys of that infidel dog Sebastião."

At the clap of the sheikh's hands, the manservant brought
out additional cushions and arranged them for us so that we
could sit comfortably on the carpet with the others.

"Who is Sebastião?" I whispered to John Frye.

"I suspect the sheikh is referring to the king of Portugal."

"That is so," confirmed Al-Rabí'a. "Know that I am vas-
sal to the sultan of Marrocos, Abu Marwan Abd al-Malik,
may Allah's blessing be upon him. My lord has a nephew, Abu
Abdallah Mohammed, who is desirous of the throne. Recently
this nephew journeyed to Lisboa to beg an army from the
Português king with which to press his claim. My orders are
to patrol the coast and provide early warning of an attack. We
had to be certain you were not spies for an invading fleet."

"Well, sir, we are English sailors, plain and simple," I

repeated.

"This is now clear. Thanks be to Allah the merciful that I do not have to stake you in the sand for ants and buzzards to devour."

As the sheikh finished speaking, the manservant carried in a heavy ceramic platter with a conical lid, which he lifted away in a flourish of steam, revealing bubbling goat stew surrounded by heaps of boiled grain.

Everyone pressed forward to share the repast. Following John Frye's whispered instructions, I was careful to employ only my right hand while eating. Using a scrap of bread as a spoon, I brought a serving of meat and gravy to my mouth.

The first bite stuck in my throat due to the inordinate amount of pepper and spice in the recipe. Swallowing did not get any easier with a second bite nor with a third even though I washed each down with water.

"Are you not enjoying the *tagine?*" asked Sheikh Al-Rabí'a, observing me wiping tears from my eyes while John Frye regarded his own portion of stew with a stunned expression.

I knew it was never polite to speak ill of your host's table and that it was particularly imprudent to do so if he commanded armed men.

But I did not want the sheikh to like me. There was something in his look that made me uneasy, a proprietary warmth I thought should be more properly directed at a woman and not at a member of the male sex.

"In all sincerity, sir," I replied, "I would not recommend the dish. For one thing, the seasoning was added with too heavy a hand, especially the turmeric, cloves, cardamom, and paprika. There is also an abundance of dried lemon rind. I imagine this was meant to hide the fact the meat is off but you can still taste the rankness on the back of your tongue."

John Frye was elbowing me to keep quiet well before I completed my review. The sheikh listened silently as the interpreter finished translating and stared at me with a stony expression while the other men muttered angrily at my unkind appraisal of the meal.

Then Al-Rabí'a exploded in laughter. "*Bismillah!*" he exclaimed. "Is it not said, *Good food praises itself*? Your words are just, *Inglês*, and I cannot find fault with them. A knowledgeable cook is that rarity among rarities and worth his weight in rubies. Mine own is as ignorant of taste as a blind man is of sight but I have been unable to replace him with anyone better. Surely Allah himself has sent you to me for a reason."

"I am honored, sir," I answered quickly, disliking the sound of this declaration. "But General Drake is not remaining long at Mogador. We must make haste back to our ship. Is that not so, John?"

"Aye, mate. Blacollers said we would sail on New Year's Day."

"Do not worry, *Inglês*," the sheikh assured Frye. "My men will escort you to the coast. If your captain has departed, we will procure you a berth home on another vessel. There are usually one or two European traders passing by. Please accept this small token as repayment for any inconvenience you have suffered."

A servant counted a dozen coins onto Frye's palm. I could tell by the clink they made against one another and by the pleased expression on Frye's face that they were gold. Then the sheikh regarded me.

"As for you, my precious jewel," he said fondly, "I would no sooner part with you than I would part with a pearl of perfect roundness! From this point forward, through all the days of our lives, until we are separated by the Destroyer of Delights and Sunderer of Society, you will live with me and be my cook."

This avowal did not come as a complete surprise since I was already suspicious of the Moor but even so I was unprepared for such profoundly bad news. With a sinking feeling I saw that the sheikh's eyes were glowing with a gastronomical passion so intense that it was unlikely any protest on my part would be heard. Even so, hoping to appeal to his honor if not to his reason, I said:

"I have another master, Sheikh Al-Rabí'a. It would not be justice to steal me from General Drake. Nor do I care to be your slave."

"Slave? No, *Inglês*, you will be my very son and I will cherish you as if you were born of my own blood."

These kind words, although meant to be soothing, only increased my alarm. Whether as son, cook, or slave, I did not enjoy the idea of living my life a thousand miles from England and from everyone I knew and every place I had ever known.

"Sir, I cannot accept your generosity!" I argued but the sheikh refused to listen. With a curt gesture he forbade further debate and insisted we instead discuss his favorite menus, a subject he did not tire of for several hours. Then he yawned behind his hand.

"Pray do not consider it an insult that I keep you under guard," apologized Al-Rabí'a. "My soul would be made desolate should you accidentally wander off from the wadi to perish."

Our escort was the same man who was my enemy—Mohammed, the others called him, a name evidently beloved by Moors since every second person seemed to carry it. He gave me a peremptory push into the tent John Frye and I were to share.

"*Você vá para dentro!*" Inside!

"Watch yourself," I answered, turning him a long look. "Did you not hear your master, Sheikh Al-Rabí'a? I am like his very son, do you understand? *Eu sou seu filho. Filho!*"

"*Você é o filho de um cão, Inglês,*" Mohammed replied, cursing me as the son of a dog, apparently a great insult. Then he turned his back to me and settled himself on his heels before the entrance to the tent, where he fell asleep and began snoring. Discerning the direction of my thoughts, Frye said:

"Do not even think of it. Escape is impossible."

"Listen to him rumble! If his own noise does not wake him, nothing will. We could be well away long before we were missed."

"You, mate, not I."

"Of course—how could I forget? Are you not being set free with a dozen gold angels in your pocket?"

"That is not the point. Why do you think we have not been warded more vigilantly? Only a fool would brave the desert without a guide."

"Aye, no doubt," I admitted grudgingly. "But what am I to do?"

"Sometimes there is naught to do," Frye answered. "Castaways must adjust to circumstances when they are on the beach."

"So I am to become a Moor?"

"I have been assured the procedure only stings a moment."

"Procedure?" I asked. "What procedure?"

"Why, did you not know? Moors are like Jews insofar as male members of both races reef their spritsails."

"Reef their spritsails?" I repeated, not understanding what he meant until I remembered exactly where the spritsail was situated aboard a sailing vessel—it hung below the bowsprit at the very stem of the ship. And reefing was the process by which sails were shortened to reduce their exposure to wind during a gale. My hand dropped to my waist in an involuntary gesture of protection. "You do not mean to say they—"

"Aye, every man. It is a symbol of obedience to Allah."

"Exactly how much is—reefed?"

"Just a bit off the head, mate," he answered, meaning the forward part of the sail. "You will never miss it."

"That is easy for you to say," I muttered, the prediction providing me small comfort, and I lay awake well past moonset, my mind filled with a succession of dangerous plots, each one more worthless than its predecessor. John Frye was right. Even if I succeeded in escaping, there was little possibility I could retrace the route through the desert to Mogador or evade the hunters who would be sent after me. But I could not resign myself to becoming a Moor and a slave to the sheikh, no matter how Al-Rabí'a promised to gild my cage and to call me his son. I had to act, and soon, if I were to have any hope of rejoining the fleet.

Hours passed and still I remained awake. Eventually, remembering its soothing effect on my crew mates, I reached for the spice with which I had been gifted. Perhaps, I thought, the smoke would have the same effect on me as it had had on the others and allow me to sleep.

But I let my hand fall back without opening the pouch. Suddenly it had come to me what I must do if I were to gain my freedom.

Most of the chunk of spice remained. The amount already consumed, perhaps a fifth of the total, had been sufficient to make drunk a half dozen sailors. The rest, I hoped, would be more than enough for what I had in mind.

It would have to be enough.

Just before dawn we were roused by the men who were to conduct John Frye to the coast. They had saddled a camel for him and brought the beast before the tent, where it knelt with a melancholy groan.

The morning was so bitterly chill that our breath was visible in the air. Frye clasped my hand in both of his and held the grip while he spoke.

"Have no fear, mate, I will get word to Drake of your plight," he told me earnestly. "The general will surely negotiate with the sheikh for your freedom when we return this way again."

"Aye, if you say so," I replied, knowing that Frye meant to ease my spirits, and liking him for making the effort, although the unspoken truth between us was that there was little chance of his optimistic forecast ever coming to pass. "But if not, John, there is a kindness you could do me."

"I will help in any way."

"You will be returning to Plymouth?"

"Aye, no doubt, with the right wind, God willing."

"I have friends there, who should be notified of my situation. Inform them I am alive and well and in good spirits. I would not want them to be troubled on my account."

"You may depend on me," Frye promised, repeating the names Audley and Winston several times in order to commit them to memory. Then his camel unfolded its legs, stood erect, and began following the other animals into the desert. Once Frye twisted around to wave but soon he was veiled by distance and I saw him no more.

I was careful to take exact note of the direction in which the camels had headed. That would be the straight course back to the sea.

In order to throw off pursuit, I would have to go another way. Instead I would bear south and veer toward the coast only when I was far from the direct route.

Mohammed, my guard, was a vigilant warder and allowed me little privacy even at the latrine ditch, where he stood entirely too close by while I did what I must. Then he led me to the kitchen tent and settled himself on a stool while the interpreter introduced me to the cook, a hugely fat man in a white frock colorfully patterned with grease and blood and other culinary remains. It was clear from his sullen expression that this man—Selim—resented my presence even more than Artyur had begrudged my being placed above him aboard the *Benedict*. Now, however, I was not particularly concerned with being liked.

Speaking slowly through the interpreter, I told my new assistant: "The sheikh has commanded a banquet for the entire company. All must be finished before sunset so we must work diligently. Your first duty is to slaughter a kid and butcher the meat. Bring me the bones since I require them for broth. We also need a half dozen chickens, plucked, washed, and trussed. Can you do this?"

"Yes, master."

"Then get to work. Did I not say time is essential?"

Next I turned to Mohammed. "If I am to serve the sheikh, I require my knife. Return it at once."

This request was not well received. It was only after I threatened to complain to Al-Rabi'a that Mohammed reluctantly withdrew the blade from his belt. Rather than put it into my hands, however, he scowled and dropped it to the ground, making me stoop to retrieve it.

The kitchen tent was an open sided awning protecting sacks of dry goods, mainly beans, grain, and flour. There were also baskets of vegetables, some familiar and some new to me, as well as jugs of oil and black olives. Just outside the tent a cooking pit had been dug and paved with stone. Beside it, also made of stone, was an oven in the shape of a beehive. I had lit fires in both by the time Selim delivered the bones of the kid, which I set to boil with some onions and thyme. I fried the meat in an iron skillet and then placed the browned cubes in a clay pot to braise slowly. My goal was to duplicate the meal I had been served the previous evening, only using good culinary sense to balance flavors properly, adding spices in judicious amounts rather than by the fistful. Soon the air was fragrant with the scents of garlic, cumin, pepper, coriander seed, and oregano. Out of the corner of my eye I caught sight of my assistant taking a piece of meat from the pot.

I stopped his hand before it reached his mouth. "Tell this

cur I will cut off a finger the next time I catch him stealing," I directed the interpreter, forcing open Selim's grip over the pot so that the pilfered meat fell back into the stew. "No one is to touch so much as a bean without permission. That applies to you, too," I continued, addressing Mohammed. "This is my kitchen, do you follow me? Here I am sheikh."

"I do not take orders from an infidel dog. I will eat what I want."

"Then you will eat with your left hand since you will have naught but stubs on your right."

At this Mohammed gripped the handle of his sword— my cutlass—with such intensity that his knuckles whitened but somewhere he found the strength not to draw it. I did not know where I found the strength to meet the devil's glare until his hand dropped from the weapon.

Then I released Selim and with a rude shove set him to kneading dough for the flat bread Moors favored. If my assistant had hated me before, now he truly despised me. But both Selim and Mohammed must remain hungry until the meal was done and the final ingredient added. Then they could stuff their bellies without care.

By nightfall all was prepared except for a last addition to the main course. Stirring the sauce with a wood spoon, careful to keep my back to my companions, I opened the leather pouch around my neck.

Had not John Frye said the spice was as potent when it was eaten as when its smoke was breathed in? Hoping my memory was accurate, I broke apart the chunk with my thumbnail and crumbled the hashish into the braised kid. Soon the entire piece was lost in the stew.

I placed a conical lid over the *tagine*—this, I had learned, was the name of the pot as well as the name of any meal cooked within it—and allowed the dish to simmer awhile longer. Then I cuffed Selim to get his attention and to further infuriate him.

"I will now join the sheikh. Carry in the meal when you are sent for. Take care not to spill a drop, or I swear you will be begging Allah for forgiveness, do you understand? Make sure the bread is warm. And keep your fingers out of the pot. I dislike imagining where they have been."

I did not know how long Selim hesitated before helping himself to a portion of kid after I left the kitchen but I doubted he wasted much time. Mohammed, too, appeared anxious to relieve himself of my custody. He led the way to the tent of the sheikh so hurriedly that I had to stretch my legs in order to keep up. Once I was inside, he departed with equal haste, presumably to join Selim in disregarding my instructions. So far, at least, events were proceeding as I had anticipated.

Except for the sentries on duty, everyone else had crowded into the main tent. The men sat in a half circle facing Al-Rabi'a, who indicated that I should take the cushion at his side. Despite my ignorance of the language, I sensed an air of expectancy among both the captains and the ordinary soldiers. I could not decide, however, whether they were looking forward to supper or fearing it.

"There is no might save in Allah, the glorious, the great," proclaimed the sheikh to the assembly, evidently words of a Moorish ritual, since the others repeated them back to their leader. Then Al-Rabí'a bade that the meal begin.

First Selim brought out the accompaniments and laid the platters on the carpet before the sheikh—rice cooked with pistachio nuts and orange rind, a puree of beans with olive oil and garlic, and a bowl of vegetables that I had grilled and marinated in vinegar and salt. Then he carried in the steaming *tagine* of braised kid. The burst of vapor released when the lid was removed caused everyone to lean forward and inhale deeply.

"By Allah!" exclaimed Al-Rabí'a, "the very aroma has made me hungrier than I have ever been. O *Inglês*, pray take up your portion without delay so that the rest of us may eat."

These were instructions I had not wanted to receive. "With all respect, sir," I answered, "in England 'tis not customary for the servant to dine before the master."

"Nor is it in Marrocos," said the sheikh, giving me a keen look. "My inflexible rule, however, is for all my food to be tasted by its cook before it is served to me. *Bismillah!* Do I not have as many enemies, wives, children, and relations as there are grains of sand in the desert? *At the narrow passage there is no brother, no friend!* It is not that I distrust you, *Inglês*. It is that I trust no one. Eat."

I took a round of bread from the basket, tore off a piece, and scooped up a mound of rice, which I chewed deliberately, allowing everyone to see it in my mouth. I did the same with the beans and grilled squash and with the chicken baked in a crust of sesame seeds.

Next I had to sample the main dish of kid and hashish. I plucked a bit of meat from the pot, taking care that little liquid adhered to it since I figured the strength of the spice would be in the sauce.

"Have another bite," insisted the sheikh. "Here is a choice tidbit." He wrapped up a large volume of goat and gravy in bread and presented the package to me. I could not decline the offer.

The sheikh permitted some minutes to pass in order to allow me time to display adverse symptoms. Then, assured of my health and of the meal's purity, he led his henchmen in devouring the food before them.

What I did not know was that hashish, when ingested, required time to take effect.

It was also more potent when eaten than when smoked, particularly when leavened with opium.

There was no conversation in the tent, which evidently was a situation so unusual that the camp sentries poked their heads inside to investigate. Seeing the concentration with which their comrades were approaching the meal, and fearing that nothing would be left for them by the end of their shift, they made sure to fill their own bowls before returning to their posts.

This would have been a stroke of good fortune had there been any indication whatsoever that the hashish was having an effect.

But I thought my scheme was stillborn as I watched the Moors consume the kid without noticeable consequence.

Nor did I myself feel any different although I attributed this to the fact that I had taken in little of the sauce compared to Al-Rabi'a and his men, who were spooning it freely over their rice.

While employed at the Jack and Rasher, helping my mother in the back room while my father served beer, cider, and wine out front, I had learned that a kitchen must be flexible in order to oblige the needs of its clientele. Patrons were by nature perverse, fickle, and irritable, and often revised their requirements at a whim. It was a given, for instance, that more guests would always appear at a gathering than the kitchen had been told to expect. Thus a prudent cook, such as I strove to be, must be prepared at all times to feed extra mouths.

There were sixteen gentlemen, soldiers, and servants in the camp. I had made enough food for twenty men.

Even so not even a bit of gristle remained of the *tagine*. A single smear of sauce indicated that the pot had not recently been scoured clean.

Such ravenous gluttony, I discovered, was an effect of the spice. Another was a sort of dreamy melancholy. I found myself staring with great interest at the flame of an oil lamp, amazed by how vivid its color was and by how serenely the fire pulsed around the floating wick.

Al-Rabí'a released a long belch behind a napkin and wiped his beard and mustache with the cloth before reclining against his cushion with a satisfied groan. "There is no god but Allah and Mohammed is his prophet," he declared. "Only because I breathe do I know I have not been transported to paradise. Tell me, *Inglês*, what miracle did you perform to render the kid so delectable? I have not had better in Fez or Marrakesh."

His speech came to me from a great distance. I did not know where I found my own voice since my entire body felt strange and light, as if I had been relieved of half my weight.

"'Tis a matter of balance, do you see?" I answered dreamily. "Sweet must be paired with sour, thus the fig must be matched with verjus, which is the sour juice of grapes—with *husroum*. There must be salt but not too much. Most importantly the spices should be cooked to release their fragrance and added in sufficient quantity to stimulate the palate without overwhelming the natural flavor of the meat. I learned this principle from my own mother, who was a wonderful cook, did you know that, sheikh? She taught me all I know, God rest her soul."

Evidently another effect of the hashish was to make its user long-winded, boring, and overly familiar. Fortunately Al-Rabí'a was himself by this time in good spirits.

"As Allah is my witness, I would kiss the feet of the woman who brought you forth," swore the sheikh. "Nay, I would wash them with my own hands and massage them with oil and dry her toes with soft towels." Although I could not follow the language, I could tell that Al-Rabí'a was having difficulty speaking correctly. The old interpreter, too, was slurring his words.

I leaned so far forward in order to hear properly that I tipped over and sprawled upon the carpet, where I lay giggling while staring up at the tent roof, enrapt by the way the material rippled when a breeze caressed it and by the play of light and shadow upon the felt.

This was when I realized I was in the grip of the hashish.

I had eaten very little but even a little had been enough to make me drunk. Having gorged themselves to repletion, my companions were utterly intoxicated. Many of the men were carrying on animated conversations in loud voices with exaggerated gestures. Not a few were laughing for no apparent reason. Others were already asleep.

No matter how much I wished to close my eyes, however, I knew I must remain awake. My liberty, if not my life, depended on keeping a clear head. So I struggled to concentrate on what I must do.

In mid sentence Sheikh Al-Rabí'a's chin dropped upon his chest. He slumped against the interpreter and they began wheezing in rhythm, beards intertwined, white pressed against black. I pushed myself onto my knees and blearily surveyed the tent. Only two men remained conscious. Neither one paid me any attention as I picked my way through the tangle of slumbering bodies. I was staggering from drunkenness and despite my best efforts I trod on more than one finger during this passage but even so I reached the exit without waking anyone.

In the kitchen tent Selim and Mohammed were sleeping side by side, each with an empty bowl by his hand.

"Shame on you, sir," I chastised Selim with intoxicated indignation while rolling him aside, an arduous task considering the size of my subordinate. "Did I not provide clear orders not to sample the *tagine*? And you, Mohammed," I continued, giving him a mean kick in emphasis, unable to stop myself from talking, perhaps because of the hashish, perhaps because of fear. "You are a vile wretch. But I believe there is one way you may make compensation to me for your rudeness."

First I retrieved my cutlass from his waist and buckled it back on my own. Then I stripped him.

Mohammed's clothes consisted of a leather vest and a broad belt of woven leather strips with a round brass buckle, a cotton shirt, and pair of loose pantaloons. I robbed him of all but his loincloth and his sandals since his feet were smaller than mine. The rest of his garments fit well enough. It was distasteful putting on another man's personal apparel but even in my drunken state I knew I must. Although I would never be mistaken for a Moor upon close inspection, hopefully Mohammed's attire would allow me to pass for one at a distance.

In Barbary, no matter the heat of the day, the temperature dropped dramatically after sunset, and I pulled my *cheche* tighter around my neck against the chill as I slunk through the tents toward the outskirts of the camp. The moon was at half roundness and shed barely enough light to allow me to pick out my path but not enough to prevent me from actually tripping over the sentry who was supposed to be guarding the camels. Thankfully the man had eaten well of the *tagine* and did not wake despite the rough handling I gave him.

The camels were hobbled with short lengths of leather to prevent them from straying. I untied them and slapped each beast on the rump, sending them ambling off in random directions, a tactic that would, I hoped, slow down the Moors who inevitably would be pursuing me, if only by the time required to round up the animals.

I kept for myself the camel I had ridden earlier, which I recognized by the surprised white rings around its eyes. I had treated the beast courteously since John Frye had said camels remembered grudges. I prayed this one would remember a kindness.

"Hello there, you know me, I am Perry, we have met before," I whispered in a soothing voice. "To your knees, that's a good lad. Here is a fine fat fig for you. Why, you are indeed a handsome creature. I believe I will call you Hal, after a friend of mine, since your noses are quite similar both in length and in shape."

I accompanied my words with the clicking noises I had heard the Moors use to control their mounts. I did not know what precisely convinced the camel to obey but to my relief Hal went to his knees and allowed me to bridle him and belt on a saddle, procedures with which I was familiar due to my acquaintance with Barnabas and Chompers on the road to Mortlake. Then Hal stood erect. I turned his head away from the coast and urged him with my heels to proceed south.

Within fifty paces the camp was invisible except for a couple bright spots where torches burned. Soon these, too, vanished from sight.

In the wan light of the half moon the landscape was reduced to a blur of shadow and darker shadow. The night sky was tinged with purple and somewhere far off an owl made a plaintive cry. The wind began to blow, scattering sand across exposed rock with a soft scratching noise.

Never had I felt so alone. I was astride a strange mount in a strange land with enemies at my back and trackless wild before me. That I carried on with my reckless scheme was due in large part, I suspected, to the hashish and opium coursing through my veins rather than to any innate determination of character. But I went forward despite my fears, hoping to put as much distance as possible behind me by daybreak.

As I have mentioned, navigation at sea was a practical art. At night mariners found their way across the dark ocean by using the stars as guides. The foremost of these was known as the North Star, or Polaris, the same star Drake had emblazoned on his cutlery and on the pennants flying above the *Pelican*. Blacollers had pointed out the star to me not a week before, when I brought him a cup of hot cider while he was standing watch on the half deck. "Bless you, lad," the boatswain had said, continuing the maritime education he had threatened to provide when I first came aboard the ship, "do you see the formation known as the Big Dipper? Well, draw a line straight through the two stars of the dipper edge and toward the handle of the Little Dipper. The orb at the end of handle is the one you want. Find it and you will never be lost."

"Why is that, sir?" I asked.

"'Tis because when you are facing Polaris, you are looking toward true north. Thus the other points of the compass become known and you can find your direction. West will be on your left hand and east will be on your right hand. Tell me, lad, where will you find south?"

"At my rear."

"That is perfectly correct. South is through your arse."

In England both the Big Dipper and its smaller companion were positioned fairly well up in the sky but in Barbary they were almost flat against the horizon. It was impossible to keep to a straight course due to natural obstacles such as gullies, boulders, and dunes of sand too steep to cross. Even though I had traveled at least a league by sunrise, which was January 1st, 1578, the morning of New Year's Day, I doubted more than half of that distance was in a clear line.

This worried me since I had hoped to be farther from the sheikh and his men, who would be waking soon, if they were not already up and wondering where I was. I was also becoming sober and losing the confidence that had sustained me through the harrowing night.

Eventually the sky paled so much that the stars faded into the background wash of light. For a while Hal and I traversed a plain of gravel and sand and then several miles of broken rock interspersed with deep fissures. Next the landscape softened into a succession of low hills covered with dry brown grass and dotted with curious twisted trees with long branches. In several of these perched goats, a half dozen balancing on a single limb and munching contentedly on the foliage, as if they were a flock of birds. This meant there were shepherds nearby and from that point forward I tried to keep an eye out on both sides as well as over my shoulder. Unhappily, my vigilance was rewarded when I spied a man lying beside the remains of a fire not a hundred yards off my course. I would have continued past without rousing him except his dogs noticed my presence and began barking.

Fighting the natural impulse to slink down in the saddle and hurry on by, I instead sat upright and waved broadly while calling:

"*Assalamu alaikum.*"

Luckily distance swallowed the flaws in my pronunciation and the shepherd returned my greeting before settling back in his blanket.

Soon after dawn the temperature had climbed high enough that I began to sweat despite the wind. I also was becoming increasingly nervous at being out in the open. The sky was now a cloudless blue and the air was so pure that I knew I could be seen for miles.

I reined in Hal at the next gully sufficiently deep to

hide us and fed him half a skin of water before hobbling him and turning him loose to graze. Then I climbed to the top of the ridge and peered through the scrub back the way we had come. That I saw nothing unusual was not reassuring. I knew Sheikh Al-Rabí'a would be relentless in his effort to recapture me and regain my services. The real question was whether my simple ruse had deceived him into believing that I had taken the direct route to Mogador. This worry and others kept me awake almost until noon but ultimately fatigue overcame me and I fell asleep until nightfall.

I set out again when the North Star rose above the horizon, covering what I estimated to be six miles by midnight, when I decided it was safe to change direction and head toward the shore.

According to the sailors aboard the *Pelican* with African experience, for the next fifty leagues the fleet would have to follow the coastline almost within hailing distance in order to evade contrary winds and so as to more easily put in at welcoming ports and trade for victuals. If I were to have any chance, however slim, of rejoining the adventure, I would have to move quickly since the fleet would be now at least a day's sail from Mogador. Giving Hal an encouraging tap with the stirrups, I set him plodding somewhat faster through the night.

By morning I could hear the pounding of surf although the beach was hidden from view by a barrier of sand fifty feet high. Hal's paws slipped among the loose stuff but he kept his footing and ultimately carried me to the peak of the dune.

In the clear air I could see all the way to Mogador, more than fifteen miles. I could even make out a white line of breakers against the black island where the fleet had anchored. Now the moorage was vacant.

In the other direction, however, and almost equally far distant, I saw white sails upon the water.

For the first time I began to believe my desperate effort could succeed and I allowed myself to hope I would not be living the days of my life in captivity as a Moor.

Not that the path ahead was free of obstacles. Far from it. First I must overtake the ships, which meant hard riding, perhaps several days in the saddle, depending on whether the wind was with the fleet or against it. Then I had to devise some means to signal to my companions from shore so they would send a boat to retrieve me. Or perhaps I could sail out to them. There were sure to be fishermen along the coast. I should have no trouble bartering Hal for passage once I no longer required his services.

With these pleasant calculations filling my thoughts, I flicked the reins and began looking for a way down to the beach.

Than an awful yipping split the air. A man on camel back, brandishing a sword, came racing toward me from out of the ocean of sand. I could not mistake my pursuer.

It was Mohammed.

Temptation on the White Cape

January 2, 1578 – January 17, 1578
Cape Blanco

The vengeful Moor came at me with maddened speed, sand erupting into the air around the paws of his racing camel. My own mount, however, did not appreciate the urgency of the situation. It required several kicks to prod Hal into a reluctant trot.

"Faster!" I told him, emphasizing the command with a thwack of the reins. "You can do better, you great misbegotten beast!"

Ultimately Hal actually began to gallop but by then it was too late to outrun Mohammed. I glanced over my shoulder and saw I was sure to be overtaken and that violence was inevitable. From the fury twisting the face of my pursuer, it was plain Mohammed did not have orders to return me alive to Sheikh Al-Rabí'a or else was determined to disobey any such instructions. In either case I knew I must defend myself and I looked around desperately for some advantage, no matter how slight.

To my right the crest of the dune broke into a gentle slope to the beach while in the other direction there was an abutment of rock.

Here the footing was more difficult. Chips of stone and gravel shot from beneath Hal's paws, creating avalanches of loose grit. Then the edge crumbled away into a ravine with a thin stream at its bottom. There would be no going forward.

I drew my cutlass and raised it just in time to deflect the vicious slash Mohammed aimed at my head. Without thinking, as Thomas Doughty had taught during military exercises aboard the *Pelican*, I hacked back at my opponent, forcing him to retreat.

Then Mohammed unsheathed a dagger and, in a display of ominous dexterity, came at me with a weapon in each fist.

"*Die infiel cão!*" he swore, an expression I would have understood even had I not been somewhat conversant in Portuguese. But "*Eu irão alimentar o seu fígado e seus olhos para os suínos*" was too difficult to translate in the heat of the moment although I knew it was a threat and that the phrase had something to do with livers, eyes, and pigs.

Mohammed slashed with his sword, targeting my neck. I beat the blade out of line and cut down at his left hand, causing him to drop the dagger.

This tactic provided me additional seconds of life.

I had to use them well.

Our brief exchange of swordplay had proven Mohammed to be a veteran murderer. It was inevitable that I would die under his blade if we continued at close quarters.

When hard pressed by the Spanish lieutenant at San Juan de Ulua, Pascoe Goddy had slain his attacker with a pistol. I did not have a gun.

With my free hand I groped blindly in the saddlebag for something to throw. My fingers closed upon a jar of olive oil stoppered with cork.

Mohammed was almost upon me. "Take this, you bastard," I cursed, heaving the jar with all my strength and catching him full in the chest. To my dismay, however, the impact did him no harm. He shrugged off the projectile as you might ignore a fly and went on the offensive, forcing me to defend myself with utter concentration against a flurry of steel. Thus I did not notice the jar shatter beneath the paws of his camel, spilling the oil and making the footing so slick that not even so nimble a creature could maintain its balance.

With a startled bray the camel began slipping backward over the cliff, forcing Mohammed to release his sword so that he could hold on.

The camel began screaming in earnest while scrabbling for purchase with its forelegs, spraying dirt everywhere. In an incredible display of agility, Mohammed got both feet under himself and perched upright on the saddle, so that he could use it as a platform from which to spring to safety. But in another instant the camel carried him over the edge.

The animal cried until it hit the ground. Mohammed made no sound during his own descent.

I remained astride Hal awhile longer to get my wind back and to allow my heart an opportunity to stop galloping.

Then I sank to my knees and thanked God. It was evident to me that my own abilities, by even the most generous estimate, were inadequate to account for the fact I was still alive. Nothing less than divine intervention could explain how I had survived such a perilous encounter and how I had overcome such an implacable opponent.

Finally I crossed myself and inched cautiously to the verge and peered down.

The camel had shattered its spine upon the rocks below. Mohammed was hanging by his fingers from a ledge only inches wide.

"God's blood!" I swore, almost losing my own footing as I went for my cutlass. "What the devil are you doing there?"

Mohammed did not answer. He had enough strength to hold on and nothing to spare.

From the look in his eyes it was clear he expected me to cut his hands or wrists and send him to his death. Instead I sheathed the cutlass and squatted as close to the edge as I dared.

The ledge from which Mohammed hung by bloody fingertips was a foot beneath me. I could see the strain in his forearms as he fought to maintain his grip. It would not be long before he fell.

"Look, you," I told him, "I did not ask for an enemy but you made yourself mine. By all rights I should leave you to your business and be done with you. God bless Lackland, the poor bastard, he would be shaking his head in disgust right now and calling me a fool, but I cannot just let you die. Take my hand before I change my mind. *Take it!*"

The hopelessness left Mohammed's eyes when he saw I meant to help. I could not imagine how he summoned the courage and trust required to let go of the ledge and to catch hold of the hand I offered.

"Come on now," I said, returning his grip with all my might, "a single good heave and the job is finished. On my mark."

Mohammed may not have understood English but he followed my meaning and scrambled upward when I pulled. For a terrible instant I thought his weight would bring me down with him but then our combined effort succeeded in getting his head over the verge, and then his shoulders. He froze in this position, part above and part below the brink, until I seized his other arm and dragged him the rest of the way.

The struggle left us both spent and we lay side by side for some time while regaining our breath.

"God's truth," I said when I could speak, "that was certainly a—" I searched for a word to describe what I had experienced but could not find one. Finally I had to settle for an expression of my own devising. "God's truth," I repeated, "that was a bloody *ledge-hanger.*"

Eventually I regained the strength to stand. Instead of getting to his feet, however, Mohammed knelt and placed his head under my foot while repeating what sounded like a ritual phrase. Attempting to explain, he said in Portuguese: "*Você salvou a minha vida. Eu sou seu servo.*"

You saved my life. I am your servant.

"Nonsense," I answered, removing my leg from his embrace and assisting him upright. "Do not forget you rescued me from the viper," I went on. "That surely would have been my end, no question. So we are quits, do you hear? One deed cancels the other. You are not my servant. You owe me nothing."

Then an idea occurred to me. I faced Mohammed squarely and said, "But if you would grant me a favor, as a friend, I would not refuse. Help me rejoin my companions. *Ajude-me a alcançar meus amigos. Lá fora.*"

I accompanied my request with gestures toward the sails of the fleet. To my relief the ships had not yet reached the southern horizon. It was apparent they were fighting the wind and making slow headway.

Mohammed nodded in comprehension. "*Temos pressa. O xeque e os seus homens não estão muito distantes.*"

The sheikh was five miles behind us. Perhaps less.

"Then let us be off quickly, sir," I told him. "I do not enjoy thinking about the welcome I will receive from Al-Rabí'a should we meet again."

It soon became obvious why Mohammed had caught up with me so readily. I was, of course, woefully ignorant of woodcraft due to having been born and raised in Plymouth, a modern city. Although I thought I had been careful to hide my tracks, I had actually left a trail behind me as plain as writing upon a page and as simple to read. Mohammed, however, was a professional ranger. He was also familiar with the area and took us by a devious and roundabout route away from the ocean and then south once more and parallel to the water. For the entire course Hal's paws rarely touched sand since Mohammed was particular about keeping to rock and hard ground. On occasion we proceeded at a walk so he could sweep behind us for several score yards. He also picked a type of nettle we came upon, crushed the bulbs carefully between stones, and scattered the thorns along our path as a deterrent to dogs.

These measures succeeded in that we returned to the shore the next morning without ever having caught sight of Sheikh Al-Rabí'a and his men. I did not doubt, however, that I would have been recaptured without Mohammed as a protector.

The sun had risen above the mountains behind us when we arrived at the beach. It was impossible to see any great distance in the dawn haze and I could not make out any trace of the fleet.

This was because I was looking in the wrong direction.

We had managed good speed despite our efforts at stealth and had gone ahead of the ships by several miles. I saw them when I looked north. Their sails were high enough to catch the first light of the new day, which made brilliant the scarlet crosses centered in the top canvas. As I watched, the fleet changed direction in unison, a maneuver known as *tacking*, by which they were able to proceed slowly forward despite the wind coming against them.

Mohammed drew my attention away from the distant ships to an ancient single masted boat pulled up on the sand not far from us. Her owners, three scrawny men wearing only loincloths and head scarves, were loading the decrepit vessel with nets, poles, baskets of bait, and other items of fishing gear. They stopped their work when we approached and touched their foreheads in greeting. Despite their simple dress, however, these men were sharpers rather than simpletons, and they drove a hard bargain for taxiing me out to the *Pelican*, profusely calling on Allah to witness the justice of their extortionate demands while tearing at their beards to underscore their sincerity. Although they first demanded Hal in payment for their services, Mohammed eventually haggled them down and they settled for the sack of victuals I had stolen.

"*Bismillah!*" Mohammed said and spat on the ground. "These dogs are thieves and pirates, *Inglés*. They will cut your throat when you are out of sight. I have told them one must remain behind as a pledge for your safety. Send back to me proof you were delivered without harm." He glowered at the

man who was to stay, and said, "*Vou matar esse cachorro lenta-
mente deverão prejudicar você.*"

I will kill this dog slowly should they injure you.

"Let us pray that will not be necessary," I replied. Then
I said, "The sheikh will not be happy should he learn you gave
me aid, Mohammed. Come with me to the *Pelican*. General
Drake will welcome a good man to the crew, particularly when
I explain the situation, I am certain of it."

"Allah forbid! I am no sailor, *Inglês*. No, I will return to
my tribe and Al-Rabí'a will never trouble me. Many months
have passed since I have seen my flock and my wives and both
are lonely for my attention."

Mohammed clasped my shoulders and held me at arm's
length. "I will remember your kindness," he said. "Tell me your
name so I may bestow it upon my next male child."

"I am Perry—Peregrine James," I answered.

"Peregrine James bin Mohammed bin Khalid Al-Fulan.
This is what I will name my son."

"It is a good name," I said, touched by the sentiment.
"Aye, it is a fine name! Peregrine James bin Mohammed. I am
honored."

Only now did Mohammed release me. "*Assalamu alaikum, Inglês*," he said while helping me over the gunwale into
the old fishing boat.

"Peace be on you, too," I answered.

The two fishermen rowed through the breakers but
brought their oars inboard once we were past the waves and
hoisted canvas to catch the wind. The water was choppy and
there were scattered whitecaps and the small boat had to fight

to make headway, her triangular sail bent in a deep bulge and the port gunwale tipped almost to the waterline. Slop spilled into the boat and I bailed steadily to prevent us from flooding.

It felt strange to have hope once more and to look forward to freedom instead of servitude.

I thought I had resigned myself to living in a strange land as a slave to a foreign master. As we approached the *Pelican*, however, a burden of a thousand pounds lifted from me. The ship had become my home during my months aboard her and I had feared I would never see her again nor enjoy the fellowship of my companions. Perhaps it was a measure of my relief that I was happily anticipating renewing my acquaintanceship with Lancelot Garget and enduring his grumbling and his boiled beef.

Taking up a strip of white canvas, I waved it in an attempt to draw attention to myself.

"Hello! Hello!" I cried with all my voice. "Come on, you see me!"

Leading the fleet was a vessel I did not know. She was the length of the *Benedict* but lower to the water. It was not until she had closed to within a hundred yards that I realized this was the pinnace that had been under construction on the black island off Mogador when I was kidnapped by the sheikh. Now she was armed with a brass bowchaser—a small cannon pointing forward. She was also outfitted with breach-loading mankillers mounted on swivels.

I saw a burst of black smoke explode from the starboard gun before I heard the report. A half dozen irregular holes appeared in the sail above my head. The mankillers were loaded with pebble or iron scrap.

The two fishermen dove for the bilge. I waved the white canvas even more frantically. "Hey, there," I yelled. "Do you not have eyes? It is Perry James! I have returned!"

Another warning shot drowned out my words. This one was aimed lower than the first.

"Heave to, you scum, or you will receive the next in your guts," called the gunner behind the mankiller. "Strike your damn sail!"

Someone threw over a grappling hook and drew the vessels together until their hulls touched.

Then the captain stepped across the gunwale with a hanger in his hand. This was John Winter, who usually commanded the *Elizabeth*.

A decade younger than either Drake or Doughty, Winter was the son of George Winter, clerk to the royal navy, as well as the nephew of Sir William Winter, surveyor of the Queen's ships. Not unnaturally, many of the crew believed he owed his captaincy to familial connections. Unlike the other gentlemen accompanying the expedition, however, most of whom had never left England before, Winter had put to sea as a boy and had worked as an ordinary sailor for many years. That he had been placed in charge of the pinnace was proof of Drake's confidence in him. Sailing at the head of the fleet, the small vessel would be first to encounter an enemy ship and to engage in military action.

Like his sailors Winter was wearing padded leather armor and an iron helmet with a sharp brim, which could be used as a weapon to slash an enemy in close combat. He did not recognize me.

"How dare you bastards approach an English ship!" he snapped, putting the tip of the hanger to my throat while I backed away with my hands in the air. "What are you damned pirates up to? Speak, you black devil. You have until the count of ten. Two. Three. Four—"

The attack startled me and it was not until Winter reached the number nine that I finally found my voice.

"We are not pirates, sir," I protested. "Look around and you will discover little except spoiled herring and even more rotten mackerel. My companions are fishermen and I am Perry James from the *Pelican*. Now could you remove your point from my neck before I am cut?"

Winter reluctantly allowed the sword to drop. "All fishermen are naught but pirates who lack opportunity," he muttered, agreeing with Mohammed's earlier observation. Then he gave me a hard stare. "You are the cook from the landing party that was attacked in Mogador," he said. "We have met before."

"Aye, sir."

"I hardly recognize you," Winter said. "You are as dark as a Moor and dressed like one to the hilt. Your mother herself would not know you as an Englishman."

"It was a necessary disguise, sir," I replied. "I was being pursued."

Borrowing a penny from one of the crew, I gave the English coin to the fishermen as a token to prove my safe delivery to Mohammed so he would release their companion who was hostage on the beach. Then I accompanied Winter in a longboat to the flagship. Francis Drake and Thomas Doughty were on the half deck by the mizzenmast. Several other gentlemen were sitting on stools in the shade of the canvas while Parson Fletcher, as usual, paced back and forth across the beam of the ship, his black canvas coat flapping around his calves. Diego, the Cimarron, stood behind Drake. His face was impassive but his eyes never left mine. I could not decide whether he suspected who I was.

"What is it, Mr. Winter?" asked Drake. "Why was this man not released with his boat?"

"This is no ordinary Moor, general. Take another look."

It required several more seconds of study before Drake knew me. "God's blood!" he swore. "'Tis young Perry James! Do you see, Tom?"

"I will be damned."

"Aye, who could misread such sweet features even under so much grime! Not to mention the peculiar headdress and heathen costume. Where have you been, lad? We thought you were lost to us."

"It is a long story, general. I will provide every detail but first I must beg of you something for my thirst. Barbary is a dry place."

"By God, I bet it is!" declared Drake. "Blacollers!"

"Aye, general," the boatswain replied from the waist.

"Beer for all hands. We are celebrating, do you hear? Our mislaid sheep has come back to the fold."

I followed Drake into the grand cabin and was told to sit at the end of the table opposite him and his captains. A boy brought in refreshments and I drank a pint of beer before finishing what I had to say. "There is not much more to tell," I ended, placing the mug on the oak table and straightening in my chair. "With Mohammed for a guide I was able to reach the coast, where I hired a boat. You know the rest."

For a moment no one spoke. Then Drake threw back his head and laughed with the same exuberance he had displayed at the Plymouth whipping post upon hearing my request to join his crew. "God damn me!" he roared and slammed both fists on the tabletop while rising to his feet. "Did you hear, Tom? What we had was a failure to communicate. The entire affair was naught but a misunderstanding. This Moor captain—what was his name?"

"Sheikh Al-Rabí'a."

"This sheikh was actually our comrade. Any foe of Lisbon is a good friend of mine, by God! The Portuguese king Sebastião is the worst of Papists. Tom, you are the university man here. What is the saying the Moors have? Tis on my tongue but I cannot recall it."

"*The enemy of my enemy is my friend,*" Doughty quoted.

"Aye, the very proverb I meant. And damned appropriate, too!"

Once again I was struck by the dissimilarity of the two captains. Drake was compact and swaggered with energy in the plain leather jerkin of a common mariner while the taller Doughty moved with languid calculation and dressed in style even though we were a thousand miles from England. I did not understand how such opposite men could be friends but they seemed to suit one another.

Perhaps, I thought, they worked together well precisely because they were so different. Each had qualities the other lacked.

"What do you think happened to the other sailor?" asked Winter. He had tilted his mug far back to drain it and soaked the bottom of his mustache with foam.

"I do not know, sir," I answered. "Frye left the encampment ahead of me and we saw no more of one another. I am afraid he encountered some misfortune on the way back to the coast."

"More likely the fellow had second thoughts about rejoining our adventure," said Doughty. "Did not Mr. Frye have a gift of gold from the sheikh and the promise of a free ticket home if he missed the fleet?"

"Aye, sir."

"Exactly. You have proven my point."

"God's blood, I pray you are right, Tom," Drake swore. "Let us hope the lucky bastard is returning to England a wealthy man even as we speak. As may we all, every gentleman and sailor, and even the worst boy here!" Then Drake pushed away his chair and came around the table. I stood hastily.

Our general was not a tall man nor was his hand large but he had the same iron strength Blacollers possessed. Exposure to sun during the voyage had tanned Drake's skin the dark red of a ripe apple while brightening the gold in his beard. His eyes were the piercing blue I remembered, round and ringed with white.

"Welcome back aboard the *Pelican*, Mr. James," he told me. "We are glad to have you with us again."

These were simple words. They would have meant little coming from another man. But Drake did not give compliments idly.

"Thank you, sir," I replied, speaking carefully so as to not seem foolish by stammering. "To be honest, I do not think

I would have made a good Moor. There is no doubt I would have tired of cooking goat, which is their favorite meat. They also take inappropriate liberties with an area of the male body that should not be touched by a knife. Aye, captain, let me say I am very glad to be back myself."

At that moment all I wished for was to wash Barbary off my skin and to find my pallet and sleep until morning. This was not to be, however, since the other sailors wanted to hear about my experiences, even Lancelot Garget. "Why, is it not pretty boy," he observed when I passed the fire box on my way below. Pushing the sweat sodden brim of his wool cap up his forehead, Garget regarded me with a quizzical expression while rubbing his chin between thumb and forefinger. "Frankly, I did not expect to see you again," he continued. "What happened? Did you tire of buggery? Or did the Moors tire of you?"

Pleased by his own humor, Garget was beset by a bout of thin laughter. Peter Corder, who had overheard him, said:

"For Christ's sake, Lance. Quit picking at the lad. Your needling is neither necessary nor kind."

Garget was not abashed by the reprimand. "If I were you, Corder," he replied, "I would look carefully at what I put in my mouth. There is no accounting for what falls accidently into the pot."

"With you cooking, offal might be the healthier choice. Come, Perry," Corder went on, "better company waits below."

For the next several hours I was plied with drink while I repeated my story and answered a hundred questions. By the time I satisfied the curiosity of the last man, I had taken aboard so much beer that I needed assistance getting from my seat. Peter Corder hefted my left arm over his shoulders and Pascoe Goddy did the same with my right arm and together they steered me to my place among the dried peas. The cotton roll stuffed with straw that was my bed was where I had left it but not the canvas bag given to me by Hal Audley.

This contained almost everything I owned.

"Where are my belongings?" I mumbled, shaking free of my companions and throwing open my bedroll although it was plain nothing was hidden inside. "What has been done with them?"

"Calm yourself," said Goddy. "No need to become excited."

"Aye, Perry," agreed Corder. "I am sure everything will be replaced none the worse for wear."

"What do you mean, sir?" I asked. There was no question the drink had slowed my wits.

"It was like this. You told us yourself you lack living family so we shared out your property among your friends. It was only fair since everyone desired a memento to remember you by."

"I myself have one of your shirts, Perry," said Pascoe Goddy. "'Tis a bit tight but I vowed to wear it in your honor no matter the discomfort."

"That was indeed generous of you. But I think you might have waited somewhat longer before giving me up for lost."

"What were the chances you would return?" Corder asked. He lifted a pail with his toes and spat into it. "That much."

Even my unhappiness with the situation could not keep me up and I fell asleep almost instantly. When I awoke just past daybreak, my mouth was dry and my head hurt. How many toasts had I given and received? I could not remember although I was certain of a dozen. Vowing never to drink so deeply again no matter the celebration, I took firm hold of a barrel and pulled myself to my knees and staggered erect.

My sea bag was once more on its peg in the bulkhead. All my clothing, too, had been returned, if not folded properly.

Going forward so I could have privacy in the shadow of the forecastle, I dropped a bucket over the side, hauled up seawater, and scrubbed with brine until I was free of the last grain of sand encrusting me. Then I rinsed with fresh water, dried myself, and dressed in my own clothes for the first time since I had stolen Mohammed's garments while he slept under the influence of the kid *tagine* infused with hashish.

These ablutions cleared my head and I felt somewhat less ill.

Not a minute later I felt a bite on my buttock. The next was under my arm. The third was just above my ankle.

After that I stopped counting.

Fleas.

"Some kind bastard has gifted me with vermin," I complained, rubbing at the most irritating spot, which was next to my navel.

"We all are infested," agreed Rich Joyner, the carpenter whose tools I had borrowed to discover the spoiled victuals provided by James Stydye. At some point in his woodworking career Joyner had lost the thumb and first finger of his right hand but this did not prevent him from vigorously employing the remaining three to scratch his own itches. "No one is free of the affliction," he went on. Then he exclaimed:

"I have the knave!"

Pinned between Joyner's pinky and the next finger was a wriggling black dot, which he deposited over the side with great care. "The mites are hard to crack and might escape to bedevil us another time," he explained. "Drowning is the more certain death."

"I will keep that in mind," I replied, digging again at my stomach. Then I forgot the throbbing in my head and my fleas when I saw on the horizon a mountain with an entire upper face as pure white as the belly of a salmon, the eastern flank luminous in the dawn. A veil of clouds streamed around the summit like the finery of a rich woman.

"Is that snow?" I said out loud. "I would think the stuff would melt, considering Barbary's heat. Yet what else could it be?"

"It is indeed snow, my son," answered Francis Fletcher. With his habitual economy of motion, the parson had joined me at the railing without advertising his arrival. As he pointed to the distant spire, his black sleeve slipped upward to reveal a shirt cuff that had been darned many times with thread of different colors. "The Lord has seen fit to raise the mountain peak into the cold region," Fletcher explained, "so the reflection of the sun never comes to it from the face of the earth. This permits frozen matter to accumulate rather than dissolve, even in summer. Enterprising merchants mine the snow for profit and sell it in the markets of Barbary, where the Moors mix it with drink to prevent bodily contagion since a steady diet of hot liquids is unhealthy. I have encountered the same practice in Seville, where the weather is equally warm, and in Russia, which is cold in winter but oppressive in summer."

"Is there no place you have not visited, sir?" I asked.

The parson allowed himself a grim smile. "The world is wide, Peregrine James. A man could travel ten times more than I have and still not have seen one tenth of God's creations, nor brought His word to the least part of those in need of hearing it."

My next destination was the waist of the ship, where I would begin the routine expected of me by Lancelot Garget. To my confusion, however, I discovered the cooking box already winched on deck and one of the ship's boys listlessly stirring the porridge while gazing in another direction. Lancelot Garget was prying meat out of a barrel with a metal fork and dropping the pieces into a tub of water, beginning the process of shifting, which would rid the flesh of salt and make it palatable.

"Why are you sniffing around, pretty boy?" Garget asked. "I warn you, do not think to presume on our relationship, which was never cordial. I will neither serve you early nor provide you with a portion larger than the next man's, no matter how you plead for favor."

"I do not want your favor, sir," I replied, "nor do I care for your porridge, which the lad appears to be singeing. I am here as usual, Mr. Garget, to be your servant."

"Have you not heard, pretty boy? You have been relieved of that duty, thanks be to God. Report to the general for instruction, and good riddance to you, that is what I say. At least Horsewill lacks the wit to be contrary. Horsewill! Horsewill! The devil condemn you to misery, you ugly whelp, stir the pot with vigor. Must I do everything myself?"

Despite its size the main cabin felt as cramped as the gun

deck since it was shared by a dozen men and cluttered with their belongings. Due to the earliness of the hour most of the gentlemen were still asleep. Leonard Vicarye, the lawyer, lay wrapped in a blanket on the grand table while Diego, the Cimarron, slept beneath it, his head pillowed on his boots. Three men had rigged hammocks for themselves while the remainder of the company lay on the planking wherever there was space.

The door to Drake's private chamber was open and through it I saw him shaving before a round mirror hung from a peg in the starboard bulkhead. Squinting into his reflection, he drew a razor against his skin and carefully scraped away soap and hair in an outline around his beard, wiping the blade clean on a towel after each stroke. Then he dried his face, combed his golden sideburns with his fingers, and gave his image a last inspection before coming into the main cabin.

"There you are, lad," Drake said in a low voice. "Let us go where our conversation will not disturb the others."

I followed him onto the exterior balcony that was built out from the stern of the ship. This was an exclusive area reserved for officers and gentlemen. The narrow walkway was a man's height above the water and protected from rain by ornate eaves. At intervals were benches with cut-outs that allowed for the completion of the natural functions common sailors performed at the head of a vessel or into buckets.

Drake took the railing with both hands and sucked a deep breath into his lungs with relish. "Damn my eyes, that tastes good!" he exclaimed. "There is an overabundance of farting down below during the watches of the night. After a supper of salt pork and beans, gentlemen stink no less than ordinary seamen."

Then Drake regarded me soberly. "God's truth, Perry James," he continued in a more serious voice, "I thought little of you when we first met in Plymouth but it has become clear that you are a brave and resourceful boy! I did not imagine we would meet again once you were taken captive by the Moors, yet here you are, returned from Barbary."

"The lord indeed showed me mercy!" I admitted, attempting to meet his look with a blank expression so as not to betray the delight I felt at the compliment. "I also relied on the tenderness of strangers."

"Even so, I am impressed!" Drake went on. "You have courage, Perry, and ingenuity, which are both fine qualities. I need sharp fellows in my crew, by God! A captain is not well served by fools."

He took my shoulders in his grip and stared directly in my eyes. Although Drake was not a tall man I was unconscious of having to look downward to meet his gaze.

"Aye, you have the makings of a true sea dog after my own heart," he continued. "This is why I have decided to send you to the pinnace commanded by Captain Winter. She will be the first ship of the fleet to see action. You will receive a valuable education aboard her under fire and become of better use to yourself and to me."

Flattered by my superior's appraisal while at the same time unsettled by the prospect of being thrust to the forefront of danger, I said, "With respect, sir, I am a cook, not a fighter."

"And you will be a cook again, never fear! For now, however, you are to be apprenticed to a more bloody trade."

Drake turned me so that I looked away from the *Pelican* toward the open sea. Standing at my back, he spoke into my ear while we stared into the distance together. "The worst threat to an expedition such as ours, Mr. James, is not foul weather nor shoal water," he said quietly. "Nor is it scurvy or rotten victuals. No, lad, upon the deep it is mutiny that must be feared above all other dangers."

"Mutiny," I repeated, disliking the very sound of the word.

"I can tell you no more about our charter than I have already said publicly," Drake continued, "but given the stakes of our adventure, treachery is certain. Damn him to hell, James Stydye was not the only traitor among us! There are sure to be others, creatures of the queen's enemies or agents of the Spanish or Portuguese. These dogs are biding their time but we will hear from them sooner or later, perhaps before we begin the Atlantic passage, while we are in the Cape Verdes. At the brink of the abyss morale will be at an ebb. Sailors and gentlemen alike will be second guessing their commitment to our voyage. This will be the moment when turncoats and cowards announce themselves."

Appalled by the idea that any of the crew, much less any of those who had become my friends, would connive against the rest of us and seek our ruin, I asked, "Why are you telling me this, sir?"

"I must have honest men on each ship in the event of treason. I need to know I can count on you, Perry James. I need to know you are prepared to defend my authority."

"Aye, I am, my word on it!" I said at once. "You are my

master, sir, and I owe you respect and obedience! Nor can I forget your kindness. Did you not take me into your adventure even though I had fresh stripes on my back? I am in your debt, General Drake, now and always."

He gave a bark of amused laughter. "Gratitude is the most transient of emotions," he said. "Still, Perry, I do not doubt you."

Once again Drake turned me around, so that we faced one another. For long seconds I was forced to suffer his scrutiny while he weighed my character and decided whether I was trustworthy. Finally he said, "How could I not love such an honest boy? Hear me, Perry James, I will remember your loyalty when the time comes to calculate our profits! Aye, and these will not be insignificant, I swear it! Now get yourself to the pinnace, where Captain Winter is expecting you. Say nothing of our conversation to anyone. Let me hear good report of your efforts."

Drake, of course, understood me as well as he could understand a broadsheet printed in plain English and spread open along every crease. With a little flattery, some vague talk of peril, and some equally vague promises, all of which cost him very little, he had ensured my absolute fidelity and commitment. Once again I foolishly imagined myself to be a player in larger schemes, a vital participant in the adventure, and I was determined to do my utmost to make Drake proud of his belief in me. At the end of this conversation my head was so swollen by vanity and inflated self esteem that I never stopped to remember the hard lesson I had learned on the road to Mortlake and in the shallows of Mogador.

Among Francis Drake's crew, it was dangerous to be both insignificant and expendable.

After going below to fetch my sea bag, I claimed a seat on the longboat that served as a courier for the fleet, ferrying men, supplies, and documents from ship to ship. The pinnace was the next stop after the *Elizabeth* and the *Marigold*. When I disembarked from the longboat, John Winter was standing with the helmsman at the tiller, which was a shaft of oak with one end carved to resemble a clenched fist. Despite the heat Winter wore armor, as did the other sailors. There was a pike every yard along the railing and piles of arquebuses and muskets on the deck. Fire pots smoldered beside the bowchaser and the mankiller, ready to ignite the powder in the cannons.

"You are not quite the heathen you were yesterday," Winter remarked. "Still, I would not easily think you an Englishman."

"I am from Plymouth, sir," I said, "as were my father and his father before him. Is this sufficient pedigree or do you require further detail?"

"What I require of you, Mr. James, is service and attention. Drake has ordered that you are to be made into a fighter, only God knows why, since your history is not inspiring. The stench still lingers in my nose from the table you set in Plymouth."

Plainly John Winter considered me either simple, ignorant, inept, or avaricious. "In any case," he went on, "I will do as the general asks or you will die trying." Then, raising his voice, he called, "Pascoe Goddy!"

"Aye, sir."

Apparently Pascoe, too, had been drafted from the *Pelican* to serve aboard the pinnace. As usual he was passing the time by tying a complicated knot, this one in the shape of a star burst. After putting it down delicately so that the weave would not unravel, he shambled to the stern and touched his forehead before Winter in a gesture that was more a casual greeting than the proper salute due an officer. This slight was not lost to Winter and he gave Goddy a stern frown.

"We know how to rid a man of insolence in the royal navy," he observed. "The lash cures all ailments, including disrespect."

"Aye, sir! No doubt, sir!" Pascoe replied. "You have pointed out the very reason I have never myself enlisted in the queen's service! Ordinary men are not so easily abused aboard merchant vessels and privateers."

"Jesus save me, you are a rude dog," Winter said with exasperation. "Still, rumor has it you are as murderous as you are impolite. I am giving the lad here into your charge. If it is at all possible, keep him alive. Be assured, though, I will not blame you if you fail."

"Perry is a ready fellow, sir!" Goddy said briskly to Winter. "We will make a man of him, never fear." Then he addressed me. "Arm yourself at once," he instructed. "The Spanish are known to frequent these parts. We are entering dangerous territory."

Although the fleet had fought contrary weather for days, now the wind turned and propelled the ships southwest over a calm sea that was more green than blue. The coastline consisted of wide beaches bordered by sand hills, behind which were slopes covered with scrub. We remained several miles offshore to avoid shoals, the pinnace at the point of the procession, prepared to intercept approaching vessels.

By afternoon we were nearing *Cap de Guerre,* the Cape of War.

This was a broad hump of terrain against which the

waves seemed to crash with particular vehemence. Even from afar I could see foam and spray burst into the air from the surf while a flock of gulls wheeled overhead and fed on baitfish stunned by the breakers.

"Aye, I recollect this place," mused Pascoe Goddy. Perhaps remembering the ill fated expedition with John Hawkins, he absently reached under his long gray hair to stroke the ear he no longer possessed. "There is a reef on the north shore so we will soon be veering to avoid the rocks," Goddy predicted. "Ah, here we go."

The helmsman steered wide to round the point. When we came to the other side, three vessels became visible in the shoal water in the lee of the land. John Winter called out:

"Stations, gentlemen! Ready the bowchaser and mankillers. Prime your arquebuses but do not fire without my word."

Like the other sailors I was wearing a padded leather vest reinforced with steel plates. My helmet was a steel bowl with a chin strap and internal stuffing meant to reduce the force of a blow to the head.

Gripping the hilt of my cutlass, I realized the sword no longer felt strange in my hand. I had used the weapon before.

Goddy yawned and returned to his seat on the planking. "You might as well sit down, Perry," he instructed. "There will be no excitement today. Those are naught but *canteras*. Fishing boats."

He was correct in this identification but even so we continued forward. Canteras were single masted vessels, each carrying two or three men. Their sails were quilted with irregular patches of canvas and it was apparent the boats were neither new nor well maintained. Their crews had been fishing with angles and bait in the calm water but they wound in their lines as we neared them. Several sailors climbed into the rigging to get a better look at us while their companions waved heartily and called: "*Hola, señores! ¿Quién eres y dónde eres? ¿Adónde vas?*"

"'Tis God damned Spanish, what else?" growled Winter. "Mr. James! You speak the language."

"Aye, captain."

"Tell these pirates to lay down their weapons and prepare to be boarded. Promise them blood if there is trouble."

Winter, it appeared, held fishermen of all nationalities in low esteem. I replaced my cutlass at my waist and cupped my hands around my mouth to propel my voice across the intervening water.

"*Somos un buque Inglés,*" I called. "*Pon tus armas. Preparar a bordo. Al dolor de la muerte, no resistir.*"

"But we have no weapons, *Inglés,*" replied the fishermen, "just gaffs and small knives for filleting our catch."

"Let the captain see you put down the knives and gaffs to convince him of your obedience. It might also be wise to place your hands where they may be seen to be empty."

"Mr. Shelle!" barked John Winter. "Do you think you are on holiday, sir? Get your tail off the deck and stand straight. You and Mr. Goddy, and you, too, Perry James, accompany me. Mr. Danielles—"

Winter was addressing the helmsman.

"*Oui, mon capitaine.*"

"Let us come to within grappling distance of the second boat."

"I will make it so, *mon capitaine.*"

Renold Danielles plucked his moustache and beard in a thin line to surround his mouth and chin in an oval as perfect as the gold hoops piercing his earlobes. His lips pursed with concentration as he worked the tiller, controlling our drift until our waist scraped the hull of the Spanish fishing boat.

"*Nous sommes ici!*"

Winter leapt from the pinnace into the smaller vessel before the gap between them closed completely. Goddy, Will Shelle, and I went over the gunwale after him, our cutlasses drawn. This proved an unnecessary precaution, however, since the Spanish sailors were cringing in the bow with their fingers laced behind their heads.

"Please, *señor* pirate, we own nothing of value," begged the leader, a swarthy man with a long chin and dark eyes. He and his crew wore red scarves around their necks and wool shirts striped white and blue. "In the name of Jesus, in the name of Mary, mother of God, do not kill us."

Winter hung his sword at his hip and began stroking the curve of his fancy mustache while regarding the Spaniards with a cold stare. "Bind their wrists, Mr. Shelle, and take them before the general," he instructed. "Mr. James, you and Mr. Goddy transfer the victuals to the *Pelican*. Leave nothing behind."

He meant the fishermen's catch.

The deck was slick with the blood and guts of fish and crowded with baskets of cod, bream, and hake, some still thrashing. The filleted sides of other fish, rubbed with herbs and salt, had been spread open on wood skewers and hung from the rigging in order to air dry in the sun. The hold contained a half dozen barrels packed with salted fish. Two others, almost full, were on the deck.

Turning to Goddy, I said, "I do not like stealing from these men. They are ordinary seamen and we are depriving them of all they have."

Goddy shrugged. "Aye, there is little profit is robbing beggars. Let us hope for better game soon. A fat Spanish merchant would do."

"You are not getting me, Pascoe. It is one thing to take from the wealthy, who can absorb the loss, but another to take from the poor. That is not honest profit in my opinion."

"Do not trouble your conscience, Perry. The Papist bastards would do the same to us were our situations reversed, as I well know. Besides, our need is greater than theirs. If what I think is true, we will require every scrap of victual we can get. Now here. On the count of three."

Goddy had gone down into the hold and was preparing to lift a barrel of salted fish up to me. There was no winch.

"What do you imagine, Pascoe?" I asked.

"*Two*," he grunted, bringing the barrel as high as his knees. "Do you know Bill Lege?"

"Only by sight. He is a blacksmith."

"*Three*."

Goddy hoisted the barrel to his chest and I grabbed hold and wrestled it onto the deck. Then we began the process again.

"Lege is a cooper," Goddy corrected me. "The thing is, he was talking to Chris Hals, who overheard Blacollers with Tom Cuttill. Cuttill told Blacollers to oil his jacket since we were all heading for a damned wet place. Blacollers laughed and said, aye, he figured as much, knowing the general, and

Cuttill laughed himself and said, aye, Drake was a bold bastard, the very son of the devil."

"I fail to see your point, Pascoe," I said. "The general's character is common knowledge."

"Is it not obvious? Mr. Cuttill is a pilot and all pilots are as thick as thieves. In whom else would Drake confide a plot of the voyage?"

"So we are heading for a wet place? There are a thousand such."

"But none wetter than *Cabo das Tormentas*. The Cape of Storms."

"I have never heard of it."

"In order to deceive simple mariners, the Portuguese renamed it the Cape of Good Hope."

"Aye, that I have heard of. Is this cape not at the end of Africa?"

"'Tis at the very spot where the Atlantic meets the Indian Ocean. The mating of currents engenders bad weather and furious tempests. The cape has been the death of countless ships."

A longboat arrived to accept the provisions we were stealing from the Spanish fishermen. As Goddy and I began loading the barrels over the side, I shook my head and said, "I do not know, Pascoe. You are making very much from very little."

"Perhaps. But past the cape lies the Malabar coast and the islands of the Moluccas, which are home to all manner of spices. The damned Portuguese have had the trade to themselves for fifty years and slay any who attempt to break their monopoly. It would be just like the general to be the first Englishman reach India by water. Christ's blood, Perry, think how much return there would be on a cargo of pepper or nutmegs? We could all retire as gentlemen on the proceeds in manors of our own."

"Aye, dream on, Pascoe."

"Laugh if you will. But heed my words, we will all be drenched to the skin soon enough and sufficiently hungry to enjoy a portion of 'tweendeck venison."

For the next several days, however, the weather contin- ued fair and the wind filled our sails and sped us south and west along a coast that became increasingly barren until the last suggestion of life was left behind and there was only sand and rock for endless miles. On January 13th, a Friday, we ar- rived at the mouth of a wide bay known as Rio del Oro, al- though there was neither gold nor fresh water here but only a brackish inlet, where we surprised a small Spanish merchant vessel. To the disappointment of my companions, her cargo was salt, which was too bulky to bother stealing although we made her men into prisoners and kept them with the other fishermen in the orlop of the *Pelican*, where a storage locker had been fitted with a bolt to make it into a jail.

According to Pascoe Goddy, Rio del Oro lay just under the Tropic of Cancer, an imaginary line drawn horizontally through the globe a thumb's width above the equator. "'Tis the northernmost point at which the sun may appear directly over- head at noon although I have no damned idea why such reck- oning is important to navigators," Goddy explained. "You have seen Drake and Mr. Cuttle on deck with their Jacob's staff?"

"The nautical instrument shaped like a cross with rul- ings?"

"That is the one. At night it is used to determine the height of the North Star in the sky. During the day it provides the same measurement for the sun. Once the pilot has a sighting, he may calculate where the ship lies north or south, which is known as *latitude*. Unfortunately, 'tis impossible to figure out *longitude*, or east and west, with any certainty. Most navigators simply guess."

"That is not a comforting thought, Pascoe."

"Aye, it is not, is it."

From Rio del Oro the bleak coast continued to trend westward. For most of the afternoon we passed a succession of white sand downs with flat summits. These were followed by fields of rubble and then by more sand. On January 15th we rounded Cape Barbas, a cliff with a square top, where the *Marigold* took a Portuguese caravel, which was a type of merchant ship, although her cargo, too, proved of little value. By the time we reached Cape Blank, the White Cape, our fleet had grown from five to eleven vessels. The captive canteras and caravels, manned with skeleton crews of English sailors, trailed behind the larger ships like goslings following their parents.

Cape Blank was a sheer white wall rising from the surf at the furthest point of a long spit of land. I had not seen any vegetation for miles, nor a stream or river. A tongue of mud and reef extended from the point and we stayed well offshore until we came around into the mouth of the bay, where we discovered a Spanish caravel at anchor. Her crew fled to land when they sighted our sails except for two men who were left behind either through haste or because there was no room for them in the longboat carrying their companions to safety.

"Mr. James," instructed John Winter, "go below and report back as to the contents of the hold."

"Aye, captain."

The caravel was fifty feet long but wide for her length, a design that made the ship look fat and graceless but provided stability at sea as well as ample storage room for bulk goods, which was an important consideration for a merchant vessel. The fact that the caravel was riding low in the swells indicated she held a full load of cargo and I was not surprised to find the main hold crammed with barrels.

What was surprising was that almost all the containers held not wine or beer or some valuable commodity but only plain water.

"Water, by God!" exclaimed John Winter when I communicated my discovery. "What could be more worthless? A man must be dying of thirst to touch the stuff."

"It is for the Moors, *señor*," explained one of the Spanish sailors. "This country is cursed of God. There is not a spring nor a well within leagues of here. Since the heathens have naught else to drink but camel's milk, which is a sour beverage, they will pay dearly for even a little quantity of fresh water."

"Will they?" asked Winter, now more interested in the conversation. "What do they offer in return?"

"*Pescados, señor. Mucho pescados.*"

Fish.

"The Moors also pay with musk and ambergris and with black slaves," continued the sailor. "We are not far distant from Guinea and there is much trafficking of men in this region. The trade is profitable."

Winter delegated three sailors to bring the caravel along with the fleet as we traveled deeper into the bay, which the Spanish called the *Baie de Cansado*, or Bay of Weariness, and then instructed me to deliver our newest guests to the *Pelican*, where they would join the prisoners already incarcerated in the flagship. By the time I discharged this duty, the fleet had come to anchor in five fathoms of water a hundred yards from a low sand point on which was a large encampment of tents and several dozen beached fishing smacks painted the same pale blue as those we had seen earlier at Asafi.

Noticing my return on deck, Thomas Blacollers called: "God's blessing, Mr. James. I was about to send word to the pinnace for you but here you are and now I am spared the trouble!"

"What would you have of me, sir?"

"On Mr. Doughty's orders you are to go below and make a tally of the victuals. Be ready with the information by noon since you are to join the landing party going ashore and that is when it leaves."

My recent visit to Barbary had not made me eager to return to the country any time soon. Nor did I wish to associate closely with Mr. Doughty, who had not used me well—not at Sutton Pool, nor on the road to Mortlake, nor in Mogador. This history had taught me to avoid the man but there was no way out of the assignment and so I went to the orlop and conducted the requested inventory. Although inroads had been made into the salted meat and fish, I estimated enough remained to last several months. The biscuit, too, was dry and free of maggots. But almost all the fresh vegetables and fruit had been consumed and the little that was left was bruised and moldy. I had expected nothing different since we had been at sea for five weeks and, as every cook learns, it is the nature of all food to rot.

Last I went to the armory and used a whetstone on my cutlass.

Parson Fletcher, his sword flat upon his knees rather than at his waist, was already seated in the longboat when I arrived. The rest of the contingent were men I knew to be experienced marines—Tom Moone; Great Nele; Diego, the Cimarron; and Oliver, the master gunner. Each had a musket or arquebuse as well as a blade. Several carried pistols. Thomas Doughty ordered the bow and stern ropes to be thrown down and grimly examined the shore.

"Supposedly the locals are accustomed to trade," he said as we cast off from the *Pelican* and began rowing toward the beach. "Remember, however, what occurred at Mogador. Be prepared for treachery."

Our approach was noted immediately and a throng of men in white robes hurried down from the camp to the waterline. They were clearly excited by our arrival and called out with words borrowed from a half dozen languages while waving what I assumed to be articles of merchandise in our direction. Observing our weaponry, they kept their distance while we ran the longboat onto the sand and pulled her above the high tide mark. Soon, though, their avarice overcame their fear and the Moors pressed in among us and sought to direct our attention to the goods they had to offer by shoving their wares under our noses and by plucking at our clothes. Some had brought livestock with them and some had brought slaves, men as dark as Diego with wooly hair, who had to shuffle as they walked due to the iron collars on their ankles. The beggars in the crowd all made the same pleading gesture, forming cups with their fists and pretending to drink in order to demonstrate their need for water. Several held upside down their leather canteens, known as *alforges*, to show that the bags were empty of liquor.

"Get your damned hands off me," Gregory Raymente swore at a particularly importunate solicitor. "How many times must I tell you I do not desire your skinny chicken?"

"I do not want it, either," said Tom Moone when the Moor turned to him. "Remove the thing from my face before I shove it up your arse."

The man may not have understood the words but he understood the menace in Moone's tone and glumly went elsewhere with his poultry. Another opportunist took his place in the mistaken belief we had traveled hundreds of leagues with the express intention of purchasing a brace of dead weasels. A third Moor, whose face was dyed blue in an unflattering fashion, held out a basket containing a mound of pinkish yellow wax with a rank odor. Raymente wrinkled his nostrils in disgust and hefted his arquebuse in order to push the man away with the butt of the gun but Francis Fletcher placed a hand on his arm to restrain him.

"That is ambergris, my son," explained the parson, "which may only be exhumed from the skulls of dead whales. It is the essential foundation of all perfumery and worth its weight in gold in Paris or Rome."

The blacksmith shook his head in disbelief. "The stuff resembles what a dog leaves behind after a bad meal," he muttered.

"Aye, Gregory," agreed Oliver, eying the ambergris skeptically. "Still, what harm is there in learning how much the fellow wants for it?"

Once it was clear the locals were more interested in commerce than in robbery, Doughty detailed two men to guard the longboat and allowed the rest of the party shore leave except for Tom Moone and myself. Following him, we pushed clear of the crowd and climbed the dune to the encampment, discovering it to be an established market with a caravanserai and a stable of slave pens at its northern extremity. Hard packed lanes of crushed shell separated the stalls and tents from one another and the place had an air of permanence although there were no solid structures. The moment we halted to look around, we were again besieged by entrepreneurs and beggars, who dispersed only after Tom Moone lifted the most aggressive of them by the collar of his robe with one hand and tossed the man ten feet.

Doughty turned to Moone and said, "Drake plans to remain here a week in order to refurbish the ships before crossing to the Cape Verdes."

"Thank God for that. Moors keep their whores well hidden but there are sure to be one or two about. Given enough time, we will find them."

Doughty ignored the ribaldry. "What we have, Mr. Moone, is an excellent opportunity to exercise the men in formation maneuvers, which are impossible to practice aboard ship. They must learn to work together as a unit on land and not only on the water."

"Aye, captain, you are right," answered Moone with the seriousness that practical men use when discussing murder. "Sailors are convinced they may do as they like when they are on the beach. It is best to dissuade them from this notion. What do you require?"

"Each afternoon while we are here assemble a squad of thirty men from among those not employed in the careening. Arm them with pikes and half-pikes but do not ask them to wear armor." He pointed toward the plain of shingle and sand extending behind the camp toward the horizon. "I will drill the first group over there as soon as possible. Make sure to bring enough beer for all since it will be damned hot work."

Next Thomas Doughty addressed me. "You inventoried the victuals as instructed, Mr. James?"

"Aye, sir."

"Then you are aware of what we lack. Go among the Moors and make the best bargain you can for our necessities. You are authorized a budget of three pounds in silver coin or an equivalent in trade goods. Be warned, I will expect an accounting for any expenditure."

"I will itemize every penny, sir," I promised.

"Of course you will, Mr. James," Doughty said, regarding me with an odd smile I neither understood nor liked. Then the three of us parted ways and I wandered the alleys of the market and inspected the merchandise at different stalls until I had a sense of what was available and a fair idea of the prevailing prices. This was a procedure I had learned from my father while at the Jack and Rasher. In Plymouth it was usual for purveyors to charge more than appropriate if they had the slightest suspicion their customer was ignorant of the going rate. I doubted affairs were any different in Barbary.

Most of the vendors knew a little Spanish or Portuguese so communicating my requirements was less difficult than I feared it would be. I almost purchased a basket of salted cod from one supplier and one of onions from another but walked away from both deals when neither man would come down far enough from his opening figure. It did not take long, however, for news of my stubbornness to get around and soon I began to receive reasonable quotes.

One prosperous merchant invited me into his tent and we drank an infusion of mint from bronze cups while negotiating our transaction.

"I can have all the fish you need delivered to your ships either in salt or in brine," Ali bin Ishmael told me. "Sadly, it is Allah's will that neither I or anyone else can do much for you in the way of meat or produce, which we must import ourselves since there is no water here."

"Aye, sir, so I have heard," I said. Then, thinking of the cargo aboard the Spanish caravel we had taken, I mused, "It could be we have sufficient water ourselves to part with some for the right inducement. Were you interested, I could raise the matter with my superiors."

"Please, I would be most appreciative if you were to do so."

Ali bin Ishmael was a plump man somewhat past middle age with an evident taste for expensive things. The large pipe on the carpet between us was blown of green glass delicate enough for you to see the liquid inside bubble when a stream of smoke was pulled through the globe. The bowl held hashish.

In Plymouth it was a common stratagem of unprincipled purveyors to ply clients with strong drink in order to sway their purchasing decisions. Moors, it seemed, were no more scrupulous than Englishmen.

"No, thank you, sir," I said when my host passed me the flexible tube used to draw the fumes. "I have had experience with the spice and am wary of its influence."

"But there must be some way I can repay you for your kindness," insisted the merchant. After reflecting a moment, he spoke to the servant, who went away and returned in the company of a lad no older than Lackland. The youth's chest, arms, and legs glistened with oil and he was wearing only a white loincloth, which barely concealed his haunches. He smiled shyly at me, fluttering lashes longer and more lustrous than Beth Winston's, and bowed his head.

Spreading his hands in a gesture of invitation, Ali bin Ishmael said, "I hope the child is to your taste. It is common knowledge English sailors enjoy nothing so much as the caress of a beautiful boy."

"I do not know who told you such a story, sir," I answered hastily, "but you have been misinformed. At least on my account."

"Please forgive me," bin Ishmael apologized, dismissing the painted lad and summoning in his place a figure garbed from head to toe in black garments so shapeless I could not determine the sex of whoever was inside them. But I did not doubt the wily merchant was now tempting me with the charms of a woman since this also was a tactic employed by certain vendors in Plymouth. I could remember several occasions on which I had been promised liberties by pretty farmers' daughters in return for looking favorably on their fathers' goods.

It had not required any great store of integrity on my part to resist these advances. The girls in question stank of the sty.

The woman in black, however, bathed in roses.

Behind a curtain someone began beating a drum while someone else played a wild melody on a pipe.

The woman extended her arms, her hands trembling like the wings of a bird and the gold bracelets girdling her wrists jingling in counterpoint to the rhythm of the instruments. Her hips began to sway.

"Yasmin is quite skillful, is she not?" bin Ishmael observed.

I forgot my answer the moment the words left my mouth. I was too busy watching the dancer discard her robes. She was naked beneath them except for bangles and tatters of lace embroidered with sequins.

Shaking back her mane of glossy dark hair, Yasmin gave me a seductive look and held my eyes with her own while she began moving her body, controlling every part independently of the rest with mysterious acumen.

"You like her, yes?" bin Ishmael whispered in my ear.

"Aye, sir," I mumbled. "She is very beautiful."

The music quickened. The ruby in Yasmin's navel caught the light and sparkled each time her belly quivered.

The merchant smiled and patted my arm familiarly, confident that I would soon be in his debt.

"She is yours for the night," he said.

Parrots of the Cape Verdes

January 17, 1578 – January 29, 1578
Cape Blank, Boa Vista, Maio

Surrounded by a cloud of gossamer, Yasmin twisted in front of me like a dancer in a dream. Her hips and breasts undulating slowly, she sank to her knees and leaned backward until she touched the carpet behind her head with her fingers.

Still shivering in time to the music, the tiny bells sewn to her belt tinkling, Yasmin tipped her pelvis upward without modesty or reticence. I could not help but notice that her femininity was hidden by a pelt of fur as dark as the tresses of hair swirling around her face.

Then she came forward until her cleavage filled my vision. Her legs straddled my lap while she ground her body against mine as if she were crushing pepper between us.

"*Si*," Yasmin breathed in Spanish. "*Sim*," she said in Portuguese. Then she flicked out her tongue and caressed my ear with its velvet tip while whispering in sweetly accented English, "Yes."

By my physical reaction to her proximity it was becoming clear to me that the reason I had been able to resist similar temptation in the past was because I had not been seriously tested.

I was also learning that there was no polite way to extricate yourself from the embrace of an unclad woman intent on mischief. Yasmin's flesh was slick with oil and sweat and my hands slipped along the curves of her body when I tried to get a grip. Misinterpreting my purpose, she stepped up her efforts to rob me of any vestige of restraint.

Somehow I found the power of will to turn away from her and address bin Ishmael. "Sir, thank you for your courtesy but I cannot accept the lady's favors."

"Are you certain, my friend?" asked the merchant. "From personal knowledge I may provide favorable report of her abilities."

To my shame I was by no means certain.

In my pride as a young man I had thought I was experienced with women but now Yasmin was teaching me that I knew little about them. I never could have imagined Annie, back in Plymouth, lifting my hand to her mouth and nibbling gently on my knuckles before sliding my fingers between her lips and sucking on them one by one while staring without blinking into my eyes. Nor could I have ever dreamed of Annie taking the hand she had moistened and placing it where Yasmin did or of Annie sighing with the same passion at my touch.

Then I remembered advice Beth Winston had once given me.

My friend had done for a living what other women did in wedlock or for love. Attempting to provide for my worldly education in the absence of my parents, she had spoken frankly about her profession. "You are such a handsome lad, and so sweet natured, I doubt you will often have to pay for affection," Beth had said. "But if you must seek such consolation, Perry, do not ever mistake a whore's moan for the real thing, no matter the delivery. We are all players and our compensation depends on our ability to lie."

Yasmin, without question, was among the most fluent of liars.

Her sigh of disappointment when I withdrew my fingers was so convincing, I almost believed her and put them back where they had been. Instead I said:

"Take no offense, please, but I really must go—"

"What is this abomination! Release him, harlot!"

Francis Fletcher had noticed my predicament through the open tent flap and come inside after me. "I had expected better of you, Peregrine James," the parson said sadly. "You appeared to be an honorable lad with higher moral principles than the usual mariner. I was mistaken."

"The situation is not as you imagine, sir," I protested, still unable to extricate myself from Yasmin's embrace since she had trapped my chin between her breasts, their fragrance proving she bathed not just in roses but also in orange essence. "We are discussing victualling," I said. "My host is a wholesaler of salted fish and other commodities."

Fletcher, however, remained convinced of my low character.

"The good lord has seen fit to provide me with eyes, my son," he said. "I repay his kindness by believing what I see. Come, let us leave this den of iniquity at once."

I did not know to what extent Ali bin Ishmael understood this exchange but he recognized that Francis Fletcher was a man of God although of a different faith than his own. "Tell your priest I would never under any circumstances condone immorality," bin Ishmael explained. "Since Allah in his wisdom has forbidden intimate congress outside the bounds of matrimony, you must, of course, marry Yasmin before you may enjoy her. I will speak the necessary words for you myself."

Considering the parson's severe expression, I did not think it prudent to translate bin Ishmael's offer.

"Your pardon, sir," I replied, "but I do not wish to be engaged, not even to such a pretty girl. Marriage is a great obligation."

"Of course it is!" agreed the merchant. "That is why Allah, the source of all blessings, has decreed divorce to be the right of all men. The marriage will be annulled as soon as you have had your pleasure."

Fletcher's stern expression did not encourage me to translate this proposal, either, and we returned to the beach together in silence. By the time we reached the waterside, however, the parson had regained his humor and regarded me with no more severity than was usual for him. "I was young once myself," he said, "and I understand the urges of virile men, particularly sailors. But as Christians, having been called to a gracious state, we must overcome our lusts and obey God's commandments else we will be no different than the inhabitants of this loathsome cape. In the future, Peregrine, seek my counsel when you feel the needs of the flesh. We will pray together."

"Aye, sir," I said. "Thank you for the advice."

"Here is further guidance," the parson went on with the practicality I had come to expect of him. "If prayer alone proves insufficient and animal instinct threatens to overcome your higher nature, I suggest you take yourself in hand privately and do what you must alone. Onanism is a lesser offense than fornication and corrupts only one person instead of two.

Are you familiar with the practice to which I refer?"

"Yes, sir," I mumbled. "I believe I am."

"If you had said otherwise, my son," said the parson, "I would know you to be as much a fraud as you are a lecher."

We were able to walk out to the *Pelican* without wetting our boots since she had been brought in close to shore and anchored in water shallow enough to strand her on dry land as the tide retreated. This had been done in order to expose the ship's underside to the air so it could be cleaned of worms and vegetative growth, a process known as *careening*. Because the *Pelican* was resting on her side, the deck listed twenty degrees, which made the world feel out of joint. Every so often the breeze brought with it the stink of the boiling tar being applied to the hull as protection against barnacles and seaweed.

Francis Drake and Thomas Doughty listened to my report on the half deck. "The local purveyors have an abundance of dried fish for sale but not a lot else," I told them. "Mostly the place serves as a transshipment depot for slaves."

"There is good money in black ivory, by God," Drake exclaimed. "But it is a perishable cargo and hard to unload, thanks to the dons, may they all rot in hell. What of meat and victuals?"

"Both are scarce, captain. I have placed orders for what is available but I cannot promise much. This is a bleak coast."

"That it is, lad. As bad as Ireland, am I right or wrong, Tom?"

"Ireland was purgatory, Francis. Cape Blank is the inferno itself. Two men passed out during drill this afternoon even without armor."

"Aye, at least Ireland was wet. In Barbary you piss sand."

"Speaking of water, sir," I continued, "it is a valuable commodity here. A local merchant is interested in purchasing our surplus."

As I had, Drake thought of the cargo aboard the caravel we had taken the day before at the point of the cape. "Do we not have a full hold of the sorry stuff, courtesy of our Spanish guests?" he mused.

"Aye, sir. Fifty-three barrels. I counted them personally at the order of Captain Winter."

"Excellent! Hold back enough to top off our supplies, Mr. James, but sell every extra drop. God's wounds, there is nothing as satisfying as making a profit at your enemies' expense. What do you say, Tom?"

"I agree."

"But I do not."

Francis Fletcher removed his black hat, revealing a scalp that was bald except for a couple straggling white locks, which he combed across his cranium from left to right.

"The Papists may see fit to profit on human misery but we should not follow their example," warned Fletcher, mopping his pate carefully with a handkerchief so as not to disturb the arrangement of the few hairs he had left. "There is a very heavy judgment of God upon these people. It would be wrong to add to their burdens. Give the water away."

The suggestion took Drake aback. "Without charge?" he asked. "Tom, what do you make of the parson's recommendation?"

"When I was ashore, a black beggar came up to me. Her dugs were so dry, her babe could not drink. It was a pathetic spectacle."

"Thomas Doughty sentimental? This is not the man I know."

"You did not see her, Francis. Besides, to provide for free what the Spanish sell would only add to our credit while damaging theirs."

"That is a cunning idea. I like it, by Christ, particularly since our generosity will cost us nothing. Blacollers!"

"Aye, general!" answered the boatswain.

"Send a gang to the Spanish caravel and unload the ship. Set up the barrels on the beach and offer drinks to everyone. Turn no one away and do not request payment. Are you satisfied, parson?"

"I am, Captain Drake," answered Fletcher. "Whatever the imperfection of our motives, it is always best to do the right thing."

We were to remain at Cape Blank somewhat less than a week, until the 21st of January. Most of this time I worked alongside my crew mates aboard the pinnace, cleaning the small ship and making her seaworthy, but on the third morning I was assigned to a fishing party going out in a longboat into the channel, which abounded with mackerel and herring and the larger predators that hunted them. We pushed off just at dawn, rowing across water that was absolutely flat except for the ripples caused by the dipping of our oars. Then we let the boat drift as we readied our gear. My angle was a springy piece of ash seven feet long to which was attached a reel holding a hundred yards of line. We speared whole sprats and chunks of clam on our hooks but neither of these baits interested fish and after several hours we had taken aboard only one nondescript tunny.

I was sharing a bench with Peter Corder, who held his angle with his feet rather than with his hands, twitching his line with his toes in order to animate the bait.

"If not for our bad luck, we would have none at all," Corder muttered in disgust.

"Stop complaining," said Luke Adden. "A poor day of fishing is still better than a good day of any other activity."

"Except for drinking," corrected Bill Lege.

"Or fornicating!" said Powell Jemes. "Christ, I could do with a bit of something tight right now. It has been too long."

"No question!" Peter Corder suddenly became alert and studied his line. "I thought I had a bite," he explained when several minutes passed and nothing more happened. Relaxing again with the angle gripped between his insteps, Corder returned to the subject of women. "You know you have been at sea too long, gentlemen," he said, "when you begin to display an inordinate interest in the crack of dawn."

"Or in black wenches."

"Oh, Moor women are not bad. As long as they keep their veils on."

"Just be sure to keep your eyes closed in case the veil comes loose."

"God forbid that happened. It would be enough to make a man swear off romance. Shit—"

Corder lunged and caught his angle before it was wrenched over the gunwale by the fish that had stuck his bait. For a moment the pole bent in half but then it sprang straight. Winding in the line, Corder retrieved an empty hook. "Ah, well," he mused philosophically, putting on more clam. "At least we know they are out there."

Powell Jemes, an armorer, was another of those who had sailed with Drake during the famous raid on Nombre de Dios six years previously. He tarred his beard in two stiff spikes beneath his jaw and shaved his skull in order to display the design inked on the skin of his crown, the head of a serpent whose tail twisted down his neck onto his shoulders. Giving his angle a bored shake, Jemes said:

"I heard from Mr. Cuttill we will soon be throwing back our catch of Spaniards and Portugals."

"It was a waste of effort to take such small vessels in the first place," said Bill Lege.

"There you are wrong," replied Peter Corder. "Do you not see? By taking the Spanish captive, we prevented advance word of our presence getting out along the coast. No matter how brisk the wind, a sailing ship will always be outrun by men on horseback."

"Even so," muttered Lege, "they are all poor craft and barely seaworthy. Nor can we crew them all."

"Too many ships, too few sailors. That is often the problem," Powell Jemes concurred. He curled his left spike of beard around a finger. "I remember we had the same situation in the Gulf of Darien back in seventy-two," he mused. "After a month of raiding we had captured two Spanish coastal barks, one off Cartagena city and the other off Santa Marta. Both prizes were seaworthy and well furnished but neither was a fighter. The general wanted to sink one and to make the other into a storehouse, which would free their crews to reinforce our important ships, but he knew the men would object to mistreating such pretty vessels. So Drake called Tom Moone to his cabin."

"Aye, I know this story," said Lege.

"Do not reveal the ending since I have not heard it," said Corder. "Go on, Jemes."

"Where is the Gulf of Darien?" I asked.

"It is in the crook of the elbow between the Isthmus of Panama and the Spanish Main," explained Bill Lege. "'Tis a hell-ish maze of swamp and reef, lad. Pray to Christ you never visit."

"As I was saying," Jemes continued after I had received this geographical advice, "the general sent for Tom Moone, who at the time was the carpenter of the *Swan*, which was one of the ships in question. 'Tom,' said Drake, 'go down secretly into the well in the middle of the second watch. Bore three holes with a spike-gimlet as near the keel as you can. Then lay something against it, that the force of the water entering the ship might make no noise nor be discovered by boiling up.'

"As you may imagine, gentlemen, Moone did not en-joy receiving these instructions. 'Captain,' he said with dismay, 'the *Swan* is strong and has many voyages left in her. Besides, the rest of the company will be unhappy with me should they learn of my role in her sinking.'

"But there was no arguing with the general—"

"Aye, is there ever?" laughed Luke Adden.

"—and Moone did as he was bid. Drake waited until morning to let the ship fill somewhat and then ordered me to ferry him over to her from the admiral in a pinnace. Have I mentioned that Drake's brother, John, was the *Swan*'s master?"

"The master?" said Peter Corder. "The general drowned

his own brother's ship? That was cold."

"What happened next was colder." Powell Jemes began winding both spikes of beard together while reflecting how best to tell the tale. "Drake invited John to come fishing—"

"No, he did not!"

"God's truth, Mr. Corder. But his brother was too busy to join us so Drake had me row a little distance from the ship and we fished a quarter hour while waiting for John to get ready. Then the general pretended to notice that the *Swan* was riding low in the water. He turned to me and asked very casually, as if to make little of the question: 'Powell, why do you think the bark is so deep?'

"'I cannot hazard a guess, captain,' I answered, since I was as much in the dark about what was going on as everyone except for Drake and Tom Moone. 'She is a sound ship and empty of cargo,' I said.

"There was no denying, however, the *Swan*'s gunwales were almost awash. So the general called to his brother, who sent a steward below to investigate. The man returned wet to the waist and crying that the scuttle was flooded. 'I do not understand it,' said John Drake. 'We have not pumped twice in six weeks but now there is six feet of water in the hold.'

"'It is indeed strange,' agreed the general, feigning perplexity so well that we were all deceived. 'Come, Powell,' he told me, 'let us go aboard the *Swan* and provide what assistance we may.'

"'No, stay,' said John. 'We have enough men for our needs. Continue fishing, that we might have some part of your catch for dinner.'

"'So be it,' said Drake and we dropped our lines over the

side and resumed angling as the *Swan*'s crew tried to save her. Every once in a while the general called out encouragement to the men, telling them to work the pump harder and offering suggestions as to where the leak might be found. But by three in the afternoon they had not freed above a foot and a half of water, nor had anyone discovered the holes drilled by Tom Moone. Finally it became clear the ship must be abandoned.

"'Damned bad luck to lose so sweet a bark!' the general said, clapping an arm around his brother in counterfeit sympathy. 'Perhaps it would be best to start unloading her now before she goes under. Let everyone take what they lack or like and find berths on the other vessels. As for you, John, you may have my place as captain of the flagship until we capture a better prize for you to master.'"

"Why, that was a kind offer," observed Peter Corder.

"Aye, was it not." Powell Jemes shook his head appreciatively. "The general got exactly what he wanted and no one was the wiser. I stood right beside him in these very boots, and we watched that sweet ship settle to the bottom, and I did not think for a second he was gaming us. You have to respect the man."

"Aye, no one surpasses the general in cunning," agreed Bill Lege.

"Thank God for that," said Corder. "A fool will not make us rich."

"Aye, a fool will get us murdered or blown against a lee shore."

"Christ save us from all evil destiny!" prayed Luke Adden.

I gave my angle an upward jerk and discovered that my bait had been stolen while I was absorbed in Powell Jemes's anecdote. I had not liked the story, which seemed to demonstrate an implacable self interest more worthy of Thomas Doughty than Francis Drake. Perhaps I was as naive as Lackland claimed but it did not seem proper justice to use your own men and family with the same ease that you would use an enemy.

"How did the truth come out?" I asked when I had replaced my bait and returned my line to the depths.

"Oh, the trick was too good to keep secret. The general told the story himself although he waited until his brother was dead, which was not long afterward, God rest the poor bastard. Fever, I think. Or was that Drake's other brother, Joseph? They both died on that deplorable coast—watch your angle, Perry!"

I stopped the pole just before it went into the water.

Something large was on the hook.

The line on my reel was spun of fiber that had been oiled and waxed to protect the thread from damp and rot. Supposedly it would resist a hundred pounds of pressure before snapping.

Even so I did not think the line would long withstand the anger of the fish at its other end.

"Bring up the tip!" exclaimed Peter Corder. "Get the God damned tip up before he shakes the hook!"

"Jesus, look at the bastard tear off line."

"Slow him, Perry. Christ, how big is that thing?"

I was by no means an expert angler but I was not completely inexperienced since I had fished with my father on the Plym and Tamar rivers outside Plymouth, mostly for salmon, which were large animals although not in the league of the monster I had on now.

I understood enough to know the key to angling success was to tire the fish by making him work hard to pull away from you. This was accomplished by letting the line out bit by bit very carefully since too much pressure would snap the thread while too little tension would do nothing to fatigue your opponent and allow him to spit out the hook.

The fish charged the longboat and I took in slack frantically. Then he dove straight down, stripping line with a hiss.

"Pump the angle, Perry," instructed Corder. "Work the bastard up."

"I am trying! He does not wish to come."

My angle was bent double and my arms were on fire with strain as I struggled to wrestle the fish to the surface. Fifteen minutes passed before we could see the beast in the water.

"Christ in heaven," said Powell Jemes. "He is a hundredweight if he is an ounce!"

"Add fifty pounds, that is my estimate," said Corder. "Come on, lad. I have the gaff ready. Do not let us down now."

"I will not, sir," I muttered, so caught up in the excitement of the struggle that I did not feel the pain in my wrists and in my fingers, which had been cut by friction as I tried to slow the line.

The fish was taller than my arms outstretched. He was the color of quicksilver except for a lining of brilliant yellow along his fins and except for his eyes, which were as black as charcoal. Lancelot Garget, of course, would boil most of the meat but I resolved to save a thick chop for myself and to grill the piece until it was just cooked and still red.

Then the fish breached and leapt into the air.

In that moment, as he hung suspended before falling back into the water, he fixed me with a glare so despairing, and yet so fierce and proud, that I could no longer think of him as food.

"I have the bastard!" said Peter Corder, thrusting with the spear, but the fish was too deep and the barb did not penetrate. "Hoist him a hair, lad," Corder said, preparing to stab again. "Aye, that should do it."

Suddenly I did not want any part of killing so valiant a creature. I hunched over, as if being pulled off balance by the fish, which screened what I was doing from the other men.

Hugging my angle and pretending the rod was in danger of being torn from my grasp, I maneuvered in such a way as to catch my line against the edge of my knife, which was at my waist.

After Mr. Stydye noticed its dullness on my first day aboard the *Pelican*, I had taken care to keep the blade sharp.

The thread parted instantly.

The tip of my angle shot skyward and I stumbled back until I landed on my rump against the far gunwale.

The fish sounded and was seen no more.

"Rotten luck, Perry," said Luke Adden. "You have lost him."

"Tell me about it," I complained. "He was too strong for the line."

"Aye, the ones that get away always are," agreed Bill Lege. "Next time be easier with the drag."

"Aye, Perry," said Powell Jemes. "Fish are like women, do you see? Both are spoiled by too heavy a hand."

"I will remember what you say," I replied, tying on a new hook and spearing a sprat on it to show I was determined to catch a fish to replace the one that had escaped. I was not sorry, however, when I did not get another bite the remainder of the afternoon even though my companions all landed several tunny before we returned to the *Pelican*. Theirs were big fish but none approached the dimensions of the one I had lost, which grew larger whenever my companions told what happened, so that by the next day everyone in the fleet thought I had engaged a leviathan.

"How big was it, pretty boy?" asked Lancelot Garget, who was standing beside me on the plain north of the Moor encampment, where we had been instructed to assemble with thirty other men. It was our turn to receive martial instruction from Thomas Doughty.

Each of us had been issued a twelve-foot pike. Garget stroked his suggestively. "This big?" he asked.

"With all respect, sir, you are a filthy person," I answered.

"Aye, and proud of the fact. It is my firm opinion that what is worth saying is worth saying obscenely."

"You cannot fault a man for practicing his philosophy," observed Pascoe Goddy, who was on Garget's other side. "God damn, it is hot. Where is Captain Doughty? Were we not told to group at four o'clock?"

"'Tis just like the bastard to keep us waiting in the heat." Garget removed his wool cap to reveal a scalp almost as bald as Francis Fletcher's. I had put on my *cheche*, which was more practical in the searing climate than English headgear although the scarf reminded me of an adventure I would rather forget. "Gentlemen take pleasure in nothing so much as the discomfort of ordinary seamen," Garget went on, mopping his forehead with the back of his hand and flinging away the sweat without thought of those around him. "Bugger them all."

"Aye, Lance," agreed Goddy. "Do you know, yesterday I was scraping the deck with holystone, which is always thirsty work in the sun, and that little nose drip Gregory Carey called me over to where he and his cronies were drinking ale in the shade of the poop. 'Say, man, you missed a spot there,' he told me. 'Do try not to be so careless.' Carey thought the remark very amusing, too, as did his friends, and they all had a fine time watching me work while they sat on their tails and did nothing. I do not know why the general endures such worthless fellows."

"'Tis because of money, why else?" volunteered Gregory Raymente, who had overheard our conversation. "Drake must please his investors. How better to flatter them than by allowing their useless offspring and poor relations to come along on the adventure?"

"Quiet, everyone!"

Thomas Doughty now stood before us. In respect of the heat he had replaced his customary finery with a linen suit and he wore a hat with a sweeping brim to shield his face from the glare. Gripping the hilt of his rapier with one hand, he placed the other upon the opposite hip and regarded the assembly with obvious displeasure.

"Line up in orderly ranks six across," he instructed and waited until we had done so before continuing. "You are all mariners and by nature cantankerous and accustomed to laxity," Doughty said, clearly unconcerned about endearing himself to the men. "Drake may permit such freedom shipboard but on land I am in command. Mark me, gentlemen. I love you all as dear friends but I will not listen kindly to grumbling, backbiting, or insolence of any stripe. Here you are soldiers, not sailors. Today you will learn how to withstand a cavalry charge."

Men on horseback, he explained, made quick work of infantry except when the men on foot stood together. The only way to break a mounted attack was to present the enemy with a wall of unyielding steel. Although their human riders might wish to continue forward into harm's way, horses—as I had learned during my association with Barnabas—were smart animals and would refuse to impale themselves.

First we practiced marching in unison and then we rehearsed a variety of defensive formations. The pike was an unwieldy weapon and hard to control. Within an hour my arms hurt from repeatedly raising and lowering the thing and my jerkin was sodden with sweat. Beside me, Lancelot Garget maintained a constant stream of invective, maligning Thomas Doughty and other gentlemen under his breath until he no longer had the wind to complain.

Then he let his pike slide from his grasp and keeled sideways on the shingle. His face was chalk white and very dry and he was breathing quickly. Although his eyes were partly open, he was not conscious.

"The man has been struck by the sun," said Thomas Doughty. "Give him shade and beer."

"Aye, captain," I replied.

I brought over a full dipper from the barrel, cradled Garget's head in a comfortable position for drinking, tipped the ladle against his lips, and allowed liquid to spill into his mouth.

He began to choke. The coughing, however, roused him.

Garget's eyes snapped open and he looked up at me.

"I am dead and in hell," he declared.

"No, sir," I answered. "You are in my arms."

"That is what I meant, pretty boy."

Reassured by his spite that Garget was on the mend, I helped him to his feet and we continued the drill another hour, until twilight, when Doughty dismissed the company. We were all begrimed and hot and I doubted there was a man in the fleet, mariner or gentlemen, who was unhappy to leave Cape Blank behind when we set sail the next day at high tide. No one could remember visiting a country as ugly and so utterly lacking in redeeming qualities.

As Powell Jemes had foretold, we freed the Spanish and Portuguese fishermen before departing although we did appropriate one of the canteras for ourselves, giving her owners the *Benedict* in exchange since their ship was the newer and better vessel. Drake also instructed one of the Portuguese caravels to accompany the fleet because her captain, a man named Gomez, claimed to know the location of a large cache of dried goat meat on Maio, which was one of the Cape Verde islands.

These lay five hundred miles in the Atlantic off the westernmost point of Africa. They had been settled by the Portuguese for a century and served as way stations for oceanic traffic, providing outbound ships with water and provisions for the long crossing, and offering returning vessels welcome relief after weeks or months of privation at sea. According to the men who had traveled the route before, the Portuguese colonists refused to supply any ships except their own and those flying Spanish flags.

"Ten, fifteen years ago, we could deal under the table

with the locals," said Christopher Waspe, another veteran mariner. "We would sail up and fire a cannon or two in the general direction of shore, which allowed the townspeople to pretend we held them hostage and to claim they conducted business with us under duress. But the dons clamped down on the practice and no longer permit trade whatever the excuse."

Waspe was a wiry man several inches under five feet in height. Despite his age, and he was well past fifty, he could clamber the ratlines faster than I could run on flat ground. He amused himself while we spoke by repeatedly flipping a dagger into the air with such precision that it landed point first in the deck every time.

"What will we do for victuals if we cannot trade?" I asked. "I purchased what I could at Cape Blank but little was available."

"Oh," said Waspe, "the general will make the Portugals a proposition they cannot turn down. Be sure of it."

"Aye, Chris," agreed Pascoe Goddy. "Drake will not accept any discourtesy. Not when we must prepare for the hard haul to the Malabar coast. 'Tis a damned long way to Calicut and Binny."

"Calicut, man?" laughed Waspe. "Binny? When will you get it through your head that we are headed for the *West* Indies, not the *East* Indies?"

"So you say but I do not."

"Stay, both of you!" I put in. "Pascoe, I thought you said the route to Asia was around the Cape of Storms—the Cape of Good Hope—at the bottom of Africa. Are we not sailing in the opposite direction, toward the Americas?"

"Aye, true enough. But were you a sailor—"

"Not I, sir! I am a cook."

"—*were* you a sailor, Perry, you would understand we are taking a necessary detour. Do you see, there is no safe course directly south down the African coast. Past Cape Verde is the land of Guinea and the shore becomes a festering labyrinth of brown water and reef. Worse, the prevailing wind beats up the beach and you have to fight for every yard of headway. Generally the Portugals steer west almost to the Americas in order to avoid Africa altogether. Then they catch an easterly breeze in the southern latitudes of Brazil and this carries them back around the cape into the Indian Ocean."

"Why go to the trouble?" Waspe objected. "God's body, man, the Spanish Main is half the distance of Kerala. Moreover, gold and silver make better cargo than even the best pepper or cinnamon."

Goddy scratched under his long gray hair while mulling over Waspe's argument. "Your logic is compelling, Chris," he admitted after a while. "Perhaps there is something to what you say. Still, my money is on Malabar or the Moluccas."

For the next several days the wind continued to blow from the northeast and east northeast, propelling the expedition south and west away from coast. As before, the pinnace led the fleet. Looking astern, I could see the sails of the other ships behind us towering from the blue like banked clouds, every yard of canvas set, even the topgallants. The ocean rolled under our keel in long swells, lifting the pinnace up and then lowering it into troughs so deep that we were surrounded by walls of brine taller than our masts. On the third morning we encountered a school of large fish with blunt snouts, which accompanied us for the better part of the day. Effortlessly matching our speed, some swam ahead of the pinnace, playing in the foam pushed forward by our bow, while others flanked us on either side. There were times the waves raised the fish higher than the deck of the ship, so that we could stare at each other eye to eye even though I was at the railing and they were in the water.

As day after day passed without sight of land, a grim mood settled upon my companions, even the most optimistic. Pascoe Goddy left his marlinspike in his belt and devoted his free hours to cleaning and readying his weaponry instead of to tying knots. Christopher Waspe practiced dagger throwing with such monotonous accuracy that a single square inch of planking, about a dozen feet from his usual seat beside the mainmast, became deeply pitted with scars while the decking around this inch had not one scratch. There was less conversation, too, and what little there was focused on the perils of the Atlantic crossing. Those who had made the voyage before, about a third of the crew, seemed to take a morose pleasure in explaining to the rest of us the hardships we were soon to encounter.

"The Portugals are famous for their cruelty and even more treacherous than the Spanish," said Powell Jemes, plunging a cloth down the muzzle of his arquebuse with a metal rod and swabbing out the bore for the hundredth time in succession. "'Tis unwise to have dealings with the fiends except at the end of a gun. Unfortunately, they infest the route we are sure to take. The Cape Verdes belong to them, as does Brazil." Perhaps to emphasize his point, Jemes scratched vigorously at a flea bite under his armpit. The action reminded other men of their own itches, and we all used the moment to tend to our personal irritations.

When the scraping died down, Bill Lege said, "There is no doubt Portugals derive uncommon satisfaction from drawing and quartering, as well as from flaying and flensing. I have heard that if a plantation slave manages to escape them, rather than fleeing the vicinity, the poor wretch will remain nearby so as to be in a position to inflict vengeance on his former masters. Can you imagine such dislike? 'Tis hard to appreciate."

Jemes shook his head solemnly and tugged at the twin spikes of tarred beard projecting beneath his chin. "Do you know, lads, the last time I came this way, the passage took eighty-five days. Eighty-five stinking days. We were becalmed for three straight weeks without a breath of wind. Nor was there a drop of rain for nearly a month. Mark me, death from thirst is not pretty. First your tongue swells. Then it turns black, as does your piss, what little leaks from your spout, which itself shrivels up from lack of use. Two men died after drinking seawater. Brine is not a healthful beverage. They did not go gently."

"Only two!" Pascoe Goddy said, slowly drawing a file along the edge of his cutlass, which lay flat across his lap. "We lost ten times that many from thirst returning with Hawkins from Mexico back in sixty-eight. An equal number starved. God speed us across the burning zone."

"God speed us," muttered many of the sailors in the audience at the same moment. Several made the sign of the cross.

"Aye, but here is the problem," Powell Jemes continued, evidently determined to outdo Goddy's pessimism. "There is no regularity to the weather along the equator. For weeks on end there will be squalls and storm and then, suddenly, for an equal length of time there will not be a breeze nor a cloud, only doldrums. A lucky captain with a good pilot can make the Atlantic voyage in less than a month. An unlucky captain, however—" Jemes shrugged and did not complete the sentence. "Eighty-five stinking days without sight of shore," he repeated.

"Thank God the general is a lucky bastard," said Bill Lege.

"He is a fine navigator, too," observed Will Shelle hopefully. "Drake will keep us heading straight."

After a week without a glimpse of land, on January 27th, we sighted the first of the Cape Verdes, which was known as Boa Vista. This was a small island with white beaches surrounding a mountainous interior, very beautiful to look at but dangerous to approach due to extensive rocks and shoals, so we remained well away from shore while passing along its eastern coast. By dusk Boa Vista had fallen behind and we continued sailing through the night, keeping on a southwesterly course. Late the next afternoon, a vast bank of fog became visible on the horizon. The mist shredded apart, revealing Maio, an island about four leagues in length with high ground toward its center. We anchored in seven or eight fathoms of water off a sandy bay just as the sun was setting.

John Winter called the crew together and addressed us from the helm of the pinnace. "Ready yourselves, gentlemen," he instructed. "We are going ashore and it unlikely that we will receive a friendly reception. The Portugals are not known for their hospitality."

"Bugger them all if they cannot be civil," growled Pascoe

Goddy, strapping a brace of pistols across his chest. He had tied his hair back to keep it out of eyes, revealing the scar he had received from the Spanish lieutenant at San Juan de Ulua.

"That is the spirit, Mr. Goddy," said Winter. "You may be a gruff dog but occasionally I do enjoy your attitude."

"Thank you, sir. Much obliged, sir," Pascoe said out loud while ducking his head and touching his fingers to his brow in order to hide his expression from Winter while he muttered under his breath, "And bugger you too very much, sir."

Following his example, I put on my steel helmet and padded leather brigandine, took up my cutlass, and found a seat in the longboat. Goddy sat beside me and patted my wrist with a callused hand. "Do not be anxious, lad," he said.

"I am fine," I replied.

"Whatever you say. Still, Perry, keep close and do as I do and all will be well. Do not forget you are in my charge! It will reflect poorly on me should you die on my watch."

We rowed across the glossy dark water and beached the longboat beside the three that had already arrived from other vessels. The moon had yet to rise and the night was black but we were forbidden to light torches or lanterns so as to not advertise our presence. Seventy men were milling about on the sand in the murk, waiting for orders. Half carried arquebuses or muskets while the rest were armed with swords or pikes. Whispered instructions passed through the crowd and we assembled around Thomas Doughty and John Winter, who had with them the captain of the caravel that had been taken captive in Barbary. "According to Mr. Gomez here, there is a town on the other side of the point," explained Doughty, pitching his voice loud enough to carry through the crowd but no further. "Supposedly the locals maintain a store of dried meat with which to supply their king's ships. Our task is to convince the Portugals to part with the victuals we require."

As he spoke, the moon lifted above the horizon, bringing the landscape out of darkness and allowing me to see that Doughty had replaced his elegant attire with a steel jacket and a skirt of chain mail. Like Goddy, he carried a brace of pistols as well as his sword.

"A word of caution, gentlemen," Doughty continued. "We want these people to fear us, not hate us. There is to be no killing unless it is absolutely necessary. Furthermore, it is critical that silence be maintained if we are not to lose the advantage of surprise. I will deal severely with any man breaking the quiet, this is a promise on which you may rely. Does everyone follow?"

No one answered.

"Excellent. Line up two abreast, pikes to the fore, arquebuses and muskets to the rear. Mr. Gomez, lead the way."

I fell in beside Pascoe Goddy and we trailed the men ahead of us, Powell Jemes and Ned Bright, away from the beach, through a screen of trees, and across a broken plain. The going was difficult despite the moonlight and I kept my eyes on the ground in order not to stumble but did so more than once. The Portuguese town lay three miles off, an hour's walk under ordinary circumstances, yet we did not reach it until long after midnight since we were crossing unfamiliar territory in gloom while burdened with armor and weaponry. Then we were deployed in a loose circle around the place and told to wait.

The sky brightened and the stars paled and our surroundings came into definition. Twenty small houses with
stone walls and thatched roofs became visible. In the center of
the town was a white washed church with a bell tower three
stories high. Somewhere a rooster began crowing.

"It should not be long now," whispered Pascoe Goddy.
"Remember, Perry, stay near."

"Aye, Pascoe," I whispered back, gripping my cutlass tightly. The cord wound around the hilt absorbed the sweat from my
palm, preventing the weapon from slipping in my grasp.

John Bruer, who had been Lackland's master, raised a
trumpet to his mouth and blew a staccato succession of notes.
Two other members of the musical company began beating
out a martial rhythm on drums slung from their hips. This
was our signal.

"God save the queen and deliver her enemies to hell!"
called Thomas Doughty, raising his sword to the sky and striding forward.

"God save the queen!" we roared in return and began advancing into the town after him, all of us walking at the same
pace so as to maintain a cordon without gaps through which
an enemy could escape our gauntlet.

Despite what I had said earlier to Pascoe Goddy, my
pulse was hammering in my ears and my mouth had gone
so dry that I could neither swallow nor wet my lips. I had
believed my experiences in Mortlake and along the coast of
Barbary had accustomed me to violence yet there was a very
different sensation about advancing deliberately into battle.
At first I thought I must be afraid and I worried that I would

prove to be a coward when put to the test but then I began to understand that what I felt was excitement. With every step I became more charged with tension and I found myself going ahead on my toes, unable to place the soles of my feet flat on the ground. My cutlass, many pounds of metal, seemed to weigh no more than my kitchen knife. Nor was I conscious of the heaviness of the brigandine across my shoulders.

I would have thought the peal of the trumpet and the rattling of the drums, not to mention the bellowing of English voices, would have summoned the townspeople from their homes.

Yet no one appeared.

Unable to stop myself, I made directly for the nearest building. Only Pascoe Goddy's hold on my arm prevented me from entering. "Do you want to die?" he growled. "Never pass through a strange door without first making sure what is behind it. Jemes, your pike!"

"Aye, Pascoe." Powell Jemes slammed the butt of the weapon against the wood panel and the door burst back off its hinges.

Within was a small room empty of both occupants and fittings except for fragments of broken furniture. The place stank of mold and rot and the floor was littered with animal droppings. Much of the thatch had fallen from the roof, admitting a dank light and making very clear that the place had not been inhabited for months or years.

"Where are the bastards?" Jemes muttered. Moisture dripped from the points of his beard and his shaven head was flushed red. A vein throbbed in the skin beneath the dragon inked on his scalp, making the image seem alive and pulsing.

Returning outside, we joined the rest of the company in the square. No one had discovered any more evidence of the Portugals than we had. Francis Fletcher, sword in hand, came down the steps of the church, kicking ahead of him a half dozen squawking chickens. "The foul edifice is abandoned," the parson said with satisfaction, tugging at his white collar to loosen it around his neck. "It is naught but a fold for goats and a roost for hens. The only sacrifices offered here for some time have been the dung of one and the excrement of the other. God damn all Papists."

"Where, sir, are the inhabitants?" Thomas Doughty asked the Portuguese captain, Gomez.

"I not know, *senhor*," answered the other with obvious perplexity. "*Esta cidade,* she had many peoples *na minha última visita.*"

"And the store of *cabritos* you promised to discover for us?"

Gomez pointed at a building to the right of the church, which was somewhat more substantial than the others and had rusty bars on its windows. "*Armazém do rei,*" he said. The king's warehouse.

"Well, now it is as empty as the rest."

There was a splash as Ned Bright dropped a bucket down the well in the center of the square. He pulled it back hand over hand, lifted the brim to his lips, and instantly spat out what was in his mouth. "Salted, by God!" he exclaimed. "The damned Portugals have soiled the water."

"Captain! Captain! Look what I have here!"

Christopher Waspe came into the square, prodding ahead of him with the point of his dagger a barefoot and shirtless man in threadbare pantaloons that once had been dyed blue but that were now bleached almost white by sun and brine. "The bastard was skulking in the bushes and spying on us," Waspe explained, giving his captive a kick and sending him sprawling in the dust at Doughty's feet. "Should I hurt him, captain?" Waspe asked, taking the man by the hair, lifting his head, and placing the knife to his throat. "Just say the word."

"Your enthusiasm does you credit, Mr. Waspe," Doughty replied. "But let us first discover whether the fellow will speak of his own accord. Mr. Gomez, if you would, translate."

"*Sim, senhor.*"

The captain knelt beside his fellow Portugal and began talking with him in their own language. "*Este homem*, he says his peoples, they have fled to the hills *com seus animais*," explained Gomez. "The coast became *muito perigoso*. Very dangerous. The peoples, they were in fear for their lives and commodities. *Não há uma peste sobre esta ilha.*"

There is a scourge upon this island.

"A scourge, sir?" asked John Winter. "What manner of scourge?"

Gomez spoke a few more words to the man, whose eyes never stopped rolling with dread as he looked up at us from his position on the ground beneath Christopher Waspe's dagger. A thread of crimson trickled where the steel had nicked his skin.

Then Gomez nodded in understanding, regained his feet, and brushed his knees and hands clean. His answer consisted of one word.

"Parrots."

The Taking of the *Santa Maria*

January 30, 1578 – February 1, 1578
St. Jago

"Parrots, by God!" exclaimed Thomas Doughty. "Did you say—parrots?"

"*Sim, senhor,*" replied the Portuguese captain. "These parrots, they roost on the Guinea coast and descend on this island in great flocks, murdering the peoples, fornicating with the womens, and stealing the *animais*. They are an awful plague."

"I imagine they would be," agreed John Winter. Like Doughty, he wore steel breast and back plates and chain mail although he carried a solid hanger rather than the slimmer rapier the other preferred. Absently curling the point of his mustache between his fingers, Winter stared skyward. Nor was he alone in examining the heavens. Everyone else had their heads craned back, looking worriedly for any sign of threat from above. "Christ's body," Winter continued, "these must be damned monstrous birds, Mr. Gomez—"

"With your permission, sir," I interrupted. "I do believe the Portugal has erred in his translation. He does not mean *parrots*. He means *pirates*. Is that not correct, *senhor*?"

"*Sim.* Parrots."

There was more than one exclamation of relief when this confusion was resolved. Thomas Doughty laughed. "My thanks, Mr. James," he said. "For a moment I feared we were sailing with Sinbad rather than with Francis Drake." This was a reference I did not understand until later, when Parson Fletcher explained Sinbad was a Moor seaman who had encountered enormous hawks, known as *rocs*, during his travels. "Let the man rise," Doughty continued. "Assure him we are not parrots. Tell him we will pay for any victuals. Here," he finished, tossing a small piece of silver. "Take this in good faith."

Christopher Waspe lowered his dagger reluctantly and the man scrambled to his feet, clutching the coin in his fist. A second later he was showing us his heels as he sprinted away.

"We will never see that fellow again, Tom," observed Winter.

"Perhaps," replied Doughty. "Still, we have lost nothing and it is always possible our kindness will convince his friends to deal with us."

"Possible, sir, but unlikely."

Suddenly, even with the warmth of the morning, I felt chilled to the bone and very tired. My teeth chattering against one another, and my body shivering violently, I sat down so that I would not lose my balance. Noticing my discomfort, Pascoe Goddy went to his knees beside me, removed my helmet, and began mopping my brow with the cuff of his sleeve while saying, "Breathe deeply, lad. That is it. Slow and steady."

"What seems to be the problem?" asked Thomas Doughty. "Has Mr. James taken ill?"

"No, captain," replied Goddy. "Perry is suffering from an excess of martial passion. I have seen the condition before in other brave men. He should recover soon, God willing, as the fever discharges from his blood. "

As Goddy predicted, I soon stopped yawning and was able to resume my place among the company. Dividing into two groups, half of the men followed John Winter west along the shore while the rest of us trailed Thomas Doughty inland. The soil under our boots was rich brown loam, which supported a profusion of plant life. Everyone was amazed that even though it was January, the dead of winter in England, here the vegetation was flourishing as if it was summer, with both green and ripe fruit growing on the same plant at the same time. There were innumerable fig trees and once we discovered a bower of Muscatine grapes, which were as sweet as any I had tasted, and which Parson Fletcher pronounced to be the fairest he had seen in all his travels. We also came across large broad leaved bushes that bore tubular fruit, called *plantanes*, clustered together like puddings. In many places there were groves of the tall trees I had seen from afar in Barbary. These had neither leaves nor boughs until the crown, where there was a clump of fronds. The fruits of this plant were each as big as a man's head.

"They are *cocos*," said the Portuguese captain. "*Muito delicioso.*"

"Aye, but difficult to harvest, I am sure," replied Doughty since the lowest hanging fruit were still more than twenty feet above the ground.

"Permit me to try, captain," said Christopher Waspe. "I can do it."

Removing his boots, Waspe flexed his toes, clamped his dagger between his teeth, and began the ascent. Even lacking handholds, he climbed the tree with the same ease that he scaled the ratlines aboard the *Pelican*. At the top he cut free a dozen *cocos* and let the fruit fall to the ground. Thomas Doughty took one and split open its hard green shell with a slash of his sword, revealing an inner cavity lined with white meat and containing a pint of milky liquor.

Notwithstanding the assurances of Captain Gomez that the flesh was fit to eat, no one wanted to be the first to have a taste.

"Let Perry try the thing," someone suggested. "Is he not a cook?"

"Aye, so goes the rumor," agreed an anonymous wit, and I was pushed forward by helping hands to the front of the group. Thomas Doughty gave me the *coco*. "Thank you for volunteering, Mr. James."

"My pleasure, sir," I replied. Tilting the strange fruit against my lips without further deliberation, I drank the juice. Then I scooped out a lump of meat with my knife and began chewing.

"Your opinion, sir?" asked Doughty.

"It is indeed delicious, captain. The milk is vaguely sweet and refreshing to the tongue. The rind has the texture of hard cheese but the flavor of curds leavened with honey. I suspect *cocos* could be made into excellent puddings or added to pastries. It is also likely the fruit does well in storage because of its hard shell. We should gather as many as we can and bring them back to the ship."

Only a couple other men, however, sampled the fruit in spite of my favorable verdict. Nor did anyone seem particularly relieved that the *coco* had not sickened me or caused my death.

Marching inland again, we kept on the look out for

both meat and water but found neither until we climbed into the hills that filled the center of the island. These were treeless wrinkled hummocks of rock, gravel, and dry red soil. The tough grass growing on their flanks was closely cropped by droves of wild goats, wily and suspicious creatures who fled to higher ground at our approach, perching nimbly on ledges so precarious that I would not have thought an eagle could balance on them. Bill Lege, the cooper, priding himself on his competence with a musket, asked Doughty to allow him to take down one of the beasts.

"You have my permission, sir," Doughty replied. "In all honesty, though, I do not foresee your success. The distance is too great."

"A penny says Lege does it," declared Luke Adden. Another man said:

"Three pence swears he does not."

There was a flurry of betting and soon everyone had odds one way or the other. Even Thomas Doughty was caught up in the spirit of the moment and relaxed sufficiently to promise a shilling purse of his own money should Lege hit the target.

"The prize is already in my pocket, captain, many thanks," the cooper answered, loading his weapon with powder, ball, and wadding.

A musket fired two ounce lead shot. Since the weapon weighed more than twenty pounds, it had to be supported on a stand in order to be held comfortably. Lege stuck the metal rod meant for this purpose securely in the dirt and rested his gun in the socket at the top of the pole. He licked his index finger and held it up to learn the direction of the wind. Then he put his shoulder to the stock and squinted along the barrel.

The weapon had an effective range of eighty yards and the goat at which Lege was aiming was at least that far away. Making the target would be a remarkable demonstration of skill.

He pulled back the serpentine, cocking the musket. Although I had not placed a wager, I found myself as curious as the others and held my breath while Lege sighted and squeezed the trigger.

The instant the report rang out a shaggy billy goat bellowed with anguish and rolled down the hillside. *Baa*ing in alarm, the rest of the flock bounded away, jumping from foothold to foothold with such alacrity that they appeared to be dancing on air.

Now even more skittish than previously, the animals refused to allow us to get within shooting distance of them again, and we returned to the fleet without provisions but for the single goat Lege had killed and some baskets of figs, grapes, *cocos*, and *plantanes*. John Winter and his men had encountered no better luck than our group excepting that they came across a pile of dried *cabritos* placed in their path on a bed of fronds, clearly an offering from the inhabitants of the island.

"The kid was so putrid, we left it behind," Winter complained. "Nor was the quantity generous. Evidently the locals were less than impressed by your kindness, Tom."

"I will not argue, sir. Portugals are a damned churlish lot."

"What of water, gentlemen?" asked Drake.

"No satisfaction there," answered Doughty. "The wells have been salted and the only springs we found were so inaccessible that it would be impossible to take the liquid away in barrels."

"Sorry news, by God," Drake said. "I had hoped to resupply here and bypass St. Jago, which is strongly defended. Ah, well, a mariner must either sail with the wind or beat against it. Blacollers! Order the crews to the ships. We leave at once."

"Aye, sir. Bless me, men, you heard the general. Get moving!"

St. Jago lay a dozen leagues to the west. With fair winds filling our sails, we sighted the island just past noon the following day, which was January 31st. It was the largest of all the Cape Verdes, ten leagues in length from north to south and five leagues in breadth. Even more mountainous than Boa Vista or Maio, St. Jago was not as green as either. A dry haze covered the upper slopes and fingers of reddish mist reached down the hillsides into the coastal valleys.

As usual, prepared to receive attack, the pinnace sailed ahead of the fleet as we followed the shore south and west.

Rounding a broad point, we came upon a town built in the bottom of the bay. The seaward approach was guarded by a stone blockhouse and I could see the black muzzles of cannon poking from between the crenellations of the fort. Apparently the defenders kept their weapons loaded and primed at all times. Less than a minute passed before the battery fired. The bloom of smoke when the guns discharged was visible immediately but seconds went by before we heard the noise of the barrage echo across the harbor.

"They know they cannot touch us," said Pascoe Goddy as the cannon balls plunged into the water a quarter mile short of our position, sending spouts of foam into the air. "The Portugals are simply expressing their joy at our arrival, God rot them all. Now sit your arse down, Perry. You are interfering with my view."

"My apologies, Pascoe," I said, taking a place beside him under the mainmast. "I have never been shot at by heavy artillery before."

"Get used to it, lad. We are sailing with Francis Drake."

Two other towns shelled us as we continued voyaging down the coast of St. Jago but neither salvo landed any nearer than the first. The shore became very low as we advanced although a tall conical peak could be seen hanging in the sky many miles to the north. On almost every point of land the inhabitants of the island had erected large wood crucifixes to announce their piety, and on several capes they had raised crude lumber statues meant to represent Christ or a saint who had expired in pain. We were passing the fifth or sixth of these icons when I noticed a longboat putting out from the *Pelican* and heading toward the beach.

In spite of the distance Francis Fletcher was unmistakable due to his stern posture and the large black hat he wore. For obvious reasons hulking Tom Moone was equally recognizable.

"What do you suppose they are after?" I asked, waving toward the longboat, which was now being dragged up the shingle.

Goddy placed the flat of his hand above his eyes and squinted. After a moment he exclaimed: "No, the bastards would not!"

The men of the shore party had looped a noose around the timber cross and were hauling together at the rope in an effort to tear the thing down. Parson Fletcher had the first position on the line and was evidently exhorting the others to pull harder although I could not hear his voice because of the separation between us.

"This is not right," Goddy went on, shaking his head in disapproval.

"What are you, Pascoe, a God damned Papist?" asked Powell Jemes. "Why should you care what happens to a God damned idol?"

"Bugger your holes both fore and aft," Goddy snapped. "Any man who calls me Papist must back his words with steel."

Powell Jemes was six inches taller and ten years younger than Goddy but the older man had a lethal reputation matched by few others in the fleet. "I meant no offense," Jemes said hurriedly.

"None taken. Still, 'tis a bad idea to meddle with sacred relics of any faith. No good can come of such desecration."

"Aye," agreed Willan Smythe, who had been the master of the cannon crew to which I had been assigned aboard the *Pelican*. Now he had responsibility for the bowchaser of the pinnace. "The parson's iconoclasm is sure to cause hard feelings," Smythe went on. "I will not name names, but everyone knows certain of our mates are sufficiently misguided as to profess the Roman superstition."

"That is their business, Smythe," said Peter Corder. "As long as a man watches my back, and hauls on the bowlines with good cheer, I could care less if he prays to Jesus or to the devil."

"Do not let the general hear you hold such an opinion," cautioned Powell Jemes. "He is as strict as Fletcher in matters of faith."

Just then a cracking noise snapped across the intervening water. The crucifix broke free of its foundation and tumbled into the surf and split apart into fragments. Goddy shook his head again and made the sign of the cross. Other men imitated him, equally disturbed by the destruction. Soon, however, we were sailing around the cape and our attention was diverted by a new scene.

Approximately four miles off our bow two Portuguese merchant ships were heading westward into the Atlantic away from land.

"Now this is more like it," Goddy said, rising to his feet and going forward in order to have a better look. "Aye, lad, do you notice how low the Portugals are riding? Both are heavily burdened. It will be interesting to learn just what cargo they carry."

The bay from which the merchantmen were departing held the largest settlement we had encountered in the Cape Verdes, several dozen buildings contained within sturdy ramparts. Castles at each end of the seawall protected the harbor with cannon, which began firing soon after our approach was observed. By this time I understood the guns could not reach us and I paid them little notice. Following the lead of my companions, I donned my armor and hung my cutlass from my belt after running the blade a couple times against a stone to whet it.

John Winter, hanger in hand, stood beside the tiller. "Steer for the outermost ship, Mr. Danielles," he ordered the helmsman. "We will take the larger vessel first and then return for the smaller one."

"*Oui, mon capitaine*," Danielles answered, putting his weight against the wood shaft and pointing the nose of the pinnace several degrees to starboard.

"Corder! Powell Jemes!" Winter called. "Ready the mankillers."

"Readying the mankillers," they answered, going to the railing and loading the swivel guns with bits of rusty iron scrap kept for that reason in buckets on the deck. Both lit slow matches from the smoldering clay pots beneath the weapons.

"Mr. Smythe! Fire a warning shot from the bowchaser."

"Aye, captain! Firing a warning shot!"

With the same care to detail that he had exercised aboard the *Pelican* while attending to Fat Jane, the demi-culverin, Willan Smythe adjusted the elevation of the smaller gun now under his command. The bowchaser was cast iron instead of bronze and was known as a *minion*. Its barrel was six feet long and it fired iron balls weighing three pounds.

Satisfied with his calculations, Smythe placed a match to the touch hole at the precise instant the pinnace, coming down on a swell, was level with the Portuguese galleons.

The minion roared and threw itself back while venting a dark cloud of smoke. A plume of water erupted directly between the fleeing vessels.

"Excellent, Mr. Smythe," said Winter. "That should send a message requiring no translation."

I would have thought so, too, but the Portuguese ships stubbornly refused to strike their sails. Instead they put on every yard of canvas their masts could carry, spritsails as well as topgallants.

"So the bastards wish to be difficult," said John Winter. "Give them another volley, Mr. Smythe. Singe their beards."

"Aye, sir," Willan Smythe growled. At his gesture subordinates sponged out the bore of the minion and rammed home a new load of powder and iron. Then they hauled the cannon tight against the gunwale.

Muttering, "God damn all Portugals," Smythe put the match to the touch hole again and the minion exploded a second time, sending a ball directly across the bow of the forward galleon.

Still the Portuguese ships failed to surrender. They were, however, merchantmen and designed for the accommodation of cargo rather than for velocity or war while our pinnace, on the other hand, had been built to be fast, maneuverable, and deadly. Within a quarter hour we closed with the leading vessel, which had a burden of one hundred and fifty tons and was the length of the *Pelican* but somewhat wider abeam. According to the white lettering across her stern, her home port was Lisbon.

She was the *Santa Maria*.

When we were twenty yards to starboard, Winter said, "Mr. James! This is their last warning. The Portugals must come about."

"Aye, sir," I said and relayed his demand in a loud voice, circling my hands around my mouth in order to throw my words to the other ship. I could see a dozen men on her deck, half of them sailors and the rest merchants and gentlemen. The latter were standing in a group by the mizzenmast, apparently arguing with one another about how to respond to our ultimatum. The ship's master, who wore a black leather vest over a gray tunic, said a word to the helmsman and then raised his arm and shook his fist at us. To make his meaning absolutely clear, he put two fingers together and jabbed them furiously at the pinnace.

"What is the fellow saying?" asked John Winter.

"I cannot tell exactly, sir. He appears to be expressing a desire to engage in conjugal relations with your mother."

Winter was not entertained. "Powell Jemes!" he ordered. "Give the Portugals a taste of ginger. Take down the main, hear me! Take it down."

It was four o'clock in the afternoon and the cloudless sky allowed the full force of the sun to beat upon the surface of the sea, which broke the light apart into a thousand bright reflections. The dragon on Powell Jemes's bare scalp seemed to breathe fire as he hunched over the mankiller and swiveled the flared muzzle of the weapon at the galleon. Then he touched the sparking match to the breach.

The mankiller gave an angry belch and sprayed a swathe of iron scrap into the Portuguese main course, cutting a hundred holes in the canvas. Within seconds the pressure of the wind burst the entire thing to pieces, and the tatters writhed across the deck like enraged vipers.

"Should I offer them another taste, captain?" Jemes inquired, feeding his gun a load of metal.

"No, I do not believe that will be required," Winter replied. "It appears the Portugals have finally come to their senses."

In order not to overshoot the *Santa Maria*, we lowered our own canvas when the Portuguese merchantman furled hers. Winter sent a dozen men to the oars and we rowed the pinnace across the remaining distance to where the other ship was wallowing in the swell.

"Pollmane, Lege!" Winter ordered. "Grapples."

Robert Pollmane and Bill Lege began whirling their iron hooks. Then they slung them up and over the gunwale of the galleon.

Winter settled his helmet and gave his mustache a satisfied stroke. "Goddy, Adden, Lege, Cooke—and Perry James, as well—to the Portugal. You have my leave to be as cruel as necessary. These fellows have annoyed me."

Drawing my cutlass, I joined the rest of the boarding party behind John Winter on the poop, the only part of the pinnace high enough off the water to reach the deck of the *Santa Maria*, which was a much larger vessel. Once again I began to fill with the tension I had felt during the attack on the abandoned town on the island of Maio, and I had to deliberately tell myself to calm down and not to launch myself into action ahead of my friends. Pascoe Goddy punched my arm and grinned.

"Try not to slay them all, lad," he said. "Leave some for the rest of us. Now come on, Perry. It is time we earned our wages."

John Winter pointed his hanger skyward, the steel catching the sun and sending splinters of brilliance in all directions.

"After me, gentlemen," he commanded.

We fanned out across the deck of the *Santa Maria* with our weapons drawn. The Portuguese crew retreated with their hands in the air, swarthy men in dark blue pantaloons, striped shirts, and wool caps dyed pink. Their expressions were murderous but only one of them, a petty officer, had sufficient courage to speak his mind.

"Lutheran pirates," he spat in passable English. "God send you to hell and show you no mercy while you suffer."

Pascoe Goddy rewarded this bravery by slamming the metal basket of his cutlass across the man's jaw and hammering him to the deck, where he lay with blood drooling from his lips onto the ivory that had been knocked from his mouth.

"Does anyone else wish to share their opinion?" Goddy asked.

No one answered. Two of the crew lifted their companion upright and began shaking him awake while another sailor scuffed the dislodged teeth into the scuppers.

"All right then," Goddy said. "Into the forecastle. Move your tails!"

Aboard the *Santa Maria* the forecastle was employed as a storage compartment for bulk commodities of little value. When I had translated Goddy's instructions, the crewmen dropped their knives and sharp tools on the deck and filed inside the gloomy space while glaring sullenly at us. After the last man entered, Pascoe slammed the door shut and jammed his marlinspike into the latch to prevent it from opening again. Then he turned to Bill Lege, who was armed with an arquebuse. Unlike a musket, the weapon was light enough for Lege to aim without a stand, couching the curved stock under his armpit.

"Remain on guard, Bill," Goddy said. "Let no one pass."

At the stern of the ship the merchants and gentleman had also been relieved of their arms, mainly rapiers similar to the one Thomas Doughty owned and expensive pistols with scrollwork engraved on their barrels. Despite being hundreds of leagues from their home country, these men were as stylishly outfitted as they would be in Portugal, their pants and cods stuffed with bombast, ruffles at both their necks and wrists, their moustaches and beards trimmed and oiled to a sophisticated gloss. Although a few seemed fearful, most were furious at being inconvenienced by our boarding of their vessel. Wagging their fingers eloquently under our noses, they expressed their dissatisfaction in an excited jabber of Portuguese, Spanish, and French. From what I could decipher, some were offering us bribes, others were making threats, and a fair number were providing candid opinions, generally unflattering, about our dress, deportment, probable antecedents, and aroma.

At a nod from John Winter, Pascoe Goddy drew a pistol and fired over their heads. Then Winter said, "Whoever next speaks without leave takes it in the gut. Make sure the Portugals understand, Mr. James."

Next Winter addressed the man who had goaded us while we chased the galleon. "You, sir, are a damned fool. How dare you disregard my order to come about. Did you think I would forget such disrespect?"

"Get off my ship, Lutheran dog," hissed the other through clenched teeth. As I would learn, Nuño da Silva was both the captain and the pilot of the *Santa Maria*. He also had his own money invested in the cargo and thus faced not only professional humiliation but financial ruin if the vessel were to be stolen. He was in his late fifties with gray hair and a white beard, which was cut in a flat line two inches under his chin. Anger had pinched his eyes into slits and wet his lips with spittle. "I will see you hanged, pirate!" da Silva continued. "*Sim, senhor*, and your men, too, every one. Get off my ship!"

Equally incensed, Winter lifted his clenched fist to strike da Silva but did not do so, controlling himself with an obvious effort of will. Allowing his hand to drop, he told da Silva, "I do not have the leisure for this. But I assure you, sir, we will continue our conversation."

Less than five minutes had passed since we boarded the *Santa Maria*. In that interval the second Portuguese galleon had managed to steer around and was now heading back to shore.

"She must be stopped before she comes in under the harbor guns," Winter said. He studied the horizon, estimating the distance of the *Pelican*, the *Marigold*, and the *Elizabeth*, whose sails were only now arriving into view around the point. "They will not reach her in time," Winter concluded. "Mr. Cooke—"

"What say, John?"

"I am taking the pinnace after the other Portugal. I leave you in command here. Mr. Goddy is your second. Heed his suggestions since he is an evil ruffian with deplorable instincts. As for these popinjays—" Winter meant the Portuguese merchants and gentlemen—"secure them in the main cabin but do them no injury unless they offer resistance. Nor is the cargo to be touched. Drake will want a record of every item when he comes aboard. Do you understand?"

"Absolutely and completely, John," Cooke replied.

With a last hard stare at Nuño da Silva, Winter returned to the pinnace and set off after the retreating galleon.

John Cooke was a gentleman rather than a mariner and had come from Plymouth aboard the *Elizabeth*, where he was known to keep his distance from the sailors, preferring the company of Emmanuel Wattkyns, Leonard Vicarye, and persons of similar standing. Below deck it was rumored Cooke had backed the voyage with three hundred pounds of his own capital, which made him a wealthy man although only a minor investor in the expedition, but no one was sure since such information was confidential. He was in his thirties, clean shaven, and possessed a nose as long as Hal Audley's although Cooke's was as thin as a knife.

Turning to Goddy, he said, "You heard Winter. What say you do me service and lock these gentleman away. But not him—" Cooke meant da Silva. "We need to talk."

Six men altogether had been left behind on the *Santa Maria* to guard the ship while we waited for the rest of the fleet to arrive. Two watched over the prisoners, Bill Lege at the forecastle and Luke Adden before the cabin in which the gentleman were confined. Rob Pollmane took over the helm while Christopher Waspe climbed the mainmast to the topgallant spar in order to serve as lookout. John Cooke, Pascoe Goddy, and I remained with Nuño da Silva.

"Where is the manifest?" Cooke asked while I translated. "The bill of lading, sir. Do not pretend to misunderstand. We wish to examine this document at once. Speak up, sir. I say, speak up."

The Portuguese captain displayed no more affection for John Cooke than he had shown for Captain Winter. "Eat what falls from my tail onto the anchor links, Lutheran," answered da Silva. "I will not help you."

Folding his arms across his chest, he turned his back in defiance of us and refused to utter another word.

"Have you ever encountered such pigheadedness?" complained John Cooke. "What say, Goddy? Should we chastise the scoundrel until he becomes more forthcoming?"

"An excellent suggestion, sir," Pascoe said. "Unfortunately, Captain Winter ordered us not to harm the bastards without reason. This would seem to specifically rule out strict interrogatory techniques."

Cooke sighed and bit his lip while mulling over the situation. "I fear you are right," he admitted at last. "Still, I am curious to discover just what the Portugals are hiding. What say we dispatch the boy below to conduct an inventory."

Pascoe considered the idea. When he eventually nodded approval, I went to the hatch leading down into the hold. Before I began the descent, however, the noise of an explosion stopped me.

Turning around, I saw blossoms of smoke expand before the castles in the harbor. Their guns fired again, and again, until the barrage was a constant roll of thunder.

The second Portuguese galleon was racing toward land. If she could get in close to shore, the coastal artillery would protect her against the pinnace sailing hard in her wake. A half mile still separated the vessels.

"Do you think Captain Winter will catch the Portugal?" I asked.

Pascoe studied the scene thoughtfully before passing judgment. "Winter is a humorless bastard," he observed, "but you cannot fault his seamanship, lad. I would say the odds are dead even."

As on the *Pelican*, the hold of the *Santa Maria* was a dark crowded warren, noisy with the ebb and flow of water against the hull and with the creaking of timber and with the jangle of loose hardware. Removing a lantern from a peg by the ladder, I began moving cautiously among the aisles of barrels and crates.

The merchant ship had been bearing west when we encountered her, beginning the long journey across the Atlantic to Brazil. Thus I was not surprised to discover her laden with goods desired by colonists on a frontier, commodities they could not manufacture and for which they would pay dearly. The first several chests I opened contained fishhooks, knives, rapiers, combs, and scissors while the next three were packed with nails. Others held bundles of linen and brocaded fabric, which would appeal to the wives of the settlers and to their mistresses. One crate was full of hats, each as gaudy as the one that had flown from my head in Plymouth Sound. There were also stacks of tanned leather, jars of olive oil, and huge bales of folded sailcloth and netting fringed with cork.

It was not until I began sampling barrels at random that I realized the true value of the cargo.

"God's body," I said aloud, closing the spigot and tapping another barrel in order to assure myself I was not mistaken. "No wonder the Portugals were so cautious. There is a treasure here."

Knowing my companions would wish to be informed of my discovery, I made my way back to the hatch leading above deck.

This slammed shut before I reached it.

The same instant I heard English oaths and the boom of an arquebuse being discharged. Bill Lege was under attack.

"Take the pirates alive!" someone commanded in Portuguese, probably Nuño da Silva. "We will need prisoners."

"What of the Lutheran in the rigging, *capitão*? And the lad below?"

"Four hostages should be sufficient. The other two are common sailors. Dispose of them."

At once there were pistol reports and I knew Christopher Waspe had been targeted by the men on deck. A moment later the hatch opened and someone came down the ladder into the hold to seek my life.

My opponent, one of the Portuguese gentlemen, wore a smart red jacket accented with purple edging and tight silk hose with a herringbone weave. But his expression was grim and he held a cocked gun in each hand. While his vision was acclimating to the murk, I kicked a piece of scrap skittering along the deck. As I hoped, the sound drew his fire.

Before the flash and noise died away, I took up my cutlass and raised it for a ferocious slash.

I failed, however, to take into account the lack of headroom. The point of my sword jammed into the planking above me and stuck fast in the wood. Dropping his spent pistols, the Portugal unsheathed a rapier. Then he lunged, thrusting sharp steel straight toward me.

I managed to wrench loose my cutlass in time to survive the assault, and hammered the heavy pommel of my sword against the neck of the rapier in an attempt to shatter the lighter weapon. This failed.

Nor was I able to take the offensive since I was hemmed in by crates and barrels and unable to wield the cutlass properly.

When the Portugal lunged again, I could not react fast enough to beat the blade away. The rapier pierced my brigandine above the heart.

I was saved from abrupt death by one of the metal plates sewn into the lining of the vest, which prevented the point from entering. The rapier bent into a half circle under the pressure of the thrust and then relaxed into a straight line when the Portugal stepped back.

It was becoming painfully clear to me that a rapier was the weapon of choice in confined quarters. Aware of his advantage, the Portugal smiled while making beckoning gestures with his free hand.

"Come to me, Lutheran," he said. "Do not be afraid. Dying will take you to a blessed place where you will enjoy the loving-kindness of God throughout eternity. Unless, of course, you go to hell."

A strange rash part of myself wanted to accept the invitation and engage my enemy no matter the consequences. A more reasonable voice, however, told me this would a serious lapse of judgment. In our brief passages of arms it had become obvious the Portuguese gentlemen was as dangerous as he was stylish. Without a tactical edge, I was certain to meet my doom under his sword.

I retreated backward into the shadows.

"Is there a problem, Anselmo Godinho?" someone called down from above. "Do you require assistance?"

"No, no, thank you for your courtesy, *Senhor* Pinto. It should not take long to dispatch this dog."

"Do not toy with the Lutheran. Finish the business and come topside. Da Silva wants all hands on deck."

"You have my promise, *senhor*, I will not delay."

True to his word, Godinho came after me without further hesitation. I had just reached one of the chests I had opened earlier, which contained combs, scissors, pins, and other steel items.

Throwing up the lid, I rummaged desperately among the contents until my fingers closed on the hilt of a rapier.

I had never handled the weapon before but I had watched Thomas Doughty and his brother practice on the half deck of the *Pelican* so often that I knew how the sword should be held.

Turning sideways in order to present as thin a target as possible, I put my left arm behind my back and advanced on the Portugal with the blade extended. Godinho clucked his disapproval.

"Your attitude is sloppy, Lutheran," he admonished me. "To master the rapier requires years of effort. I myself have studied the weapon since childhood in order to attain my present level of expertise."

"I figure what I know is sufficient to do you harm, *senhor*," I replied, lying unreservedly in a vain effort to intimidate my enemy.

Defense in an engagement between rapiers relied on the wrist. When Godinho lunged, I spun my sword in an arc and forced his blade to miss me by a fraction of an inch. According to orthodox practice, my next move should have been to bring my point back into line. Instead I closed with Godinho and slapped his face with my left hand.

When I had taken the rapier from the chest of metalwork, I had also appropriated a cushion stuck with needles. This I had kept hidden in my fist behind my back until now.

A hundred steel splinters pierced the Portugal's skin and pinned the cushion to him when I let go. Howling in surprise and pain, Godinho ripped the pillow from his cheek, leaving half the needles behind in his flesh. Blood trickled from the punctures.

My trick distracted the Portugal barely long enough.

We were too close together for me to use the rapier so I dropped the sword and hoisted up a firkin, a small barrel laden with thirty pounds of iron nails, and rammed it into Godinho's stomach.

The impact knocked him backward and expelled the breath from his chest in an anguished gasp. Before he could recover, I struck him with the firkin again, and his eyes closed. I did not know if Godinho was alive or dead and I did not care. To be sure he would not trouble me further, I pulled down a stack of cartons and buried him beneath them.

I had to help my friends but I did not know how. Only a miracle had allowed me to save my own life.

"What is going on, Anselmo?" someone inquired from above.

"*Nada, senhor,*" I answered, praying that distance would muffle my accent and make the Portugal believe I was his comrade. "*Um minuto mais é tudo o que necessitam.*"

A minute more is all I require.

"Get on with it. Da Silva is asking for you."

I cast the light of the lantern around the hold, searching for a better weapon than the sword in my hand.

An arquebuse or musket would be excellent. Or a brace of pistols.

Grenades would be perfect, I thought wistfully. The lethal clay pots were just what a single man needed when he was outnumbered.

There were hundreds of grenades in the armory of the *Pelican.* Each contained black powder, pebbles, and glass shards and was ignited by a short fuse. When one exploded, it rained deadly shrapnel in a fifteen foot radius, maiming or killing anyone within that zone.

Being a merchant vessel, however, the *Santa Maria* did not carry artillery, grenades, or small arms except for the personal weapons of the crew and gentlemen and except for the swords in her trade goods.

Then the beam of the lantern fell on the ship's iron fire box and on the locker in which the *Santa Maria*'s cook stored his herbs, spices, salt, sugar, and other valuable culinary ingredients.

Some irritation, perhaps a speck of dust, caused me to sneeze.

At that exact moment inspiration struck.

Before my eyes cleared, I was already looking through the locker. The first two drawers held only cloves, cinnamon, and nutmeg.

But the third drawer held a quantity of dried scarlet fruit, famous for their piquancy, which were native to the Americas. In the fourth drawer I found several pounds of black kernels imported from the Moluccas.

I decided to use both the red and the black.

The cook of the *Santa Maria* kept his utensils arranged neatly in a wood box. I could not help but admire his professional discipline as I tore apart the tool kit while searching for the articles I required, a mortar and pestle. A second after I found them, I had heaped the small dark nuts and the reddish rinds in the marble bowl and started grinding frantically.

The next item I needed was a bellows. To my relief it was precisely where it should be, hanging from a hook in the side of the fire box.

Giving the leather lungs an exploratory squeeze, I poured

the powder I had ground down the throat of the bellows and stuck the stone pestle into my belt. Then I went to the ladder, climbed a few rungs, and peered on deck cautiously.

Guarded by Portuguese sailors, my companions were sitting beside the mainmast, their hands tied behind their backs with leather straps. On the afterdeck the Portuguese gentlemen gathered around Nuño da Silva. All were talking at once while making passionate flourishes with their fingers. From what I could overhear, they were debating whether to barter their English captives or to kill them and dump the bodies overboard to lighten the ship.

Then da Silva asked, "*Onde está Anselmo Godinho?*"

Where is Anselmo Godinho?

"He has yet to return, *capitão.*"

"God curse the son of a bitch! Pero, Jorge, go and summon him."

"What if he has not finished with the Lutheran?" Pero asked.

"Then end the matter yourself."

I ducked down the ladder as two gentlemen separated themselves from the crowd around da Silva and approached the hold. Both were dressed in outfits as fashionable as the one Godinho had worn, Pero stuffing his cod with so much bombast that it appeared to enclose a third leg rather than a natural appendage. Despite this foppery, I had no doubt these men were as expert with the rapier as my first antagonist.

Anticipating danger, they descended with their swords drawn.

"Where are you, Anselmo?" called Pero. "Da Silva is sour

with vinegar and piss and he is being even more impolite than usual."

"The *capitão* is indeed impossible," agreed Jorge. "Come, Anselmo. Where is the Lutheran hiding?"

"Here, damn you," I said, pumping the bellows directly in their faces while emerging from concealment. Air blasted from the nozzle, enveloping them in red cayenne pepper and pulverized black Moluccan peppercorns. This mixture had an instantaneous effect on the Portugals.

Both men screwed their features in agony and could not stop themselves from discarding their weapons so that they could bring their hands to their eyes and rub them. At the same time they were crying and sneezing so single mindedly that they could not scream.

Taking the pestle from my belt, I clubbed them unconscious.

Less than ten minutes had elapsed since Godinho had entered the hold to end my life. When I returned back on deck, I learned that the pinnace was still racing the smaller Portuguese merchant ship to land. The vessels were now a mile off the shore, coming fast within range of the coastal artillery. Two other ships of the fleet joined the chase while the rest, led by the *Pelican*, sailed toward us.

The noise of cannon fire covered the sounds I made as I sprinted for the mainmast. I had to cross fifteen feet of empty space. My presence was noted before I took two steps.

"Mary, mother of God!" said one man. "Where has this rascal come from? And of all things, why is he carrying a bellows?"

"Shoot him first, Nicolau. We can ask questions afterward."

"But then he will be in no condition to satisfy our curiosity."

"Sadly, my friend, even the best laid plans have unwelcome consequences. Manoel, Paulo, fill the pirate with lead."

The range of my improvised weapon was no more than a yard. The Portuguese sailors began reaching for the pistols strapped across their striped shirts when I was three times that distance away.

Before I could squeeze the bellows, however, my foot slipped on a wet patch of planking and I went flying in one direction while my weapon flew off in another. One man got off a shot as I fell and I could have sworn the lead ball grazed my temple but it must have missed me since I was still alive as I skidded on my back across the deck.

Then the Portugal clubbed me with the gun. The blow did not knock me out but it took the fight from me and I could not lift a finger in resistance as I was dragged to Nuño da Silva. There was a bloody gash in my forehead and I had to blink to clear my eyes.

"This is the Lutheran who slew Anselmo Godinho," volunteered Manoel, the sailor twisting my right arm behind my back. "*Sim*, and Pero and Jorge, too, may the blessed virgin have mercy on their souls."

"Your men are not dead, *senhor*," I explained in halting Portuguese. "I did not treat them gently but they should wake soon enough, never fear. I am no murderer."

Da Silva ignored my explanations. He looked past me toward St. Jago, evidently calculating the distance separating the *Santa Maria* from the approaching English fleet. "The cursed pirates will understand we have retaken our ship the moment we raise sail," he muttered. "It is unlikely that we can outrun them whether we bear to sea or attempt to gain the harbor. This leaves only one option."

"What is that, *capitão*?" asked a gentlemen, tugging nervously at his cod, which was embroidered with red hearts and stuck with sequins.

Da Silva gave me a dispassionate stare, obviously weighing my worth. "Signal the Lutherans that we wish to negotiate," he instructed. "Then hang the lad from the mainsail yard."

"Ah, *Capitão* da Silva, you are truly Machiavellian!" another gentlemen said admiringly. "Such meanness will indeed provide us credibility with the heretics. They will know us to be serious men and will not dare to risk the remaining hostages."

I raised my voice to protest this plan but no one listened to my complaints. A sailor fetched a length of rope from a storage locker and began tying a special knot, known as a collar or hangman's noose, looping the working end of the rope into a bight and coiling the loose end thirteen times around the center strands. After fitting the noose over my head, he pulled the rope snug around my neck with the knot pressing against my left ear. Then he threw the rope's other end over the spar.

Da Silva nodded approval. "Hoist the Lutheran high," he ordered.

The Portugals holding me let go, allowing the line circling my throat to lift me from the deck. I gripped the noose with both hands and tried to pull it apart but the knot's friction, combined with my weight against the rope, prevented the loop from opening. The coarse fiber bit into the soft skin beneath my jaw.

"*Senhor capitão!*" I cried before the collar closed on my pipes and cut off my wind. "This is not justice. Did I not spare your men when they were at my mercy? There is no honor in killing an unarmed prisoner."

Da Silva gestured to the sailor hauling on the rope to ease the upward pressure. His smile was bleak. "I have no intention of killing you, pirate," he said in so grim a voice that I took little comfort in the promise. "You may die, of course. In fact, it is probable. My main intention, however, is to cause you harm for as long as you live."

Two other sailors joined the man on the rope and they all hauled together, jerking me from my feet so that I dangled by my neck a yard in the air. To my humiliation I could not stop from kicking desperately in a futile effort to find purchase. Then the sailors hauled again, raising me higher, until I was suspended just below the spar.

"Dance, *Inglês*," da Silva called. "Let your friends feel your pain."

In a proper hanging death results not from strangulation but from the fall from the gallows, which breaks the neck of the condemned man. Soon I began to regret I had been denied such a quick passing.

My hands had been left unbound not from kindness but in order to extend my torment. By holding onto the rope above my head, I was able to partly relieve the strain against my throat and lengthen my agony. Even so I could not take in enough air to stay alive.

Darkness closed in from the edges of my vision and strength slipped from me like water through a sieve while my heart hammered in my rib cage and my chest heaved in a vain struggle to draw breath.

The Taking of the *Santa Maria*

At some point I thought I died. Unfortunately, I was mistaken.

I came awake believing I was drowning, which was not an unnatural assumption since I was dripping wet, chilled through, and coughing up brine, having been doused with a bucket of seawater.

Once more I was hoisted skyward. My struggles set me spinning back and forth in a sickening arc. I felt the gorge rise in my stomach but I fought down the need to retch since I knew that surrendering to the urge would cause me to choke on my own vomit. Through bloody tears I saw that the *Pelican* was almost within hailing distance of the *Santa Maria*, close enough that I could make out the men on her half deck.

Drake was there, as were Tom Moone, Parson Fletcher, Diego, the Cimarron, and Tom Blacollers, the boatswain.

Knowing I was in full view of my commander encouraged me to resist despair. I swore to myself I would not give my master or my companions cause to be ashamed of me. Nor would I allow my suffering to provide the Portugals any entertainment.

I would not be made a spectacle!

Somehow I found the courage to stop fighting for survival. I let my legs go limp and dropped my hands from the collar, permitting the rope to clamp down on my windpipe and throttle me. Although I could not suppress the involuntary twitching of my body in its death throes, I made no effort to resist the process of dying.

They would not see me dance!

Again darkness closed in. Again I was revived with seawater.

Da Silva knelt at my side and pried up my eyelid with a thumb, presumably to judge if I was healthy enough to be tortured. "You are young and strong, *Inglês*," he told me. "You will live awhile longer." Then he addressed his men. "Another time!"

"Bugger you, *senhor*," I cursed da Silva, giving in to hatred, and vowing to revenge myself against him although I had no idea how I would ever manage to do so. "I will not forget this," I croaked. "I promise you, sir, you will regret having mistreated me."

Da Silva thought so little of my threat that he did not bother to acknowledge it. The noose constricted and I was raised to the yardarm. This time I neither kicked nor fought the rope.

Thankfully, darkness fell quickly.

Pascoe Goddy, who watched this painful episode from beside the mainmast, told me later that da Silva attempted to revive me again so I could endure a fourth hanging but I remembered nothing of what took place since I was insensible and oblivious to the world. After several buckets of brine failed to rouse me, my inert hulk was rolled aside and I was left in a sodden heap beside the gunwale.

No one expected me to recover. A half hour later, however, I returned to consciousness. My neck was scalded but unbroken. Every breath burned in my throat but I was alive.

Thinking it best not to betray that I had come to, I remained quiet, moving not a muscle while cautiously peering around.

Shouting in a mixture of English and Portuguese carried from the stern and although I could not decipher what was being said, I recognized both Drake's voice and da Silva's. I did not doubt, though, that the Portugal was bargaining the hostages for his ship's freedom, confident that his misuse of me had demonstrated his ruthlessness, and that this would provide him an advantage during negotiations.

The bellows still lay in the scuppers where it had landed after flying from my grasp. Since the Portugals had not seen it used as a weapon, they had failed to recognize that the implement was dangerous, evidently assuming that I had bludgeoned Anselmo Godinho and the other gentlemen in the hold with the pestle.

Murmuring a prayer of thanks to God for his kindness, I wormed my head free of the noose. I had to consciously slow myself since I was filling again with the strange excitement that came upon me at the approach of peril. I could only open my eyes half way due to the dried blood sticking the lids together but even so the acuity of my vision seemed to have increased, so that I was aware of every detail around me with astonishing precision, the grain of the scoured deck, the fact that the nearest Portugal sailor was spitting sideways through his teeth, the flash of sunlight off the dagger at his waist.

Pascoe Goddy, Luke Adden, and the rest of the prize crew remained under guard by the mainmast. My first task, I knew, was to free them and deprive Nuño da Silva of his hostages.

As I launched myself toward the bellows, time, too, seemed to fracture, each second breaking into a dozen parts as long as an hour. Then the bellows was in my hands and the present sped up again.

"Shut your eyes and hold your breath!" I shouted in English, flinging myself forward and squeezing the handles with all my strength, pumping a red and gray cloud at the

Portugal guards until they succumbed to the toxic concoction and began clawing at their faces while disgorging streams of snot and tears.

Going to my knees beside Pascoe Goddy, I began cutting his wrists free of their bindings. The straps had been wet with seawater so they would shrink when they dried and grip the skin cruelly.

"What kept you, Perry?" he asked while I sawed at the leather. "I did notice you hanging about having fun, and thought it spiteful of you to ignore your shipmates."

"Aye, Pascoe," I whispered, unable to speak aloud due to the rawness of my throat, "I was indeed having fun, sir, that I was. But now it is time for *Senhor Capitão* da Silva to be entertained, my word on it. I have sworn to repay his hospitality."

"I am with you, lad!" Goddy replied. Then he leapt upright and bludgeoned the Portuguese crewmen with one of their own pistols while I attended to releasing the other men. As the fourth Portugal collapsed to the planking, Goddy reversed the gun and aimed it at the gentlemen on the half deck, who had just begun to understand something was wrong. He shot, missed, and dropped the empty weapon to retrieve another. Before he could aim again, however, Bill Lege stopped him.

"Give that to someone who knows how to use it," said Lege.

"Aye, you may have the honor," Goddy agreed, exchanging the pistol for a rapier. "Christ, I hate these things," he muttered.

Bill Lege gripped the pistol with both hands to steady the weapon.

All of the Portuguese gentlemen had scattered except

for Nuño da Silva, who was so consumed with fury that he was unconcerned by danger. Reaching into his leather vest, he revealed a pistol of his own and pointed the muzzle at us while cocking the serpentine.

"Die screaming, Lutheran dogs," da Silva hissed.

Lege fired first.

His shot struck the Portugal's pistol directly in the breach, shattering the weapon while ripping it into the air. Part of da Silva's index finger accompanied the gun as it flew into the sea.

"My God," I whispered hoarsely. "I did not believe such accuracy was possible, Mr. Lege."

He shrugged modestly and replied, "I cannot take credit for the shot, lad. Particularly considering I was aiming for the bastard's gizzard."

A motion above my head drew my attention upward. Christopher Waspe was descending from the topsail spar, riding the backstay downward so quickly through the sails that I could not imagine why his palms were not smoking from friction. He halted twenty feet above the deck and took a knife from the sheath under his jerkin. Hanging by one hand, Waspe threw the dagger with the other.

His target was a Portuguese gentlemen wearing a particularly fine beaver pelt garnished with a peacock feather.

The blade sliced off the showy plume before the point buried itself in the shoulder of the man under the hat. Screaming, the Portugal plucked out the steel thorn and pressed a silk handkerchief illustrated with flowers against the wound, striving to stanch the flow of blood.

John Cooke had armed himself with a rapier. There were spots of color in his cheeks and the tip of his sharp nose was equally red.

"What say we have at the scoundrels," he proposed.

"Aye, sir, a superb idea," Goddy agreed. He turned to the rest of us and instructed: "Let me hear you, gentlemen. Who is our general?"

"Francis Drake!"

"Who is our queen?"

"Elizabeth Regina!"

"God damned right. For Drake and Elizabeth!"

"For Drake and Elizabeth!" we answered.

Then we followed his lead and stormed the afterdeck.

Some Fine Cuisine

February 1, 1578 – February 2, 1578
Fogo

"Christ's bloody globes," Drake swore, approaching John Winter and forcing him to back away in order to maintain conversational space between them. "Why did you not first take the leeward vessel? Tell me, sir, for I wish to fathom your reasoning."

Winter had failed to intercept the second Portuguese merchantman. She had reached the protection of the coastal fortifications before he caught up with her, and a deadly rain of lead shot had torn the sea between the ships into froth, forcing the pinnace to surrender the chase.

Never before had I seen Francis Drake in such foul temper, not even when James Stydye's treachery with the provisioning of the victuals had been exposed while the *Pelican* was anchored in Sutton Pool.

"I thought it more important to prevent the larger vessel from escaping into open water, where we might have lost her spore," Winter said stiffly, his face immobile although the beads of sweat above his moustache advertised his discomfort.

"You thought wrong," Drake snapped. "Any of our ships could have overtaken this scow regardless of her head start! No, the harbor cannon were the issue! You did not see this?"

Winter refused to meet Drake's white-ringed stare.

"I did not, general."

"So much is damned obvious, sir."

The five ships of the fleet were riding the swell a hundred yards off our stern. The sun was sinking toward the horizon and the green and gold streaks coloring the sky promised a breathtaking sunset.

Drake now turned to Goddy, who was holding Nuño da Silva by the collar while pressing a knife into his kidney.

Our general was not pleased by what he had learned of the events that had transpired aboard the *Santa Maria*.

"You have disappointed me, Pascoe," said Drake, shaking his head sadly. "Explain how you managed to lose control of the prize to the Portugals, and do not plead senility. You may be getting long in the tooth but I know you are still the mad dog you always were."

"Three of the bastards were hiding in the forward sail locker and discovered themselves only when the pinnace had cast off," Goddy explained. "I should have conducted a more thorough search before they surprised us, general. It is my fault."

"By my life, it is your fault, Pascoe! I have half a thought to bind you to the mainmast and lay stripes on your back personally! For dereliction of duty, do you hear! Not to mention stupidity."

"Aye, sir, and it would be no better treatment than I deserved, too."

Until I watched Goddy squirm under Drake's appraisal, I had not thought such a grizzled mariner could be capable of embarrassment, but now he was hangdog, refusing to raise his eyes and instead inspecting the deck in the vicinity of his boots with minute thoroughness.

Drake allowed Goddy to suffer his scrutiny awhile longer and then regarded John Cooke. Apparently noticing something he disliked in the other's expression, he said:

"Do not play the innocent, sir. It would be a grave error to assume you were above account because of your investment in our enterprise. In my company I hold gentlemen as bound to obligation as sailors."

"I hear you, Captain Drake," Cooke answered, managing to remain as composed under censure as John Winter although his nose became bright red along its entire length.

Then Drake looked carefully around the assembly, studying each of us in turn until his eyes settled on my face.

"It is a damned sorry state of affairs when the only one here who does not stink of shit is the least boy among us," he said with disgust. "If not for Mr. James, you all still would be hostage to the Portugals. Nor would I have paid ransom for any man, my oath on it, not a penny!" Then Drake clapped my shoulder and gave me a rough shake. "Pepper, by God!" he said. "A clever scheme, lad. How did you hit on it?"

I shrugged, unsure myself. "I am a cook, sir. My mind naturally tends to a culinary point of view. There is also the fact I sneezed at an opportune moment."

"Opportune! I should say so! God's wounds, we could do with a few more lucky lads like you aboard, Mr. James!"

I was not enjoying being praised while my companions were being reprimanded. "Thank you, general," I said, "but you give me more credit than is due. Retaking the prize was a group effort."

"Aye, perhaps," Drake replied doubtfully. "Still, lad, you did well. God's wounds, it pained me to watch you hang!"

With a final shake, he released my shoulder and focused on Nuño da Silva, who returned the inspection with a dour frown.

"Will you swear your parole, captain-pilot?" Drake asked the Portugal after indicating that I should interpret. "I dislike mistreating a fellow mariner, no matter his flag."

Da Silva shrugged, as if resigning himself to an unkind fate. "*Sim, senhor,*" he said. "You have my word I will not resist your robbery nor seek to escape your depredations. What choice do I have, pirate?"

"Pirate!" Drake said, offended by the term. "I am no pirate! Listen well, sir. Nine years past, at San Juan de Ulua, I was caused serious harm by one of your countrymen, the treacherous dog Don Martin Enriquez."

At the mention of the viceroy of New Spain, Goddy loudly cleared his throat and spat a large mess onto the deck as he had sworn to do when telling of his duel with the Spanish lieutenant aboard the *Minion*.

"In compensation for my injury," Drake went on, "the queen of England, my sovereign lady, has herself granted me license to come into these parts and seek revenge against any Spaniard or Portugal I encounter. I do regret possessing myself of anything that does not belong exclusively to Enriquez or to King Philip, for it grieves me that their vassals should be paying for their crimes. But I am not going to stop until I have collected the money I lost, aye, and what was lost by my cousin, John Hawkins, as well. I have legal right to your ship and to your cargo. They are both mine to do with as I will."

This observation was clearly meant to impress upon the Portuguese captain the understanding that resistance was futile. Drake, however, had not counted on da Silva's obstinacy. Ignoring the fact that he was our prisoner and held harmless by a blade to his vitals, he cleared his pipes even more noisily than Pasco Goddy and toasted the deck himself.

"Your queen has no jurisdiction here," da Silva snarled. "These are the territorial waters of the king of Portugal, given to our country by the holy father himself. Taking my ship is an act of piracy. By all that is sacred, you will burn for your sins, Lutheran, preferably after hanging."

I would have expected such truculence to inflame Drake but instead he chuckled. "Only rovers who return to port as paupers do the marshal's dance and drink the tide," he told da Silva. "Were I one, and I am not, never would I make that mistake and kick my heels at Wapping shore."

This was so dreadful a place that even Nuño da Silva, a foreigner, had heard of it.

Drake was referring to the London neighborhood that was home to the Admiralty's Execution Dock, where pirates and mutineers were hanged for their crimes. Often those convicted of piracy were suspended by short ropes, a practice that denied them quick deaths and meant they strangled slowly while thrashing out a bizarre jig. By law the corpses must remain on display until the Thames washed over them three times.

Taking da Silva by the arm, Drake pushed the Portugal ahead of him into the main cabin of the *Santa Maria*, which was even more extravagantly furnished than the similar space aboard the *Pelican*. The officers' table was built of mahogany rather than oak, an actual chandelier hung from the ceiling in place of brass lanterns, and the cutlery was not plain silver but silver inlaid with gold.

With a nod to me that I should translate, Drake said:

"Sir, I will have your rutter, along with any maritime treatises, charts, and instruments in your possession. Be so kind as to retrieve these items at once."

As I have mentioned, a rutter was a pilot's most valuable belonging. It was a diary of his travels, sometimes spanning decades, in which he wrote down the particulars of his voyages, taking note of wind direction and speed, the strength of tides and currents, soundings and bottom structure, and the appearance of important landmarks from various distances and angles at sea. A pilot relied on his rutter as a map to find his way to places he had been and to find his way back home after sailing into the unknown. Sometimes a pilot would share his rutter with another as a professional courtesy but more often he would keep his book secret. It was not unheard of for the pilot of a defeated vessel to be robbed of his rutter by his captors.

This was what da Silva feared even more than he feared losing his ship and the goods she carried.

"Would you rape me of my very livelihood?" he protested.

"Calm yourself, captain-pilot," Drake replied. "You have my promise I will steal none of your personal belongings. We will make copies and return the originals to you when we are done."

Finally da Silva shrugged and grudgingly accommodated himself to the inevitable. Offering Drake a stiff nod, he stalked into his quarters and returned with a leather notebook and an envelope containing parchment diagrams. Our general studied the documents briefly before handing them to Diego, the Cimarron, for safekeeping.

Then he once more addressed da Silva. "Now, sir, let us discuss your cargo. What is your lading?"

The Portuguese captain did not answer immediately and it was clear he was debating whether to keep silent or to lie. Before he could come to a decision, I spoke up, happy to be in the position to discomfit da Silva. "At Mr. Cooke's request, general, I have already conducted an inventory. Let me tell you, sir—there is a treasure here!"

"A treasure! I like the sound of that. Did you hear, Tom? The lad said there is treasure."

Thomas Doughty, John Winter, and Tom Moone had followed Drake and da Silva into the cabin.

"Tell me, Mr. James," Doughty asked. "This treasure, is it gold?"

"No, sir."

"Silver, then?" asked Drake. "Silver is good. I prefer ingots to coin but either will do. Which is it?"

"General, I saw no silver."

"No silver, no gold. I will be damned—you have discovered precious stones! Are there emeralds, lad? Or rubies?"

"Neither, general," I admitted. "I saw no jewels of any sort."

"Then in God's name, Mr. James, just what exactly did you find?"

"Wine, sir."

"Wine!"

"Aye, there are at least one hundred and forty casks of wine in the hold. Most appear to contain Canary or Madeira although there are also pipes of sack and claret."

"Did you say one hundred and forty casks?" asked Drake.

"More or less," I agreed, nodding. "I am not sure precisely because I did not have time to complete the tally."

Tom Moone was shaking his head in wonder. "Why, 'tis enough liquor to keep every man in the crew drunk day and night even were our adventure to encompass the entire world around," he mused. "One hundred and forty casks! The lad is right, general. It is indeed a treasure."

"I will fetch a barrel at once for inspection," volunteered Pascoe Goddy. "Is it not our duty to appraise the vintage to ensure it is worth drinking? Just say the word, general, and I will go below."

"Hold a moment, sir," Drake replied with a laugh, amused by Goddy's selflessness. "Important matters must be decided before we may rule on the cellar. First, Mr. Moone, you and Pascoe escort the Portugals to the *Pelican* and confine them in the orlop. Allow them personal items but no weapons. Captain-pilot da Silva may have his own cabin and the freedom of the ship but keep him under guard."

Tom Moone grunted acknowledgement, touched his forehead, and stooped low in order to pass through the exit from the cabin. Pascoe Goddy shoved da Silva after the giant and I prepared to follow them on deck but Drake stopped me from leaving with a gesture to remain where I was. Our general sat at the head of the table in the chair that had obviously belonged to the Portuguese captain.

"Damn this cargo!" Drake said. "It is as much a curse as a blessing."

"Aye, Francis," agreed Doughty. "No offense intended, but all mariners are drunkards and a majority are pilferers as well. There will be bedlam should the men get into the liquor."

"You will hear no argument from me!" Drake replied. "I know my crew, Christ love the bastards. I am tempted to empty the entire consignment into the sea except we are on the brink of the Atlantic gulf. There is no telling when we might be in need of every drop of fluid, particularly in the burning zone. But the wine cannot be stored on the *Pelican* or on the *Elizabeth*. That would be asking for trouble. Nor is there room for it all in our holds."

"Leave the liquor here in the merchantman and bring the Portugal along with the fleet as a warehouse," Doughty suggested.

"Aye, I have reached the same conclusion, that is what we must do. There is no other way to protect the cargo. You will command the prize, of course, and govern with my authority. We will call her the *Mary*, since *Santa Maria* is too Papist for my taste. What do you say?"

"It is a good English name, I agree. Who will I have for a sailing master and pilot?"

"John Hughes. For boatswain I will give you my brother Thomas. He is not the sharpest knife in the sheath but he is a good sailor. And for cook, why not Tom Hogges. His assistant can take over the mess on the *Benedict*. The Hollander lad—what is his name, Mr. James?"

"Artyur, sir."

"Aye, evidently Artyur's skills have improved to the point where Barty Gotsalk no longer fears death from poisoning."

Doughty stroked his beard thoughtfully. "Tom Moone has described Mr. Hogges's mess and the details are not appetizing. If it is all the same with you, Francis, I would prefer a different cook."

"Well, we can decide the issue later. Mr. Winter—"

"Yes, general?"

"Ferry ten casks of wine to the *Pelican*, five to the *Elizabeth*, and two casks to each of the other ships. I am declaring a holiday. The crew are to be allowed a gallon per man, both this evening and tomorrow as well. No, on second thought, make that two gallons."

"Is not the amount somewhat excessive?" asked Doughty.

"Absolutely. Mariners are not soldiers, Tom. They are as fond as gossip as women and as quick to take offense. They also measure generosity with an exact plumb line. By now every sailor in the fleet has heard about the Portugal spirits. They are all eager for a good carouse and will become bitter if they are not treated liberally."

Then Drake addressed me. "Perry James!"

"Aye, captain?"

"Complete the inventory requested by Mr. Cooke. Deliver it in writing before noon tomorrow. Mark down every item without exception. I warn you, lad—do not accidently fail to include a barrel or two in order to reserve the liquor for your private enjoyment."

Going through the hold of the *Santa Maria* required the

rest of the evening and the better part of the morning, which meant I had no opportunity to sample my ration of wine and thus was still sober when I rowed from the merchantman over to the *Pelican* with the completed list. Everyone else, however, had been drunk since the night before and the ship was noisy with singing and loud conversation. Lancelot Garget was swilling sack contentedly beside the cooking box while Horsewill, his assistant, relieved himself into the embers of the fire. Even Blacollers, normally a strict taskmaster, was sipping from a jack of Madeira while turning a blind eye to what was going on around him. As I crossed the deck, I had to step over men sprawled asleep on the planking, a liberty never permitted under normal circumstances.

Pascoe Goddy was drinking in the shade of the mainmast with a couple other sailors. He had retrieved his marlinspike and was using the point of the tool to work a loop of cord through the knot he was tying. Apparently this was intended to represent a fish but Pascoe had lost track of the weave and his creation looked more like a toad than a tunny.

"Hello, Perry!" he said as I came up to the group, lifting his jack to me in a casual toast. "Do you know, mates, the lad threw himself at the Papist bastards armed only with a pestle."

"A bellows, Pascoe. Not a pestle."

"Do not confuse me," Goddy said and proceeded to describe what had occurred on the *Santa Maria* during the retaking of the ship. Being a natural raconteur, Pascoe could not stop himself from embellishing the facts until his tale was so florid and ingenious that I could not recognize myself in it. The bored looks of the other listeners suggested that they had already heard the story at least once already, and their skeptical expressions proved they were also having difficulty willingly suspending their disbelief although Christopher Waspe corroborated the fable with drunken sincerity, as did Luke Adden.

On the half deck several gentlemen and petty officers were lounging with cups of wine beside a barrel of Canary set on end and tapped with an iron spigot. They were all as drunk as the ordinary seamen. Noticing my arrival, John Cooke said: "What say, fellows! It is Pepper James."

"Perry James, sir," I corrected him but Cooke would not listen.

"Well, I prefer *Pepper*," he insisted stubbornly. "Did you not oppose the Portugals with nothing but a grinder in your hand?"

"It was a bellows, sir."

"As you like. But from now on you are Pepper James, and that is my final word on the subject." Cooke lifted his mug in a salute, slopping wine onto his sleeve. "What say? Let us have a loud hurrah for Pepper!"

One or two of the rest took Cooke's suggestion and gave a ragged cheer but most continued their conversations and paid me no attention. Entering the main cabin, I found Drake, Thomas Doughty, and some other men sitting across the grand table from the Portuguese gentlemen and Nuño da Silva. Despite their incarceration overnight in the orlop, the Portugals had managed to maintain their finery in presentable condition and had attended to each other's barbering as well.

Thinking it best not to interrupt the conference, I stood with my back against the starboard bulkhead to wait unobtrusively but Drake waved his tankard to indicate that I should approach the table.

Our general had been partaking as steadily of the Canary as everyone else. His vest was open and so was his collar, revealing a chest that was startlingly pale against the red tan of his neck.

"Put down the damn papers and pour yourself a drink, lad," Drake told me. "Then inform these gentlemen they are to be released—although we are appropriating their ship and cargo since we have need of both. In exchange they will be given our pinnace when the artillery is stripped from it, as well as sufficient victuals and wine to reach St. Jago."

At this information the Portuguese gentlemen began muttering among themselves while scowling and shaking their heads. Drake, however, had even more unwelcome news for Nuño da Silva.

"You, captain-pilot, are to remain aboard the *Pelican* as my guest and continue with us on our journey," he told the Portugal. "I have examined your rutter and know you are an experienced and careful navigator. Your guidance along the American coast could prove invaluable to our adventure. I cannot afford to let you go."

Da Silva placed his palms flat on the tabletop and leaned forward. Blood began to spot the linen bandage around his injured finger but he ignored the pain and fixed his eyes on Drake. "You are robbing us of our vessel and of our commodities, leaving us nothing," da Silva said, speaking deliberately so I could interpret each word. "You may have my parole, Lutheran, but I will never assist you."

"Aye, you say that now," Drake replied. "Only remember,

senhor, there are two courses a man may steer, with the breeze or against it. Do not force me to instruct you which way the wind blows."

Tilting his mug, Drake drained it of Canary. "In the meantime," he continued more mildly after wiping his lips and beard dry with the back of his wrist and handing his cup to a boy for refilling, "there might as well be peace between us. Have more wine, captain-pilot. I insist."

Neither da Silva nor his companions had touched what had already been poured for them. I did not suppose they were overwhelmed by Drake's largesse since the liquor came from their own stock.

Then Drake raised his voice so that he could be heard on deck. "Blacollers!" he called.

The boatswain poked his head through the cabin door and peered inside blearily. "Bless you, general!" he said after a pause to pull from his jack of Madeira. "What would you be wanting of me now?"

"Instruct the galley to prepare supper for our Portugal guests," Drake said. "Since I have been forced to pinch them by their purses, 'tis only fair we send them off with a kind memory of English hospitality. Tell Garget to prepare boiled beef and onions. It is his signature dish."

"Alas, sir, Lancelot is out cold," Blacollers replied, holding on to the door frame in order to steady himself although I had seen him surefooted in bad weather countless times and now there was flat calm. "We could not rouse the scrawny little angel even were we to shave his belly with a rusty knife."

"I will send for Rich Writ," volunteered John Winter,

referring to the cook of the *Elizabeth*. "Writ does a pudding of suet, raisins, and biscuit that is quite delicious. Hopefully he will not yet be drunk."

"What about Tom Hogges?" suggested Leonard Vicarye, who was sitting at Doughty's right hand. The lawyer was dressed as finely as the Portugals although he stuffed his pants with less bombast. "Hogges has a recipe for stewed bacon and cabbage as delectable as any I have tasted."

This was the moment Thomas Doughty interfered with my life another time and proved again that he was not my friend. Taking a measured sip of sack from his tankard, he studied me thoughtfully.

"Is it not Mr. James's responsibility to serve visiting dignitaries?" Doughty observed. "Equally important, Francis—the lad is sober."

"That is true, by God!" Drake agreed, and turned to me. "What are you waiting for, Perry? You heard Mr. Blacollers, Garget is indisposed and you must cover his watch. Go forward and get busy."

Nuño da Silva gave me an ugly look when he understood the situation. He recognized my face from the *Santa Maria* and clearly disliked me for my role in seizing his ship. He also distrusted my competence. Determined to be unpleasant, da Silva stood from the table and bowed with such exaggerated courtesy that the gesture was transformed from a compliment into an insult.

"You are gracious, *senhor*," he told Drake, "but I prefer not to suffer the ministrations of your—sea cook, who is clearly an ignorant boy and certain to be unskillful. It is also well known that the food of your country is objectionable to cultivated palates. Instead allow me to offer the services of my own chef. Thus I will be assured of one last decent meal before I am kidnapped and ill used."

As da Silva intended, Drake was not pleased by the request. "Did you hear the surly rogue?" he asked Doughty. "In a single breath the Portugal has insulted my personal table and the cookery of our people as a whole! Still, I do not care to refuse the bastard outright since I hope to cultivate his good will. What should we do?"

"Accept the offer half way," Doughty suggested. "Allow da Silva's man to serve us but insist Mr. James attend the Portugals. If we must have the victuals of their country, they must endure ours."

"Tom, by God, you are Solomon himself!" Drake said admiringly. Then our general came to a decision with his customary energy despite having recently consumed at least four mugs of Canary. "Do you understand what is going on, lad?" he asked me. "The Portugals hope to prove us to be bumpkins and sorry hosts. You must dish them out a good English meal and confirm otherwise."

"I promise to make it so, general," I said although I did not look forward to cooking for the Portugals since I was sure they would not appreciate my efforts. Nor did I like the idea of serving Nuño da Silva in any capacity, the ring of scabbed blood around my neck a reminder of how he had used me aboard the *Santa Maria*.

Nuño da Silva plainly had mixed feelings about the compromise since it meant that he must submit to the indignity an English supper. On the other hand it allowed him an opportunity to advertise the superiority of his national cuisine and to further offend his captors. With a brief grim cleaver of a smile, he gestured to a man on his left.

João Longo Prata rose from his chair.

Prata was two decades my elder and walked with a limp since he lacked a left foot below the knee and stood on a peg. Loose pants hid the straps securing the false limb to his stump but his truncation was betrayed by the thud of wood against wood as he crossed the deck and came around the table. Sweeping his hat off his head, he, too, bowed fulsomely and said, "It is my honor, *senhor capitão pirata.*"

Then Prata addressed me in a kind voice. "The morning porridge proved that you are in dire need of remedial instruction in the basics of cookery, *jovem.* I urge you to attend closely to what I do, so that you may be instructed by my example."

Prata's criticism did not annoy me since it was based on the mistaken belief that I was responsible for his breakfast. I also suspected I would have shared his unflattering judgment had I, too, recently eaten a meal prepared by Lancelot Garget.

By this time, however, I had finished my own Canary and I felt the wine loosening my tongue and encouraging me to speak up when I should have remained quiet.

"Thank you, *Senhor* Prata," I replied, attempting to match his civility while being equally condescending. "I doubt, though, there is much you could teach me. In my opinion Portuguese fare relies overmuch on stockfish and anchovies."

Although I would have expected my mean remarks to offend Prata, he was so secure in his self regard that instead of being affronted, he only smiled with a confidence that was, unfortunately, fully justified.

João Longo Prata, after all, was the man whose professionalism I had admired while I searched through his tool kit for the means to save my life in the hold of the *Santa Maria*. While I had studied my trade at my mother's knee in the dirt floored kitchen of the Jack and Rasher, a small tavern in an English port, Prata had apprenticed under master cooks and pastry chefs in the finest houses of Lisbon, a world capital. Nor, as I would learn, did he usually work as a ship's cook.

Prata was traveling to the Americas to assume the position of personal chef to Don Luis de Velasco, prefect of the City of Mexico. He had accepted employment from da Silva partly to defray the cost of passage but mainly to keep occupied during the Atlantic crossing.

"Come, *jovem*," João Longo Prata said, stumping to me and grasping my arm. "I will serve your *capitão* and you will serve mine. We will discover who is worthy of credit and who is not."

The Portugal's frankness amused Drake. "Well spoken, sir!" he told Prata. "I caution you, though. Do not dismiss Mr. James so easily. The lad may be a sea cook but he is an English sea cook, by God!"

Our general no doubt meant to be encouraging and I was grateful for his confidence even though it quickly became apparent that the Portuguese chef was my superior in every regard.

Blacollers accompanied us from the main cabin into the waist and seated himself on a barrel beside the cooking box. As the boatswain had said earlier, Lancelot Garget was senseless with liquor and I had to roll him aside and prop him against the forecastle bulkhead so he would not be stepped on. Horsewill, although drunk, was still on his feet.

"Shovel out the ashes and light a new fire," I told the boy. "Then make yourself useful to *Senhor* Prata and fetch him what he needs."

As was only to be expected, our activity drew a curious audience and a half dozen men settled down in a semi circle to drink Canary and watch us work. Prata bowed to the sailors with the showmanship of a player in a theater, took a strop from his tool chest, looped it around his fist with a flourish, and began stroking his knife against the leather. Then he plucked a dark hair from his scalp and let the thread fall upon the blade. The strand's own weight parted it in two.

"I will prepare an Iberian specialty known as *petiscos*," Prata explained. "These are savories, each one different, allowing the diner to experience a medley of flavors and textures, which is essential for gastronomical satisfaction. What will you serve, *jovem*?"

"I have not yet decided," I admitted.

"Heed my words. *Capitão* da Silva is partial to saffron and travels with a private hoard of the spice for his personal enjoyment. Any dish containing this ingredient is sure to meet with his approval."

Another man might have been trying to mislead me with bad counsel but I was certain João Longo Prata felt no need to be dishonest. Pascoe Goddy, however, had a different idea as to what I should prepare.

"Fry up the Portugals a brace of bangers with a side of peas," he said when I had interpreted Prata's remarks. "Aye, and do not forget to include a portion of mashed."

"Bangers and mashed," agreed Peter Corder, lifting his jack into the air with his toes in a salute to the dish. "'Tis a true English glory. Too delicious for foreigners."

"What about pasties?" asked Gregory Raymente. "I personally am quite partial to them, especially as they are made in Yarmouth, stuffed with chopped rutabaga and herring." He, too, lifted his jack skyward. "I dearly love a pasty," Raymente hummed, "a hot and leaky one. With carrots, maybe turnips, parsley, and onion."

"Ah, pasties," mused Pascoe Goddy approvingly. "'Tis a meal close to mine own stomach. Did you know, gentlemen, my dear sweet mam prepared them every Sunday without fail, God bless the woman."

"It is news to me you had a mother," remarked Corder.

"You are a funny fellow, sir," Goddy answered without heat since they were old comrades and had sailed together under various captains for many years. "Still, you would be much funnier without a tongue."

Corder was unabashed. "Cut off your other ear if you do not care to hear me," he replied. "The amputation could only make you prettier."

Despite a barrage of encouraging suggestions I could not decide what to serve Nuño da Silva and his gentlemen. I feared any dish I put before them would suffer in comparison to what João Longo Prata presented Drake, shaming me and embarrassing our general, as well as harming the reputation of my home country. So I went forward to the head as if to answer a natural urge although what I really needed was a moment of quiet in which to focus my thoughts and to figure a way out of the predicament I was in.

Then a boney arm clasped me close before I could button my pants.

Francisco Albo pressed his grizzled cheek against mine and breathed winey fumes into my face. "Little time remains, *filos*," he said earnestly. "Tomorrow we set off into the deep brine of the burning zone, with salt on all sides and naught a drop of water fit to drink for two thousand miles. Are you prepared? Have you made peace with God and given your soul into the care of Jesus?"

Facilities for seamen on a galleon consisted of a narrow ledge at the bow of the ship. Handholds in the hull allowed users to keep their perch while balancing over the edge. Because of its exposed position, anyone employing the latrine was wet by spray even in fair weather. I could not escape Albo's embrace in the precarious space.

"I suppose I am prepared as any aboard," I answered and then had to grab for support when a swell threatened to propel us both into the Atlantic. My reply entertained the drunken mariner.

"A brave boast, lad," he said with a cackle. "Well, we will learn what stuff you are made of, aye, that we will. Tell me, when the water is stinking and all our victuals are foul, how much will you charge your mates for a bit of warm gristle? On the *Victoria* rats sold for a half crown each, and the price was paid gladly. The cook died a rich man. What of you, lad? Will you die in poverty or in wealth?"

I did not care to dwell on either outcome. "Whatever the circumstances, Mr. Albo," I said, "I would not seek payment from my friends for doing them service."

As I spoke, I remembered my first conversation with Lancelot Garget after joining the crew of the *Pelican*, which had taken place in the murk of the orlop while he held a squirming rodent by the tail and tortured the poor brute with his dagger. What had I said then? It would be an interesting challenge to make such poor fare palatable.

This was when I understood the menu I must prepare in order to preserve my credit. I was embroiled in a contest that I could not win. I could not equal João Longo Prata at fine cuisine so I would not try. As Drake had observed, I was indeed a sea cook, an English sea cook, by God, and I would serve the Portugals a good English supper.

Nor could I think of any better method of repaying Nuño da Silva for the hanging I had undergone. In my opinion there was no other man more deserving of being served such a repast.

Several more minutes passed before I managed to escape Francisco Albo without sending us both plummeting to our doom from the head into the sea. Descending below deck, I began hunting for the ingredients of the recipe I was determined to cook. A dozen hens and as many pigeons remained of the flock we had brought from Plymouth. The birds squawked and fluttered their wings nervously as I went among their cages with my knife until I cornered the animals I wanted behind some bales of straw meant to be used as livestock feed or as bedding for the crew. Soon I had five plump carcasses on a cutting board.

I deboned them and chopped the meat finely, blending the mince with currants and prunes, salt and pepper, ground cinnamon, and a pinch each of cloves and mace. In another bowl I kneaded together flour, eggs, lard, and water, and rolled out the dough into two large rounds, using one to line the bottom of an iron skillet. After packing the meat into the pan, I moistened the filling with mustard and beer and covered the pie with the second pastry sheet, crimping the edges of the crust with the tines of a fork and pricking it all over so that steam could escape. Finally I carried the skillet above deck, placed it in the fire box, and banked embers around it to ensure even baking.

João Longo Prata was grilling whole fish on skewers directly over the coals while tending a half dozen pans containing as many different dishes and a deep pot of hot olive oil in which codfish croquettes were frying. With the proficiency of long practice, he adjusted the pans so that each received the proper amount of heat and cooked at the correct speed. By the time my pie was ready, Prata had a full supper of many courses, some hot and some cold, arranged with flair on decorative platters. After placing a sprig of rosemary atop a composition of *chouriço em vinho tinto,* smoked sausage poached in red wine, the Portugal regarded the finished *petiscos* with a satisfied air while stroking his sideburns with the same fondness that John Winter displayed for his elaborate mustache.

"Damn me if those sprats do not look tasty," remarked Gregory Raymente, referring to a dish of *enguias de escabeche,* which was actually composed of small eels, not sardines. These had been simmered in broth and garnished with crisp shreds of leek.

"Aye, and I could do with a bit of the boiled ham," said Pascoe Goddy although the meat in question had been salt cured and air dried, not cooked in liquid. Prata had sliced the pale pink flesh as thinly as paper and wrapped the pieces around figs and fresh melon, tying the morsels closed with stalks of green onion and sprinkling them with coarsely crushed black pepper.

In the grand cabin the table was set with silver service. A brass candelabra with eight branches augmented the wan daylight admitted through the leaded glass of the latticework windows in the port and starboard bulkheads. John Bruer, who had been Tobias Lackland's master, was picking a melody from a lute but doing a bad job of making music since his fingers were clumsy with drink and he was hitting one wrong note after another. Holding the pie in a towel so that the pastry would stay warm, I interpreted for João Longo Prata as he laid out an array of *petiscos*, condiments, and sauces on the gleaming oak.

"These are *bolhinos de bacalhau*," Prata explained, introducing the cod fritters, tasting one himself to prove it was healthy. "They are best with a squeeze of lime juice and a dollop of roasted garlic creamed with pimiento. And here are *amêijoas à bulhão pato*. The mussels are very fresh. We took them aboard only yesterday at St. Jago, and they have been steamed with cilantro and ginger shavings."

Again Prata ate a mussel himself before offering one to Drake. Our general sucked down the flesh and broth from the shell in one gulp.

"Not bad, by God!" he said, dropping the husk and taking another. "Not bad at all. You must try one, Tom."

More than a dozen plates were arranged upon the table by the time João Longo Prata finished displaying the meal he had prepared. Each dish was attractively garnished, tantalizing to the eye, and aromatic. That he had put together so appetizing a feast in such a short time and under such rough conditions was incontrovertible proof of Prata's creativity and expertise. Even Thomas Doughty, a sophisticate, was appreciative of the achievement. Using the point of his dagger, he speared a sliver of *torresmo*, which was a crisp bit of pork, and chewed admiringly.

"I never thought to be dining this well at such a remove from London," Doughty admitted. "Perhaps we should insist *Senhor* Prata join our adventure along with his captain."

"A damned fine idea, Tom—although I doubt Prata would care much for it," Drake laughed. Then he asked Nuño da Silva: "Pray tell, *senhor*, what do you have in your hand. It looks interesting."

The Portuguese captain had taken a grilled fish from the platter on which Prata had arranged them, all the size of fingerlings, with green olives and slices of browned onion. "It is *sardinha assada*," explained da Silva. "João Longo prepares the dish exactly as it is done in Sonsonata, which is a town in—"

"I know where Sonsonata is located," Drake interrupted brusquely. "You are familiar with the area, *senhor*?"

Da Silva nodded. "*Sim*," he answered. "For five years when I was a young man, I was employed as a pilot all along that coast, from Colima to Bahia Saluda and every point in between. Sonsonata was my favorite port, however. Not only was the cookery exceptional but the women—ah, *senhor*, you have not lived until you have had your bilges pumped by a whore from Sonsonata. They have a special manner of working the handle that is unforgettable."

Drake ignored the advice. "You must have become familiar with the route," he said, giving da Silva an intense look.

"There was no better pilot!" da Silva boasted. "Even after twenty years, I would wager as many crowns that I could navigate those waters without a compass. *Sim*, and blindfolded, too. Sadly, my employers and I had a disagreement over certain, shall I say, accounting matters. I have not returned since. It would not be healthy."

I do not blame myself for missing the significance of this brief conversation between Drake and the Portuguese captain. Although I had gleaned a smattering of geography from the other men during the voyage, I was still largely ignorant of the world's finer details. How could I have been expected to know the position of three small Spanish ports out of the hundreds of similar insignificant settlements across the globe? Nor would it be reasonable to have expected me, until recently a landsman who had never gone to sea, to guess what da Silva's earthy reminiscences meant to Drake or to imagine the awful consequences they would have, months later and thousands of miles away. Outwardly showing nothing of the furious calculations that must have been filling his head, Drake addressed me.

"What have you there, lad? Let us see."

This was the moment I had been hoping to avoid. Even if my menu were to be well received by the Portugals, I knew I would have difficulty with my superiors once they learned what I had done.

Placing the skillet on a trivet before Nuño da Silva, I stripped away the towel and revealed the pie I had baked.

"Here, sir, is the work of an English sea cook," I said.

Some Fine Cuisine

Tobias Lackland, God rest him, had been a grudging accomplice on the last occasion I had served a similar meal. Now I was on my own.

In a sorry attempt at matching Prata's theatrics, I stropped my knife against a steel rasp to hone the edge. Then I cut into the dome of the crust and used the flat of my blade to serve myself a portion, which I chewed and swallowed deliberately. To my relief, it was not bad. Resisting the urge to wash the bite down with Canary, I had another, and a third, before slicing wedges for da Silva and his gentlemen.

"Umble pie may be a simple dish but it is an excellent meal," I assured them. "A flaky shell is ensured by using lard rather than butter in the dough. You must also cut a sufficiency of vents in the lid else it will become soggy. As for the filling, well, many recipes call for deer or boar but I prefer smaller animals."

With regretful glances at the delicacies before Drake and Doughty, the Portugals took up their forks without enthusiasm and began eating the meal I had prepared them. Anselmo Godinho, the man who had tried my murder in the hold of the *Santa Maria*, was seated beside da Silva. One side of his face was a solid bruise where I had struck him with the firkin of nails. "These English are being intentionally offensive, *capitão*," he declared angrily, stirring the piece on his plate with his knife while giving me an evil look. "This is food for peasants."

The Portuguese captain, however, was in better humor than his associate. For the first time since I had met the man, da Silva smiled. It was clear he enjoyed having publicly advertised the quality of his own table while highlighting his host's lack of refinement. "You expected better from Lutheran pirates?" he asked. "Come, Anselmo, eat your fill. The pastry has a certain—bucolic charm—and it is apparently the best fare the heretics can provide. I am enjoying mine."

Da Silva ate with gusto, pretending enthusiasm in order to be as offensive as possible. This fact was not lost on either Drake or Doughty.

"Mr. James," asked Doughty, "tell us why you thought serving our guests umble pie would be a good thing."

What he meant was the dish was typically a repast of the poorest people since it was cheap to make, the filling being in large part composed of umbles, the innards of game.

Drake was equally direct. "Did I not explain the bastards sought to discredit us and make us out to be bumpkins? Look at them—even now they are sniggering. Why did you not prepare something more special? Umble pie, by God! The Portugals will think we are paupers."

In the candlelight I could not decide whether the color in Drake's cheeks was caused by the Canary or by irritation. In an apparent effort to calm himself, he took a bite of João Longo Prata's *choquinhos fritos*, which were tidbits of fried squid immersed in a sauce of their own ink.

Before I could answer Drake, however, the door to the cabin was flung open and Lancelot Garget staggered inside. It was a miracle that he could stand upright, much less walk. Managing to reach the table, he nearly overbalanced while giving Drake an offhand salute.

"Begging your pardon, general, sir," Garget muttered, "but I thought I smelled dinner. Ah, yes, do you mind very much, sir? I am famished."

Without waiting for leave, he pinched a bit of *chouriço* and popped it into his mouth only to spit out the bite after just one chew. "Jesus," he exclaimed, "there is enough garlic to kill a man. Did you commit this misdemeanor, pretty boy? I would not put the crime past you."

"No, sir. I prepared the umble pie."

"Umble pie, that sounds better. Let us pray you have not ruined an honest dish with the irresponsible invention for which you are famous."

Perhaps from hunger one or two of the Portuguese gentlemen had eaten second helpings of the pastry. Garget's gaze fixed on the single remaining slice. Lurching erratically, he made his way to the skillet and grabbed the wedge with a pleased air of accomplishment before I could stop him. In seconds it was gone into his maw. His Adam's apple had hardly stopped bobbing before he was licking crumbs from his fingers.

After a satisfied belch, Garget offered me his highest compliment. "Praise be to God, 'tis almost up to the measure set by my dear departed mother," he admitted with amazement. "The only fault is too high a proportion of meat to umbles, which accounts for a certain blandness, as the pie should taste more of organ, particularly kidney and lights. Even so, the good woman would have approved, I think."

Garget gripped me with drunken sentiment. Then his eyes rolled up into his head and he folded to the deck, slumping against the carved wainscoting of the cabin bulkhead.

Given the circumstances, neither Drake nor Doughty shared Lancelot Garget's appreciation of my efforts.

"We are still awaiting an answer, Mr. James," Doughty reminded me. "Explain why you have damaged our reputation with such sorry fare. Did you think the Portugals would enjoy offal?"

"Aye, lad," Drake agreed. "Umble pie is not an inspiring dish. 'Tis naught but venison entrails, by God."

"Sir," I replied, "we have no venison."

This was when my superiors began to understand what had gone into the recipe. Addressing Nuño da Silva, I said in Portuguese, "I am explaining my selection of ingredients to General Drake. Chiefly I relied on—how do you say it in your tongue? *Coelho*."

"*Coelho* is indeed a common staple of beggars and vagabonds," da Silva observed, not without a little satisfaction at this further proof of the vulgarity of English cuisine.

"Mr. James, correct me if I am mistaken," said Thomas Doughty, "but I do not remember any rabbits being included among the victuals. Pigeons, yes. Hens, yes. But no rabbits or other game."

"Aye, sir," I answered. "Fortunately, there is a surfeit of wildlife aboard the ship. Particularly in the orlop."

Once more I saw Drake's pupils become surrounded by white as he rose from his chair while gripping the edge of the table with such strength that the knuckles went as pale as his eyes.

"God's wounds, lad, do you mean to say—"

"Exactly, general," I admitted. "The umble pie consisted principally of water coney, or 'tweendeck venison, as it is also known."

No one spoke for some time after this revelation. Drake's voice was dangerously conversational when he finally addressed me.

"You thought it permissible to serve such a bill of fare, Mr. James?" he asked. "It was all right with you to risk our reputation with such ingredients? It met with your approval, sir, to gamble with my name and credit? To make a laughing-stock of my ship and the table I set?"

I had known that I would have to suffer our general's displeasure but even so I was ill prepared to receive the full brunt of his anger.

The fact that Drake's tone remained level during this tirade was a disturbing indication of the depth of his fury since he would have been roaring had he been less enraged. Resisting the futile temptation to turn on my heels and flee the grand cabin, I said:

"With respect, general, let us be honest. I am a sea cook, sir, while *Senhor* Prata is a chef of experience and talent. It was obvious my best efforts could not hope to equal his least work. There never was a chance the Portugals would appreciate any menu I served."

"Aye, and so what? You have still fed our guests—"

"A good English meal, which they will be happy to disparage at length, as they would have done in any case, although they did finish the entire thing. Do you see my point, sir? The Portugals have dined on umble pie. All of it. Every last bit, even the tail and squeak."

Thomas Doughty was the first to follow my line of reasoning. "Aye, they have truly eaten humble pie, Mr. James," he said with a snort of laughter, adding an initial *h* sound to the word to make his meaning clear. Meanwhile Drake's complexion was reddening further, convincing me that I was about to be sentenced to another lashing or to some worse punishment. Then our general began studying the overhead planking and whistling tunelessly through his front teeth. After a few seconds, however, Drake could no longer contain his amusement at the situation.

"Bugger my arse with a stiff timber," he swore. "You have cooked up a fine mess, lad! I tell you, though, I cannot decide if I care for the trick. By God, even Portugals do not merit such tainted fare."

"Tainted fare?" I objected at once. "Your pardon, general, the umble pie was wholesome and palatable. Did not Mr. Garget himself approve, and his blessed mother, too?"

Drake remained unconvinced. Remembering the question posed to me by the ancient mariner, Francisco Albo, while we wrestled in the head, I marshaled my final argument and said:

"I also wished to demonstrate my readiness for advancement, sir. There is the need for a chief cook aboard our new prize. Even though I am not a senior man, I would like to be considered for the job."

"Your point being, lad," Drake answered carefully, "that by serving an umble pie of water coney, you would prove your ability?"

"Exactly, general! It is all very well and good to prepare an elegant feast, as *Senhor* Prata has done, in calm seas and fair weather. But when the water is foul and the victuals are stinking, would you not like to know that your cook, your English sea cook, could put together an acceptable meal from whatever is at hand, however noxious? I trust I have demonstrated this skill to your satisfaction."

My effrontery astonished everyone except the Portugals, who were chatting among themselves in their own language and oblivious to our conversation since they did not understand it. Drake studied me while he took a drink of Canary, the tankard hiding his expression so that I could not suspect what he was thinking until he put down the mug.

"Aye, lad," he said with a sobriety at odds with the amount of wine he had consumed in my presence, "I do believe you have made such a demonstration. Particularly convincing was the fact you had sufficient faith in your own cooking to dine with the Portugals. I would not care to eat umble pie myself, Mr. James, but if a time comes when I must, on my oath, I would rather be served the dish by your hand than by any other."

"Hopefully, General Drake, that time will never come."

"Aye, lad," he said, "but there is no telling when a ship may run afoul of a lee shore or contrary winds. God have mercy on all mariners!"

Then Drake addressed Doughty. "What is your opinion, Tom? The lad has my endorsement but it is your decision since you are the *Mary*'s captain. Are you willing to have Mr. James as your man?"

Thomas Doughty drank sack while mulling over the question. It was evident he was debating the wisdom of employing a cook known to serve water coney from his galley, no matter the justification for the menu.

As I met his gaze, I could not help but remember the first occasion we had met, while I hung from the whipping post in Plymouth and awaited the stroke of the lash. I had not liked him then and I did not trust him now. By his own confession, Doughty was a practical man, and he had twice used me for his own ends. But it was too late to retrace the dangerous course on which I had embarked, nor was it possible to retract the vain words I had spoken.

At last Doughty nodded slowly. "Francis, you are right, Mr. James has indeed earned the position. He may be a headstrong and ambitious lad but he has proven himself to be a good cook as well as a cunning scoundrel. I do, though, have one inflexible stipulation."

"What is that stipulation, Mr. Doughty?" I asked.

"Never, without permission, are you to serve umble pie again."

No one volunteered to enlighten the Portugals as to what exactly they had eaten at our table and they remained happily ignorant although Nuño da Silva, since he was to travel with the adventure many months, eventually learned the truth and from that point forward he hated me as unrelentingly as I hated him. By the time the Portugals left the main cabin, however, news of the unusual meal had spread among the crew. As our guests crossed the waist, they were greeted with smiles and extravagant bows.

"I hope you enjoyed your supper, you damned Papists," said Pascoe Goddy in a sweet tone while taking off his cap and scraping before the gentlemen as they began clambering over the side of the ship into the boat waiting to ferry them to the pinnace. "Aye, sir, there is nothing as toothsome as a bit of good water coney, is there!"

"Tell me, *senhor*," said Peter Corder to another Portugal,

trusting that the man he addressed would not comprehend him, "does vermin truly taste like poultry? I have heard this rumor."

"We could ask Lance Garget when he wakes," suggested Gregory Raymente, going to a bucket and dipping himself a cup of wine.

"No, that would be cruel. What about it, Perry? What do you say?"

Everyone stopped talking to listen to my answer. "To be honest, gentlemen," I replied after considering the matter, "the meat rather more resembles veal than chicken although it does possess the gaminess of pheasant. It is also tough. Had I more time, I would have hung the flesh a week to allow it to mature. I pray the Portugals were not disappointed."

Goddy almost choked on his liquor. "Have you ever met as spunky a lad," he said when he had recovered, coming over to me and slapping my back with such camaraderie that half my drink flew from my mug. Then he lifted his own jack. "To Peregrine James," he declared, "who is a God damned cook without compare and a true sea dog in the making! And let us drink to all Portugals, Spaniards, and Papists! Dead rats!"

"Aye! Dead rats!" the men answered.

This was the first toast of many and I was unsteady on my feet by the time the last one was finished. Climbing the ladder to the forecastle, I went to the bow of the *Pelican* and leaned against the railing and looked into the distance while trying to clear my head. Although it was the second day of February, the breeze was warm and the sun burned bright in a cloudless sky. The island of St. Jago had disappeared behind our stern during the night and there was only blue sea to the horizon on every side. A light breeze teased the canvas, and the spritsail, hanging beneath the bowsprit, flapped erratically along the luff, or forward edge, as the wind hit from off side, propelling the ship westward toward the vast abyss of ocean that lay between the continents.

Then I noticed a darkening in the distance.

At first I thought we were sailing toward a storm but soon I realized I was looking at a mountain on fire.

It rose at least a mile into the air, a vast hummock of black rock ringed by beaches of black sand. From the top spat billows of smoke and soot while rivulets of flame ran from the lip of the crater down the slopes to the plains of the shore. Flashes of light illuminated the dark underbellies of the clouds above the peak.

"The burning island," explained Francis Fletcher, joining me at the railing. "The Portuguese call it Fogo."

"I never imagined such a thing could exist," I said in amazement.

"Aye, my son, Fogo far exceeds Aetna, which I have also seen, and it is growing taller. Notice how the flinders cool when they hit the air and fall down the side of the spire. Inch by inch they build it up and continually increase the size of the hill."

As we neared the island, ash began falling like snow and drifts of the stuff began building up on deck. Mixed in with the powder were chunks of larger residue. The gray stones had pockmarked shapes and were very light for their size. Landing in the sea, they floated upon the surface of the water with a buoyancy quite unnatural for rock.

"Pumice," said the parson, taking his leather notebook from a coat pocket and opening it to a blank sheet. "Being born of fire, the mineral partakes of its nature and resists the pull of gravity."

Then he removed a jar of ink and a quill from another pocket and began to sketch the mountain, delineating its triangular figure with quick strokes and penning a dozen upward lines to represent the material erupting from the top. It was painfully apparent, however, that Parson Fletcher was not an artist.

Peering over his shoulder, I asked, "What are those tiny circles, sir? I cannot make them out."

"They are boulders, my son."

"And the crosshatchings?"

"That is the vegetation on the north flank."

"Ah, yes, I do see, sir. It helps to squint a little."

Fletcher closed the book after making sure the ink was dry and would not blot. "You are kind, Peregrine," he said, "but I know my own abilities. I do not draw for pleasure, however, but to document the wonders I witness during my travels lest I forget them as I grow older. Memory fails as a man ages. Already I cannot remember scripture I memorized when I was young. I know I once knew certain passages but I do not know them now. It is frustrating."

Then a different expression lit the parson's face and he was no longer a paternal clergyman but the wary journeyer who had survived a lifetime of wandering far from home. "I also make a strict record of what I see for another reason," Fletcher continued. "You will learn, my son, that there are ignorant men who enjoy nothing better than to laugh at the reports of travelers. Even though the featherbed milksops may never have ventured a mile from their own doorstep, they feel competent to mock those who have dared go out into the world and explore God's great and marvelous works. Well, should I meet one of these misguided know nothings, I will take out this diary, turn to the appropriate page, and say, 'This is what I saw when I was there. Now wipe the icicles off your nose and admit your blind error.'"

"God's truth," I agreed. "I do not think my own friends will credit me when I tell them what I have seen on our voyage. If you had said to me in Plymouth, 'Perry, soon you will be sailing along Barbary with a rough crew of sea dogs bound for God knows where,' well, sir, I would have guessed you were out of your mind and laughed in your face. Yet here I am. It is a great mystery."

Fletcher chuckled and replaced his notebook in a coat pocket. "The lord has a plan for each of us," he explained. "There are neither accidents nor coincidences, my son. Mystery is but another name for miracle."

This observation remained with me after the parson went below. Alone at the bow except for the man on watch taking soundings, I watched the burning island pass to starboard and looked back on the three short months since I first met Francis Drake and Thomas Doughty. In that brief interval I had known more hardship and danger than in my entire past life. I had almost died from accident or by murder on more occasions than I cared to count and I had lost one friend to the sea while another had disappeared among the Moors in the sands of Africa.

Francis Fletcher was right. My survival was both a mystery and a miracle. Nor did I imagine the future would be any less perilous.

In the morning, led by the *Pelican*, the tiny fleet of wooden ships would embark across the Atlantic. Should we live through the passage, menace would face us wherever Drake steered. Far from being a peaceful merchant venture bound to trade in currants, as I had earnestly assumed at the outset of the journey, it was now clear we sought more dangerous cargo. Every man's hand would be turned against us and the Spanish and the Portugals would receive us with powder and shot.

Even so I found myself grinning as I leaned against the railing and watched the foam curl from the bow as we headed onward into the brine across a hundred colors of blue.

"Twenty fathoms. Black gravel and oyster shell," called the sailor with the plumb line. In the waist someone began singing *Drunken Sailor* until someone else drunkenly commanded him to stop. Beyond the bowsprit the horizon receded endlessly for thousands of miles.

I could not help thinking that much had changed in the same brief space of time since that moment on the quay side of Sutton Pool. Then I had been a convicted felon without prospects, penniless and heartbroken. Now I had earned the confidence of my masters and would soon take control of my own galley aboard the prize vessel *Mary*.

Here was both another mystery and another miracle.

I was no longer the least boy of the adventure.

On the Edge of the Abyss

February 3, 1578 – February 4, 1578
Brava

I f this was not a narrative of a real voyage, I would end my story here at this happy moment with the fleet poised to venture across the Atlantic and with my personal history at a high point. However, as Parson Fletcher would say, God's plan continues to be revealed and for honesty's sake I must continue the tale somewhat further. When I awoke the next morning, which was February 3rd, I was pleased with myself and with my prospects, smugly satisfied that I had a galley of my own to run, and determined to repay my masters' trust to the best of my abilities. How could I suspect that soon I would be disgraced before my companions and despised by the man I most admired?

Climbing on deck, I dipped a bucket over the side and rinsed my face. I had refrained from Canary the previous evening in time to fall asleep sober and so I was clearheaded as I gathered my belongings and prepared to leave for the prize vessel and assume my new duties.

No one else had exercised similar restraint. Crossing the waist, I had to step carefully to avoid puddles of piss and vomit as well as the bodies of drunken mariners. The few men who were awake were in pain.

"Could you not tread more lightly, Perry?" groaned Pascoe Goddy, gingerly massaging his forehead with his fingertips. "The entire ship echoes with your stomping about."

"I am sorry," I whispered but evidently did not speak in a sufficiently quiet voice since not only Goddy but several other sailors all moaned with anguish at the sound. Rich Joyner lurched to his feet and began discharging the contents of his belly in thin streams against the mainmast until Blacollers took hold of the carpenter by the scruff of the neck and pulled him away from the nasty business.

"Enough!" said the boatswain. "The celebration is over and proper discipline is again the order of the day. Use a bucket or visit the head to empty yourself. Then find a mop and swab up this mess. The poor *Pelican* is a disgrace, that she is."

"Ah, bugger off, old man," Joyner said, wrenching free of Blacollers with an angry shrug.

The boatswain's first blow took Joyner in the stomach. The second, a hook from the left, caught him in the jaw and lifted him an inch off the planking. Then the carpenter was stretched out flat on his back while Blacollers stood over him, rubbing his hands as if they stung.

"Bless you," he said, "the sad truth is I am an old man. Still, it was not kind to remind me of my mortality, Mr. Joyner. Nor was it respectful to ignore the instructions of a superior. On the next such occasion, despite my great affection for you, I will be obliged to take official notice and mention your behavior to the general. Are we understood, sir?"

Joyner was too inebriated to be swayed by reason. "Bugger the general, damn him, and bugger the ship the bastard sailed in on," he said, struggling erect and flailing at Blacollers, who easily dodged the wild swings. Clenching his fingers together so tightly that the joints popped as his hands balled into fists, the boatswain struck the carpenter twice more very deliberately, once in the sternum and once in the temples.

Joyner pitched sideways and did not move. Blacollers brought his knuckles to his mouth and sucked them clean of blood. "That was no way to speak of General Drake, nor of his mother," the boatswain admonished the unconscious man. Then he looked around the deck. "Get your arses moving, ladies," he instructed. "Waspe, Raymente, carry Richard down to the bilge and let him sober in the scuppers. Great Nele, you and Powell Jemes fetch brooms—what are you waiting for? Christ love you all, my sister holds her drink better than any here!"

As I had mentioned to Tobias Lackland back in Plymouth while we had concocted our plan to expose James Stydye, Lancelot Garget was blessed with the constitution of a horse and he was no more harmed by liquor, however much he imbibed, than he was ever touched by seasickness. Despite his drunkenness the evening before, the man was not only awake but apparently he had been up for some time since the fire was lit and the pot of water above the flames was simmering. Putting down the sack from which he was scooping handfuls of dried oats into the kettle, Garget gestured for me to approach with the wood spoon he was using to stir the gruel.

"A word, pretty boy," he said.

"Will this take long, sir?" I replied as I came over to the cooking box, barely troubling to conceal my impatience since I was very full of myself now that I was no longer slaving for him and had a galley of my own. "I must leave for the *Mary* with the first boat."

"So I have heard. Sweet Jesus, is there no position that cannot be purchased by conscientious tail licking?" Garget jabbed the spoon under my nose to emphasize his distaste for the circumstances. "Aye, you are an ambitious scoundrel," he continued, "and arrogant beyond all credit. Do you think so little of me that you supposed I would not realize your trick? That I would not know what went into my mouth?"

"To be equally frank, sir," I answered stiffly, "I am amazed you remember anything at all of last evening. However, the meal was meant for the Portugals, not for you or any of our mates. Your drunkenness forced the situation. Do not blame me."

I thought Garget would strike me with the spoon. Instead he let the utensil drop while he leaned forward until only inches separated our faces. At such a distance I could avoid neither his sour aroma nor the warm spray of vapor he exhaled. Strangely, Garget's eyes were wet although there were no onions in evidence to account for the tears.

"No, Mr. James, I do not blame you. I wish you to know I stand by my judgment. Your umble pie would indeed have proven acceptable to my dear mother, may God rest her."

"Aye, sir?" I replied. "I mean—thank you, sir."

Then Garget surprised me by putting an arm around my shoulders and drawing me close with more friendliness than I ever would have imagined to receive from him while he was sober.

"We were a poor family," he explained, "with a room in Cheapside, which is in London, across from the bull pits. My father was a tailor but when his sight failed and he could no longer see the needle, well, the pantry was bare more often than not. Mother did what she could with the little she had but that was not much, considering there were nine of us. Although we all understood why the vicinity was curiously free of pests, even the youngest child pretended to accept her explanations as to how she secured the victuals to fill our bellies. I have always prayed the good woman went to Jesus thinking we believed her lies."

"Your mother was indeed a remarkable person," I said, touched by the confidence. Garget, however, had not finished his say.

"So you see, pretty boy," he continued with his usual malice, "do not think to deceive me. You are not so clever. When I compliment your umble pie, it is because I am a connoisseur of the dish and not because I am too dull to know what I am being served."

The piping of a whistle interrupted this unpleasant exchange, summoning the crew to the waist below the half deck, where Francis Drake stood before the mizzenmast with his hands clasped behind his back. From the brightness of his eyes it was clear our general shared Lancelot Garget's immunity to the aftereffects of wine. Leaning forward, Drake studied the men assembling slowly beneath him.

"God's blood, I have never seen such a dismal sight!" he swore, echoing Blacollers's earlier judgment. "Is there not a man here equal to his liquor? Stand straight, Powell! I do not care for slouching. And you, what is your damned name, sir? Yes, you—Minivy—is that puke on your pants or have you shit yourself? Wipe it off. No, by Mary's tits, not with your hand. With a rag!"

Under ordinary circumstances Drake's blasphemy would

have entertained the men and they would have appreciated his speaking as plainly as any sailor. Now, however, everyone hurt too much to be amused and his remarks were greeted by grumbling instead of by laughter although only Pascoe Goddy was imprudent enough to allow his voice to rise above the anonymous mutter.

"For Christ's sake, general," he asked too loudly than was wise, "why will you not allow us to die in peace?"

This insolence encouraged others in the audience to express themselves although no one spoke as audibly as Goddy and all made sure to look away while they voiced their opinions so that they would not stand out in the crowd and draw Drake's notice.

He waited until the noise quieted. Then he roared, "Damn my eyes, it makes me sick to listen to such complaining. A little wine and you are all as weak as women! I shudder to think how I will be served when there is real need. The Spanish will feed us our globes on silver platters, aye, and ask if we wish salt with our meat!"

Then Drake flung his arm forward, so that we all turned our heads and looked beyond the bow to where a small island was rising from the horizon, a huddle of green hills surrounded by cloud. "That is Brava," Drake said, "the last of the Cape Verdes. Here land ends. There is no more for two thousand miles. We are at the brink of the gulf and soon we must seek the far shore. Our voyage cannot be made by fools or by weaklings! I need dogs beside me, not a litter of mewling bitches!"

No one had the nerve to protest the unflattering description.

Drake allowed the silence to deepen and then slammed a fist into his other palm as if at an important realization. "With such a crew our adventure cannot help but come to grief," he said in disgust. "I have half a mind to turn back this very instant, by God, and spare myself the shame! There is nothing praiseworthy in failure."

This declaration was not well received by the sailors in the waist nor by the gentlemen who had gathered behind Drake on the half deck.

The latter were no better off than the ordinary men and many were holding themselves upright by hanging onto each other or to the railing. John Cooke, his pallor so complete that his nose was corpse white instead of its usual rosy color, blanched even further.

"God forbid, general," he said. "Returning to England now would mean our ruin. Our money is spent and we are empty handed. What say, sir, would you make us all into bankrupts?"

"Aye, and what of our wages?" called a sailor I could not identify since he was careful to hide himself by speaking out of the side of his mouth. According to stories I had heard, it was a common practice for seamen to be cheated by their employer if a venture proved unprofitable or not lucrative enough to satisfy the investors. Many of the crew shared his financial concern. Once again muttering broke out in the waist.

Leonard Vicarye approached Drake. The lawyer was a heavy man with loose jowls on either side of a tiny button of a mouth, which was pursed in a querulous expression. Due to the difference in our stations, we had never spoken and I knew little about him except that he was often in Thomas Doughty's company and it was said that they were friends in London. Vicarye, too, was a backer of the expedition although no one had an idea of the size of his stake. The dark bags beneath his eyes demonstrated he was as ill as the rest of the gentlemen. Even so, perhaps because of his profession, his voice was resonant.

"Sir," said Vicarye, "listen to my counsel and heed my words. It would be imprudent—nay, in my opinion it would be unlawful—to retreat at this point. According to our charter—"

"What of it!" Drake snapped. "There are but two men privy to our charter, Mr. Vicarye, and you are not one of them. Do not speak of what you do not know. God's wounds, I despise crafty lawyers!"

Dismissing Vicarye with the back of his hand, Drake surveyed the men in the waist and then the gentlemen with one long glance. Again he shook his head. "Aye, we will go on," he said, as if making an unwilling admission, "and for one reason only."

This morning Drake was wearing a simple sailor's cap of knitted gray wool. Taking it from his head in a sign of respect, he said, "It is because I have sworn an oath to her grace Elizabeth herself to go on, no matter the cost, and Francis Drake is a man of his word! With her own lips our sovereign lady charged me to succeed and I will not let her down. Nor will I allow any here to do so. Our mission is more important than can be imagined. Hear me, and I am being as honest as I may, it could be that the very future of our nation depends on what we achieve."

This patriotic appeal stirred the men despite their lethargy and several growled, "God save the queen!"

"Much more I cannot reveal, not yet," Drake went on, lowering his voice so that everyone shuffled forward to hear him. "Our bearing is a secret of state and must remain confidential for reasons you all understand. Damn the Spanish and any who kiss the Pope's ring!"

"Aye, general! Damn the Spanish!"

Drake lowered his voice even further, creating an atmosphere of intimacy, as if he were imparting a grave confidence. "Still," he said, "I do have some leeway. Tell me, who here knows of the Straits of Anian?"

Most of the men were puzzled by the question, as were the gentlemen on the half deck since none of them were seamen, much less navigators, but one or two of the sailors apparently understood the reference and were not heartened by it. Thomas Cuttill, a pilot himself although not a mariner of Drake's reputation, said:

"With respect, general, the straits do not exist. They are a myth."

"Are they, Mr. Cuttill? Well, I have been informed otherwise, and by a very good source, too—by the very best source, the most eminent scholar of the geographic arts in all England!"

I knew without his name being mentioned that our general was referring to Dr. John Dee.

"The straits do exist," Drake continued, "and they lie somewhat to the north in the high latitudes of the Americas, where they mirror the southern passage sailed by Magellan and lead directly to the Pacific. Aye, and on impeccable authority I have heard the northern straits are more friendly than Magellan's, being clear of ice and tempest and contrary current! Think of the great service we would be doing our country if we were to discover such a route! Our ships would be free to bypass the Spanish and their Portugal henchmen, avoiding both the Cape of Good Hope and the Caribbean sea. All of India would be open to our vessels, by God!—the Moluccas, too, and China! The treasure of Asia has no limit, gentlemen. Finally England would be allowed her share!"

Drake paused to allow us to consider this cheerful prospect and what it would mean to our nation as a whole as well as to our individual fortunes. "Do not misunderstand me," he went on. "I am not saying it is our duty to discover these straits. I am not suggesting the queen has ordered us to search for them, nor that she and I have ever so much as discussed the matter together. Still, if we should come across the Straits of Anian in the course of our journey, well, gentlemen, I ask you, what harm would there be in exploring the channel? Who would take issue with our returning home with a full hold of Malabar gold or cloves from the Celebes or Mindanao. Would not such a cargo be our honest due for bringing glory to our country and to her grace!"

"Aye, general!" I answered, unable to stop from joining the chorus of agreement that rose from the men in response to Drake's question.

Then, as always, I could no more resist his rhetoric than any of the crew. By the time Drake finished, my head was awash with foolish visions of heroism and fame, not to mention improbable financial reward. In my innocence I did not hear that his words were as empty of content as so much nonsense and that he had told us nothing while making it appear as if he were divulging important mysteries. In my ignorance I thought I now understood why there had been such misdirection in Plymouth about our true objectives, and why James Stydye had worked secretly against us, and why I had been waylaid on the banks of the Thames while hurrying to Mortlake. Given our ultimate destination, it was no wonder that the Spanish feared our success and had sought our doom from the very outset of the voyage.

The Straits of Anian!

Such a northwest passage would indeed end Spanish hegemony over the Americas and the stranglehold with which Portugal gripped the sea route to the Indies, China, and the Spice Islands.

If we were to claim the straits for England, every man aboard would be remembered as a hero. A wealthy hero.

Again our general removed his knitted cap. The rising sun lit his salt bleached curls and set them afire while he regarded us so that his head was framed by a halo of pale flame. Never before had I seen such determination and purpose in a man's face, and I burned with pride to be in his company and to have him as my master.

At that moment I would have given my life at Drake's command. Nor was I alone in the love I felt.

"To the straits!" called one sailor.

"Aye, and bugger all Spanish dogs," called another.

"Anian! Anian!"

The assembly disbanded much faster than it had gathered together and the crew went to their tasks with the agility of abstemious men rather than with the creaking senility they had displayed not a half hour earlier.

By the time the longboat was ready to leave from the

Pelican for the *Mary*, the waist was swept and mopped and all loose trash had been dropped overboard to the delight of the fish who followed the wake of the ship and fed on our garbage. These were ugly creatures with triangular fins and gray snouts lined by pink gums and filled with sharp teeth. They were easy to take with a hook and line since they attacked anything that fell in the water. Unfortunately, their flesh had the foul taste of piss and the brutes were not worth catching.

The Straits of Anian!

I could not keep from repeating the phrase to myself while we pulled at the oars of the longboat and headed for the *Mary*.

She had lowered her sails to allow us to approach but raised her canvas once we were aboard in order to stay in formation with the rest of the fleet. Thomas Doughty was on the afterdeck talking with John Hughes, who was the sailing master and pilot, and with Tom Drake, our general's younger brother, who had been assigned the position of boatswain. Other men I recognized included John Bruer—the leader of Tobias Lackland's musical consort—and Ned Bright, a carpenter. Altogether twenty sailors, officers, and gentlemen had been stripped from the other ships of the expedition to crew the prize vessel.

She had also been equipped with the cast iron minion and the set of mankillers that had been removed from the pinnace when it was given to the Portugals for their return to St. Jago.

In the distance the island of Brava steadily grew larger, a lonely green outcrop surrounded by blue, the last speck of land we would encounter before we reached the continent of

America, which lay hundreds of leagues away across a desert of brine.

We had failed to restock our provisions both at Mogador and at Cape Blank except for the salted fish available in the latter port. Nor had we managed to secure any of the dried *cabritos* stored by the residents of Maio for the benefit of passing Portugal vessels. Brava offered the last opportunity we would have to replenish our water and victuals until we fell to land on the other side of the ocean.

Trailing behind the *Pelican*, which now led the expedition, we followed the coastline while seeking an anchorage in which the ships could ride. No matter how many fathoms of line were let out, however, the plumb did not find bottom even within a cable's length of the island. For miles the shore met the sea in a battery of stark cliffs unrelieved by beaches of either sand or shingle.

At noon the boatswain's whistle summoned the crew to the waist. Once more dressed with his usual elegance in a suit of gray velvet with a ruffled collar and cuffs, as if he were in the hallways of power rather than at the edge of the world, Thomas Doughty flicked an infinitesimal mote from the sleeve of his jacket and cocked his hat brim against the sun's glare before addressing us.

"Gentlemen," he said, hooking the thumb of one hand in a belt loop and the thumb of the other in the basket of his rapier, "I will be brief. General Drake has given this prize into my charge, to govern and keep safe from harm. I act in his name and with the same authority that was granted to him by the queen. Does anyone question this fact?"

No one answered.

"Make no mistake," Doughty went on, "I am not so easy a master as our general, being more accustomed to the service of soldiers, not sailors. Do not think I will ignore the slightest instance of impertinence or sloth. Furthermore, and listen carefully to my warning, the cargo is not to be touched by anyone without my direct permission, not a drop of the liquor nor the least trinket of hardware. Drake has ordered to be informed of pilfering, and any mischief will be dealt with severely. I would not care to employ the lash on any here, sailor or gentleman, but I will do so, readily, if given cause. Is this understood?"

"Aye, captain," one or two of the men grumbled in response but everyone else remained silent. As for myself, I did not care to be reminded of Thomas Doughty's willingness to use a whip.

"Be honest men," Doughty finished, turning the assembly a severe look. "By God's body and by my very faith, use yourselves well and give me cause to think well of you. I make an end."

After securing pulleys to the mainmast spar, I dropped lines into the hold and hoisted the fire box on deck. The *Mary*—formerly the *Santa Maria*—was well provisioned since she had resupplied in St. Jago in preparation for the crossing to Brazil. Besides the wine that comprised much of her cargo, there was a store of dried and salted meat as well as fresh victuals, including *cocos* and *plantanes*. There were also dozens of baskets of a starchy round tuber that Diego, the Cimarron, being familiar with the vegetable in his home country, later identified as a *papa*.

The Portugals had been permitted to take their personal

possessions with them when they were put into the pinnace
and João Longo Prata had removed the crate of culinary utensils and rare ingredients that had been of such help to me
when I had been fighting for my life during the boarding of
the Portuguese merchant ship.

In its place was a bit of heavy paper bent in half.

On the top fold, printed in an even hand, were the English words, "Mister Cook."

The paragraph inside was also in English. I had not had
the least inkling of the fact, but João Longo Prata actually had
been more fluent in my own language than I was in his.

"Sir," I read, "thank you for the courtesy you showed me
aboard your vessel and for allowing me the freedom of your galley. I pray I have left mine in order for you. There is kindling in a
crate by the rice. Capers and anchovies are in jugs next to the oil.
I have also left behind a packet of nutmegs, which will always
benefit a rabbit pie, whether the animals are caught on land or
at sea. To preserve your credit, I did not announce this lack publicly. All cooks are cut equally by knives and scalded similarly by
fire and boiling water. Yours, sincerely, John L. Silver."

Apparently my culinary invention had deceived João
Longo Prata no more than it had taken in Lancelot Garget.

Yet neither had denounced me, one man because of spite
and the other because of loving kindness.

Again struck by the similarity between mystery and
miracle, I refolded the note and placed it in a pocket so that I
could keep it as a memento of God's sympathy and to remind
myself that I was not a bit as sharp as I often supposed I was.

Then my attention was drawn by noises coming from

deeper in the hold. The thudding was too loud and too regular to be made by vermin.

Taking the lantern by its cord, I let my hearing guide me through the barrels of Canary and sack to the cramped area behind the ladder reaching up into the forecastle. Beside a coil of anchor cable higher than a man was a stack of crates, the topmost of which had been removed from the pile and pried open. The noises I heard came from the hammer, its head wrapped in canvas, employed to remove the lid of the box.

Thomas Drake was bent over the container, playing the beam of his own lantern over the contents, which included steel daggers tied in bundles of a dozen, baleen combs, and bolts of silk dyed with indigo. Ignoring my arrival, the younger Drake pawed through the goods, lifting one item for inspection and then another. He gave a scissors a couple snaps and then, pleased by their action, tucked them into his vest.

I had sailed aboard the *Pelican* with Tom Drake but we had not become familiar since he bunked with the gentlemen and took his leisure on the half deck with the other notables. He was perhaps five years the junior of our general and had the same features and stocky build as his elder brother, as well as the broad Devonian burr of their native region.

"What are you looking at, James?" he asked, acknowledging my presence with an unfriendly glance. "Can you not see I am occupied? Point your light elsewhere and go about your business."

"No, sir."

"What did you say?"

Stuffing a clasp knife into his vest beside the scissors,

Tom Drake let the lid of the crate fall shut. He had his brother's burly frame and filled the narrow aisle from side to side.

"Did you say *no?*" he asked with pretended amazement, poking a forefinger into my chest to underscore the question, obviously expecting me to retreat before him. Instead I pressed ahead.

"Tom," I replied, making a point of using his personal name to advertise my determination to be rude. "Did not Captain Doughty forbid pilfering just now in a public address? Yet here you are up to your elbows in the merchandise."

"Doughty was speaking to the sailors. I am an officer."

"Perhaps you are right, Tom. Perhaps the captain did not specifically include each man aboard in his remarks."

"Exactly. You are only a cook and cannot be expected to understand everything you hear. Now return to your duties. It is getting on toward supper and I am growing hungry although I am not hoping to be fed well. I asked Francis—" Tom Drake, too, was making a point by using his brother's given name—"to assign us Lancelot Garget, whose boiled beef is famous, but he would not listen. Go along, James. Off with you."

I shook my head stubbornly. It galled me to see a man who had played no part in the ship's capture help himself to the cargo for which I had bled and almost died.

"Not until you replace what you have taken," I told him.

Equally stubborn, the younger Drake said, "These are small souvenirs and hardly worth mentioning. Discuss the matter with Doughty, if you like. It will earn you nothing but a stripe or two to match those he already laid on your back." Tom Drake laughed. "Aye, do not think I am ignorant of what took place in Plymouth before we sailed. Who will believe a thief, Mr. James? No one will credit what you say."

Then he knocked me aside with a shoulder, pushed past, and climbed from the hold without returning the scissors or the knife.

I went back to the fire box and resumed preparing the meal but I could neither concentrate on the task nor enjoy my work although I did have the good sense not to rush forward with my accusations. Displaying a prudence that Tobias Lackland would have admired, I decided to give Tom Drake time to reconsider his actions.

For supper that afternoon I made a simple dish of salted cod baked with butter and Canary wine and accompanied by carrots mashed with mace and nutmeg. Just past five o'clock I rapped my spoon against the bell that summoned the crew to eat. The *Mary*, trailing the *Pelican* and the *Elizabeth*, was still coasting along Brava in search of anchorage and the bulk of the island blocked the setting sun, so that we were sailing in shadow although the sky was still light overhead. Led by the officers and gentlemen, a line formed before the fire box while I dispensed the meal, ladling portions into the tin bowls held out by the men as they passed. Tom Drake was third in line.

"What do you think this is?" he asked John Bruer, who was next to him, poking at the cod with a hunk of biscuit. "I cannot tell."

"I cannot tell, either, Tom," agreed the musician, eyeing the fish and vegetables in his bowl with exaggerated suspicion. "Nor can I say that what I see looks appealing."

John Bruer was the same age as the younger Drake but thin instead of broad and pale instead of ruddy. His beard was brushed into a sharp point and the end had an upward flip not unlike a goat's. He was wearing a suit of black linen with loose sleeves from which poked long white wrists and fingers unmarked by scars or callus except at their very tips.

I had been told by Lackland that his master was a good friend of Francis Drake's. Apparently he was also the younger brother's crony.

Refusing to be goaded, I bit my lip, choked back what I wanted to say, and wordlessly returned Tom Drake's mocking stare until he dismissed me with a contemptuous snort, convinced that I was cowed by his position and lineage and that I lacked the nerve to protest both his insults and his larceny. Laughing together, he and John Bruer carried their bowls to the half deck and contented themselves with disparaging the supper while they ate it. Seething inwardly, I served the remainder of the men, banked the fire, and had my own meal beside the cooking box while sitting on an upended barrel and watching Brava pass by to starboard, sheer cliffs surmounted by fissured green hills.

Then Tom Drake reached into his vest and retrieved the knife he had taken from the hold. He began paring an apple while chuckling at something Bruer said. This was when I knew I could no longer hope he would reconsider and do the right thing.

Perhaps if Francis Fletcher had been aboard the *Mary*, his wise advice might have dissuaded me from the course I decided to take. The parson, however, was sailing on the *Pelican*, and I made the grave error of relying on my own conscience as a guide. Lackland, God bless him, would have been beside himself with mirth at my foolishness when I rapped on the door of the master cabin, which had belonged to Nuño da Silva and now was Thomas Doughty's personal quarters. Although the compartment was the largest aboard the *Mary*, the space was cramped and most of the interior was taken up by a narrow bed covered by a heavy green spread fringed with gold brocade. Doughty was sitting in a chair with padded arms, reading a Bible by lantern light and idly scratching flea bites. He closed the book upon a finger to hold his place.

"Your pardon, captain," I said. "May I have a moment?"

"What is so important that it cannot wait until tomorrow, Mr. James?" he asked, impatient at being interrupted at his leisure.

"It has to do with your instructions regarding the cargo, sir," I replied. "I have discovered thievery and thought it my duty to bring the situation to your attention."

Thomas Doughty's face darkened as I explained how I had followed the sound of hammering into the hold and had come across the rifled crate. Before I finished, he slammed the holy book against the armrest and half rose from his seat. "They are determined to test me!" he said, not troubling to hide his irritation. "By my faith, sailors are unruly mongrels and bite their leash with impudence. Well, I always knew I would have to make an example of someone. I just did not guess the time would come so soon. Who is this man? Provide me his name."

"Tom Drake."

At my response the anger in Doughty's face was replaced by a perturbed expression. He put down the Bible so that he could stroke his beard while he regarded me without speaking. Finally he said, "Do you know, Mr. James, I have always thought you to be a sly fellow. Now, however, I suspect I was mistaken and that I confused sincerity with calculation. It seems you are indeed the honest lad you appear to be. Unfortunately, honesty is a dangerous principle when pursued without restraint. Worse, I am beginning also to suspect you are an idealist."

"I am not familiar with the term, captain," I said.

"An idealist is a person who follows his beliefs without concern for consequences," Doughty explained. "He is generally accounted a danger to himself and others. Tell me, Mr. James, did you ever pause to consider how our general would react to having his brother accused of theft?"

"Aye, sir," I replied. "General Drake has often spoken of how we are all comrades together in our adventure, sailors and officers alike. I supposed he would want his kin to be held to the same standard as the rest of the men and gentlemen."

Doughty arched an eyebrow skeptically and shook his head. "You supposed wrong. Drake would not be at all happy if I mentioned his brother's indiscretion. More likely he would suspect my motives and think I plotted against him. Listen carefully, Mr. James. The balance between commanders is always uneasy, especially on a journey such as ours. On Magellan's voyage the mutineers included two captains as well as a priest. I assure you, our general is familiar with the story. He has a copy of Pigafetta's journal in his cabin and has read it many times."

This reference escaped me since I was not a sailor and I did not learn until afterward that Doughty was referring to a survivor of the first and only circumnavigation of the world,

Antonio Pigafetta, whose diary had been translated into a dozen languages and published in as many countries, including England, during the past half century.

"Do not raise this subject again," Doughty finished. "I caution you, Mr. James, it would not be prudent."

These instructions ended our conversation and I returned to my duties knowing that I had once more revealed the earnestness of which Tobias Lackland had often accused me. Was it not, after all, the privilege of those with rank and connections to enjoy considerations unavailable to those of lower station? In a kitchen, the chief cook dined on food fresh from the pan while the pot scrubber fed on scraps and leftovers and no one, myself included, would ever think of complaining since this was the proper order of things. It was right and natural that Tom Drake's behavior would be overlooked. Only a fool or an idealist, to use the unflattering phrase, would have expected a different outcome. Nor could I fault Doughty, ever the practical man, for being wary of Drake. Our general was indeed alert for treachery. Had he not personally ordered me to be on guard against cowards and turncoats?

Upon the deep mutiny must be feared above all other dangers.

Taking Doughty's warning to heart, I fully meant to heed his orders and to forget the incident.

As it happened, however, I was noticed leaving the main cabin.

The younger Drake correctly assumed I had dared report his misdemeanor but he underestimated Thomas Doughty's realism and wrongly believed the captain would act upon my complaint.

The next morning, as I was hoisting wood on deck for the breakfast fire, a longboat arrived from the *Pelican*. Flanked by his favorite henchmen, Tom Moone and Diego, the Cimarron, and followed by another half dozen men, including Parson Fletcher and John Winter, Francis Drake came aboard the *Mary*. Last to clamber over the gunwale was the carpenter, Ned Bright, another friend of Tom Drake's. Since I had served Bright supper myself the evening before, I knew he must have gone over to the *Pelican* sometime during the night. I could not say why, but I did not think Bright had visited the flagship on an idle errand.

Our general noticed me at the fire box. "Summon Mr. Doughty," he instructed. "I would have a word with him."

Although I did not hesitate to obey, I did not act fast enough for Drake, and he was at my heels by the time I reached the captain's quarters. Doughty answered before I finished knocking.

With Drake directly behind me, I was trapped between the two men, unable to escape the door frame without offending one or the other.

"Captain Doughty, sir," I said, not knowing what else to do but follow orders, "General Drake asked to speak with you."

Doughty looked past me at Drake. Neither man moved aside to let me leave. "What is the emergency?" he asked.

"I have received a troubling report," Drake replied. "It appears I have been betrayed by a trusted friend."

"Who is this friend and how has he done you harm?"

Drake did not answer immediately. Nor did he shift from where he stood and permit me to go. I could feel his angry presence at my back even though we were not touching.

"You are that friend," Drake said at last.

A thin smile flickered across Doughty's lips but there was no amusement in his eyes. "Francis," he said, "I am not your enemy."

"By God, I would like to think so! But I must know why you chose to ignore my orders the very day you were given your own command."

"Of what exactly am I supposed to be guilty?" Doughty asked.

"There are witnesses who have said you took from the cargo for your personal enrichment." Drake pressed against me impatiently, forcing me around Doughty and into the cabin. "Did you think our friendship exempted you from my instructions?" he asked.

I did not doubt Thomas Doughty was offended by the accusation, which struck at his integrity as a man and at his honor as a gentleman. Nor did I doubt his rapier would already have been drawn to defend his reputation had any other person been before him but Francis Drake.

Even so his expression revealed nothing of what he must have felt.

"Where are these witnesses?" Doughty asked. "Let them step up and have their say to my face."

Ned Bright and several other men from the *Pelican* had followed our general into the captain's quarters. The carpenter shuffled forward.

"There are the items, sir," Bright volunteered, peering over Drake's shoulder and pointing at Doughty's bedside. "Notice the suede gloves. Anyone can tell they are fine Spanish work. Unworn, too. And the money, general. That is not English silver. He received the coin from the Portugals before we sent them away in the pinnace. I saw the transaction myself. Aye, as did Mr. Bruer, who was with me. Is that not so, John?"

Belatedly I understood why Bright had left the *Mary* after dark the night before and traveled to the *Pelican*. He had been sent by Tom Drake to bear false testimony against Doughty. Evidently fearing that his own crime would be exposed, the younger Drake sought to divert attention away from himself by having his friends defame an innocent man.

Listening to Bright's lies, I could not forget that I, too, had recently been accused of a crime I had not committed.

Putting aside my better judgment, and disregarding the good counsel I had been given, I decided to say what I must. Despite my personal dislike for Thomas Doughty, I could not remain silent.

"With respect, general," I said, "Mr. Doughty is not the one whose activities should be questioned. You must look elsewhere for thievery."

At my statement the cabin became so still that even the normal sounds of the sea seemed hushed. Drake turned deliberately.

"Explain yourself, lad," he said. "Where exactly should I look?"

The evenness of his voice brought home to me the gravity of the situation I was in, causing the words I meant to utter to catch in my throat. Once again I found myself in the unhappy position of attempting to return Drake's cold blue stare without flinching.

"Out with it, Mr. James!" he ordered. "You have made a serious charge. Speak plainly. I do not appreciate innuendo!"

"It was your brother, sir," I blurted out. "Tom Drake. He was the one who went into the cargo. I saw him myself."

"That is a damned lie!"

The younger Drake had entered the cabin in time to hear my accusation and rudely shouldered aside Parson Fletcher in his haste to reach the forefront of the group. He turned me an ugly glower while taking his elder by the arm and saying in a confidential tone, "I did but avail myself of a few trifles with the full knowledge and permission of Captain Doughty. You have my word on it, Francis."

"Is this true, Tom?" Drake asked.

Doughty shrugged, as if the business were beneath him. "Of course," he replied, keeping his eyes straight on me while he spoke the lie. "Your brother has always had my confidence. I explained as much to Mr. James. I do not understand why he has chosen to raise the issue."

Then Doughty took up the suede gloves and gave Ned Bright a scornful look while saying to Drake, "I should not have to defend myself against gossip but I will do so to clear the air. These gloves were not part of the cargo. They belonged to one of the Portugals, who offered them as a gift for a small favor I did him. This was his privilege since they were his personal property. The coins, too, lack value. They are bits of copper and worthless except as curiosities."

Drake did not bother to examine either the gloves or the money. Instead he turned on Bright.

"God's wounds, Ned," Drake swore, "why should I not string you to a spar right now for slander!"

Bright gulped. "I meant no slander, general! I told you what I saw, sir! Nothing more."

"You carried an idle tale, by God! If I thought you did so from malice—" Drake paused, as if unable to describe the punishment he would inflict under such circumstances. Then he shrugged with disgust. "As it is, I cannot believe you are anything more than foolish. Drag your arse from my sight, Ned. I am displeased with you."

Drake returned to Doughty. "Tom, I rushed to judgment without informing myself of the facts."

"You are a man of action, Francis. It is your defining quality."

"Aye, perhaps." Drake's laugh was without humor. "Did I not say this prize would cause trouble? Her cargo is too rich and there are too many envious eyes on her. No matter whom I left in charge, there was bound to be poor talk about him. It was unfair of me to burden anyone with such a responsibility." He paused a moment in thought and then came to a decision. "The only thing to do is to take the helm myself. Do you see, Tom, this is the only way to put an end to rumor."

"I will not argue," Doughty said in a flat voice. "Of us all, Francis, only you are above suspicion."

"My very point! Now, lest any one suggest we are not friends, you are to go to the *Pelican* and take over as captain of the flagship in my place. This will prove that you have my confidence. Are we agreed, sir?"

Doughty nodded. Then Drake's attention settled on me.

"I am usually an excellent judge of men, Mr. James," he said, repeating what he had told me the day we met, while I was chained to the post beside Sutton Pool. "With you, however, it appears I have stumbled. From the first Mr. Doughty cautioned me about your character but I did not heed him. No, I said, Perry is a willing and loyal lad. I did not suspect you were biding your time for the opportunity to wrong me."

"That is not the case!" I protested, aghast at his appraisal. "On my life, General Drake! I have always tried to be of service to you, sir. Nothing more, sir. You are my master."

His eyes narrowed. "And you show your respect by touching at my brother? By shooting at his credit with a bald lie? No, Mr. James, there is some further meaning to this matter."

Drake took my collar in his fist and curled the material in a knot as he drew me toward him. "Let us discuss James Stydye," he said. "You were working together all along, is that how it was? But you fell out. He was not paying you enough. Or was Stydye about to reveal your treachery? Which was it? Answer me, lad!"

"Neither, sir! I was only thinking of our adventure, I swear it."

"And what of Lackland?"

"Lackland, sir?"

"Aye, Tobias Lackland. Were you not the last person with the boy before he drowned? What did he know about you, Mr. James?"

"Lackland was my friend, general! I tried to save his life."

"I wonder. Aye, and I also wonder if Cape Blank was actually as barren of commodities as you led us to believe. Or did you have orders to interfere with our provisioning, so that we would starve upon the brine? Is that it, Mr. James? You have been paid for."

"No, general! I am loyal to you and no one else."

Drake was unmoved. "You may or may not be a traitor," he told me. "What is plain, however, is that you are not trustworthy. Nor is there room in my company for a man I cannot trust. Diego, accompany Mr. James while he collects his belongings. Allow him sufficient victuals to last a week, as well as a pistol, powder, and fifty rounds of shot. He will not be accompanying us. We are quits."

"Do not do this, general," I pleaded. "I am your honest servant and always have been!"

Drake held up his palm to cut me off. "Enough," he said. "I did once believe you but I do not now. Count yourself lucky not to receive sterner treatment. It is only because I am a forgiving man that you are leaving us with both ears and your tongue. Now away with you, Mr. James. I have no further need of your service."

Drake turned his back in dismissal and Diego's massive brown hand settled on my shoulder.

"*Hijo*, get along," he urged. "There is nothing more for you here."

"Aye, and good riddance to a farting talebearer," added Tom Drake.

I knew tears stained my eyes but I swore I would not let them fall. Somehow I managed to hold myself upright as I was pushed from the cabin out into the waist of the ship.

Every man on deck watched as I retrieved my sea bag

from beside the fire box but no one spoke to me. They had all heard Drake. Everyone was sure I had betrayed the adventure.

For the first time in living memory Christopher Waspe's dagger missed its mark. Instead of hitting the square inch of scarred wood that was its target, the knife flew wide and buried itself beside my foot.

"Damn it, Waspe!" I said. "That was not amusing!"

"No, not half as amusing as seeing you left behind," he answered. "Where will you spend your filthy pay now, lad?"

"Aye, good question, Chris," put in another man. "Brava is deserted even of Portugals. I hope Mr. James enjoys his own company. It will be a long time before he has any other."

We were a mile off the island, the last land before the Atlantic gulf, a bank of sheer cliffs wrapped in mist. With this lonely place as my prison, I knew it was unlikely I would ever see another English face.

Diego, the Cimarron, pushed me to the railing.

"Into the boat, *hijo*," he said. "We do not have all day, no."

Below, her prow scraping against the hull of the larger ship, was the longboat that was to remove me from the *Mary* and take me into exile. Before I went over the side and down to her, however, I saw Francis Fletcher come out on deck from the main cabin.

"Parson!" I called desperately. "A moment, please, sir!"

"Yes, Peregrine?" he asked.

"You are a man of God, sir. The general respects your opinion. He will listen to you, I know he will. Tell him—tell General Drake I meant to do the right thing, that is all. I had no other motive."

On the Edge of the Abyss

"Our general is convinced of your guilt," Fletcher replied. "Nor will he hear any ill of his brother." The parson's lips pursed in disapproval. "Tom Drake is an ungodly lecher and known to be a thief, Peregrine, but it was unwise of you to air the matter. Still, I will do what I can."

He gripped me by both shoulders. "May God be with you," he said. "Trust in his grace, and all will be well." Then, with his usual practicality, the parson finished, "Aye, and take care to keep your powder dry, my son. There may be Papists in those hills."

A quarter hour later I was standing in ankle deep water on a beach of rough gray shingle. My bag and small sack of provisions had been thrown behind me on the rock above the high tide line.

There was little surf since the depth of the water around the island calmed the waves that hit it, allowing the wake of the longboat to remain visible on the surface of the ocean almost until the fleet hoisted sail.

The *Pelican* was the first to raise her canvas. The great white sheets seemed to burst into being when they filled with wind. Soon they were taking her away from land and out into the fathomless blue.

One by one the other ships followed her.

By noon the horizon was empty.

I was marooned on the edge of the abyss.

The End

*The adventures of Peregrine James
will continue in the second book
of the Drake circumnavigation,*
Desperate Bankrupts.